Year's Best SF 2

Edited by David G. Hartwell

Year's Best SF
Year's Best SF 2

Published by HarperPrism

Year's Best SF 2

EDITED BY

David G. Hartwell

HarperPrism

An Imprint of HarperPaperbacks

HarperPaperbacks
A Division of HarperCollins*Publishers*
10 East 53rd Street, New York, N.Y. 10022-5299

Individual story copyrights appear on page 316.
Copyright © 1997 by David G. Hartwell

ISBN 1-56865-438-3

Cover illustration by Bob Eggleton

First printing: June 1997

Printed in the United States of America

*To Judith Merril; Harry Harrison
and Brian W. Aldiss; Terry Carr;
Donald A. Wollheim.
The best, every one different.*

Again I would like to acknowledge the contribution of Mark Kelly, whose *Locus* columns I found helpful. The magazine reviews in *Tangents* are also, I feel, a valuable contribution to the ongoing dialog about quality in short fiction in the SF field. And of course to the magazine editors, who accomplish so much more than they are ever paid.

Table of Contents

xi   Introduction

1   Dave Wolverton
After a Lean Winter

23   Terry Bisson
In the Upper Room

43   John Brunner
Thinkertoy

55   Gregory Benford
Zoomers

65   Sheila Finch
Out of the Mouths

89   James Patrick Kelly
Breakaway, Backdown

97   Yves Meynard
Tobacco Words

123   Joanna Russ
Invasion

131   Brian Stableford
The House of Mourning

145 Damon Knight
Life Edit

149 Robert Reed
First Tuesday

165 David Langford
The Spear of the Sun

173 Gene Wolfe
Counting Cats in Zanzibar

189 Bruce Sterling
Bicycle Repairman

221 Gwyneth Jones
**Red Sonja and Lessingham in
Dreamland**

237 Allen Steele
Doblin's Lecture

249 Kathleen Ann Goonan
The Bride of Elvis

267 Kate Wilhelm
Forget Luck

281 Connie Willis
Nonstop to Portales

303 Stephen Baxter
Columbiad

Year's Best SF 2

Introduction

First, the usual caveat: this selection of science fiction stories represents that best that was published during the year 1996. In my opinion, I could have filled two more volumes this size and then claimed to have nearly all of the best—though not all the best novellas.

Second, the general criteria: this book is full of science fiction—every story in the book is clearly that and not something else. I personally have a high regard for horror, fantasy, speculative fiction, and slipstream and postmodern literature. But here, I chose science fiction. It is the intention of this year's best series to focus entirely on science fiction, and to provide readers who are looking especially for science fiction an annual home base.

And now for the year 1996.

One theme that was particularly evident in this year's fiction was respect for the forefathers of science fiction. Since it was one hundred years after the first publication of H. G. Wells' *The War of the Worlds*, an original anthology was conceived in honor of the occasion, and the stories in that book filled many magazine pages as well before the book appeared. The gimmick was irresistible to writers: tell a story of the Wellsian Martian invasion in the literary voice and style of a writer contemporary of Wells. Another idea that attracted first-rate writers was to write a story in honor of Jack Williamson, the living Grand Master of SF whose contemporary career began in the 1920s and is still going strong. In addition to these anthologies, there were individual books such as Stephen Baxter's *The Time Ships*, a sequel to Wells' *The Time Machine*; and Richard Garfinkle's *Celestial Matters*, an alternate science alternative history of space adventure among the crystalline spheres of the Ptolemaic universe that looked to the past with respect and wonder.

Stephen Baxter, David Langford, and others wrote more individual stories about Jules Verne, Wells, G. K. Chesterton, as forefathers. Perhaps it is a signal of a new evolutionary stage in the literature that the field is aware of diverse literary traditions and of the historical figures, styles, and ideas that have made science fiction what it is today.

There was a relative crash in mass market distribution in 1996 that affected all genres, and that hurt SF, too, leading to some fewer titles in mass market by the end of the year and more titles announced in trade paperback—but not as many in 1997 as in earlier years in mass market size. The major magazines were all in transition, with *Analog* and *Asimov's* sold to another publisher, *Omni* ceasing print publication in favor of online issues—a move followed by A. J. Budry's magazine, *Tomorrow*, at the end of the year. Gordon Van Gelder took over as the new editor of *Fantasy & Science Fiction* as of January 1997. *SF Age* was the only magazine that didn't appear to go through some difficult transition in 1996, achieving a new level of quality that challenged both *F&SF* and *Asimov's*. The smaller professional magazines were all hurt by the relative collapse of small press distribution over the last few years that continued in 1996. *Absolute Magnitude* and *Pirate Writings* continued to publish, as well as *On Spec* in Canada and *Interzone* in England, but in spite of editorial excellence, none of them thrived—just survived. *Interzone*, as usual, maintained its leading position in speculative fiction, and published several fine science fiction stories in the mix.

The trend toward novellas I mentioned last year ceased abruptly, with many fewer fitting into the magazines after page cutbacks and fewer individual issues this year (now most monthly magazines publish eleven times a year, including one big double issue). On the other hand, it was a particularly good year for the science fiction short story, with excellent work appearing every month. And I wish to point out that with the exception of anthologies such as the two mentioned above, Ellen Datlow's hybrid reprint/original, fantasy/SF *Off Limits*, and Patrick Nielsen Hayden's fine *Starlight I* (the beginning of a new series of original anthologies of new short SF and fantasy), and the long-awaited, extraordinary *Tesseracts Q*—SF from the French–Canadian for the first time in English—it was another year in which the magazine editors outperformed the anthologists.

The world stayed turned upside-down in that the average issue of the major magazines was better than the average contents of the original anthologies. Perhaps one beneficial effect of the distribution cutbacks will be fewer original anthologies and a resurgence of quality control (by which I mean editing) in them. The history of science fiction is filled with landmark anthologies, whose story notes and introductions tell the real history and evolution of the literature. We need more good ones.

But now for the stories. . . .

David G. Hartwell
Pleasantville, N.Y.
January, 1997

After a Lean Winter

DAVE WOLVERTON

Dave Wolverton won a Writers of the Future prize at the start of his career and has gone on not only to write many novels and stories of science fiction adventure, but to head the Writers of the Future contest and edit their anthologies himself for the past few years. He is one of the most talented writers of entertaining adventure among younger SF writers, the new generation that appeared at the end of the 1980s. This story is particularly interesting in that it is written as if by Jack London. It was composed for inclusion in *War of the Worlds: Global Dispatches*, edited by Kevin Anderson, though it first appeared in *Fantasy & Science Fiction*. The idea was that writers would write reports of the Martian invasion from parts of the world other than Wells' England (an exception is made for Mr. Henry James) as if witnessed by other famous historical personages, such as Pablo Picasso or Albert Einstein. But the writers often took on another challenge: "After a Lean Winter" is a Jack London story in the style London would have written it. Other interesting pieces in the book in this vein include Robert Silverberg's Henry James, George Alec Effinger's Edgar Rice Burroughs, and Gregory Benford and David Brin's Jules Verne. Wolverton delivers a virtuoso performance here, an SF writer writing as another SF writer (those of you who have missed London's SF may be in for a treat), in the world of a third writer.

Pierre swept into Hidden Lodge on Titchen Creek late on a moonless night. His two sled dogs huffed and bunched their shoulders, then dug their back legs in with angry growls, hating the trail, as they crossed that last stubborn rise. The runners of his sled rang over the crusted snow with the sound of a sword being drawn from its scabbard, and the leather harnesses creaked.

The air that night had a feral bite to it. The sun had been down for days, sometimes hovering near the horizon, and the deadly winter chill was on. It would be a month before we'd see the sun again. For weeks we had felt that cold air gnawing us, chewing away at our vitality, like a wolf pup worrying a shard of caribou bone long after the marrow is depleted.

In the distance, billowing thunderclouds raced toward us under the glimmering stars, promising some insulating warmth. A storm was chasing Pierre's trail. By agreement, no one came to the lodge until just before a storm, and none stayed long after the storm began.

Pierre's two poor huskies caught the scent of camp and yipped softly. Pierre called "Gee," and the sled heeled over on a single runner. Carefully, he twisted the gee-poles, laid the sled on its side next to a dozen others. I noted a heavy bundle lashed to the sled, perhaps a moose haunch, and I licked my lips involuntarily. I'd pay well for some meat.

From out under the trees, the other pack dogs sniffed and approached, too tired to growl or threaten. One of Pierre's huskies yapped again, and Pierre leapt forward with a dog-whip, threatening the lean beast until it fell silent. We did not tolerate noise from dogs anymore. Many a man would have pulled a knife and gutted that dog where it stood, but Pierre—a very crafty and once-prosperous trapper—was down to only two dogs.

"S'okay," I said from my watch post, putting him at ease. "No Martians about." Indeed, the frozen tundra before me was barren for miles. In the distance was a meandering line of wizened spruce, black in the starlight, and a few scraggly willows poked through the snow along the

banks of a winding frozen river just below the lodge. The distant mountains were dark red with lush new growth of Martian foliage. But mostly
the land was snow-covered tundra. No Martian ships floated cloudlike
over the snowfields. Pierre glanced up toward me, unable to make out my
form.

"Jacques? Jacques Lowndunn? Dat you?" he called, his voice muffled
by the wolverine-fur trim of his parka. "What news, my fren'? Eh?"

"No one's had sight of the bloody-minded Martians in two weeks," I
said. "They cleared out of Juneau."

There had been a brutal raid on the town of Dawson some weeks
before, and the Martians had captured the whole town, harvesting the
unlucky inhabitants for their blood. We'd thought then that the Martians
were working their way north, that they'd blaze a path to Titchen Creek.
We could hardly go much farther north this time of year. Even if we
could drag along enough food to feed ourselves, the Martians would just
follow our trail in the snow. So we dug in, holed up for the winter.

"Ah 'ave seen de Marshawns. Certayne!" Pierre said in his nasal voice,
hunching his shoulders. He left the dogs in their harness but fed them
each a handful of smoked salmon. I was eager to hear his news, but he
made me wait. He grabbed his rifle from its scabbard, for no one would
walk about unarmed, then forged up toward the lodge, plodding toward
me through the crusted snow, floundering deeper and deeper into the
drifts with every step, until he climbed up on the porch. There was no
friendly light behind me to guide his steps. Such a light would have
shown us up to the Martians.

"Where did you spot them?" I asked.

"Anchorawge," he grunted, stamping his feet and brushing snow out
of his parka before entering the warmer lodge. "De citee ees gone,
Jacques—dead. De Martians keel everybawdy, by gar!" He spat in the
snow. "De Martians es dere!"

Only once had I ever had the misfortune of observing a Martian. It was
when Bessie and I were on the steamer up from San Francisco. We'd
sailed to Puget Sound, and in Seattle we almost put to port. But the
Martians had landed, and we saw one of their warriors wearing a metal
body that gleamed sullenly like polished brass. It stood watch, its curved
protective armor stretching above its head like the chitinous shell of a
crab, its lank, tripod metal legs letting it stand gracefully a hundred feet
in the air. At first, one would have thought it an inanimate tower, but it
twisted ever so insignificantly as we moved closer, regarding us as a
jumping spider will a gnat, just before it pounces. We notified the captain, and he kept sailing north, leaving the Martian to hunt on its lonely
stretch of beach, gleaming in the afternoon sun.

Bessie and I had thought then that we would be safe back in the Yukon. I cannot imagine any other place than the land near the Circle that is quite so relentlessly inhospitable to life, yet I am intimate with the petty moods of this land, which I have always viewed as something of a mean-spirited accountant which requires every beast upon it to pay his exact dues each year, or die. I had not thought the Martians would be able to survive here, so Bessie and I took our few possessions and struck out from the haven of San Francisco for the bitter wastes north of Juneau. We were so naive.

If the Martians were in Anchorage, then Pierre's tidings were mixed. It was good that they were hundreds of miles away, bad that they were still alive at all. In warmer climes, it was said, they died quickly from bacterial infections. But that was not true here by the Circle. The Martians were thriving in our frozen wastes. Their crops grew at a tremendous rate on any patch of frozen windswept ground—in spite of the fact that there was damned little light. Apparently, Mars is a world that is colder and darker than ours, and what is for us an intolerable frozen hell is to them a balmy paradise.

Pierre finished stamping off his shoes and lifted the latch to the door. Nearly everyone had already made it to our conclave. Simmons, Coldwell and Porter hadn't shown, and it was growing so late that I didn't anticipate that they would make it this time. They were busy with other affairs, or the Martians had harvested them.

I was eager to hear Pierre's full account, so I followed him into the lodge.

In more congenial days, we would have had the iron stove crackling merrily to warm the place. But we couldn't risk such a comforting blaze now. Only a meager lamp consigned to the floor furnished any light for the room. Around the lodge, bundled in bulky furs in their unceasing struggle to get warm, were two dozen stolid men and women of the north. Though the unending torments of the past months had left them bent and bleak, there was a cordial atmosphere now that we had all gathered. A special batch of hootch warmed on a tripod above the lamp. Everyone rousted a bit when Pierre came through the door, edging away enough to make room for him near the lamp.

"What news?" One-Eyed Kate called before Pierre could even kneel by the lamp and pull off his mittens with his teeth. He put his hands down to toast by the glass of the lamp.

Pierre didn't speak. It must have been eighty below outside, and his jaw was leather-stiff from the cold. His lips were tinged with blue, and ice crystals lodged in his brows, eyelashes, and beard.

Still, we all hung on expectantly for a word of news. Then I saw his mood. He didn't like most of the people in this room, though he had a warm spot in his heart for me. Pierre had Indian blood on his mother's side, and he saw this as a chance to count coup on the others. He'd make them pay for every word he uttered. He grunted, nodded toward the kettle of hootch on the tripod.

One-Eyed Kate herself dipped in a battered tin mug, handed it to him. Still he didn't utter a word. He'd been nursing a grudge for the past two months. Pierre Jelenc was a trapper of almost legendary repute here in the north, a tough and cunning man. Some folks down at the Hudson Bay Company said he'd devoted a huge portion of his grub stake to new traps last spring. The north had had two soft winters in a row, so the trapping promised to be exceptional—the best in forty years.

Then the Martians had come, making it impossible for a man to run his trap lines. So while the miners toiled in their shafts through the dark winter, getting wealthier by the minute, Pierre had lost a year's grub stake, and now all of his traps were scattered in their line, hundreds of miles across the territory. Even Pierre, with his keen mind, wouldn't be able to find most of those traps next spring.

Two months ago, Pierre had made one desperate attempt to recoup his losses here at Hidden Lodge. In a drunken frenzy, he started fighting his sled dogs in the big pit out behind the lodge. But his dogs hadn't been eating well, so he couldn't milk any fight out of them. Five of his huskies got slaughtered in the pit that night. Afterward, Pierre had left in a black rage, and hadn't attended a conclave since.

Pierre downed the mug of hootch. It was a devil's concoction of brandy, whiskey, and hot peppers. He handed the cup back to One-Eyed Kate for a refill.

Evidently, Doctor Weatherby had been reading from an article in a newspaper—a paper nearly three months old out of southern Alberta.

"I say, right then," Doctor Weatherby said in a chipper tone. Apparently he thought that Pierre had no news, and I was of a mind to let Pierre speak when he desired. I listened intently, for it was the Doctor I had come to see, hoping he would be able to help my Bessie. "As I reported, Doctor Silvena in Edmonton thinks that there may be more than the cold at work here to help keep the Martians alive. He notes that the 'thin and rarefied air here in the north is more beneficial to the lungs than air in the south, which is clogged with myriad pollens and unhealthy germs. Moreover,' he states, 'there seems to be some quality to the light here in the far north that causes it to destroy detrimental germs. We in the north are marvelously free of many plagues found in warmer lands— leprosy, elephantiasis, and such. Even typhoid and diphtheria are seldom seen here, and the terrible fevers which rampage warmer climes are almost unknown among our native Inuit.' He goes on to say that, 'Contrary to speculation that the Martians here will expire in the summer when germs are given to reproduce more fervently, it may be that the Martian will hold forth on our northern frontier indefinitely. Indeed, they may gradually acclimatize themselves to our air, and, like the Indians who have grown resistant to our European measles and chicken pox, in time they may once again venture into more temperate zones.' "

"Not a'fore bears grow wings," Klondike Pete Kandinsky hooted. "It's cold enough to freeze the balls off a pool table out thar this winter. Most like, we'll find them Martians all laid out next spring, thawing in some snowbank."

Klondike Pete was behind the times. Rumor said that he'd struck a rich vein in his gold mine, so he'd holed up in the shaft, working eighteen-hour days from August through Christmas, barely taking time to come out for supplies. He hadn't attended our previous conclaves.

"Gads," Doctor Weatherby said, "I say, where have you been? We believe that the Martians came here because their own world has been cooling for millennia. They're seeking our warmer climes. But just because they are looking for warmer weather, it doesn't mean they want to live on our equator! What seems monstrously cold to us—that biting winter that we've suffered through this past three months—is positively balmy on Mars! I'm sure they're much invigorated by it. Indeed, the reason we haven't seen more of the Martians here in the past weeks seems blatantly obvious: they're preparing to migrate north, to our polar cap!"

"Ah, Gods, I swear!" Klondike Pete shook his head mournfully, realizing our predicament for the first time. "Why don't the Army do somethin? Teddy Roosevelt or the Mounties ought to do somethin."

"They're playing at waiting," One-Eyed Kate grumbled. "You know what kinds of horrors they've been through down south. There's not much the armies of the world can do against the Martians. Even if they could send heavy artillery against the Martians in the winter, there's no sense in it—not when the varmints might die out this coming spring, anyhow."

"There's sense 'n it!" one old timer said. "Folks is dyin' up here! The Martians squeeze us for blood, then toss our carcasses 'way like grape skins!"

"Yeah," One-Eyed Kate said, "and so long as it's the likes of you and me that are doing the dying, Tom King, no one will do more than yawn about it!"

The refugees in the room looked around gloomily at one another. Trappers, miners, Indians, crackpots who'd fled from the world. We were an unsavory lot, dressed in our hides, with sour bear grease rubbed in our skin to keep out the weather. One-Eyed Kate was right. No one would rescue us.

"I just whist we 'ad word on them Martians," old Tom King said, wiping his nose on the sleeve of his parka. He looked off into a corner with rheumy eyes. "No news is good news," he intoned, the hollow-sounding supplication of an atheist.

None of us believed the adage. The Martian vehicles that fell in the southern climes were filled only with a few armies and scouts. Thirty or forty troops per vehicle, if we judged right. But now we saw that these were only the advance forces, hardly more than scouts who were meant, perhaps, to decimate our armies and harass the greater population of the world in preparation for the most massive vehicle, the one that fell two months later than the rest, just south of Juneau. The mother ship had carried two thousand Martians, some guessed, along with their weird herds of humanoid bipeds that the Martians harvested for blood. The mother vehicle had hardly settled when thousands of their slaves swarmed out of the ships and began planting crops, scattering other-worldly seeds that sprouted nearly overnight into grotesque forests of twisted growths that looked like coral or cactuses, but which Doctor Weatherby assured us were more likely some type of fungus. Certain of the plants grew two hundred yards high in the ensuing month, so that it was said that now, one could hardly travel south of Juneau in most places. The "Great Northern Martian Jungle" formed a virtually impene-trable barrier to the southlands, a barrier reputed to harbor Martian bipeds who hunted humans so that their masters might feast on our blood.

"If no news is good news, then let us toast good news," Klondike Pete said, hoisting his mug.

"Ah've seen dem Marshawns," Pierre said at last. "En Anchorawge. Dey burned de ceety, by *Gar,* and dey are building, building—making new ceety dat is strange and wondrous!"

There were cries of horror and astonishment, people crying out que-ries. "When, when did you see them?" Doctor Weatherby asked, shout-ing to be heard above the others.

"Twelve days now," Pierre said. "Dere is a jungle growing around Anchorawge now—very thick—and de Marshawns live dere, smelting de ore day and night to build dere machine ceety. Dere ceety—how shall I say?—is magnificent, by *Gar!* Eet stands five hundred feet tall, and can walk about on eets three legs like a walking stool. But is not a small stool—is huge, by *Gar,* a mile across!

"On de top of de table, is huge glass bowl, alive with shimmering work-lights, more varied and magnificent dan de lights of Paris! And under dis dome, de Marshawns building dere home."

Doctor Weatherby's eyes opened wide in astonishment. "A dome, you say? Fantastic! Are they sealing themselves in? Could it keep out bacteria?"

Pierre shrugged. "Ah 'uz too far away to see dis taim. Some taim, maybe, Ah go back—look more closer. Eh?"

"Horse feathers!" Klondike Pete said. "Them Martians couldn't raise such a huge city in two months. Frenchie, I don't like it when some pimple like you pulls my legs!"

There was an expectant hush around the room, and none dared intervene between the two men. I think that most of us at least half believed Pierre. No one knew what the Martians were capable of. They flew between worlds and built killing death rays. They switched mechanical bodies as easily as we changed clothes. We could not guess their limitations.

Only Klondike Pete here was ignorant enough to doubt the Frenchman. Pierre scowled up at Pete. The little Frenchman was not used to having someone call him a liar, and many honest men so accused would have pulled a knife to defend their honor. A fight was almost expected, but in any physical contest, Pierre would not equal Klondike Pete.

But Pierre obviously had another plan in mind. A secretive smile stole across his face, and I imagined how he might be plotting to ambush the bigger man on some dark night, steal his gold. So many men had been taken by the Martians, that in such a scenario, we would likely never learn the truth of it.

But that was not Pierre's plan. He downed another mug of hootch, banged his empty mug on the lid of the cold iron stove at his side. Almost as if magically summoned, a blast of wind struck the lodge, whistling through the eaves of the log cabin. I'd been vaguely aware of the rising wind for the past few minutes, but only then did I recognize that the full storm had just hit.

By custom, when a storm hit we would set a roaring blaze and lavish upon ourselves one or two hours of warmth before trudging back to our own cabins or mine shafts. If we timed it properly, the last of the storm would blanket our trail, concealing our passage from any Martians that might fly over, hunting us.

Still, some of us were clumsy. Over the past three months, our numbers had been steadily diminishing, our people disappearing as the Martians harvested us.

My thoughts turned homeward, to my own wife Bessie who was huddled in our cabin, sick and weakened by the interminable cold.

"Storm's here, stoke up the fire!" someone shouted, and One-Eyed

Kate opened the iron door to the old stove and struck a match. The tinder had already been set, perhaps for days, in anticipation of this moment.

Soon a roaring blaze crackled in the old iron stove. We huddled in a circle, each of us silent and grateful, grunting with satisfaction. During the storms, the Martian flying machines were forced to seek shelter in secluded valleys, it was said, and so we did not fear that the Martians would attack. The bipeds that the Martians used for food and as slaves might attack, I suspected, if they saw our smoke, but this was unlikely. We were far from the Martian Jungles, and it was rumored that the bipeds held forth only in their own familiar domain.

After the past two weeks of damnable cold, we needed some warmth, and as I basked in the roaring heat of the stove, the others began to sigh in contentment. I hoped that Bessie had lit our own little stove back in the old mining shack we called home.

Pierre put his gloves back on, and the little man was beginning to feel the effects of his drinks. He weaved a little as he stood, and growled, "By *Gar*, your dogs weel fait mah beast tonait!"

"You're down to only two dogs," I reminded Pierre. He wasn't a careless sort, unless he got drunk. I knew he wasn't thinking clearly. He couldn't afford to lose another dog in a senseless fight.

"Damn you, Jacques! Your dogs weel fait mah beast tonait!" He pounded the red-hot stove with a gloved fist, staggered toward me with a crazed gleam in his eyes.

I wanted to protect him from himself. "No one wants to fight your dogs tonight," I said.

Pierre staggered to me, grabbed my shoulder with both hands, and looked up. His face was seamed and scarred by the cold, and though he was drunk, there was a cunning glint in his eyes. "Your dogs, weel fait, my *beast*, tonait!"

The room went silent. "What beast are you talking about?" One-Eyed Kate said.

"You looking for Marshawns, no?" he turned to her and waved expansively. "You want see a Marshawn? Your dogs keeled mah dogs. Now your dogs weel fait mah Marshawn!"

My heart began pounding, and my thoughts raced. We had not seen Pierre in weeks, and it was said that he was one of the finest trappers in the Yukon. As my mind registered what he'd brought back from Anchorage, as I realized what he'd trapped there, I recalled the heavy bundle tied to his sled. Could he really have secured a live Martian?

Suddenly there was shouting in the room from a dozen voices. Several men grabbed a lantern and dashed out the front door, the dancing light throwing grotesque images on the wall. Klondike Pete was shouting, "How much? How much do you want to fight your beast?"

"I say, heaven forbid! Let's not have a fight!" Doctor Weatherby began saying. "I want to study the creature!"

But the sudden fury with which the others met the doctor's plea was overwhelming.

We were outraged by the Martians for our burnt cities, for the poisoned crops, for the soldiers who died under Martian heat beams or choked to death in the vile Black Fog that emanated from their guns. More than all of this, we raged against the Martians for our fair daughters and children who had gone to feed these vile beasts, these Martians who drank our blood as we drain water.

So great was this primal rage, that someone struck the doctor—more in some mindless animal instinct, some basic need to see the Martian dead, than out of anger at the good man who had worked so hard to keep us alive through this hellish winter.

The doctor crumpled under the weight of the blow and knelt on the floor for a moment, staring down at the dirty wood planks, trying to regain his senses.

Meanwhile, others took up the shout, "There's a game for you!" "How much to fight it? What do you want?"

Pierre stood in a swirling, writhing, shouting maelstrom. I know logically that there could not have been two dozen people in the room, yet it seemed like vastly more. Indeed, it seemed to my mind that all of troubled humanity crowded the room at that moment, hurling fists in the air, cursing, threatening, mindlessly crying for blood.

I found myself screaming to be heard, "How much? How much?" And though I have never been one to engage in the savage sport of dogfighting, I thought of my own sled dogs out in front of the lodge, and I considered how much I'd be willing to pay to watch them tear apart a Martian. The answer was simple:

I'd pay everything I owned.

Pierre raised his hands in the air for silence, and named his price, and if you think it unfairly high, then remember this: we all secretly believed that we would die before spring. Money meant almost nothing to us. Most of us had been unable to get adequately outfitted for winter, and had hoped that a moose or a caribou would get us through the lean months. But Martians harvested the caribou and moose just as they harvested us. Many a man in that room knew that he'd be down to eating his sled dogs by spring. Money means nothing to those who wish only to survive.

Yet we knew that many would profit from the Martian invasion. In the south, insurance hucksters were selling policies against future invasions, the loggers and financiers were making fortunes, and every man who'd ever handled a hammer suddenly called himself a master carpenter and sought to hire himself out at inflated prices.

We in this room did not resent Pierre's desire to recoup his losses after the most horrible of winters.

"De beast has sixteen tentacles," he said, "so All weel let you fight heem with eight dogs—at five t'ousand doughlars a dog. Two t'ousand doughlars for me, and de rest, goes for de winner, or de winners, of the fait!"

The accounts we'd read about Martians suggested that without their metallic bodies, they moved ponderously slow here on Earth. The increased gravity of our world, where everything is three times heavier than on Mars, weighed them down greatly. I'd never seen a bear pitted against more than eight dogs, so it seemed unlikely that the Martian could win. But with each contestant putting in two thousand dollars just for the right to fight, Pierre would go home with at least $16,000—five times what he'd make in a good year. All he had to do was let people pay for the right to kill a Martian.

Klondike Pete didn't even blink. "I'll put in two huskies!" he roared.

"Grip can take him!" One-Eyed Kate said. "You'll let a pit bull fight?"

Pierre nodded, and I began calculating. If you counted most of my supplies, I had barely enough for a stake in the fight, and I had a dog I thought could win—half husky, half wolfhound. He'd outweigh any of the other mutts in the pit, and he pulled the sled with great heart. He was a natural leader.

But I caught that sly gleam in Pierre's dark eyes. I knew that this fight would be more than any of us were bargaining for. I hesitated.

"By Gol', I'll put in my fighter," old Tom King offered with evident bloodlust, and in half a moment four other men signed their notes to Pierre. The fight was set.

The storm raged. Snow pounded in the unbounded avarice, skidding across the frozen crust of the winter's buildup. One-Eyed Kate lugged a pair of lanterns into the blizzard, held them over the fighting pit. At the north end, a bear cage could be lowered into the pit by means of a winch. At the south end, a dog run led down.

Klondike Pete leapt in and flattened the snow, then climbed back up through the dog run. Everyone unhitched and brought their dogs from the sleds, then herded them down the run. The dogs smelled the excitement, yapped and growled, stalking through the pit and sniffing uneasily.

Someone began winching the big cage up, and the dogs settled down.

Some of the dogs had battled bears, and so knew the sound of the winch. One-Eyed Kate's pit bull emitted a coughing bark and began leaping in excitement, wanting to draw first blood from whatever we loosed into the pit.

It was a ghoulish mob that stood around that dark pit, pale faces lit dimly by the oily lanterns that flickered and guttered with every gust of wind.

Four men had already lugged Pierre's bundle around to the back of the lodge. The bundle was wrapped in heavy canvas and tied solidly with five or six hide ropes of Eskimo make. A couple of men worried at the knots, trying to untie the frozen leather, while two others stood nearby with rifles cocked, aimed at the bundle.

Pierre swore softly, drew his Bowie knife and sliced through the ropes, then rolled the canvas over several times. The canvas was wound tight around the Martian six turns, so that one moment I was peering through the driving snow while trying to make out the form that would emerge from the gray bundle, and the next moment, the Martian fell on the ground before us.

It burst out from the tarpaulin. It backed away from Pierre and from the light, a creature frightened and alone, and for several moments it made a metallic hissing noise as it slithered over the snow, searching for escape. At first, the hissing sounded like a rattlesnake's warning, and several of us leapt back. But the creature before us was no snake.

For those who have never seen a Martian, it can be difficult to describe such a monstrosity. I have read descriptions, but none succeed. My recollections of this monster are imprinted as solidly as if they were etched on a lithographic plate, for this creature was both more than, and less than, the sum of all our nightmares.

Others have described a fungal green-gray hue of the creature's bulbous head, fully five times larger than a human head, and they have told of the wet leathery skin that encases the Martian's enormous brain. Others have described the peculiar slavering, sucking sounds that the creatures made as they gasped for breath, heaving convulsively as they groped about in our heavy atmosphere.

Others have described the two clumps of tentacles—eight in each clump, just below the lipless V-shaped beak, and they have told how the Gorgon tentacles coiled almost languidly as the creature slithered about.

The Martian invites comparison to the octopus or squid, for like these creatures it seems little more than a head with tentacles. Yet it is so much more than that!

No one has described how the Martian was so exquisitely, so gloriously alive. The one Pierre had captured swayed back and forth, pulsing across the ice-crusted snow with an ease that suggested that it was acclimated to polar conditions. While others have said that the creature seemed to them to be ponderously slow, I wonder if their specimens were not somehow hampered by warmer conditions—for this beast wriggled viciously, and its tentacles slithered over the snow like living whips, writhing not in agony—but in desperation, in a curious hunger.

Others have tried to tell what they saw in the Martian's huge eyes: a marvelous intelligence, an intellect keen beyond measure, a sense of malevolence that some imagined to be pure evil.

Yet as I looked into that monster's eyes, I saw all of those and more. The monster slithered over the snow at a deceptively quick pace, circling and twisting this way and that. Then for a moment it stopped and candidly studied each of us. In its eyes was an undisguised hunger, a malevolent intent so monstrous that some hardened trappers cried out and turned away.

A dozen men pulled out weapons and hardly restrained themselves from opening fire. For a moment the Martian continued to hiss in that metallic grating sound, and I imagined it was some warning, till I realized that it was only the sound of the creature drawing crude breaths.

It sized up the situation, then sat gazing with evident maleficence at Pierre. The only sound was the gusting of wind over the tundra, the hiss of frozen snow stinging the ground, and my heart pounding.

Pierre laughed gleefully. "You see de situation, mah frien'," he addressed the Martian. "You wan' to drink from me, but we have de guns trained on you. But dere ees blood to drink—blood from dogs!"

The Martian gazed at Pierre with calculating hatred. I do not doubt it understood every word Pierre uttered, every nuance. I imagined the creature learning our tongue as Pierre talked to it and his dogs on the lonely trail. It knew what we required of it. "Keel dem if you can," Pierre admonished the creature. "Keel de dogs, drink from dem. If you ween, Ah weel set you free to fin' your own kind. Ees simple, no?"

The Martian expelled some air from its mouth in a gasp, an almost mechanical sound that cannot adequately be described as speech. Yet the timing of that gasp, the pitch and volume, identified the beast's intent as certain as any words uttered from human lips. "Yes," it said.

Haltingly, with many a backward glance at us, the Martian slithered over the ground on its tentacles, entered the bear cage. Klondike Pete went to the winch and lifted the cage from the ground, while Tom King swiveled the boom out over the floor of the pit, then they lowered the cage.

The dogs sniffed and yapped. Snarls and growls mingled into a continuous sound. One-Eyed Kate's pit bull, Grip, was a grayish creature the color of ash, and it leapt up at the cage as it lowered, growling and snapping once or twice, then caught the alien's scent and backed away.

Others were not so circumspect. Klondike Pete's dogs were veterans of the ring, used to fighting as a team, and their teeth snapped together with metallic clicks as we lowered the Martian into the pit. They jumped up, biting at the tentacles that recoiled from them.

When the cage hit the floor of the pit, Klondike Pete's huskies snarled and danced forward, thrusting their teeth between the pine-wood bars at each side of the bear cage, trying to tear some flesh from the Martian before we pulled the rope that would open the door, freeing the Martian into the ring.

The dogs attacked from two sides at once, and if it had been a bear in that cage, it would have backed away from one dog, only to have the other tear into it from behind. The Martian was not so easily abused.

It held calmly in the center of the cage for half a second, observing the dogs with those huge eyes, so full of malevolent wisdom.

Klondike Pete pulled the rope that would spring the door to the cage, releasing the Martian to the pack of dogs, and what happened next is almost too grisly to tell.

It has been said that Martians were ponderously slow, that they struggled under the effects of our heavier gravity. Perhaps that was true of them when they first landed, but this creature seemed to have acclimated to our gravity very well over the past few months.

It became, in an instant, a seething dynamo, a twisting, grisly mass of flesh bent on destruction. It hurled against one side of the cage, then another, and at first I believed it was trying to demolish the cage, break it asunder. Indeed, the Martian was roughly the size and weight of a small black bear, and I have seen bears tear cages apart in a fight. I heard timbers crack under the monster's onslaught, but it was not trying to break the bars of its cage.

It was not until after the Martian had hurled itself against the bars of its cage that I realized what had happened. Each of a Martian's tentacles is seven feet long, and about three inches wide near the end. With several tentacles whipping snake-like in the air, striking in precision, the Martian had snatched through the bars and grabbed one husky, then another, and pulled, pinning the dogs helplessly against the sides of the bear cage where it held them firmly about their necks.

The huskies yelped and whined to find themselves in the Martian's grasp, and struggled to pull away, desperately scratching at the beast's tentacles with their forepaws, tugging backward with their considerable might. These were not your weak house dogs of New York or San Francisco. These were trained pack dogs that could drag a four-hundred-pound sled over the bitter tundra for sixteen hours a day, and I believed that they would easily break free of the Martian's grasp.

The door to the cage began to drop open, and with one tentacle, the Martian grasped it, twined the tentacle about the door, and held it closed as securely as if it were held by a steel lock, and in this manner it kept the other dogs somewhat at bay.

The other dogs barked and snarled. The pit bull lunged and experimentally nipped the tentacle that held the door closed, then danced back. One or two dogs howled, trotted around the pit, unsure how to proceed in their attacks. The pit bull struck again—once, twice—and was joined quickly by the others, and in a moment three dogs were snarling, trying to rip that one tentacle free of the door. I saw flesh ripped away, and tender white skin, almost bloodless, was exposed.

The Martian seemed unconcerned. It was willing to sacrifice a limb in order to sate its appetite. Holding the two huskies firmly against the cage, the Martian began to feed.

It must be remembered that Pierre had held this Martian for nine days without food, and any human so ill-treated perhaps would also have sought refreshment before continuing the fight. It has also been reported that Martians drink blood, and that they used pipettes about a yard long to do so. From other accounts, one might suppose that such pipettes were metallic things that the Martians kept lying about near their vehicles, but this is not so.

Instead, from the Martian's beak, a three-foot long rod telescoped, a rod that might have been a long white bone, except that it was twisted, like the horn of a narwhal, and its tip was hollow.

The Martian expertly inserted this bone into the jugular vein of the nearest husky, who yelped and snarled ferociously, trying to escape.

A loud, orgasmic slurping issued from the Martian, as if it were drinking sarsaparilla with an enormous straw. The dog's death was amazingly swift. One moment it was kicking its hind legs convulsively, bloodying the snow at its feet in its struggles to escape, and in the next it succumbed totally, horribly, and it slumped and quivered.

The tiniest fleck of blood dribbled from the husky's throat as it ceased its frantic attempts at flight.

In thirty seconds, the feeding over, the Martian twisted with a snapping motion, inserted its horn into the second husky, and drank its blood swiftly. The whole process was carried out with horrid rapidness and precision, with as little thought as you or I might give to the process of chewing and swallowing an apple.

By now, the other dogs had gotten a good portion of the flesh on the Martian's tentacle chewed away, and as the Martian fed upon the second of Klondike Pete's prize-fighting huskies, the Martian struck with several tentacles, pummeling the dogs on their snouts, frightening them back a pace, where they snarled and leapt back and forth, seeking an opening.

The Martian stopped, regarded Klondike Pete balefully, and tossed the body of a dead second husky a pace toward him. The look in the creature's eyes was chilling—a promise of what would happen to Klondike Pete if the Martian got free.

The Martian exhaled from its long white horn, and droplets of blood sprayed out over our faces. The sound that this exhalation—this almost automatic cleaning of the horn—made was most unsettling: it sounded as a trumpeting, ululating cry that rang through the night, slicing through the blizzard. It was a mournful sound, infinitely lonely in that dark setting.

At that moment, I felt small and mean to be standing here on the edge of the pit, urging the dogs to finish their business. For their part, the other six dogs backed away and studied the monster quietly, sniffing the air, wondering at this awe-inspiring sound that it made.

A biting gust of wind hit my face, and for the first time during that fight, I realized just how cold I was. The storm was blowing in warmer air. Indeed, I looked forward to the next few days under the cloud cover. But the wind was brutal. It felt as if ice water were running in my veins, and the bitter weather drove the breath from me. I hunched against the cold, saw how the dogs quivered with anticipation in the pit, the breath steaming hot from their mouths.

I wanted to turn, rush inside to the warm stove, forget this grisly battle. But I was held by my own bloodlust, by my own quivering excitement.

There were six strong dogs in the ring, dogs bred to a life of toil. They growled and menaced and kept their distance, and the Martian retracted its horn back under that peculiar V-shaped beak, and flung open the doors of the bear cage, surging forward. Its appetite for blood had been sated, and now it was ready for battle.

In a pounding, quivering mass it rolled forward over the ice, staring into the eyes of the dogs. There was a look of undaunted majesty in those eyes, an air of mastery to the creature's movements. "I am king here," it was saying to the dogs. "I am all you aspire to be. You are fit only to be my food."

With a coughing bark, Grip lunged for the Martian, its gray body leaping silent as a spectre over the snow. It jumped in the air, aiming a snapping bite at the Martian's huge eye. I was almost forced to turn away. I did not want to see what happened when that pit bull's monstrous, vise-like jaws bit into that dark flesh of the Martian's eye.

In response, the Martian dropped down and under the dog with incredible speed. It became a whirling dynamo, a vortex, a living force of incredible power. Reaching up with three tentacles, it caught the pit bull by the neck in midair, then twisted and pulled down. There was an awful snapping as the pit bull hit ground, bounced twice. The pit bull slid a few feet over the snow, its neck broken, and lay panting and whining on the ice, unable to get up.

But the huskies were undaunted. These were the cousins to wolves, and their bloodlust, the primal memories passed through generations, overcame their fear. Four more dogs lunged and bit almost simultaneously, undaunted by the spectacle of strangeness and power before them. As they latched onto a tentacle, twisting, trying to rip and tear at the Martian as if it were some young caribou on the tundra, the Martian would convulse, pull its limb back rapidly, drawing each dog into its clutches.

In seconds, the Martian had four vicious, snarling dogs in its grasp, and its tentacles wound about their necks like a hangman's ropes.

There was a flurry of activity, of frantic writhing and lunges on the parts of the dogs. The growls of attack became plaintive yelps of surprise and fear. The eager savage cries of battle became only a desperate pawing as the four worthy huskies, these brothers of the wolf, tried to escape.

The Martian gripped with several tentacles to each dog, as a squid might grasp small fishes, and choked the fight and life from the dogs while we ogled in horrid fascination.

Soon the startled yelping, the labored breathing of dogs, the frantic tussle as the huskies sought escape, all became a stillness. Their heaving chests quieted. The wind blew softly through their gray hair.

The Martian sat atop them, slavering from its exertions, heaving and pulsating, glaring up at us.

One dog was left. Old Tom King's husky, a valiant fighter that knew it was outmatched. It paced on the far side of the pit, whimpered up at us in shame. It was too smart to fight this strange monster.

Tom King hobbled over to the dog run, grunted as he lifted the gate that would let his dog escape the pit. Under normal circumstances, this act of mercy would not be allowed in such a fight, but these were anything but normal circumstances. We would not be amused by the senseless death of this one last canine.

Klondike Pete raised his 30-30 Winchester, aimed at the Martian's head, right between its eyes. The Martian stared at us fiercely, without fear. "Kill me," it seemed to say. "It does not matter. I am but one of our kind. We will be back."

"So, mah fren'," Pierre called to the Martian. "You have won your laif. As Ah promis, Ah weel let you go now. But mah companions here," he waved expansively to the rest of us around the pit, "Ah no t'ink weel be so generous, by *Gar*. Mah condolences to you!"

He turned his back on the Martian, and I stared at the indomitable creature in the pit, lit only by the frantic wavering of our oil lamps. The storm was blowing, and the fierce cold gnawed at me, and for one moment, I wondered what it was like on Mars. I imagined the planet cooling over millennia, becoming a frozen hell like this land we had all exiled ourselves to. I imagined a warm house, a warm room, and I thought at how I, like the Martian, would do anything for one hour of heated solace. I would plot, steal, kill. Just as the Martian had done.

Time seemed to stop as Klondike Pete took aim, and I found myself croaking feebly, "Let it live. It won the right!"

Everyone stopped. One-Eyed Kate peered from across the pit. Jim cocked his head and looked at me strangely.

The Martian turned its monstrously intelligent eyes on me, and gazed, it seemed, into my soul. For once there was no hunger in that gaze, no disconcerting look of malevolence.

What happened next, I cannot explain, for words alone are inadequate to describe the sensation I received. There are those who assume that the Martians communicated through clicking sounds of their beaks, or through the waving of tentacles, but the many witnesses who observed the monsters in life all agree that no such sounds or motions were evident. Indeed, one reporter in London went so far as to suggest that they may have shared thoughts across space, communicating from one mind to another. Such suggestions have met with ridicule in critical circles, but I can only tell what happened to me: I was gazing into the pit, at the Martian, and suddenly it seemed as if a vast intelligence was pouring into my mind. For one brief moment, my thoughts seemed to expand and my intellect seemed to fill the universe, and I beheld a world with red blowing desert sands so strikingly cold that the sensation assaulted me like a physical blow, crumpling me so that I fell down into the snow, curling into a ball. And as I beheld this world, I looked through eyes that were not my own. All of the light was tremendously magnified and shifted toward the red spectrum, so that I beheld the landscape as if on some strange summer evening when the sky shone more redly than normal. I looked out across a horizon that was peculiarly concave, as if I were staring at a world much smaller than ours.

A few red plants sprouted in this frigid waste, but they were stunted things. Martian cities—walking things that traveled through great maze-like canyons as they followed the sun from season to season—were marching in the distance, tantalizing, gleaming. I craved their warmth, the company of my Martian companions. I hungered for warmth, as a starving man might hunger for food in the last moments of life.

And above me, floating like a mote of dust in the sea of space, was the shining planet Earth.

One. We are one, a voice seemed to whisper in my head, and I knew that the Martian, with its superior intellect, had deigned speak to me. *You understand me. We are one.*

Then above me—for I had fallen to the ground under the weight of this extraordinary vision—a rifle cracked, the sound of it reverberating from the cabin and the low hills. Klondike Pete cocked the gun and fired three more times, and the stinging scent of gunpowder and burnt oil from the barrel of his gun filled the air.

I got up and looked into the pit at the Martian. It was wriggling in its death throes, twisting and heaving on the ground in its inhuman way.

Everyone stood in the freezing, pelting snow, watching it die. I looked behind me, and even Doctor Weatherby had come out to witness the monster's demise.

"Right then, I say," he muttered. "Well, it's done."

I got up, brushed the snow from me, and looked down into the pit. Tom King was watching me with rheumy eyes that glittered in the lamplight. He pulled at his beard and cackled. " 'Let 't live,' says he!" He turned away and chuckled under his breath. "Young whippersnapper thinks he know ever'thing—but he don't know gol'-durned nothin'!"

The others hurried into the warm lodge for the night, and in moments I was forced to follow.

That was on the night of January 13, 1900. As far as I know, I was among the last people on Earth to see a living Martian. In warmer climes, they had all passed away months before, during that hot August. And even as we suffered that night through the grim storm, the huge walking city in Anchorage began a tedious trek north, and was never seen again. Its tracks indicate that it came to the frozen ocean, tried to walk across, and sank into the sea. Many believe that there the Martians drowned, while others wonder if perhaps this had been the Martians' intended destination all along, and so we are forced to wonder if the Martians are even now living in cities under the frozen polar ice, waiting to return.

But on the night I speak of, none of us at Hidden Lodge knew what would happen in months to come. Perhaps because of the Martian's malevolent gaze, perhaps because of the nearness of the creature, or perhaps because of our own feelings of guilt for what we had done, we feared more than ever an ignoble death in the tentacles of the Martians.

After we had warmed ourselves for a few moments in the lodge, the men all scurried away. Doctor Weatherby agreed to accompany me to my cabin under the cover of the storm, so that he might look in on Bessie. More than anything else, it was her need that had driven me to the lodge this night.

We left Hidden Lodge during the middle of the storm, let the snows cover our trails until we reached the cabin. We found Bessie gone from the cabin. The front door was open, and an armload of wood lay on the floor just inside. I knew then that the Martians had gotten her, had snatched her as she tried to warm herself. I tramped through the snow until I found her frozen, bloodless corpse not far outside the cabin.

I was overcome with grief and insisted on going out, under cover of darkness, and burying her deep in the snow, where the wolves would not find her. I did not care if the Martians took me. Almost, I wanted it.

The storm had passed. The Arctic night was brutally cold, the stars piercingly bright. The aurora borealis flickered green on the northern horizon in a splendid display, and after I buried Bessie, I stood in the snow for a long hour, looking up.

Doctor Weatherby must have worried at why I stayed out for so long, for he came out and put his hands on my shoulders, then stared up into the night sky.

"I say, there it is—isn't it? Mars?" He was staring farther south than I had been watching, apparently believing that I was studying events elsewhere in the heavens. I had never been one to study the skies. I did not know where Mars lay. It stared down at us, like a baleful red eye.

After that, Doctor Weatherby stayed on for a week to care for me. It was an odd time. I was brooding, silent. On the woodpile, the good doctor set out petri dishes full of agar to the open air. Small colored dots of bacteria were growing in each dish, and by watching these, he hoped to discover precisely what species of bacteria were destroying the Martians. He insisted that cultures of such bacteria might provide an overwhelming defense in future wars. I was intrigued by this, and somehow, of all the things that happened that winter, my numbed mind remembers those green splotches of mold and bacteria better than just about anything else.

After the doctor left, it was the most difficult time of my life. I had no food, no warmth, no comfort during the remainder of that winter. Sometimes I wished the Martians would take me, even as I struggled to stay alive.

Before the end of the cold weather, I was forced to eat my dogs, and ultimately boil the gut strings from my snowshoes to eat these at the last. I struggled from day to day under each successive frozen blast from the north.

I managed to live.

And slowly, haltingly, like the march of an old and enfeebled man, after the lean winter, came a chill spring.

In the Upper Room

TERRY BISSON

Terry Bisson slips back and forth between science fiction and fantasy in his stories and novels, but when he writes science fiction, it is full of detail and fascination with how things work, deadpan humor, wit, and stylish grace. His SF novel, *Voyage to the Red Planet*, is perhaps both the most heroic and the funniest chronicle of the first voyage to Mars in all science fiction. His *Fire on the Mountain* is an unconventional alternate history utopia, and his *Talking Man* is a wild outright fantasy. In the 1990s, Bisson began to write short stories and hit the ground running. One of his first was "Bears Discover Fire," which won the Hugo and Nebula Awards, and several others. His short fiction has been a regular fixture on award ballots during this decade. This piece is an aside set in the same future as his 1996 novel, *Pirates of the Universe,* which was one of six SF novels chosen by the *New York Times* as "distinguished" in the year. Only Bisson could have invented the idea of a science fiction story using the prose style of the Victoria's Secret catalog, and then sold it to *Playboy.* This was a year in which VR, virtual reality, was a major theme in science fiction and here is Bisson's take on it.

"You will feel a slight chill," the attendant said. "Don't worry about it. Just go with it, OK?"

"OK," I said. I had heard all this before.

"You will feel a slight disorientation. Don't worry about it. A part of you will be aware of where you are, and another part will be aware of where you really are, if you know what I mean. Just go with it, OK?"

"OK," I said. "Actually, I have heard all this before. I was on the Amazon Adventure last year."

"You were? Well, I am required to say it anyway," the attendant said. "Where was I? Oh yes, go slow." He wore squeaky shoes and a white coat and carried a little silver hammer in a loop on his pants. "If you look at things too closely at first, nothing will be there. But if you take your time, everything will appear, OK?"

"OK," I said. "What about—?"

"You won't know her name," he said. "Not in the demo. But if you sign up for a tour, you will know it automatically. Ready? Lie down. Take a deep breath."

Ready or not, the drawer started sliding in and I felt a moment of panic, which I remembered from the year before. The panic makes you take another breath, and then there is the sharp smell of the Vitazine, and there you are. It is like waking from a dream. I was in a sunlit room with a deep-piled rug and high French windows. She stood at the windows overlooking what appeared to be a busy street, so long as you were careful not to look at it too closely.

I was careful not to look at it too closely. She was wearing a sand-washed burgundy silk chemise with a sheerlace Empire bodice, cross-laced on the plunging back. No stockings. I have never really liked stockings. She was barefoot but I couldn't make out her feet. I was careful not to look at them too closely.

I liked the way the bodice did on the sides. After a while I looked around the room. There was wicker furniture and a few potted plants by a low door. I had to duck my head to step through and I was in a kitchen with a tile floor and blue cabinets. She stood at the sink under a little window overlooking a green, glistening yard. She was wearing a long-sleeved panne velvet bodysuit with a low sweetheart neckline, high-cut legs and a full back. I liked the way the velvet did in the back. I stood beside her at the window, watching the robins arrive and depart on the grass. It was the same robin over and over.

A white wall phone rang. She picked it up and handed it to me, and as soon as I put the receiver to my ear and heard the tone, I was looking up toward what seemed at first to be clouds but was in fact the water-stained ceiling of the Departure Hall.

I sat up. "That's it?" I asked.

"That's the demo," said the attendant, who hurried over to my opened drawer, shoes squeaking. "The phone is what exits you out of the system. The same way the doors elevate you from level to level."

"I like it," I said. "My vacation starts tomorrow. Where do I sign up?"

"Slow down," he said, helping me out of the drawer. "The Veep is by invitation only. You have to talk to Cisneros in client services first."

"The Veep?"

"That's what we call it sometimes."

"Last year I did the Amazon Adventure," I said to Dr. Cisneros. "This year I have a week, starting tomorrow, and I came in to sign up for the Arctic Adventure. That's when I saw the Victoria's Palace demo in the brochure."

"Victoria's is just opening," she said. "Actually, we are still beta testing sectors of it. Only the middle and upper-middle rooms are open. But that should be plenty for a five-day tour."

"How many rooms is that?"

"Lots." She smiled. Her teeth looked new. The little thing on her desk said B. CISNEROS, PH.D. "Technically speaking, the Veep is a hierarchical pyramid string, so the middle and upper middle includes all the rooms but one. All but the Upper Room."

I blushed. I'm always blushing.

"You wouldn't be getting that high in just five days anyway." She showed me her new teeth again. "And because we're still beta testing, we can make you a special offer. The same price they charge for the Arctic and Amazon adventures. A five-day week, nine to five, for $899. The price will go up substantially when Victoria's Palace is fully open next year, I can assure you."

"I like it," I said. I stood up. "Where do I go to pay?"

"Accounts. But sit back down." She opened a manila folder. "First I am required to ask a clinical question. Why do you want to spend your vacation in Victoria's Palace?"

I shrugged to keep from blushing. "It's different and that appeals to me. You might say I'm sort of a VR freak."

"Direct experience," she corrected me primly. "And the word is enthusiast," she added.

"DE, then. Whatever." Every company has its own name for it. "Anyway, I like it. My mother says I—"

Dr. Cisneros cut me off by raising her hand like a traffic cop. "This is not the answer I need," she said. "Let me explain. Because of its content, Victoria's Palace is not licensed as an adventure simulation, as are the Arctic and the Amazon. Under our certification, we can operate it only as a therapeutic simulation. Are you married?"

"Sort of," I said. I could just as easily have said, "Not exactly."

"Good." She made a mark in the folder. "Our most acceptable Victoria's Palace clients—the only ones we can accept, in fact—are married men who want to improve the intimacy level of their relationships through the frank exploration of their innermost sexual fantasies."

"That's me," I said. "A married man who wants to enter the most intimacy through Frank's sexual fantasies."

"Close enough," Dr. Cisneros said. She made another mark in the folder and slid it toward me with a smile. "Sign this release and you can start tomorrow morning at nine. Accounts is down the hall on the left."

That night Mother asked, "What did you do today? If anything."

"I signed up at Inward Bound," I said. "My vacation starts tomorrow."

"You haven't worked in two years."

"I quit my job," I said. "I didn't quit my vacation."

"Didn't you do Inward Bound already?"

"I did the Amazon Adventure last year. This year I'm doing the, uh, Arctic Adventure."

Mother looked skeptical. She always looks skeptical.

"We're going for a seal hunt along the edge of a polynya," I said.

"Who's this Pollyanna? Somebody new at last?"

"It's where the ice never freezes over."

"Suit yourself," Mother said. "But you don't need me to tell you that. You always have. You got another letter from Peggy Sue today."

"Her name is Barbara Ann, Mother."

"Whatever. I signed for it and put it with the others. Don't you think that you at least ought to open it? You have a stack this high on that thing you call a dresser."

"Well, what's for supper?" I said to change the subject.

* * *

The next morning I was first in line at Inward Bound. I was let into the Departure Hall at precisely nine, and I sat down on a stool outside my drawer and changed into a robe and sandals.

"What's the little silver hammer for?" I asked the attendant when he showed up in his squeaky shoes.

"Sometimes the drawers are hard to open," he said. "Or close. Lie down. You did the Amazon last summer, right?"

I nodded.

"I thought so. I never forget a face." He was sticking the little things to my forehead. "How high did you go? Could you see the Andes?"

"You could see them in the distance. The jungle girls wore little bark bras."

"You'll see plenty of little bras in the Veep. Five days will get you pretty high there, too. Don't look around the rooms too soon, because as soon as you see a door you'll go through it. Slow down and enjoy yourself. Close your eyes."

I closed my eyes. "Thanks for the tip," I said.

"I worked on the programming," he said. "Breathe deep." The drawer slid in. There was the sharp smell of the Vitazine and it was like waking from a dream. I was in a dark, wood-paneled library. She was standing by a Tudor window with narrow panes overlooking what appeared to be a garden. She was wearing a tangerine-seamed silk charmeuse teddy with flutters of lace trim at the sides and a low-cut bodice with covered buttons and lace-trimmed, wide-set straps. For a moment I thought I didn't know her name, but then I said it: "Chemise." It was like opening your hand and finding something you had forgotten you were holding.

I joined her at the window. The garden was filled with low hedges and gravel walks that spun if you looked too closely at them. I looked away and that's when I saw the door. It was in the far wall, between two bookcases. I ducked my head to go through and I was in a wallpapered bedroom with white-frame windows. The floor was pine with knitted throw rugs.

"Chemise," I said. She was standing between two windows wearing a bodysuit in creamy-white stretch satin, with underwire cups and a plunging V center. The cups were edged with white lace. The treetops just below the window were shimmering as if in a breeze.

I was getting higher. The sheer satin back of her bodysuit was cut in a low V that matched the V in front. I liked the way the straps did. As soon as I turned away I saw the door. It was down one step, and I had to duck my head, and I was in a long, dark room with narrow windows hung with heavy drapes. Chemise was kneeling on a curved love seat wearing a baby-blue baby doll in tulle with lace trim, over a ruffled bra and matching panties. Using one hand I pulled back the drapes. I could see treetops far below, and beneath them, brick streets wet with rain.

I sat down beside her. Her face was still turned away but I could tell that she was smiling. And why not? She didn't exist unless I was with her. She wore little slippers trimmed with lace, like her panties. I'm not into feet, but they made her feet look sexy. I lingered, letting the lace on her panties make an identical pattern on my heart. Then I thought I heard a faint voice calling for help.

I turned and saw a low, arched hole in the wall. It was hardly bigger than a mouse hole. I had to lie flat on my belly, and even then I could barely squirm through, one shoulder at a time.

I was in a concrete-floored hallway with no windows. The walls were bare. The floor was cold and it sloped in two directions at once. It was hard to stand. There was a stack of new lumber against one wall. A girl was sitting on it wearing a red hat. A baseball cap-type hat. She stood up. She was wearing a T-shirt that read:

MERLYN SISTEMS
SOFTWARE THAT WORKS HARD

I could feel myself getting confused. "Chemise?"

"Not Chemise," she said.

"Not Chemise," I said. "What are you doing here? This is my—"

"This isn't your anything," she said. "You're not in the Veep right now. You're running parallel, in a programmer's loop."

"How did you get here, then?"

"I'm the programmer."

"A girl?"

"Of course a girl." She was wearing full-cut white cotton panties under her T-shirt. "What do you think?"

"I'm not supposed to have to think." I could feel myself getting annoyed. "This is Direct Experience. And you are not one of my fantasies."

"Don't be too sure. I'm a damsel in distress. And you're a guy. You came when I called, didn't you? I need your help to get to the Upper Room."

The Upper Room! She said it so casually. "They told me it's not open yet."

"It is if you know how to get to it," she said. "There's a shortcut through the mouse holes."

"Mouse holes?"

"You ask too many questions. I'll show you. But you have to do exactly what I say. You can't be looking around on your own."

"Why not?" I could feel myself getting annoyed again. I looked around just to prove I could. I saw a door.

"Because," she said, behind me.

But I was already stepping through, ducking my head. I was in an old-fashioned kitchen with white wooden cabinets. Chemise stood at the counter stirring a pot with a pair of big scissors. She was wearing a low-cut, smooth-fitting strapless bra in stretch satin and lace with lightly lined underwire cups, and a high-cut, wide-band brief with a sheer lace panel in the front, all in white. "Chemise!" I said. I wondered if she wondered where I had been.

But of course she hadn't. Behind her someone was either getting into or out of a pantry door.

It was me.

I was wearing an Inward Bound robe and shower sandals.

It was me.

I was wearing an Inward

It was

I was looking straight up at the water-stained ceiling of the Departure Hall. "What happened?" I asked. My heart was pounding. I could hear shoes squeaking frantically. A buzzer was buzzing somewhere. Mine was the only open drawer.

"System crash," the attendant said. "They want to see you upstairs in client services. Right away."

"Our bit maps show you in places you couldn't have been," said Dr. Cisneros. She was looking back and forth between the manila folder on her desk and something on her computer screen that I couldn't see. "Areas you couldn't possibly have entered." She looked across the desk at me and her new teeth glittered. "Unless there is something you're not telling me."

When in doubt I play dumb. "Like what?"

"You didn't see anyone else in the palace, did you? Anyone besides yourself and your DE image construct?"

"Another girl?" I decided to go with my instinct, which is always to lie. "No."

"Could be a simple system error," Dr. Cisneros said. "We'll have it sorted out by tomorrow."

"How did it go?" Mother asked.

"Go?"

"With your Pollyanna, your Arctic misadventure?"

"Oh, fine," I lied. I have always lied to Mother, on principle. The truth is too complicated. "I learned to handle a kayak. Lots of open water tomorrow."

"Speaking of open water," Mother said, "I opened those letters today. Lucille says you have to get your stuff. She swears he won't hit you again."

"Barbara Ann, Mother," I said. "And I wish you wouldn't open my mail."

"If wishes were pennies we'd all be rich. I stacked them back in the same order. Don't you think you should answer at least one?"

"I need my rest," I said. "We go after basking seals tomorrow. We stalk them across the ice."

"With guns?"

"With clubs. You know I hate guns."

"That's even worse."

"They're not real, Mother."

"The clubs or the seals?"

"Both. None of it is real. It's Direct Experience."

"My $899 is real."

I was one of the first ones into the Departure Hall the next morning. I took off my clothes and sat down on the bench to wait for the attendant. I watched the other guys file in, mostly wearing parkas or safari outfits. Their attendants had them in their drawers by 8:58.

At 9:14 Squeaky Shoes showed up. "What's the delay?" I asked.

"Bug in the system," he said. "But we're getting it." He was sticking the little things to my forehead. "Close your eyes."

Bug? I closed my eyes. I heard the drawer rumble; I smelled the sharp smell of the Vitazine and it was like waking from a dream. Chemise was sitting on a brocaded settee under an open window, wearing a plum-red stretch-velvet baby T with lattice edging and elastic-trimmed neckline over matching high-cut bikini panties.

"Chemise," I said. I tried to concentrate but I couldn't help feeling I had been higher yesterday. A dog walked through the room. The window looked down on a formal garden with curving brick walkways. The sky was blue and cloudless.

Chemise was looking away. I sat down beside her, feeling restless. I was about to get up again when I thought I heard a faint voice calling for help. I looked down and saw a crack in the baseboard. It was too small to put my hand in but I was able to crawl through on my belly, one shoulder at a time.

I was in the concrete hallway again, with the stack of lumber shimmering against one wall. The girl in the red hat was yelling at me: "You almost got me killed!"

"Bug?" I said.

"What did you call me?"

"Not Chemise?" I tried. She was sitting on the stack of lumber, wearing her

MERLYN SISTEMS

SOFTWARE THAT WORKS HARD

T-shirt over white cotton panties cut high on the sides.

"Not Not Chemise. You called me something else."

"Bug."

"Bug. I like that." She had gray eyes. "But you have to quit looking around. We have to go through the mouse holes, not the doors, or you might meet yourself again."

"Then that was me I saw!"

"That's what crashed the system. You almost got me killed."

"If the system crashes you die?"

"Supposedly. Luckily I had saved myself. All I lost was a little memory. A little more memory."

"Oh," I said.

"Let's get going. I can take you to the Upper Room," she said.

I tried to sound casual. "I thought you wanted *me* to take *you*."

"Same thing. I know the route through the mouse holes. Watch me or watch the hat. Let's get moving. Clyde will get the cat out soon."

"Cat? I saw a dog."

"Oh, shit! We better get moving, then." She threw the red hat behind me. Where it hit I found a wide crack in the concrete floor. It was tight but I managed to crawl through on my belly, pushing one shoulder through and then the other. I was in a bright room with one whole wall of windows. Potted plants were stacked on boxes and on the sofa. There was no place to sit down. Bug was standing by the window, wearing a pale-peach bra with adjustable tapered straps and deep décolleté, and a matching bikini with full back. And the red hat.

I stood beside her at the window. I expected to see treetops but all I saw were clouds, far below. I had never been so high.

"That cat, that dog you saw, is a system debugger," she said. "Sniffs out mouse holes. If it finds me I'm a goner."

I liked the way her bra did in the back. "Do you mind if I call you Bug?"

"I already told you, I sort of like it," she said. "Especially since I don't remember my name."

"You don't remember your name?"

"I lost some memory when the system crashed," she said. She looked almost sad. "Not to mention the time when Clyde killed me."

"Who is Clyde? And who are you, anyway?"

"You ask too many questions," she said. "I'm Bug, that's all, a damsel in distress, and that's one of your fantasies. So let's get going. We can talk on the way."

She threw the red hat against the wall. I found it in the corner, where the wallpaper was pulled loose, revealing a crack barely large enough for my fingertips. It was tight but I was able to manage, one shoulder at a time. I was in a bedroom with a bay window. Bug was—

"Do you mind if I call you Bug?"

"I told you, it's OK." Bug was standing at the window wearing a pearl-white satin jacquard demi bra, accented with scalloped trim along the cups, and a string bikini with a sheer stretch back accented with one little bow. And the red hat, of course.

"Clyde will find me here in the Veep sooner or later, especially now that they suspect a bug. But if I can make it to the Upper Room, I can port through to the other systems."

"What other systems?"

"The Arctic, the Amazon, whatever adventures they add later. All the franchises are interfaced at the top. It'll be like life. Life after Clyde."

"Who's—?"

"Shit!" A phone was ringing. Bug picked it up and handed it to me. It was porcelain with brass trim, like a fancy toilet. Before I could say hello I found myself staring up at the water-stained ceiling of the Departure Hall.

"Client services wants to see you," said the attendant. For the first time I noticed the name stitched on his white jacket. It was CLYDE.

"You still seem to be showing up in rooms where you aren't supposed to be," said Dr. Cisneros. "On code strings that aren't connected. Unauthorized pathways." Dr. Cisneros had been eating lunch at her desk, judging by the little pile of bones at the edge of her blotter. "Are you positive you haven't noticed anything unusual?"

I had to tell her something, so I told her about the dog.

"Oh, that. That's Clyde's cat. The system debugger. He configures it as a dog. It's his idea of a joke."

Sometimes the smart thing is to act dumb. "What kind of bug are you looking for?" I asked.

Dr. Cisneros swiveled the computer monitor on her desk so that I could see the screen. She hit a key and a still picture came up. I wasn't surprised to see Bug—wearing the MERLYN SISTEMS T-shirt and the red hat, of course. She also wore baggy Levi's and glasses. "Early this year one of our programmers was caught illegally altering proprietary software, which is, as you know, a federal crime. We had no choice but to call BATF&S. But while she was free on bail awaiting trial she illegally entered the system."

"As a client?" I asked.

"As a trespasser with criminal intent. Perhaps even to commit sabotage. She may have been carrying a resedit. She may have left loops or subroutines designed to render the software unstable or even dangerous. Unexecutable routines, unauthorized pathways."

"I don't understand what this has to do with me," I said. Mother always said I was good at lying. Mother ought to know.

"The danger to you," Dr. Cisneros said, "is that one of these unauthorized pathways might lead to the Upper Room. And the Upper Room is not, at present, exitable. It's an enter-only. You may have noticed that Victoria's Palace is a one-way system, from lower to higher rooms. It's like the universe. You go until you hit an exit sequence."

"The phone rings," I said.

"Yes," said Dr. Cisneros. "That was Clyde's idea. A nice touch, don't you think? But at present there's no exit sequence, or phone as you call it, installed in the Upper Room."

"Isn't there a door?"

"There's an in door but no out door. Where would the out door go? The Upper Room is at the top of the code string. The client would be trapped. Maybe forever."

"So what do you want me to do?"

"Keep your eyes open. Rogue programmers have rogue egos. They often leave signature stuff lying around. Clues. If you see anything odd, like a picture of her, a little token left around, try to remember what room it is in. It will help us isolate the damage."

"Like a red hat."

"Exactly."

"Or her herself."

Dr. Cisneros shook her head. "It would only be a copy. She's dead. She committed suicide before we could have her reapprehended."

"Rhonda left another message on your answering machine," Mother said when I returned home.

"Barbara Ann," I corrected.

"Whatever. She says she's going to bring your stuff over here and leave it on the lawn. She says Jerry Lewis—"

"Jerry Lee, Mother."

"Whatever. Her new guy, he needs your old room. Apparently they're not sleeping together either."

"Mother!" I said.

"She says if you don't come and get your stuff she's going to throw it out."

"I wish you wouldn't play my messages," I said. "What's the point of having two machines?"

"I can't help it. Your machine recognizes my voice."

"That's just because you try to talk like me."

"I don't have to try," Mother said. "How was your day? Bash any baskin' robins?"

"Very funny," I said. "We did club a large number of basking seals today. They weren't babies though. We club the old seals, the ones that have borne their children and outlived their usefulness to the tribe."

I gave her a look but she chose to ignore it.

The next morning I was the first one in the Departure Hall. "Get squared away with Bonnie?" the attendant asked.

"Bonnie?"

"Hold still." He was sticking the little things to my forehead. "Lie down." It was like waking from a dream. I was in a library with an arched glass window overlooking faraway hills. Chemise had taken down a book and was leafing through the pages. She was wearing a black camisole embroidered with velvet jacquard on whisperweight voile, with slender straps, deeply cut cups and a full stretch-lace back. I could see that the pages were blank. "Chemise," I said. I wanted to tell her I was sorry I was neglecting her. I liked the way her cups did when she bent over, but I had to find Bug. I had to warn her that Dr. Cisneros and Clyde were looking for her.

I searched along the baseboards looking for a mouse hole until I found a crack behind a warped board. It was barely big enough to stick a hand in, but I was able to crawl through on my belly and wedge one shoulder in at a time.

I was back in the concrete hallway.

Bug was standing beside a pile of two-by-fours, wearing her MERLYN SISTEMS T-shirt over French-cut white cotton bikini panties with scalloped lace trim along the edges. And the red hat, of course. And glasses!

"What's with the glasses?" she asked me. She tried to take them off but couldn't.

"They know about you," I said. "They showed me a picture of you. Wearing glasses."

"Of course they know about me! Clyde for damn sure knows about me."

"I mean, they know you're in here. Although they think you're dead."

"Well, I am dead, but I won't be in here long. Not if we get to the Upper Room." She took off her red hat and sailed it down the hall. It landed by a break in the concrete where the floor met the wall. It was too small for even a mouse but I was able to wriggle through, first my fingertips and then one shoulder and then the other. I was in a conservatory with big bay windows overlooking bright, high clouds that looked like ruined castles. Bug—

"Do you mind if I call you Bug?"

"Jesus, I told you, it's OK." Bug was standing by the window wearing a white voile bra with lace-embroidered cups and matching panties with lace inserts on the front and sides. And the red hat. And the glasses.

"I'm willing to help," I said. "But this Upper Room stuff sounds dangerous."

"Dangerous? Who says?"

"Client services."

"Cisneros? That cunt!"

"I wish you wouldn't call her that. She says once I get in the Upper Room I can't get out. Like a Roach Motel. No phone."

"Hmm." Bug looked straight at me. Her gray eyes looked worried. "I didn't think of that. Let's go higher, where we can talk." She threw the red hat and it landed next to a little wedge-shaped hole barely big enough for me to crawl into on my belly, squeezing one shoulder through at a time. I was in a dark room with heavy drapes and no furniture except for an oriental rug on the floor. Bug—

"Do you mind if I call you Bug?"

"Will you stop it? Why does DE make people so stupid?"

"Beats me," I said.

Bug was sitting on the floor, wearing a white faux-satin bra trimmed with an embroidery edge and a matching faux-satin string bikini. "Bug is not really my name," she said. "It's either Catherine or Eleanor, I forget which. It's one of the things that goes when they kill you."

"They told me that you committed suicide."

"Suicide with a hammer, right." I liked her laugh. I liked the way the strings on her string bikini did. They were like tiny versions of the velvet ropes in theaters. "They got me arrested, that much of what Bonnie told you is true. I'd been creating illegal subroutines, mouse holes, to allow movement throughout the Veep. That's true, too. What she didn't tell you is that Clyde and I were partners in crime. Well, how could she know? That cunt. I put the mouse holes in, buried them in the mainstream code string so Clyde and I could later access the palace on our own. Blackmail and extortion was our game. Clyde designed the palace and left the mouse holes up to me. That's the way we always worked. What I didn't know was that he was already in cahoots with Cisneros."

"What are cahoots?"

Bug made a vulgar gesture with a thumb and two fingers; I looked away. "Cisneros owns 55 percent of the franchise. Which made her irresistible to poor Clyde, I guess. For months they had been playing Bonnie and Clyde behind my back, while I was busy hacking away. Anyway, when Victoria's Palace got accepted at Inward Bound, some franchise-checker dude found the mouse holes—I hadn't really bothered to hide them—and he told Cisneros, and then she told Clyde, and he pretended to be shocked and outraged. Set me up. So as soon as I got out on bail I went in to get my stuff—"

"Your stuff?"

"Subroutines, proprietary macros, picts and diffs. I was going to rip it all out. And maybe trash the place a little. I was carrying a resedit so I could rewrite code even as I was riding it. But Clyde got wind somehow. So he murdered me."

"With the little hammer."

"You're beginning to get the picture. Just opened the drawer and, *whack*, right between the eyes. What Clyde didn't know was that I could save myself. I always run with a little auto-save macro I wrote back in community college, so I lost only about ten minutes, and some memory. And my life, of course. I ducked into the mouse hole space but who the hell wants to live like a rat forever? I was waiting for my prince to come and take me to the Upper Room."

"Your prince?"

"Finger of speech. I was waiting for the Veep to open. Any dude would have done."

"Figure of speech," I said.

"Whatever. Anyway, what Cisneros doesn't know—or Clyde either—is that the Upper Room is interfaced at the top with the other Inward Bound areas, the Arctic and Amazon franchises. I'll be able to get out of the Palace. And, as more and more modules get added, my universe will get bigger and bigger. If I watch my ass, I'll live forever. Or haven't you noticed that there's no death in DE?"

She stood up and yawned. I liked the pink inside of her mouth. She took off the hat and threw it against the wall. It landed by a little opening under the baseboard. It was tight but I managed to squeeze through, one shoulder at a time. I was in a stone room with a tiny slit window and a folding chair. Bug—

"Do you mind if I call you Bug?"

"Will you knock it off? Come over here."

Bug was wearing a black lace bra with deep décolleté cups and wide-set straps, and matching black lace thong panties with little bows on the sides. And the red hat, of course. And the glasses. She made room so that I could stand beside her on the chair and see out the slit window. I could almost see the curve of the earth. I could almost feel the curve of her hip against mine, even though I knew that it was my imagination. Imagination is everything in DE.

"We're not so far from the Upper Room," she said. "Look how high you've gotten me already. But Cisneros is right about one thing."

"What?"

"You can't take me into the Upper Room. You'd be stuck. No way back."

"What about you?" I liked the little bows.

"I'm already stuck. I don't have a body to go back to. You provide this one, I guess." She peered through her glasses, down the front of her bra, down the front of her panties. "Which is why I'm still wearing glasses, I guess."

"I'd like to help you get to the Upper Room," I said. "But why can't you go in by yourself?"

"I can't move up, only down," Bug said. "I'm dead, remember? If I only still had my resedit, I could—Shit!" There was a phone. We had hardly noticed it until it rang. "It's for you," she said, handing me the receiver.

Before I could say hello I was staring up at the water-stained ceiling of the Departure Hall. I heard shoes squeaking. The attendant helped me out of the drawer. Clyde.

"4:55 already?" I asked.

"Time flies when you're having fun," he said.

"Guess who's here?" Mother said.

I heard the snarl of a toilet flushing in the bathroom.

"I don't want to see her," I said.

"She came all the way from Salem," Mother said. "She brought your stuff."

"Where is it, then?"

"It's still in her car. I wouldn't let her bring it in," said Mother. "That's why she's crying."

"She's not crying!" a deep voice called out from the bathroom.

"My God," I said, alarmed. "Is he in there with her?"

"She's not taking it back!" the same deep voice called out. Another toilet flushed. Mother has two in her bathroom, one for me and one for her.

"I'm on my vacation," I said. The bathroom doorknob started to turn and I went for a walk. When I got back they were gone and my stuff was on the lawn.

"You could dig a hole," said Mother, "and cover it."

I was the first one in the Departure Hall the next morning. But instead of opening my drawer, Squeaky Shoes—Clyde—gave me a paper to sign.

"I already signed a release," I said.

"This is simply for our own protection," he said.

I signed. "Good," he said and smiled. It was not a nice smile. "Now lie down. Now take a deep breath." The drawer slid shut. I inhaled the Vitazine and it was like waking from a dream.

I was in a formal living room with a cream-colored rug, couch and chair. Chemise was standing at the window wearing an ivory underwire bra in satin jacquard with a low-plunge center and wide-set straps and matching bikini panties with a sheer stretch panel in front. She was holding a cup and saucer, also matching. Through the window I could see rolling hills stretching to a horizon. The dog trotted through the room.

"Chemise," I said. I wished I had time to explain things to her, but I knew I had to find Bug.

I looked around for a mouse hole. Behind a lamp, in a dark corner, there was a low arch, like the entrance to a tiny cave. I could barely negotiate the narrow passage, shrugging one shoulder through at a time.

"What took you so long?" Bug was sitting in the concrete hallway on the gleaming stack of lumber, her knees pulled up under her chin. She was wearing her MERLYN SISTEMS T-shirt over a tiny thong bikini. And the red hat and the glasses, of course.

"They made me sign another release."

"And you signed it?"

I nodded. I liked the way the thong made a little V and then disappeared.

"You moron! Do you realize that by signing the release you gave Clyde the right to kill you?"

"I wish you wouldn't call me that," I said.

"Fucking Bonnie and Clyde! Now I'll never get to the Upper Room!" I was afraid she was about to cry. Instead, she hurled the red hat angrily to the floor and when I bent down to pick it up I saw a crack barely large enough for three fingertips, but I was able to squeeze through by crawling on my belly and pushing one shoulder in at a time. I was in an empty room with bare wood floors and windows so new that the stickers were still on them. Bug was wearing a coral stretch-lace bra cut low for maximum décolleté with a French string bikini that was full in the back and plunged to a tiny triangle of sheer pink lace in front. And the red hat.

I followed her to the window. Below was a mixture of seas and clouds, an earth as bright as a sky.

"We must be getting close to the Upper Room!" I said. "You're going to make it!" I wanted to make her feel better. I liked the way her bra did in front.

"Don't talk nonsense. Do you hear that howling?"

I nodded. It sounded like a pack of hounds getting closer.

"That's the cat. Search and destroy. Find and erase." She shivered quite extravagantly.

"But you can save yourself!"

"Not so easily. I'm already a backup."

I was afraid she was about to cry. "Then let's get going!" I said. "I'll take you to the Upper Room. I don't care about the danger."

"Don't talk nonsense," Bug said. "You would be trapped forever, if Clyde didn't kill you first. If only I had my resedit, I could get there by myself."

"So where is it?"

"I lost it when Clyde killed me. I've been looking for it ever since."

"What does it look like?"

"A pair of big scissors."

"I saw Chemise with a pair of big scissors," I said.

"That cunt!"

"I wish you wouldn't call her that," I began. But the phone was ringing. We hadn't noticed it before.

"Don't answer it!" Bug said, even as she picked it up and handed it to me. How could she help it? I had signed the release. It was for me, of course. The next thing I knew I was staring up at the water-stained ceiling and at the little silver hammer coming down right between my eyes.

And at Clyde's smile. Not a nice smile.

First it got real dark. Then it got light again. It was like waking from a dream.

I was in a round, white room with curved windows all around. My head hurt. Through the glass I could see gray stars in a milk-white sky. Bug—

"Over here," she said. She was standing by the window wearing periwinkle panties of shimmering faux satin, cut high on the sides and full in the back, with delicately embroidered cutouts down each side of the front panel. And nothing on top at all. No bra. No straps, no cups, no detailing, no lace.

My head hurt. But I couldn't help being thrilled at how high I was. "Is this—the Upper Room?" I asked breathlessly.

"Not quite," she said. She was still wearing the red hat and the glasses. "And now we're out of luck. In case you hadn't noticed, Clyde killed you, too. Just now."

"Oh no." I couldn't imagine anything worse.

"Oh yes," she said. She put her hand on my forehead and I could feel her fingers feel the little dent.

"What did you do, copy me?"

"Pulled you out of the cache. Barely." Out the window, far below, there was a blue-green ball streaked with white. "Hear that howling? That's Clyde's cat rooting through the palace room by room."

I shivered. I liked the way her panties did underneath.

"Well, what have we got to lose?" I said, surprised that I wasn't more upset that I was dead. "Let's head for the Upper Room."

"Don't talk nonsense," she said. "If you're dead too, you can't pull me through." The howling was getting louder. "Now we have to find the resedit. Where did you see what's-her-name with the big scissors? Which room was she in?"

"Chemise," I said. "I can't remember."

"What was out the window?"

"I can't remember."

"What was in the room?"

"I can't remember."

"What was she wearing?"

"A low-cut, smooth-fitting strapless bra in stretch satin and lace with lightly lined underwire cups, and a high-cut, wide-band brief with a sheer lace panel in the front, all in white," I said.

"Let's go, then," Bug said. "I know the spot."

"I thought we couldn't go anywhere without the res-whatever."

"Down we can go," Bug said. She threw the red hat and followed it herself. It fell near a tiny hole barely big enough for her fingertips. I squeezed through after her. I still liked the way her panties did underneath. We were in an old-fashioned kitchen and Chemise was stirring a pot with a pair of big scissors. She was wearing a low-cut, smooth-fitting strapless bra in stretch satin and lace with lightly lined underwire cups, and a high-cut, wide-band brief with a sheer lace panel in the front, all in white.

"Give me those!" said Bug, grabbing the scissors. She was also wearing a low-cut, smooth-fitting strapless bra in stretch satin and lace with lightly lined underwire cups, and a high-cut, wide-band brief with a sheer lace panel in the front, all in white. And the red hat. But where were her glasses?

"Bitch," said Chemise, softly. I was shocked. I didn't know she could talk.

"Cunt," said Bug.

Just then the dog trotted into the room from nowhere. Literally.

"The cat!" said Bug. She was trying to jimmy the lock on the pantry with the point of the big scissors.

The dog—cat—hissed.

"In here!" said Bug. She pushed me backward into the pantry while she jabbed upward, ramming the point of the big scissors into the dog's belly. The cat's belly. Whatever. Blood was everywhere. I was in a large, empty, pyramid-shaped room with a white floor and white walls rising to a point. There was one small porthole in each wall. Bug—

Bug was nowhere to be seen.

Outside the portholes, everything was white. There weren't even any stars. There were no doors. I could hear barking and growling below.

"Bug! The cat erased you!" I wailed. I knew she was gone. I was afraid I was going to cry. But before I could, a trapdoor in the floor opened and Bug came through feet first. It was odd to watch. Her arm was covered with blood and she was holding the scissors and she was—

She was nude. She was naked.

"I have erased the cat!" Bug cried triumphantly.

"It's still coming." I could hear wild barking below.

"Shit! Must be a replicating loop," she said. She was naked. Nude. Stripped. Bare. Unclad completely. "And quit staring at me," she said.

"I can't help it," I said. Even the red hat was gone.

"I guess not," she said. She was nude. Naked. She was wearing nothing, nothing at all. She ran to one of the four portholes and began prying at the frame with the point of the scissors.

"There's nothing out there," I said. The howling was getting louder. The trapdoor had closed but I had the feeling it would open again, all dogs. Or cats. And soon.

"Can't stay here!" Bug said. She gave up on the frame and shattered the glass with the scissors.

"I'm going with you," I said.

"Don't talk nonsense," she said. She put her hand on my forehead again. Her touch was cool. I liked the way it felt. "The dent is deep but not all that deep. You may not be dead. Just knocked out."

"He hit me pretty hard! And I'm trapped here anyway."

"Not if you're not dead, you're not. They'll shut down and reset once I'm gone. You'll probably just wake up with a headache. You can go home."

The barking was getting closer. "I don't want to go home."

"What about your mother?"

"I left her a note," I lied.

"What about your stuff?"

"I buried all my stuff." She was nude. Naked, except for her lovely glasses. Nothing on the bottom, nothing on top. Even the red hat was gone. The hole was barely big enough for my hand but I followed her through, one shoulder at a time. Everything was white and the howling was gone and something was moaning like the wind. I took Bug's hand and I was rolling. We were rolling. I was holding her hand and we were rolling, rolling, rolling through warm, blank snow.

It was like waking from a dream. I was wrapped in a foul-smelling fur, looking up at the translucent ceiling of a little house made of ice and leaves. Bug was lying beside me wrapped in the same smelly fur.

"Where are we?" I asked. "I hear cats barking."

"Those are our dogs," she said.

"Dogs?" I got up and went to the door. It was covered with a scratchy blanket. I pulled it back and looked out across miles of new snow to a distant line of trees, hung with vines. Silvery dogs were peeing on the outside of the little house. One was shaking a snake to death. It was a big snake.

"They all come together here," Bug said. "The Upper Room, the North Pole, the headquarters of the Amazon."

"Headwaters," I said. "Where are your glasses?"

"I don't need them anymore."

"I liked them."

"I'll put them back on."

I got back under the fur with her, curious to find out what she was wearing. There's no way I can tell you, from here, what it was. But you would have liked it, too. If you're anything like me.

Thinkertoy

JOHN BRUNNER

John Brunner was one of the finest living science fiction writers. He died
suddenly of a stroke on the Friday morning of the World Science Fiction
Convention in Glasgow, Scotland, in 1995, shocking the community. He
was the author of many first-rate science fiction stories and novels
throughout a career that began when he was seventeen in the 1950s.
Brunner was known for his vast, encyclopedic knowledge; his clever logical extrapolations; his clean, sharp style in the tradition of Asimov and
his peer Robert Silverberg; and his complex plots. His ability at charac-
terization was underrated. Among his SF masterpieces are *The Squares
of the City*, *Telepath*, *Stand on Zanzibar*, and *The Shockwave Rider*. His
last stories appeared in 1996. This story was written at the request of
Roger Zelazny who, at the time of Brunner's death in 1995, was assem-
bling an original anthology in honor of Jack Williamson. The book was
completed by Jim Frenkel and *The Williamson Effect* was published in
1996. But Brunner died before he could write his afterword to the story,
explaining its exact relation to Williamson and his work. He must have
had something clever in mind (he always did), but now we'll never know
precisely what. What is clear is that Williamson was a pioneer, in investi-
gating the idea of robots as a possible threat to human life, in such novels
as *The Humanoids*. But this piece particularly reminds me of Williamson's sharp and nasty little story about children and robots, "Jamboree."
Insight into human psychology is essential to the punch. And it packs a
real punch.

Paul Walker was afraid of his children. For months now he had been afraid for them, ever since the fatal accident, but this was different—not a rapid change, but the gradual kind that is recognized one morning as having happened.

And he and Lisa had been so proud of their outstanding intelligence. . . .

He could not tell which of them he found the more disturbing. Logically it should have been Rick because of the way the crash had altered him. He bore no visible scars, but it had done incontestable damage. Whether directly, as the result of trauma, or indirectly, through showing him his mother hideously dead, had proved impossible to establish.

Yet in many ways Kelly, two years the older, affected him worse. There was something unnerving about the composure she maintained: in particular, the way she cared for Rick now that he showed so little interest in the world. It wasn't right for a child barely into her teens to be so organized, so self-possessed: to rouse her brother in the mornings, make sure he was neatly dressed and came to breakfast on time, arrange their return home because though Paul could drop them at school on his way to the office, he was still at work when classes finished. Most days they came back by bus, now and then in the car of one of the numerous other parents living nearby who had been shocked by Lisa's death. . . . It was in principle a great arrangement; as his friends kept reminding him, it meant he could keep his job and even work overtime now and then, without worrying.

But he had worried all along. Now he had progressed beyond that. He had grown used to the sense of Rick not being wholly present anymore, yet not resigned to it. The boy went to school without protest, and endured his classes and maybe soaked up the odd droplet of information. But on regaining his room he would sit, both before and after supper unless Kelly coaxed him to watch TV, in front of his computer or his games console, perhaps with a game loaded, more often watching a net display scrolling of its own accord, looking—this had crossed Paul's mind weeks ago and fitted better than any other description—bored. Bored as though he was tired of being able to remember that he had used to operate these expensive gadgets, without recalling what he had actually done to make them work. For a while Paul had offered to partner him, but was defeated by his frustrating wall of indifference.

Every weekend he sought some stimulus that might reawaken his son's dormant personality, making a trip to a game or a show or some place of interest out of town. This time, though, Kelly had asked to visit a shopping mall, to which he gladly consented because he felt she ought to let him buy her new and more stylish clothes to keep up with her school friends. It was fruitless; she insisted on the same kind of items as usual, inexpensive, practical, plain.

However, there proved to be a compensation. He was double-checking his grocery list for the coming week before continuing to the supermarket when Kelly—in T-shirt, jeans, and trainers as she would remain until it was time for sweater, jeans, and boots—returned to him with a thoughtful air.

"Dad, I think you ought to see this."

Instantly: "Where's Rick? Why isn't he with you?"

"That's what I want you to see. Look."

And there the boy was, standing riveted before a display in a section of the mall it had not crossed Paul's mind to make for.

But why did I not think of toys? After all, in some ways he has become a child again. . . .

Hastening in Kelly's wake, he wondered what could have broken through that armor of remoteness. It must be something special, for there were as many adults and even teenagers, normally contemptuous of childish things, as there were children gathered here. A smiling salesman was putting his wares through their paces.

And quite some paces they were.

They were performing under an arch bearing the name THINKERTOY in brightly colored letters, on a display one part of which modeled a modern city block with buildings of various heights; another, a medieval castle with donjon, moat, and curtain wall; another, an icebound coastline lapped by miniature waves. All over these were roaming little machines, some with wheels, some arms and/or legs, some tentacles, some hooks and suckers for hauling themselves up cliffs or trees or vertical walls. Occasionally they came to an obstacle they could neither surmount nor traverse, whereupon, seemingly of their own volition, they repaired to a heap of miscellaneous parts at the side of the display, disconnected part of their or another's current fitments, plugged in replacements and renewed their progress. Now and then the onlookers clapped and laughed at some particularly ingenious configuration, such as a scaling-ladder. Also there were a pair of video screens showing other actions they were capable of. Paul found himself fascinated along with all the rest.

"Excuse me."

A tentative voice. The salesman deployed his broadest beam.

"Suppose you change things around."

Rick? Could it be . . . ? Yes, it was Rick who had spoken! This was fantastic!

"You mean like shifting things to new places? They keep right on going. They learn in moments. For instance—" He reached for a handful of the spare parts, then checked.

"No, kid, you can do it. Dump 'em wherever you like. When they bump into one of these bits they'll recognize it, remember it's in the wrong place, collect it, and return it to store. You'll see."

The little machines performed as predicted, watched by Rick with total attention. Meantime the man continued his spiel, while two pretty girls took station beside a credit-card reader in anticipation of impending sales.

"But you haven't seen a fraction of what Thinkertoys can do! You can find out more from the screens here, and our full-color literature." On cue, the girls fanned brilliant leaflets like oversize poker hands. "You can discover how much more fun, how much more fulfilling for adults too is life with Thinkertoys around! Want your Thinkertoy to answer your phone, and that includes videophones by the way, with any of a hundred voices and identities? Make 'em up yourself or use the ones supplied. Want your games console or computer to play against you in exactly the style of your favorite partner, only he or she is not available? Easy! Just record a sample of the games you've played together. Your Thinkertoy will analyze and duplicate anybody's style to grandmaster level and beyond. Want to integrate your computer with your stereo, your stereo with your TV, your TV with your phone—so you can call home and tell the VCR to record a program you only just found out about? Your phone with your cooker, your microwave, your refrigerator? It's done for you! And as for what two or more of these little pals can do, it's astonishing! Two Thinkertoys working together can open an icebox or freezer, read the labels on the stored food, or if unlabeled show it to a videophone for you to identify, then locate the recipe you name and prepare it against your return home, substituting if need be alternative ingredients of equal or superior quality. Thinkertoys retrieve from awkward places. They clean tirelessly and unobtrusively. They hide in corners when not required and reactivate instantly on hearing their names. No need to connect them to wires or cables, though that is an option. They communicate like portable phones, and with ultrasound, and with infrared—"

"Say!" one of the listeners burst out. "If they do all these things why call them toys?"

"They're for playing with," was the suave rejoinder. "Most people don't have enough fun in their lives. Thinkertoys are designed to put the fun back in living! And . . ." His voice dropped to a confidential level, though everyone in the small crowd still heard every syllable. "To be absolutely frank, our company was intending to introduce a family model, what you might call a more sober design, just to do dull things like help out around the house. But then this new chip came out, the very latest most sophisticated kind, and we found we could pack all these features in as well, and . . . okay, I'll let you in on the secret. Thinkertoys work so well, people buy them for their kids and wind up using them themselves, so they have to come back and buy another, catch?"

He flashed a mouthful of excellently cared-for teeth, and several people chuckled at his engaging blatancy.

"Of course," he added, "it makes sense to save yourself the second trip, and these young ladies will be pleased to show you our double packs at a net savings of fifteen percent. And of course all Thinkertoys are fully guaranteed."

"Dad," Kelly whispered, "are you going to buy one for Rick?"

The things weren't cheap, especially with the full kit of parts warranted to permit access anywhere in any house or apartment. However, the sight of Rick showing animation for the first time since he came home from the hospital. . . .

He hadn't spent the insurance he had had on Lisa, meaning to invest it until the kids were of college age. But this was a special case. Just how special became plain when, instead of showing his customary indifference, Rick made a careful selection of the optional extras. As he put his credit card away Paul's heart felt light for the first time since his wife's death.

"What's got into you?" demanded Carlos Gomez when they met during lunch break. Carlos was the firm's computer manager, and as personnel supervisor Paul worked closely with him, but they had been drawn together most of all because Belita Gomez had been a good friend of Lisa, and immensely supportive since the tragedy. It was she who most often gave Rick and Kelly a ride home from school.

"What do you mean?"

"You're looking cheerful for a change."

Paul explained, with the aid of some of Thinkertoy's promotional literature that he had in his pocket. Studying it, Carlos gave a soft whistle.

"I'd heard they were working on stuff like this, but I didn't know it was
on the market. And for kids, yet! There must be something wrong with
it."

Paul blinked. "What makes you so sure? I haven't noticed anything
wrong. In fact the opposite. Kelly has been so anxious to help Rick get
better, and this is the first real chance she's had. First thing they had to
do when they switched the gizmo on was choose a name for it, and they
settled on Marmaduke and that was the first time I've heard Rick show
any sign of amusement since . . . Well, recently. But I swear I heard
him chuckle.

"Then they settled down to try out everything in the manual, and I had
to take supper to Rick's room for them and eventually become the heavy
father at midnight. And today I've let them stay home from school, just
for once, because . . . well, because of the change it's worked on my
son." He sounded almost belligerent. "And you immediately conclude
something is wrong? I think it's all extremely right!"

"Cool it," Carlos sighed. "I didn't mean wrong from your kids' point of
view. I meant from the point of view of what they originally intended the
things to do. Maybe they're fine for home use but no good for autopilot-
ing an airliner or controlling an industrial plant."

"You ever heard of this operation before? No? Then what makes you
so positive?"

"Just the sort of things a Thinkertoy is capable of, on its own or in
conjunction with others. Paul, a chip like that simply isn't the sort you
develop for the toy market."

"During the Cold War, didn't the Soviets buy gaming machines intended for Las Vegas because that way they got their hands on electronics that were otherwise under ban?"

"Sure, but those aren't exactly toys. The gambling market operates in
the billion-dollar league. Even the biggest hits in the toy market arrive
one season, thrive for another, and fade away the next. Exceptions exist,
like Barbie dolls, but have you seen a Peppervine doll lately? Or a Captain Carapace? So I can't help wondering what the intended application
was for these things. I guess I'll ask around. Mind if I keep this?" He
tapped the stiff polychrome paper of the advertising flyer.

Paul shrugged and nodded. But he felt annoyed with Carlos. He had
spent months in a nonstop condition of worry; thought it was ended; and
now found himself given a reason to start worrying all over again.

He was still further alarmed when he arrived home to find Kelly alone
in the kitchen defrosting food for supper.

"What's Rick doing?" he demanded. "Never tell me he's bored with Marmaduke already!"

Wrestling with a too-tough plastic cover, she shook her head. "No, it's just that we've done everything in the manual that we can—you need some extra connectors to wire up the kitchen, like the oven and the broiler, and he didn't pick them up—and . . . Well, you better ask him yourself. He lost me halfway. Ah!"—as the obstinate cover finally peeled back.

"He'll lose me sooner than that," Paul sighed, and headed for his son's room.

The boy was seated contemplatively before his computer. Marmaduke squatted beside the keyboard, or rather its torso, devoid of the attachments. The screen showed mazy lines.

"Circuit diagram?" Paul hazarded.

"Mm-hm"—without looking around.

"Something wrong? Kelly said you can do everything in the manual except jobs you need special parts for."

"Mm-hm."

"So—uh—are you running an autodiagnostic?"

"Trying to. I can't get it to run properly."

"I was talking to Carlos Gomez over lunch. You know, our computer manager. He seemed very interested in these Thinkertoys. How about downloading it to him and seeing if he can help?"

"Nope." The boy's tone held the first hint of determination his father could recall since the crash. "I think I know what's wrong and I'd rather fix it myself."

He rose stiffly from his chair, as though he had been there all day.

"I'm hungry," he added. "What's Kelly fixing? Smells good."

Paul had to wait a moment before following him downstairs. His eyes were blurred with tears.

The following day Kelly said she wanted to go to school. Rick didn't. He wanted to finish solving his problem and thought he could. Unwilling to risk an argument that might make him late for work, Paul exacted a promise that he would certainly attend the next day, and was astonished and delighted when the Thinkertoy appeared unexpectedly on the breakfast counter in a quasi-humanoid configuration with two arms, two legs and one head, threw up a smart salute and shouted, "You got it, Mister Admiral, sir!"

His son had often made jokes like that, way back when . . .

In the car, he hoped Kelly's detachment might thaw, but it didn't.

Drawing up before her school, he ventured, "Buying Marmaduke seems to have been a bright idea, hm?"

With her customary abnormal gravity she shrugged. "Too soon to say."

And was gone, not pausing to kiss him goodbye.

That, though, had become the pattern.

Carlos was not in the office today—on a trip, Paul learned, to inspect a batch of expensive gear being offered second-hand at a bargain price. The seller, a bankrupt arms company, had been a casualty of the end of the Cold War. He resolved to phone him at home tonight if Rick hadn't sorted out his problem. Two days off school were enough.

And of course if there really was something wrong with Marmaduke they could always return him—it—on Saturday, under guarantee.

But, Kelly declared as soon as he entered the house, that wasn't going to be necessary. Pleased, more than a little proud of his son, who had been a real computer whiz before the accident and seemed to be recovering at last, he headed upstairs.

"Rick! Kelly tells me you figured it out," he said heartily.

"Mm-hm." The screen was acrawl with lines like yesterday, but this time the boy was using his mouse rather as though he was in Draw mode, marking a dot here and a dot there and leaving the computer to connect them.

Paul hesitated, aware that he understood far less about computers than his son, but finally ventured, "Are you repairing Marmaduke?"

"Yup."

"I didn't know you could. I mean, not on the sort of gear you have."

"He's designed that way. To be fixed in the field."

"Field?"

"Away from the shop. It's a really dense chip in there. You can write to it with real tiny currents. Amazing stuff. 'Course, reprogramming it would be a different matter."

"You're not—uh—doing that?"

"Nah. Just cleaning it up. Getting rid of some junk."

"So what exactly did you find wrong?"

Rick leaned back and stretched.

"It got damaged. Like my brain . . . Say, I'm hungry."

And after they'd eaten, he carried his plate to the sink, announcing, "Okay, well, if I got to go to school in the morning I better make sure Marmaduke is one hundred percent. See you later."

After a pause, Kelly's mood softened enough for her to concede, "I guess you were right, what you said about Marmaduke."

That was as far as she was prepared to go, but Paul passed his most relaxed evening in a long, long while.

Around ten-thirty Rick decided he was satisfied, emerged yawning from his room, took a shower, and retired peacefully to bed. Kelly decided to do the same. As she headed for the stairs there was a soft scuttling noise.

"What's that?" Paul exclaimed.

"Marmaduke, of course, this time with all his wits about him. You turning in too?"

"In a little while. I want to call Carlos, see if he's home yet—Just a moment! Do I need to set the answering machine as usual or has Marmaduke been programmed to switch it on?"

"Better than that," the Thinkertoy replied. It was perching on the newel post of the banister. "I can act as one, using whichever phone is nearest and adjusting the outgoing message to correspond with the current situation. I shall memorize your usual bedtime and rising time with allowance for weekends, but in addition I can take calls whenever the house is unoccupied and give the other party your estimated time of return. Let me know if ever you would like these parameters changed. By the way, I can also control a modem and a fax and reprogram your VCR in response to a phone call—but you've read the brochure. At least I hope you have."

"You forgot to mention," Kelly murmured, "that we've fixed you to sound like me, or Rick, or Dad, or Donald Duck, according to who the caller wants to talk to. The Donald Duck one is for telephone solicitors. In case you're interested, Dad, the voice he's using right now is a three-way mix of all of us. I told Rick it would be kind of suitable."

For a second Paul was stunned. Then he chuckled.

"Marmaduke, I think you are going to be a distinct asset to the Walker household. Good night!"

He reached for the phone. They only had the regular kind. Videophones were still very expensive, even though it was clear from the Thinkertoy literature the manufacturers took it for granted that if you could afford one you could afford the other.

Moments later Belita Gomez's drowsy voice sounded in his ear.

"No, Paul, Carlos isn't home yet. He called to say he'd closed the deal and they were all going to a restaurant. Want him to call back?"

"Don't even give him a message. It can wait until morning. The kids are in bed and I'm about to follow their example. *Buenas noches.*"

"I'm *in* bed. G'night."

Later there was the faintest beep from the phone bell, cut off so quickly it was barely audible.

Whereafter, to the accompaniment of a yawning noise: "Hello."

In a whisper: "Paul, this is Carlos. Sorry to call so late. I'll try and keep it short but you need to hear this. 'Fraid I got to keep my voice down. Belita's asleep and I don't want to disturb her."

A deep breath.

"At this company where I went today, after we agreed on a figure, I stuck around for dinner with the guys I was mainly dealing with. I happened to ask whether they knew anything about Thinkertoys. I hit pay dirt. Remember I said those chips weren't developed for the toy market even if the toys do double as home appliances? Well, this company I was at used to be in arms back in the Cold War period, and this guy says yes, he knows who made them, though he wouldn't give a name, but he did tell me what they were intended for. Sabotage! Plant 'em behind enemy lines, or leave 'em during a retreat, and they activate and start wrecking everything in reach. Electronics first, naturally—they have built-in jamming capacity. But they can start fires and foul up bearings and unscrew closed valves in chemical plants, even loosen tacks in stair carpet so people break their necks. . . . They're supposed to have been rendered harmless. Some kind of inactivation program. But this guy I was talking to: he says the security is lousy and you can get around it in an hour, or sooner if you automate the job, and the word's out on the net and you want to guess who's buying? The Sword Arm of the Lord, that's who, hoping to destroy black-owned businesses, and the Islamic League for Female Decency, and the Choosers of the Slain, and— Shit, I think I woke Belita after all. Talk to you in the morning. 'Bye."

The connection broke.

Whereupon Marmaduke went on about its proper business, the liberty for which Rick had restored.

"Sorry, *querida*—didn't mean to wake you."

"It's okay, I wasn't really asleep. . . . Who were you talking to at this hour?"

Sitting on the edge of the bed to remove his shoes: "Paul. Paul Walker. I learned something about those Thinkertoys that couldn't wait for morning."

"If it was that urgent why didn't you call from the car?"

"His home number is unlisted and I don't have it in the car memory."

"Ah-yah . . ." Belita was struggling to keep her eyes open. Then, with a sudden start: "What do you mean, it couldn't wait until morning? It'll have to anyway, won't it?"

Carlos, unfastening his tie, checked and glanced at his wife. "I don't get you," he said after a pause.

She forced herself to sit up against the pillows. "You got his answering machine, right?"

"No! I talked to Paul—"

"But he called here about ten-thirty to ask if you were home yet. When I told him no he said the kids were in bed and he was going to turn in as well. Ever know him forget to set his answering machine?"

Carlos was staring. "But I know his message! He never changes it. I must have heard it a hundred times. . . . Oh my God."

"What is it?" Belita was alarmed into full wakefulness now.

Feverishly he retrieved the Thinkertoy advertisement from his jacket. "Yes, I'm right," he muttered. "One of the things they can do is impersonate their owner on the phone."

"You mean carry on a conversation that can fool the caller?"

"No, that's the Turing test and no machine has passed it yet. But it could exploit the Eliza principle. That goes right back to the early days, but it's still used and it can sure as hell fool people, especially if they're under stress and their guard is down. . . . 'Lita, I got to go check that the Walkers are okay."

"But why should they not be?"

He told her. Before he finished she was out of bed and scrambling into whatever clothes she could reach.

Kelly and Rick, in pajamas and barefoot, stood hand in hand before their house, waiting. Hearing a car approach, they disregarded it. There were still a few people returning home even at this time, and they were concealed in the shadow of a clump of bushes.

Just as Carlos braked, there came a faint whooshing sound from the kitchen, which lay partly below the bathroom but mainly below Paul's room, the one that had been his and Lisa's. An orange glow followed, and a crackling noise. The house was largely timber-built. Later it was established that Marmaduke had loosened the valve on a cylinder of propane and ignited the leak, as it was designed to, by short-circuiting its powerpack.

The glow revealed the children.

"Madre de dios!" Belita exclaimed. "But what are Rick and Kelly doing out here? And where's Paul?"

"Save your breath!" Carlos was frantically escaping his safety belt. "Blast away on the horn! Rouse everyone you can! Call 911!"

"Carlos, don't do anything foolish—"

But he was already rushing towards the porch. Kelly and Rick recognized him and seemed to scowl and mutter. Suspicion burgeoned but he had no time. He reached the door.

It was locked. Suspicion grew brighter and fiercer like the fire within. But he still had no time. In the car he kept a baseball bat for security. He ran back for it. Thus armed, he smashed a glass panel alongside the door and managed to reach the inside lock.

By now lights were coming on, windows being flung open as the car horn shattered the night silence. Slamming shut the kitchen door, which he found open, gained Carlos a few more precious moments before heat and smoke made the stairway impassable. Three at a time he dashed up it.

The front door was not the only one that was locked.

Suspicion approached certainty, but still he had no time. He smashed the flimsy jamb, found Paul sleepily approaching the window, aroused by the horn, dragged him down the stairs and staggering into the garden. . . .

With seconds to spare. Like a puff of breath from a dragon, the gas cylinder burst and blew out all the house's doors and windows. Flame erupted through the ceiling under Paul's room.

Distant but closing fast, sirens wailed.

Paul collapsed, choking from a lungful of smoke, but Carlos managed to retain his feet. Gasping, he found himself confronting Rick and Kelly. Their faces were stony and frustrated. He whispered, "You knew, didn't you?"

Impassivity.

"Paul said you spent most of your time scrolling around the net. That must be how you found out. I guess the Thinkertoy display at the mall must have been pretty widely advertised. And like the guy said, the protection that was supposed to make the chips harmless could be easily erased."

He stood back, hands on hips, ignoring Belita, who clearly wanted to fuss over the children. He barely registered that Paul was albeit unsteadily regaining his feet. Before his friend could speak:

"But why?" Carlos pleaded.

The children exchanged glances. At length Rick gave a shrug.

"He was driving."

After which Belita's importunities could no longer be ignored.

Paul Walker was afraid of his children.

As those three words made clear, he had good reason.

Zoomers

GREGORY BENFORD

Gregory Benford is a science fiction fan who grew up to be an astrophysicist and a science fiction writer. He is the most significant hard-SF writer in the generation after Larry Niven, and one of the most eloquent and vocal advocates of hard SF today. In addition to the Nebula Award and the John W. Campbell Memorial Award, he has been given the United Nations Medal in Literature. His most famous novel is *Timescape;* his most recent, *Sailing Bright Eternity*. Benford's sequel to Isaac Asimov's Foundation series, *Foundation's Fear,* was published in early 1997. His "Zoomers" is a cyberspace romp with a hard-SF attitude. It first appeared in an anthology edited by Martin H. Greenberg and Larry Segriff, *Future Net*, devoted to stories of the "networks of tomorrow" and in a computer magazine. It's a positive, upbeat story about competition.

She climbed into her yawning work pod, coffee barely getting her going. A warning light winked: her Foe was already up and running. Another day at the orifice.

The pod wrapped itself around her as tabs and inserts slid into place. This was the latest gear, a top of the line simulation suit immersed in a data-pod of beguiling comfort.

Snug. Not a way to lounge, but to *fly*.

She closed her eyes and let the sim-suit do its stuff.

May 16, 2046. She liked to start in real-space. Less jarring.

Images played directly upon her retina. The entrance protocol lifted her out of her Huntington Beach apartment and in a second she was zooming over rooftops, skating down the beach. Combers broke in soft white bands and red-suited surfers caught them in passing marriage.

All piped down from a satellite view, of course, sharp and clear.

Get to work, Myung, her Foe called. *Sightsee later.*

"I'm running a deep search," she lied.

Sure.

"I'll spot you a hundred creds on the action," she shot back.

You're on. Big new market opening today. A hint of mockery?

"Where?" Today she was going to nail him, by God.

Right under our noses, the way I sniff it.

"In the county?"

Now, that would be telling.

Which meant he didn't know.

So: a hunt. Better than a day of shaving margins, at least.

She and her Foe were zoomers, ferrets who made markets more efficient. Evolved far beyond the primitivo commodity traders of the late TwenCen, they moved fast, high-flying for competitive edge.

They zoomed through spaces wholly insubstantial, but that was irrelevant. Economic pattern-spaces were as tricky as mountain crevasses. And even hard cash just stood for an idea.

Most people still dug coal and grew crops, ancient style grunt labor—but in Orange County you could easily forget that, gripped by the fever of the new.

Below her, the county was a sprawl, but a smart one. The wall-to-mall fungus left over from the TwenCen days was gone. High-rises rose from lush parks. Some even had orange grove skirts, a chic nostalgia. Roofs were eco-virtue white. Blacktop streets had long ago added a sandy-colored coating whose mica sprinkles winked up at her. Even cars were in light shades. All this to reflect sunlight, public advertisements that everybody was doing something about global warming.

The car-rivers thronged streets and freeways (still *free*—if you could get the license). When parked, cars were tucked underground. Still plenty of scurry-scurry, but most of it mental, not metal.

She sensed the county's incessant pulse, the throb of the Pacific Basin's hub, pivot point of the largest zonal economy on the planet.

Felt, not *saw.* Her chest was a map. Laguna Beach over her right nipple, Irvine over the left. Using neural plasticity, the primary sensory areas of her cortex "read" the county's electronic Mesh through her skin.

But this was not like antique serial reading at all. No flat data here. No screens.

She relaxed. The trick was to *merge,* not just observe.

Far better for a chimpanzeelike species to take in the world through its evolved, body-wrapping neural bed.

More fun, too. She detected economic indicators on her augmented skin. A tiny shooting pain spoke of a leveraged buyout. Was that uneasy sensation natural to her, or a hint from her subsystems about a possible lowering of the prime rate?

Gotcha! the Foe sent.

Myung glanced at her running index. She was eleven hundred creds down!

So fast? How could—?

Then she felt it: dancing data-spikes in alarm-red, prickly on her left leg. The Foe had captured an early indicator. Which?

Myung had been coasting toward the Anaheim hills, watching the pulse of business trading quicken as slanting sunshine smartly profiled the fashionable, post-pyramidal corporate buildings. So she had missed the opening salvo of weather data update, the first trading opportunity.

The Foe already had an edge and was shifting investments. How?

Ahead of her in the simulated air she could see the Foe skating to the south. All this was visual metaphor, of course, symbology for the directed attention of the data-eating programs.

A stain came spreading from the east into Mission Viejo. Not real weather, but economic variables.

Deals flickered beneath the data-thunderheads like sheet lightning. Pixels of packet-information fell as soft rains on her long-term investments.

The Foe was buying extra electrical power from Oxnard. Selling it to users to offset the low yields seeping up from San Diego.

Small stuff. A screen for something subtle. Myung close-upped the digital stream and glimpsed the deeper details.

Every day more water flowed in the air over southern California than streamed down the Mississippi. Rainfall projections changed driving conditions, affected tournament golf scores, altered yields of solar power, fed into agri-prod.

Down her back slid prickly-fresh commodity info, an itch she should scratch. A hint from her sniffer-programs? She willed a virtual finger to rub the tingling.

—and snapped back to real-space.

An ivory mist over Long Beach. Real, purpling water thunderclouds scooting into San Juan Cap from the south.

Ah—virtual sports. The older the population got, the more leery of weather. They still wanted the zing of adventure, though. Through virtual feedback, creaky bodies could air-surf from twenty kilometers above the Grand Canyon. Or race alongside the few protected Great White sharks in the Catalina Preserve.

High-resolution Virtuality stimulated lacy filigrees of electro-chem impulses throughout the cerebral cortex. Did it matter whether the induction came from the real thing or from the slippery arts of electronics?

Time for a bit of business.

Her prognosticator programs told her that with 0.87 probability, such oldies would cocoon-up across six states. So indoor virtual sports use, with electrostim to zing the aging muscles, would rise in the next day.

She swiftly exercised options on five virtual sites, pouring in some of her reserve computational capacity. But the Foe had already harvested the plums there. Not much margin left.

Myung killed her simulated velocity and saw the layers of deals the Foe was making, counting on the coming storm to shift the odds by fractions. Enough contracts-of-the-moment processed, and profits added up. But you had to call the slant just right.

Trouble-sniffing subroutines pressed their electronic doubts upon her: a warning chill breeze across her brow. She waved it away.

Myung dove into the clouds of event-space. Her skin did the deals for here, working with software that verged on mammal-level intelligence itself. She wore her suits of artificial-intelligence . . . and in a real sense, they wore her.

She felt her creds—not credits so much as *credibilities,* the operant currency in data-space—washing like hot air currents over her body.

Losses were chilling. She got cold feet, quite literally, when the San Onofre nuke piped up with a gush of clean power. A new substation, coming on much earlier than SoCalEd had estimated.

That endangered her energy portfolio. A quick flick got her out of the electrical futures market altogether, before the world-wide Mesh caught on to the implications.

Up, away. Let the Foe pick up the last few percentage points. Myung flapped across the digital sky, capital taking wing.

She lofted to a ten-mile-high perspective. Global warming had already made the county's south-facing slopes into cactus and tough grasslands. Coastal sage still clung to the north-facing slopes, seeking cooler climes. All the coast was becoming a "fog desert" sustained by vapor from luke-warm ocean currents. Dikes held back the rising warm ocean from New-port to Long Beach.

Pretty, but no commodity possibilities there any more.

Time to take the larger view.

She rose. Her tactile and visual maps expanded. She went to split-skin perception, with the real, matter-based landscape overlaid on the info-scape. Surreal, but heady.

From below she burst into the data-sphere of Investtainment, where people played upon the world's weather like a casino. Ever since rising global temperatures pumped more energy in, violent oscillations had grown.

Weather was now the hidden, wild-card lubricant of the world's econ-omy. Tornado warnings were sent to street addresses, damage predictions shaded by the city block. Each neighborhood got its own rain forecast.

A sparrow's fall in Portugal could diddle the global fluid system so that, in principle, a thunderhead system would form over Fountain Valley a week later. Today, merging pressures from the south sent forking light-ning over mid-California. That shut down the launch site of all local rocket-planes to the Orbital Hiltons. Hundreds of invest-programs had that already covered.

So she looked on a still larger scale. Up, again.

This grand world Mesh was N-dimensional. And even the number N changed with time, as parameters shifted in and out of application.

There was only one way to make sense of this in the narrow human sensorium. Every second, a fresh dimension sheared in over an older dimension. Freeze-framed, each instant looked like a ridiculously complicated abstract sculpture running on drug-driven overdrive. Watch any one moment too hard and you got a lancing headache, motion sickness and zero comprehension.

Augmented feedback, so useful in keeping on the financial edge, could also be an unforgiving bitch.

The Foe wasn't up here, hovering over the whole continent. Good. Time to think. She watched the *N*-space as if it were an entertainment, and in time came an extended perception, integrated by the long-suffering subconscious.

She bestrode the world. Total immersion.

She stamped and marched across the muddy field of chaotic economic interactions. Her boot heels left deep scars. These healed immediately: subprograms at work, like cellular repair. She would pay a passage price for venturing here.

A landscape opened like the welcome of a mother's lap.

Her fractal tentacles spread through the networks with blinding speed, penetrating the planetary spider web. Orange County was a brooding, swollen orb at the PacBasin's center.

Smelled it yet? came the Foe's taunt from below.

"I'm following some ticklers," she lied.

I'm way ahead of you.

"Then how come you're gabbing? And tracking me?"

Friendly competition—

"Forget the friendly part." She was irked. Not by the Foe, but by failure. She needed something *hot.* Where?

'Fess up, you're smelling nothing.

"Just the stink of overdone expectations," she shot back wryly.

Nothing promising in the swirling weather-space, working with prickly light below her. Seen this way, the planet's thirteen billion lives were like a field of grass waving beneath fitful gusts they could barely glimpse.

Wrong blind alley! sent her Foe maliciously.

Myung shot a glance at her indices. Down nineteen hundred!

And she had spotted him a hundred. *Damn.*

She shifted through parameter-spaces. There—like a carnival, neon-bright on the horizon of a black, cool desert: the colossal market-space of Culture.

She strode across the tortured seethe of global Mesh data.

In the archaic economy of manufacturing, middle managers were long gone. No more "just in time" manufacturing in blocky factories. No more one-size-fits-all. That had fallen to "right on time" production out of tiny shops, prefabs, even garages.

Anybody who could make a gizmo cheaper could send you a bid. They would make your very own custom gizmo, by direct Mesh order.

Around the globe, robotic prod-lines of canny intelligence stood ready in ill-lit shacks. Savvy software leaped into action at your Meshed demand, reconfiguring for your order like an obliging whore. Friction-free service. The mercantile millennium.

Seen from up here, friction-free marketism seemed the world's only workable ideology—unless you counted New Islam, but who did? Under it, middle managers had decades ago vanished down the sucking drain of evolving necessity. "Production" got shortened to *prod*—and prodded the market.

Of course the people shed by frictionless prod ended up with dynamic, fulfilling careers in dog-washing: valets, luxury servants, touchy-feely insulators for the harried prod-folk. And their bosses.

But not all was manufacturing. Even dog-dressers needed Culture Prod. *Especially* dog-dressers.

"My sniffers are getting it," she said.

The Foe answered, *You're on the scent—but late.*

Something new . . .

She walked through the data-vaults of the Culture City. As a glittering representation of unimaginable complexities, it loomed: Global, intricate, impossible to know fully for even a passing instant. And thus, an infinite resource.

She stamped through streets busy with commerce. Ferrets and deal-making programs scampered like rodents under heel. Towers of the giga-conglomerates raked the skies.

None of this Big Guy stuff for her. Not today, thanks.

To beat her Foe, she needed something born of Orange County, something to put on the table.

And only her own sniffer-programs could find it for her. The web of connections in even a single county was so criss-crossed that no mere human could find her way.

She snapped back into the real world. *Think.*

Lunch eased into her bloodstream, fed by the pod when it sensed her lowering blood sugar. Myung tapped for an extra Kaff to give her some zip. Her medical worrier hovered in air before her, clucked and frowned. She ignored it.

—And back to Culture City.

Glassy ramparts led up into the citadels of the mega-Corps. Showers of speculation rained on their flanks. Rivulets gurgled off into gutters. Nothing new here, just the ceaseless hum of a market full of energy and no place to go.

Index check: sixteen hundred down!

The deals she had left running from the morning were pumping out the last of their dividends. No more help there.

Time's a-wastin', her Foe sent nastily. She could imagine his sneer and sardonic eyes.

Save your creds for the crunch, she retorted.

You're down thirteen hundred and falling.

He was right. The trouble with paired competition—the very latest market-stimulating twist—was that the outcome was starkly clear. No comforting self-delusions lasted long.

Irked, she leaped high and flew above the City. Go local, then. Orange County was the PacBasin's best fount of fresh ideas.

She caught vectors from the county drawing her down. Prickly hints sheeted across her belly, over her forearms. To the east—there—a shimmer of possibility.

Her ferrets were her own, of course—searcher programs tuned to her style, her way of perceiving quality and content. They *were* her, in a truncated sense.

Now they led her down a funnel, into—

A mall.

In real-space, no less. Tacky.

Hopelessly antique, of course. Dilapidated buildings leaning against each other, laid out in boring rectangular grids. Faded plastic and rusty chrome.

People still went there, of course; somewhere, she was sure, people still used wooden plows.

This must be in Kansas or the Siberian Free State or somewhere equally Out Of It. Why in the world had her sniffers taken her here?

She checked real-world location, preparing to lift out.

East Anaheim? Impossible!

But no—there was something here. Her sniffer popped up an overlay and the soles of her feet itched with anticipation. Programs zoomed her in on a gray shambles that dominated the end of the cracked black-top parking lot.

Was this a museum? No, but—

Art Attack came the signifier.

That sign . . . "An old K-Mart," she murmured. She barely remembered being in one as a girl. Rigid, old-style aisles of plastic prod. Positively *cubic,* as the teeners said. A cube, after all, was an infinite number of stacked squares.

But this K-Mart had been reshaped. Stucco-sculpted into an archly ironic lavender mosque, festooned with bright brand name items.

It hit her. "Of course!"

She zoomed up, above the Orange County jumble.

Here it was—pay dirt. And she was on the ground *first.*

She popped her pod and sucked in the dry, flavorful air. Back in Huntington Beach. Her throat was dry, the aftermath of tension.

And just 16:47, too. Plenty of time for a swim.

The team that had done the mock-mosque K-Mart were like all artists: sophisticated along one axis, dunderheads along all economic vectors. They had thought it was a pure lark to fashion ancient relics of paleocapitalism into bizarre abstract expressionist "statements." Mere fun effusions, they thought.

She loved working with people who were, deep in their souls, innocent of markets.

Within two hours she had locked up the idea and labeled it: "Post-Consumerism Dada from the fabled Age of Appetite."

She had marketed it through pre-view around the globe. Thailand and the Siberians (the last true culture virgins) had gobbled up the idea. Every rotting 'burb round the globe had plenty of derelict K-Marts; this gave them a new angle.

Then she had auctioned the idea in the Mesh. Cut in the artists for their majority interest. Sold shares. Franchised it in the Cutting Concept sub-Mesh. Divided shares twice, declared a dividend.

All in less time than it took to drive from Garden Grove to San Clemente.

"How'd you find that?" her Foe asked, climbing out of his pod.

"My sniffers are *good,* I told you."

He scowled. "And how'd you get there so fast?"

"You've got to take the larger view," she said mysteriously.

He grimaced. "You're up two thousand five creds."

"Lucky I didn't really trounce you."

"Culture City sure ate it up, too."

"Speaking of which, how about starting a steak? I'm starving."

He kissed her. This was perhaps the best part of the Foe-Team method. They spurred each other on, but didn't cut each other dead in the marketplace. No matter how appealing that seemed, sometimes.

Being married helped keep their rivalry on reasonable terms. Theirs was a standard five-year monogamous contract, already nearly half over. How could she not renew, with such a deliciously stimulating opponent?

Sure, dog-eat-dog markets sometimes worked better, but who wanted to dine on dog?

"We'll split the chores," he said.

"We need a servant."

He laughed. "Think we're rich? We just grease the gears of the great machine."

"Such a poet you are."

"And there are still the dishes to do from last night."

"Ugh. I'll race you to the beach first."

Out of the Mouths

SHEILA FINCH

Sheila Finch has been writing better-than-average science fiction since the 1970s. Her first novel, *Infinity's Web*, appeared in 1985, followed by several more in the 1980s and early 1990s, but her work has had little impact on the field. "Sheila Finch is still in the wings," said *The Encyclopedia of Science Fiction* in 1992, "but gives the impression she is capable of stepping into full view at any time."

She had professional training in linguistics, which is evident in her novel, *Triad*, and since the late 1980s she has been publishing stories of the Guild of Xenolinguists. Two of these appeared in *Fantasy & Science Fiction* in 1996 and this one particularly, "Out of the Mouths," gives some evidence of the depth of Finch's real power as a storyteller. As is evident in our world today, problems of communication between cultures can be deadly. How much more so, then, between aliens and humans in the future.

Out of the Mouths

SHEILA FINCH

The old man was wading, net in hand, tending his fish ponds, when the visitor arrived. He hadn't heard the approach of an aircar. Tattered curls of autumnal mist caught in the low boughs of oak and alder; patches of night darkness still lingered on the estuary beyond the fish ponds; the rich, dark smell of river mud rose like a favorite perfume to his nose. He transferred the net to his left hand and shaded his eyes with the right, bending forward from the waist. "*Heron*," his students had once called him, affectionately mocking his awkward height. The name had stuck.

"Good morning." A small, brown, middle-aged woman stood on the opposite bank.

There was something clipped and suppressed in her speech; he understood from it that she didn't like him. By his leg, a fish jumped, a gleam of dull gold above gray glass. He watched the ripples spreading, aware the woman watched him.

"Do you know who I am?"

He sensed the itch of irritation that ran through her words. He studied the woman's face, reading small physical clues that gave the lie to words as he'd taught his students to do. The visitor was unafraid of tough decisions but not blessed with patience. She was annoyed at having to be here. Yet he'd known for a long time that she would come some day.

"You are Magistra Orla Eiluned," he said. "Head of the Mother House of the Guild of Xenolinguists."

The visitor's mouth twitched. "I remember a time when that was your title, and I was a lowly probationer, fresh from a provincial world no one had ever heard of."

"Minska. I'd heard of it."

Orla Eiluned glanced at him. When she spoke, the anger was back underneath her words. "Must we confer across this stinking water? I'm susceptible to the damp in this island, even if you aren't."

He waded out onto the bank where his visitor stood, laid the net aside, and pulled off his hip boots. He led the way up the path to the small cottage. Inside, she gazed around, and he saw it fresh through her eyes: a book-filled room with sloping roof, a long cot under a window and a cooking alcove at the rear. He thought of the ample apartment that had been his at the Mother House, overlooking the lake beneath snow-crowned Alps. He wondered if she'd brought in pictures and rugs and musical instruments of her own, as he had, though he'd brought mostly books. The memory ached this morning.

"Ten years it's been, since you were Head." She turned from a book-shelf, her face in shadow. "Do you miss the Guild, Magister Heron?"

He thought about that for a moment. "The students, perhaps." She was silent while he set tea in pottery mugs on a small table before her. At his gesture, she sat, her eyes reading his face as he had read hers a moment ago.

"You had a reputation as a good Head. It's all the more wonder to me—"

"Keri and T'biak," he said at once, because there could be no other reason. He remembered a sharply clear, end-of-winter morning, and a baby, pink and smooth as a porcelain doll, lying in his arms; he remembered how she'd smelled of milk and petals and innocence.

"Indeed," Orla Eiluned said. "And now the final chapter to this sorry experiment must be written."

"It was wartime," he said. "We took extraordinary measures for what seemed good enough reason at the moment—"

"The thought of using babies is horrifying, no matter how desperate the times or how noble the purpose!"

He bowed his head and waited.

She sighed, and for a moment seemed to set aside the mantle of her office. They sat quietly, as if they were old country wives, mending threadbare patches with their words, preparing to examine the troubled fabric of the past.

The human child had arrived first.

A cold, clear day at the end of winter. Heron stood on the porch of the secluded, centuries-old stone house that Essa had refurbished for them, the child awkwardly draped across his stiff arms. She was three weeks old, an orphan, with a tiny pouty mouth and a fuzz of almost silver hair.

"You act as if this is the first infant you've held!" Essa glanced at him from under a purple wool scarf, a spot of color in a white landscape.

"It is." The Guild discouraged parenthood for lingsters, and he, a dutiful son in the Mother House for the last five decades, had never needed to question its wisdom. But the thought made him ask, "What happened to her parents?"

"Casualties of the war," Essa answered shortly.

"Poor child. Does she have a name?"

"Keri."

Uncontrolled emotion was dangerous for a lingster at work; all his training guarded against being swept away in the storm of strong feelings. *Never let emotion color the interface,* the first rule of the Guild. He could see how that applied here too; becoming sentimental about the baby would lead to inappropriate actions that could jeopardize the project. He gave the infant back to Essa. Yet his arms retained the imprint of her tiny body long after she'd been carried into the house, an odd effect that he noted as dispassionately as he marked the snow softening underfoot as the thaw began.

Essa had found the house in a pine forest on the slopes of a mountain, not so far north that the weather would be a problem, but far enough away from the Mother House for privacy. Heron had considered going off-world, but that would create additional difficulties because of the uncertainties of civilian travel due to the war, and he'd bowed to Essa's choice. The house, which had belonged for many generations to a prosperous family, boasted several living rooms, and also bedrooms with wood-burning fireplaces, a feature that had appealed to him in these times of austerity. A large stone-flagged kitchen opened out to a greenhouse and vegetable garden behind the house; that would help keep their costs to a minimum. The fewer times he asked the Guild for money, the fewer awkward questions would be asked. He wanted to avoid the awkward questions.

Essa had filled the house with rocking chairs and antique rugs and handmade quilts, and also with dogs and cats; the children were not to be deprived of the comforts of a normal childhood as she saw it. He didn't argue, though he wondered how animals might contaminate the experiment. He recognized that he needed Essa's warmth as counterweight to his necessarily colder vision.

Three months ago, an ambassador he'd only vaguely known—but whose sister was once Heron's student—had approached him with a proposition, and excitement and apprehension had warred in his blood ever since. The ambassador had reminded him how often he'd mused with his students about such an experiment; war, the ambassador said, often allowed great leaps of scientific knowledge to happen. Why not in Heron's field too?

There was no denying the great need for such an advance. In the centuries since humans had begun to spread out to the worlds of the Orion Arm, they'd never encountered an enemy like the Venatixi. The ambassador told a disturbing tale of a race whose history, customs, and intentions toward humans were all unknown, inscrutable; only the trail of destruction and blood they left behind spoke of their fierce enmity. *"If we could crack their language,"* the diplomat said, pacing the floor in Heron's study at the Mother House, *"we could decipher their intentions and frustrate them! The Guild is our only hope."*

But the Guild lacked the nerve to do what had to be done; forcing the issue ran the risk of tearing it apart, perhaps fatally. He would never knowingly do anything to damage the Guild. For the first time in his long career, Heron knew he had to act outside the Guild.

Odysseus must have felt like this, he thought now, on the porch of the stone house: lured by the twin sirens of duty and intellectual adventure. He would never have agreed to do it for money. It was good that Essa would be the children's ombudsman if they should ever need protection; he understood that some people found him too austere. Questions there might be, in the future, but he didn't want it said he'd been cruel.

A few hours later, the Venatixi infant arrived with a face like a forest god, half fawn, half fox. He'd never seen a Venatixi before, and he was stunned by the child's beauty. He remembered Essa's comment when he'd first asked her to join him: *"They kill like demons, but they look like angels."*

The adult Venatixi male who accompanied the child resembled a vision of human perfection carved by a master sculptor. Taller than Heron, he seemed much younger in spite of his pure white hair. His skin was golden, and his dark eyes seemed to look into the deeps of space from which he had come. If Heron expected to read hostility or defiance in the alien's expression—understandable emotions for an enemy, brought here under who knew what coercion—he was disappointed. The beautiful face was blank. Or else, he thought, the play of Venatixi emotions across the face was too subtle for even a trained lingster to read. He sensed a distance in the alien, vaster than the circumstances of war demanded, or their incompatible languages.

He disliked the man on sight. This unusually strong reaction distressed him; he amended it with logic: What kind of creature delivers its young up to the enemy? How could the Venatixi be sure he didn't plan to torture the child, or even dissect it? And what was the alien's connection with the shadowy ambassador who had set the project in motion and then disappeared?

Heron never found vague unease to be a useful state of mind in which to work; he turned his thoughts back to the project in hand.

The alien attendant made it known the baby was to be called T'biak. Odd, how pointing and naming were used so often among the races of the Arm. But names were all he could be sure of at this point. Ah, but the project would rectify all that in time, he thought, and was flushed with eagerness to begin.

The Venatixi possessed the same organs that in humans facilitated speech. No struggling with olfactory cues, or intricate light pulses, or any of the half dozen or so other variations in the way communication was handled around the Arm. Yet he'd observed that the closer an alien's physiology to human, the more subtle the problem of unlocking the language. The temptation was strong to believe too quickly in surface similarities. Humans were lonely creatures, driven on an endless search across the galaxy for soulmates.

Over the years he'd developed a sixth sense for invisible problems, quirks of language that didn't easily slip from one tongue to another, hidden minefields that blew understanding sky high when least expected. The best lingsters sometimes met languages that contained obstacles all their skills couldn't overcome. Venatician appeared to be such a one. He'd studied it as best he could while he was still in the Mother House; lingsters who encountered it around the Arm sent back samples. The language was slippery; as soon as he thought he'd identified words and assigned denotation to them, they slid away, meaning changing under his fingertips even as he worked.

Inglis had retained many homonyms, despite centuries of attempts to standardize and regularize it, but he found Venatician held a more baffling mystery. It would've been daunting if it had occurred between friendly races; with a ferocious enemy like the Venatixi it was monstrous. The war that had resulted—from what? territorial imperatives? xenophobia? misunderstanding? nobody knew—had gone on too long, destroyed too many lives, and now threatened the survival of Earth itself. Time for visionary measures in the search for solutions.

"Did you stop to wonder how the ambassador got hold of an alien child? And so quickly at that!"

Essa had come back to stand beside him on the porch where he'd been gazing at the surrounding forest. She chewed at her under lip, a habit he knew she would've suppressed when she was younger for what it gave away of her inner turmoil.

"Kidnapped him, I suppose."

"You joke, Heron, but I have misgivings."

"Only partly, I'm afraid. Ugly things happen in war. Perhaps he's a hostage of some kind—"

"Where do you get such a terrible idea?"

"History," he said. "Many tribes in Earth's own past made an exchange of high-ranking children to be brought up in the enemy's camp. A good way to ensure peace between them!"

Essa shuddered.

"But I don't want to know the truth," he said. "It's a chance to explore a most promising theory, and I'm not about to lose it through needless bureaucracy." His blood began to pound; he felt flushed, giddy with the excitement of setting out in unknown territory, the Marco Polo of language. But he understood she might have misgivings. "Of course, it's natural that you'd feel some uncertainty—"

"More than that. I'm wondering whether we ought to do this at all."

"Keep in mind the great good we're doing for our world."

"How many scientists have said this down the centuries, I wonder, as they raced to damnation?"

He smiled tolerantly at her. Nothing could shake his confidence today. "Essa, you exaggerate the dangers here!"

"Do I?" she said quietly. Beyond where she stood with her back to the forest, the setting sun turned the mountain tops bloodred. "I don't know. But I think perhaps I should've turned you down when you asked me to help. I should've stayed where I was—grounded and safe in the Mother House's library until I retired!"

"In your day in the field, you were one of the best lingsters the Guild ever produced. Your skills are as sharp as ever. I need them."

"I wonder if I need this assault on my ethics."

Impatient with her hesitation, he said, "I can do this, Essa. I *know* I can!"

"Hubris, old friend," she said somberly. "Occupational hazard, I suppose."

But she gave up arguing and went inside.

The experiment he'd designed wasn't a new idea; in fact, early theoretical xenolinguists such as Elgin and Watson had discussed it centuries before. Raise a human child with an alien, and she'll have the other's language in her head from birth, as well as her native tongue. A chance to interface between languages without the programs, the drugs, the implants that lingsters normally used to forge understanding out of chaos. The theory had been well thought out long ago. But the opportunity and the resolve had never presented themselves until now.

He had the chance to save human lives from a violent enemy, and expand the boundaries of knowledge at the same time. It was hard to say which was the more compelling.

"Saving lives by sacrificing two innocent children, do you mean?" Orla Eiluned interrupted the old man's story.

He turned stiffly from the window where he'd been staring at the ponds. Sunlight played over the water now, and the fishing birds that had not yet flown south arrived to work their craft on unsuspecting carp. Perhaps, he thought with sudden insight, he devoted his last years to these fish precisely because they had no voices.

There was no point in explaining; she knew it as well as he: human children were born with a template for language, any language. The young of *Homo sapiens* learned second, third, even fourth languages rapidly, easily, while their parents labored over the grammar of a second. But there was more, something seen many times in human history. Nations were thrown together by conquest, or met in shared servitude, their languages mutually unintelligible. Pidgins developed: odd, ungrammatical mixes, bits from here or there to get the adults through the daily task of living and working together.

The next step had to be taken by the second generation, the children who invented the creole, the beginnings of a genuinely new language in the interface between the two their parents spoke. And they did it easily, compulsively, brilliantly. The mystery of how language had come into being was solved: Children were its inventors. Children had spoken those first words in the caves and around the cooking fires.

"You must return with me at once to the Mother House," Orla Eiluned said.

"I don't travel anymore."

"Nevertheless, I insist. There's much at stake." She stood, staring moodily out the window at the gleaming ponds over which a hazy net of insects hung and an occasional turquoise kingfisher flashed through shadow. "Whatever inspired you to retire to this damp island?"

"Solitude and ghosts," the old man said. "This estuary has seen the blood of a great nation's birth and passing away. It comforts me to remember how insubstantial human dreams are in the sweep of time."

"And sometimes, how unprincipled?" she suggested.

He shook his head. "Perhaps we ought never allow scientists to play with their toys unsupervised."

The Head frowned as if she wished to argue the point, then thought better of it. "Well—Go on!"

Essa had given the old stone house a name since he was last here, and the deaf old man who cooked and cleaned for them had carved it and hung it over the door: *Manhattan*.

Heron stopped at the foot of the porch steps and read it. Melting snow dripped off the house's sloping roof, and the wind soughed gently in the pine trees behind him. Beyond, in the clearing, the 'car that was his as Head of the Mother House—a luxury not granted to other people these troubled days—lifted off and went to shelter. Essa watched him, sharp-faced.

"An odd choice," he suggested. "I would have chosen something to do with mountains. Or trees, perhaps."

"You don't recognize the reference?"

He frowned. "I seem to remember something about buying an is-land— No? That isn't right?"

Essa snorted. "You read the wrong history, my friend!"

He smiled at her as they went inside. "How're they doing?"

"See for yourself."

For three years he'd divided his time between his duties at the Mother House and the children's hideaway, but his heart grew ever more firmly rooted in the stone house. In Geneva the talk was of colonies lost and cities destroyed, the war coming nearer and nearer to Earth itself. The sense of some horror creeping closer day by day, some catastrophe wait-ing to engulf them all when they were least expecting it, sapped his energy. He found himself glancing anxiously over his shoulder at shad-ows, jumping at noises, suspicious of strangers until his nerves frayed and he couldn't work. He worried whether there'd even be time to complete the language project, let alone reap any benefits from it. But in this forest he could be hopeful, dreaming of the future as if he were as young as his small subjects in a world at peace.

He never spoke of the children or the stone house when he was in Geneva, allowing the Guild Procurators to believe that when he was away he was busy writing his memoirs. When the day came that the project was revealed, he expected they would be displeased at his se-crecy, but by then the results would justify his actions.

Essa led him to the well-equipped playroom where the toddlers, al-most three years old now, spent most of their day alone in each other's company. He stared through the one-way glass, watching them; they were absorbed with each other, a head of golden curls bending close to one of dark silver. The hidden mikes picked up a steady stream of infant bab-bling; at the same time the computer recorded and analyzed the proto-speech for replay and reinforcement later.

Ideally, he would have isolated the children from all other human contact, but Essa hadn't allowed that. *"The human child will lose her humanity,"* she'd argued. *"Our culture is transmitted, not inherited. We teach our young to grow up human!"* In any case, there was a flaw in a language produced in total absence of models; even if it should work, the basic problem of interfacing afterwards with existing tongues would still remain.

He listened to the children's voices coming from the speakers, the rising and falling music of baby speech, trying with his practiced ear to catch the tonal variations, the patterns of stress and juncture that should be emerging by now, hinting at the assignment of meaning. They seemed content at their play, and they were obviously healthy—Essa saw to that. If anything, their physical progress seemed accelerated by isolation, not hindered.

He wondered idly if this was how parents felt, watching their offspring at play, a combination of pride and awe and helplessness. The Venatixi child was beautiful, but it seemed to him that little Keri was his equal. She turned now and smiled, perhaps at something T'biak said. But he felt as if she sensed his presence behind the glass wall, and instinctively he smiled back, though she couldn't possibly see him. He knew a sudden, peculiar ache in his heart, and a sadness for which he knew no cause touched him briefly.

He shook the sensations away and returned his thoughts to the project. The children were not cut off from adult contact altogether, only the language exchanges were limited. His aim was to produce speakers able to move easily back and forth from their native tongues to the creole he expected them to invent in the buffer zone between them. If his theory was correct, that new language would prove to be as rich and full of subtlety as either of the parent tongues, and it would provide the key to communication between humans and the Venatixi that was so desperately needed.

As the project had begun, he'd taken into his confidence two talented members of his faculty at the Mother House, an older man and a young woman, and they'd come to the stone house with him. When the children were fed or bathed, they were taken separately by their adult guardians and spoken to in the languages of their birth. At least, he had to assume that was happening with T'biak, since communication with the Venatixi attendant remained non-existent.

In front of him, as he stared through the one-way glass, he saw the daily working out of a miracle he'd dared to dream. Why, then, didn't he feel more cheerful? Where did this sudden, oppressive sense of loneliness come from today?

"Shall we review the observation notes first, or do you want to listen to the language samples the AI has processed so far?" Essa asked.

He'd almost forgotten her presence, and was glad to turn his attention to the choice. On each of his visits he reviewed the progress, made recommendations, but generally left day to day activities in Essa's capable hands, a task she handled well.

"The samples, of course!" He strode ahead of her to the small room at the back of the house which he used as his study. Essa fed cubes into the computer for him. The AI had analyzed the morphemes it identified in their speech, and assigned probable meaning to the combinations. He settled himself in a comfortable chair behind the desk to listen, familiarizing himself with the sounds at the same time as he studied the tentative Inglis spellings the computer had used for them. He was surprised at how few words the AI confidently identified; somehow he'd expected more by now.

Of course, so much of the verbalizing Keri and T'biak were doing remained baby babble; he knew what could be expected of toddlers, and these two were hardly different. A project like this demanded patience and time. He worked until his stomach complained that it was suppertime.

As he was about to leave the study, the young woman staff member came to find him.

"What is it, Birgit?"

"The Venatixi's missing, Magister," she said. "We need him to take T'biak out of the playroom now. The children're hungry and need to be fed."

"Perhaps Merono knows where he is?" The older lingster seemed to have befriended the alien, an action Heron approved but couldn't share.

"I can't find Merono either."

"Have you checked the outbuildings?" Essa asked. The alien never socialized with the other staff when his duties were done, and lived by himself outside the house.

"Empty too. But he's never been missing before! He always takes good care of T'biak."

"Well, let's think this through. The weather's been mild today. Perhaps he's gone for a walk?"

"Perhaps he's gone home to Venatix!" Essa said.

He glanced at her and saw she was only half joking. No one could be really sure if the Venatixi approved of what they were attempting to do here, or even if he understood. He remembered his first suspicions of the man, and Essa's unease over the manner in which T'biak had been found for the project. Perhaps she was right and the alien had tired of his role as a hostage of sorts, and had escaped? But why leave a child of his own race in enemy hands? It wouldn't make sense. At least, he amended, it wouldn't if one were human. And it would be disastrous for the project; they needed the adult Venatixi to teach the boy his own language, or the whole attempt would fail.

He ordered a search of the area around the house and the nearby forest. The days were slowly lengthening as spring approached, but darkness still fell early so far north, and there was very little daylight left. In a drift of snow turning to slush, they found the blood-soaked body of Merono who might one day have succeeded Heron as Head of the Mother House. He looked as if wolves had got him. But no wolf tears off a man's hands.

"Why was he killed?" Birgit wailed. "Merono was never anything but kind to the Venatixi. He was more like a father than a colleague to us all."

They had to wait for morning to hunt for tracks. No new snow fell overnight, yet they never found any tracks; the Venatixi had disappeared without a trace. All they learned was that the alien had taken his small supply of belongings with him. He wasn't coming back. Perhaps he'd taken his victim's hands with him too, for they were never found either.

Heron returned to the house in a somber mood. He'd lost a gentle, valuable member of his team, victim of a grisly crime, and an indispensable if unlikable alien. He wasn't at all certain what to do next.

Essa waited for him to come in, the sleepy alien boy cradled in her arms. "Now what?" she demanded, voicing his own question.

He shook his head. At that moment he felt overwhelmed with horror at the brutal murder. But he knew an even greater frustration at being blocked so near his goal; such an opportunity would never arise twice in a man's lifetime. Yet there was no way he could succeed without the Venatixi. Everything hung on the children growing up bilingual.

While he hesitated, little Keri came and clasped him about the leg. One of the pups that had attached itself to her whined softly, and she let go of Heron to pick it up. Watching the child cradling the pup, he had a bleak vision of his future: abandoning the project, returning to his sterile, bachelor rooms at the Mother House, knowing he'd never see Keri again.

The thought caught him by surprise; his project lay in ruins and he mourned the loss of contact with a child? That shouldn't have mattered at all. He was ashamed of his sentimental weakness.

"We can't abandon this precious boy," Essa said, absently ruffling the child's silver hair. "But what will we do with him?" Then he saw how to make the best of this, how to salvage something from his ambitious plan.

"We'll keep them both here. We'll work with T'biak—teach him Inglis—"

"No, Heron." Essa shook her head. "Let the children go. It's over."

"I don't accept that. We have too much at stake here!"

"How would teaching T'biak Inglis bring an end to the war? The problem of communicating with his people will still remain."

"Forget that, Essa. Think instead of the new possibilities!" His excitement grew as the new plan unfolded before him. "We have a chance to observe how an alien brain processes human language! A chance to see how much truly is due to biogrammar and whether that biogrammar itself varies from race to race."

She didn't seem to be listening. "Poor little orphan!"

"We've had experience with other races learning Inglis, of course." He was thinking aloud now, exploring the dimensions of his idea. "But how much do we really know about how they acquire language in the first place? We accept the concept of Universal Grammar because it's proved serviceable, but we don't really know how it works! Perhaps it's only a useful illusion. If we're ever going to open up the Guild to lingsters from other races, we'll have to know."

Essa wasn't impressed by his argument. "How could we teach him his own heritage? We know so little about the Venatixi!"

"Teach him whatever you'd teach Keri," he said impatiently. "It's that or perish for him. Don't you see?" His face felt flushed and a nervous energy seemed to have taken hold of his hands, which moved in an eager ballet, an emotional sign language that for once was not under his conscious control.

"It's Keri, isn't it?" she said thoughtfully. "Are you quite certain that your motive isn't to keep her here at all cost?"

"Essa! We have a chance to train our first alien-born lingster. Think how the Guild will benefit!"

"And how will we do this—with two less staff? Birgit and I and that senile old cook—I don't owe this much work to the Guild!"

"I'll find you local help with the chores. It won't be as sensational a situation as before—it won't cause as much gossip. And I'll come more often myself," he promised. It seemed very necessary that Essa be persuaded to continue; he valued her support and her intelligence.

She hugged the alien boy to her breast, looking doubtful. "I don't know. Heron—"

"Essa, old friend. Do it for me."

Unconvinced and grumbling, Essa carried T'biak off to bed. Keri trotted behind them, the pup at her heels.

He watched them go. At least she hadn't refused his request. It irritated him that Essa should think he proposed this new direction because he was so concerned with Keri. He was taken with her, yes—she was a pretty child. But obviously his first duty was to salvage something from the wreckage of the experiment. Essa herself fussed over the boy like an anxious mother bird; he wasn't convinced the child appreciated so much attention. The one thing he'd come to be certain about the Venatixi was that they didn't experience feelings the same way humans did.

Alone, he sat staring out the window at the mountains through a curtain of melted snow dripping off the roof, and planned the training of an alien lingster to serve the Guild.

"So you blame the Guild for your continuing this unethical experiment?" Orla Eiluned had been watching him intently as he spoke, as if ready to pounce on the first lie he dared to utter. "Of course, you would need to find another scapegoat once the war ended!"

The war had ended as suddenly and as inexplicably as it had begun; but it was an uneasy peace based on incomprehension and there was little room for joy in it. Humans and Venatixi remained as far apart as ever.

Outside his window, a late dragonfly hovered, admiring its own reflection in the glass. He watched until it darted suddenly away in a whir of opal brightness over the fish ponds beyond. There would be no more dragonflies this year.

"No," he said when the iridescent insect was out of sight. "I don't blame the Guild. But there was an urge in me to expand its work, and a pride in doing so. As there must be in every good Head."

She thought about that for a moment. "An 'occupational hazard,' I believe your Essa called it?"

For the first time, she smiled thinly at him.

He had hardly arrived back in Geneva when the announcement came of the truce with the Venatixi; for a moment he wondered if T'biak's attendant could have known the news before they did, but that still didn't explain abandoning the child. The ambassador's name featured prominently in the news. It occurred to Heron to wonder why, if the ambassador was capable of arranging a truce now, he'd ever come to Heron about the project in the first place. But as the diplomat never contacted Heron to officially end it, Heron felt justified that he hadn't.

It was just one more unknown in a whole disturbing catalog of unknown things to do with the Venatixi. Humans had been overdue to meet an alien they would never understand. Yet there'd been moments when he'd thought he pinned something down, captured some essence, stood on the edge of breaking through. Was there truly something to this, or was it only self-delusion?

In spite of his promise to Essa, his visits to the northern hideaway became less frequent; his responsibilities to the students in the Mother House caught up with him. There was a need to find new faculty to train the lingsters increasingly in demand around the Arm once hostilities ended, and more students than ever applied for admission and had to be tested and evaluated and counseled. New buildings had to be planned, and roofs replaced on old ones. Money needed to be found. And the dolphin tutors demanded that they be given more say in the selection of students since they felt they could better evaluate certain areas of expertise than any human faculty committee; it took diplomacy on his part to settle the dispute that resulted.

He visited briefly as often as he could, and in between he looked forward to the regular reports Essa sent, relying on them for details of the children's progress. There was a certain joy to be gained from knowing the children were thriving in their hidden sanctuary. Essa was a perfect caregiver; his presence wasn't necessary—and sometimes that thought bothered him. Alone in his chambers at the Mother House at the end of day, he took his secret knowledge out and turned it over in his mind, enjoying the bittersweet memory of Keri.

The thought of her, he sensed, was less dangerous for him than the reality which threatened to undermine his careful life, flooding him with unaccustomed emotion. He began to catch himself at odd moments, brooding over what he'd given up to serve the Guild; the disloyalty of it frightened him.

On the occasion of the fourth anniversary of the project, he returned for a visit after a months-long absence. He set the 'car down in the clearing and saw Keri outside in mild sunshine. He was eager to see her, but a vague apprehension stopped him from calling to her as he'd been about to do. Instead, he stood watching, unnoticed.

Spring this far north was a brief explosion of color and perfume, a rebellion against the punishing cold that ruled most of the year. The little girl was playing with chains of tiny wildflowers, and beside her, the dog that had been her constant companion as a pup nursed a litter of her own. He saw she'd decorated the bitch's neck with the same small blooms.

"I taught her how to make daisy chains," Essa said from the doorway.

"Daisies?"

"So unobservant, you are! Do you ever notice anything outside the library and the classroom?"

"When it's important to me," he answered honestly, then became aware she was teasing when he saw her grin. He said ruefully, "I shall be a stuffy old fool in my old age, shan't I?"

Essa indicated the bench outside the door, and they sat comfortably together, old friends watching the young ones at play. The moment of unease he'd experienced faded away.

Then Keri came to him, hands outstretched. The touch of her little fingers in his own suddenly enormous hands started a rush of tears. He still didn't know how to behave. He glanced at his old friend for help and

Essa smiled encouragement. He stooped and brushed Keri's soft cheek with his lips.

The result startled all of them. The child drew back instantly, staring at him as if she'd somehow made a mistake and given her hand to a stranger.

Before he had a chance to speculate what had caused Keri's reaction, T'biak trotted up to them, and he immediately forgot Keri's strangeness. The boy opened his small fist and revealed a dead bird—crushed, by the look of its mangled feathers and jutting bones thin as needles.

"Where did you find that dead old thing?" Essa scolded her favorite indulgently, taking the carcass away from him and brushing stray bits of feather and blood off his hand.

He had the unpleasant notion the bird had been alive when the child found it. It was a strange idea, and he had no proof; he decided not to share this with Essa.

The moment of warmth—of *family,* he thought, astonished at the word—passed. He sensed his own withdrawal back into a narrower self that for a brief second had unfurled like the petals in Keri's daisy chains. Essa threw the sorry corpse away into undergrowth, and they all went into the house.

Somber now, he moved into the office, anxious to bury himself in work and drive both the uncomfortable suspicions about T'biak and his own disturbing emotions away. A small fire murmured in the grate, filling the room with wood smoke. Birgit entered silently, bringing cubes of the children's progress as she always did on his visits; she fed them into the small terminal on his desk. He sat down at the desk, looking forward to the calm the routine of work brought with it.

Instead of leaving, Birgit stood by the desk.

He looked up. "Is something wrong?"

"Something bothers me, Magister. They still babble a lot together."

"Babble?" He frowned, unwilling to entertain doubts about the project even in this revised version.

"Babies do it. Pre-language. Made-up words. But they should've passed that stage long ago. It's as if they're still inventing their own language. Not Inglis, certainly."

He searched for an explanation. Birgit was a talented lingster and a gifted teacher, not one to come to hasty conclusions, a good counterbalance to Essa's fussy motherliness. If anything, he'd always judged her a little too calm and a bit distant.

"Maybe they're bored?" he suggested.

"You be the judge, Magister."

She left and he turned his attention to the children's language. Almost immediately, he sensed that Birgit was right: something was indeed wrong. It wasn't Inglis that poured from the speaker, nor did it seem to be the proto-language they'd started to invent before the Venatixi attendant disappeared. Yet he could have sworn it wasn't nonsense babbling either. He frowned at the catalogs of nouns and verbs the AI spelled phonetically in Inglis—an already extensive list scrolling up the data screen.

There was a certain murkiness to the computer's translations. Closing his eyes to concentrate, he listened to the high pure voices filling the room. Language was a signal, but this set of signals lacked constants; it had variable referents, moments when the ground underfoot vanished though the children strode confidently ahead. His heart constricted with the pain of being left behind.

In this queer, sad mood, he realized there was an odd something other present, like something dimly glimpsed in the dark woods outside, sensed rather than recognized. He stopped the voices and glanced quickly at the screen.

"Inglis equivalent for—" He thought for a second, then touched one of the transliterations of the babies' sounds.

The data screen divided and displayed Inglis words—six—ten—a dozen—

"Stop. They can't all be homonyms?" How could they all be equivalencies for the same word? Worse, he saw, some translations were totally opposite to each other. "How can they have made one word mean 'far' and 'near' at the same time? 'Dark' and 'light.' What am I missing?"

And then he knew. Why had it taken so long to see what was happening?

"Run comparison with Venatixi," he ordered.

The AI complied; two columns of collected data flowed over the screen.

"Probability of a match?"

"Greater than 98 percent."

Essa came into the office, having tucked the children in bed. She peered anxiously over his shoulder at the screen. "Does it matter?"

He glanced back at her. She'd always been remarkably protective of her babies. He wondered now if that wasn't a negative attribute, something he should've guarded against.

"Instead of T'biak learning Inglis so we can work with him, Keri's learning Venatixi from him," he said. "That shouldn't be possible. He lacks models for Venatixi."

Essa warmed her hands at the fire. "So? Apparently the Venatixi are born with full language capability. Not just potential like us."

She wasn't surprised, he realized. She'd known this for a long time. Perhaps she'd even been hiding it from him. "What language do they use with you? Come now, Essa. Tell me the truth."

"I know them so well, you see . . ." She hesitated, stuffing her hands into large pockets in her skirt. "We don't really have to say much to each other to get along at all! It doesn't matter, does it? They're only children, after all."

But it did matter. And perhaps at this late date he was experiencing the scruples he should've felt all along. Something of the bleak mood he'd experienced earlier on the porch came back. He said stiffly, "The boy will have to go back to his people. I'll do what I should've done before. I'll contact the ambassador."

Essa began to protest, but he waved her objections away and she ran out of the room near to tears.

Before he had a chance to talk himself out of his decision, he instructed the AI to open a channel to Geneva. Within the hour, he received an answer to the query he sent: the ambassador had been accused of treasonable activity with the Venatixi and executed.

Heron was now, by default, the boy's sole guardian.

"And even then," Orla Eiluned noted, her tone heavily sarcastic, "you didn't foresee trouble!"

She stood with one hand on the door of her aircar, waiting. The old man lowered his head. The telling of his story sucked energy from his bones like sap retreating from the leaves and branches of deciduous trees as winter conquered the land. Willow and ash, poplar and elm, the trees of the estuary bloomed and decayed, the rhythm of life. He felt his own December approaching.

"Perhaps, by then, I didn't want to see trouble," he said.

He gazed past the vehicle to the river, shining now in the full light of the low sun, as if he would never see it again and must imprint it on memory. A lone butterfly floated over the surface, and rainbows flashed into being and disappeared again as birds flew up, fish glinting in their beaks. They seemed to know the guardian of the fish was going away, leaving them to poach undisturbed. He didn't begrudge them an occasional fish. It was their nature, and nature made no moral judgments. Some lived and some died; he accepted nature's plan.

She indicated he should enter the 'car. He climbed in slowly, aware of a growing arthritic stiffness in his joints. Somewhere, a lark's song skirled down from the vast sky. It sounded like a funeral dirge.

* * *

He'd jeopardized his position at the Mother House by spending so much time away on business he couldn't explain to anyone. The death of his faculty member, which he'd managed to smooth over, was brought up again by enemies he hadn't known he'd made in the Guild. During the next year, urgent work kept him in Geneva for weeks, unable to get away. Perhaps, he admitted to himself, there was also fear of the tangle of emotions he experienced whenever he saw Keri. Easier to stay away than deal with them.

A great source of concern was the fact that T'biak grew increasingly alien before his eyes, his moods shifting quickly from light to dark. He was a very beautiful child, even more than Heron's little favorite, yet without her winning charm. But his social interaction with Heron and Essa deteriorated rapidly, and he was given to quick flashes of disapproval when crossed. Not temper, exactly, for there was no heat in them, but Heron could find no name for these outbursts, and he was coming to fear them. Things touched by T'biak ended broken and damaged more often than not—Like the bird, he thought. The child was not yet five years old.

Then one of the house cats disappeared, and this time when he found the mangled corpse under a fir tree he knew who was the killer. He'd managed to cut a little time out of his overloaded schedule to go back to the stone house, and he was prepared to stay for a while; he had a sense of things out of control, coming to a head. So he wasn't surprised to find its front paws had been hacked as if a clumsy attempt had been made to remove them.

Long ago, before she'd been blinded by love, Essa had seen the demon behind the angel eyes of the Venatixi. The uncanny echoes of the killing and mutilation of Merono chilled him even though the day was bright and warm, but he didn't know what to make of them.

The boy came up as he contemplated the body. He watched Heron, his eyes bleak as the mountains that ringed the stone house. Suddenly, Heron had no desire to move the corpse or confront the killer.

It didn't make sense. He accepted by now that the Venatixi language was inherited complete at birth and did not need to be learned from models in the inefficient way of human languages. That seemed plausible, once he thought about it. Birds still chirped even when hand-raised from hatchlings; they didn't have to be taught. Some even inherited their songs. But an entire culture, down to its rituals—and how else was he to interpret the mutilated animal than as a child's imitation of what adults do?—was unbelievable.

For several weeks he tried to explain the almost daily oddness the boy manifested as coincidence. *"We see it because we look for it,"* he told

Birgit. But he didn't believe that himself. Essa, as usual, would have none of it. *"He's just a child, Heron!"* was her constant refrain.

The summer after the children's fifth anniversary, Keri brought him the mother dog that loved her so warmly. He was in the office, going over accounts with Essa, when the child laid the body tenderly on the desk before him. He didn't need to examine it to know there were no paws at the end of the bloody stumps.

The little girl gazed at him with that pure, cherubic look he'd grown so attached to. It was a game, a mimicry of the adult behavior that had led to the killing of Merono. But he had no idea what the rules were.

He wanted to shout at her. He wanted to weep. He did neither. Angels, he understood now, were as amoral as scientists. Like lingsters, they kept emotion out of the interface.

"What have you done?" Essa exclaimed in horror.

Keri's expression clouded. Without a word, she swept the mangled dog off the desk and carried it outside. He glimpsed T'biak waiting for her under a fir, sunlight striping his cheeks like war paint. It had been some kind of test, he knew. And he'd failed it. His fists clenched with frustration but he did nothing.

Even then he wanted to believe it was a mistake, that T'biak had killed the dog and Keri was only bringing it to them. The language—well, yes, he could believe she could pick that up to the exclusion of her native tongue. But not the culture. That couldn't be transmitted without adult models. Not an entire culture!

Essa rose from her chair, her face white. "It's my fault. I've failed you. I should've seen—"

"Nobody could see this coming, Essa. Don't you think I would've made some provision if I had?"

"We must end it now."

"End it how?"

"Admit to the Guild what we've been doing here. We have no choice now, Heron! They'll find a way to return T'biak to his own people."

He could see love for the boy at war with fear of him in her expression, and wondered if she saw a similar conflict in his own eyes. "And Keri?"

"You've lost her already, Heron. If it's the last thing you do here, accept the truth!" She ran out of the house.

He knew he should go after her. But instead he sat and stared out the window at the forest where fragile wildflowers bloomed so briefly and birds darted through conifers, nest-building, scraps of fur scavenged from the household cats and dogs in their beaks. He couldn't recall ever noticing them before. So much had changed in the way he viewed the world. Hatched only a year ago, now the birds knew—all untaught—how to seize life's flickering warmth in a year mostly cold and dark. The sheer bravery of tiny things touched his heart.

He ran outside at the sound of the first scream, but he was too late to save Essa. He did, however, manage to prevent T'biak from cutting off her hands.

"The Procurators decided it was better not to let the true story get out," the old man said. "I was allowed to 'retire' from the Guild."

The 'car hummed softly, lifting over the sea to the destination the Head had coded into the onboard AI. After a while she sighed.

"And you exiled yourself on that island, far away from your life's work—"

"As penance, Magistra."

She stirred irritably at his use of the honorific. "There're better ways to make amends than becoming a hermit!"

He felt drained of words, a relief, as if he'd lanced a boil and let infection flow out. After the shock of events had begun to fade, he'd made the decision that he couldn't trust himself ever again. *Hubris,* Essa had called his crime. On his river mouth, where silent fish and noisy birds pursued their instinctual ways, he'd found healing if not forgiveness. For that, one had to pay one's debts, but it had not been possible to pay his.

"Did you ever learn why T'biak killed Essa?"

"I think because she loved him. They can't take too much love."

The Head glanced quizzically at him. "Well, we shall never know. He was returned to his people not long after."

The 'car was descending now and he recognized the autumnal gold-green dress of the Alps. They skimmed over ripe fields and flag-bedecked towns; in the distance, he saw the white buildings of the Mother House, surrounded by apple orchards. He imagined the shimmer of young voices under the heavy boughs, practicing their craft on each other, their music a reminder of how much he'd loved the Guild and its mission. Everything looked fresher, more prosperous than he remembered. The peace, incomprehensible though it might be, had held; things had improved.

"You don't seem curious to know why I came for you." Orla Eiluned waited for him to answer. When he didn't, she said: "The girl asked for you. You must find out why."

He raised an eyebrow at that.

"Oh yes," she said, misunderstanding. "We've taught Keri Inglis! She learned fast enough once the boy was gone. We have great hopes for her as a superior lingster. Something good will emerge from your abominable experiment, after all."

He saw then how she was like the man he'd once been. It was the

Guild itself that bred such ambition in its members, such proud ignorance. He could no more expect her to understand than he had in the beginning.

"I sometimes think Venatician will always remain beyond our reach," she said. "All those years, you made so little progress!"

One homonym, he thought. One connection he was sure of. But he didn't say it to her.

"Keri speaks Inglis. But does she still think in Venatician?"

She glanced sharply at him. "Her attendants say she dreams in it. They hear her talk in her sleep."

"Attendants."

She looked uncomfortable for the first time since she'd come for him. "The girl has had—some problems."

He could imagine what those problems might be. "We teach our culture to our young," he said. "It's not inherited. Not instinctive. I'll never believe that."

"But who's to say which model is learned, and when, or why?" the Head asked. "Young children bond, and the bonds are hard to educate away."

"And you need me now. Why now?"

"Well—she needs you. You'll see."

The 'car settled on a dark green lawn, folding its wings with a soft flutter. In front of him, he saw the classical lines of familiar buildings: the low roofs of the dolphin hall where the dolphin tutors taught their young pupils the restraint of physiology on concept and philosophy, classrooms where eager voices called and answered, polyphony in a dozen tongues. He'd apprenticed to the Guild at the age of ten, never wanting to be anything other than a lingster. He caught sight of the residence that had been his home when he was Head of the House, and then the library—he still thought of the library as Essa's domain though she'd been dead for a decade. His throat tightened and his eyes stung. The Guild had been his whole life for so many years, yet at its heart he'd found an aching loneliness.

Orla Eiluned touched his arm, urging him toward a building that hadn't existed in his time. Doors opened silently ahead of him and he followed their invitation slowly, down a short corridor and into a small room filled with green plants and a dazzle of sunlight. He blinked and shaded his eyes. The Head waited outside.

Keri stood by the window, her back to the light. She wore a simple white tunic that caught the light and gave her the look of an angel in a medieval illumination. His heart leaped, recognizing her instantly by her presence long before his eyes could adjust and identify her features.

When his vision cleared he saw how tall she'd grown in ten years, slim as a willow sapling, a young girl trembling on the edge of full womanhood. Her beauty took his breath away.

Yet there was some indefinable quality under the surface, as if—in spite of the robust health she displayed—she were dying. A bird, he thought in dismay, unable to break its way free of the egg that has nurtured it, would look like that. He understood why the Head had come herself to fetch him.

"My dearest child."

He opened his arms. She flowed into them in one graceful, catlike movement, and he folded her to his chest, feeling the fragile bones under skin as soft as wildflowers. Neither said anything for several moments. Then an embarrassed cough revealed the presence of another woman in the room.

"Please. Leave us alone."

"Is that wise, Magister Heron?" the woman asked.

"This is my daughter," he said simply, finally bringing himself to claim a bond of the heart if not of the blood.

The attendant looked doubtfully from Heron to Keri and back. But she went out of the room and closed the door behind her.

"You understand why I asked for you?" Keri stepped out of his embrace but kept his wrinkled old hands in her smooth young ones.

He was thrilled by her voice, low and musical like the call of a bright bird on his river. He felt himself rising to its lure. "Yes."

She studied his face. "I cannot be completely free without this rite."

He nodded, understanding. "T'biak too. But earlier?"

"Venatixi males mature faster than females. They need to. Our world is bloodier than yours."

He noted her choice of pronoun without comment; somehow, he wasn't even surprised. Her radiance held him transfixed. Perhaps the carp looking up felt this way as the kingfisher flashed overhead.

Her eyes filled with shadow, and she added: "There is no anger in the act."

"Surely a Guild lingster can understand that!" He smiled at her. "They hope you'll be a great lingster, you know."

She smiled too. "I shall. But not here. I have to go to Venatix."

"And how will you do that?"

"T'biak speaks to me. He is my mate. He'll come for me."

He thought again how much like angels they all were, and who could doubt that such superior beings moved in ways humans could never dream? Or made choices humans never faced. He remembered the way he and Essa and Birgit had searched for the vanished Venatixi in the snowbound forest after gentle Merono's murder and found no trace. He was an old man now, and such things were easier to believe than when he'd been young.

She lifted his hands and studied them thoughtfully, and the touch of her fingers burned. He tried and failed to suppress a shiver.

"I'm old. I have no regrets. But—my hands—" He broke off. It was irrational. "An old man's whim."

"Inglis too is full of metaphors about controlling hands," she said gently, letting go. "But I'll grant you them."

She drew him slowly toward her by his arms. His nose filled with her scent of milk and petals, and he thought suddenly of innocence as the river understood it, the cycle of life and death that nature wrote. He couldn't say whether he'd created an angel or a demon, nor did he care. The universe was more complex than the Guild recognized. But the Guild was young; he hoped it would learn.

As her face swelled in his vision, he saw her eyes brimming with love. "Father," she said.

Love and death, the only Venatician homonym he was certain he understood; they were intimately connected in the languages of Earth too.

He had the sense of a debt paid. He was at peace.

Breakaway, Backdown

JAMES PATRICK KELLY

James Patrick Kelly wrote "Think Like a Dinosaur," which was the lead
story in *Year's Best SF* last year, and which won the Hugo Award. In
introducing that story, I said that Kelly seems to be coming into full
command of his talents in the 1990s. Although a writer identified with
the Sycamore Hill workshop in the 1980s, the hotbed of Humanist oppo-
sition to the cyberpunks, he was also chosen as one of the original
cyberpunks by Bruce Sterling for inclusion in *Mirrorshades: The
Cyberpunk Anthology.* Much of his fiction has a serious hard-SF side that
appeals broadly to all readers in the field.

His novel, *Wildside*, which includes his novella "Mr. Boy," appeared in
the early 1990s and since then he has been publishing more frequent
short stories. In 1996 he published at least three, of which "Breakaway,
Backdown" is clearly the best. This is a story by a writer who was once,
for five minutes, included as a core cyberpunk. It has the hip, dark,
druggy attitude, the techno-wizardry, the post-adolescent angst of the
Blade Runner/Neuromancer future, but also O'Neill colony hardness, and
New Wave strangeness and stylistic ambition reminiscent of Samuel R.
Delany's classic, "Aye, and Gomorrah." It's all one side of a conversation, exposition and all. This guy can really write. If there is a new synthe-
sis in 1990s SF, it is at the point where Benford, Kelly, and Sterling meet.

You know, in space nobody wears shoes.

Well, new temps wear slippers. They make soles out of that adhesive polymer, griprite or griptite. Sounds like paper ripping when you lift your feet. Temps who've been up a while wear this glove thing that snugs around the toes. The breakaways, they go barefoot. You can't really walk much in space, so they've reinvented their feet so they can pick up screwdrivers and spoons and stuff. It's hard because you lose fine motor control in micro gee. I had . . . have this friend, Elena, who could make a krill and tomato sandwich with her feet, but she had that operation that changes your big toe into a thumb. I used to kid her that maybe breakaways were climbing down the evolutionary ladder, not jumping off it. Are we people or chimps? She'd scratch her armpits and hoot.

Sure, breakaways have a sense of humor. They're people after all; it's just that they're like no people you know. The thing was, Elena was so limber that she could bite her toenails. So can you fix my shoe?

How long is that going to take? Why not just glue the heel back on?

I know they're Donya Durands, but I've got a party in half an hour, okay?

What, you think I'm going to walk around town barefoot? I'll wait—except what's with all these lights? It's two in the morning and you've got this place bright as noon in Khartoum. How about a little respect for the night?

Thanks. What did you say your name was? I'm Cleo.

You are, are you? Jane honey, lots of people *think* about going to space but you'd be surprised at how few actually apply—much less break away. So how old are you?

Oh, no, they like them young, just as long as you're over nineteen. No kids in space. So the stats don't scare you?

Not shoe repair, that's for sure. But if you can convince them you're serious, they'll find something for you to do. They trained me and I was a nobody, a business major. I temped for almost fifteen months on *Victor*

Foxtrot and I never could decide whether I loved or hated it. Still can't, so how could I even think about becoming a breakaway? Everything is loose up there, okay? It makes you come unstuck. The first thing that happens is you get spacesick. For a week your insides are so scrambled that you're trying to digest lunch with your cerebellum and write memos with your large intestine. Meanwhile your face puffs up so that you can't find yourself in the mirror anymore and your sinuses fill with cotton candy and you're fighting a daily hair mutiny. I might've backed down right off if it hadn't been for Elena—you know, the one with the clever toes? Then when you're totally miserable and empty and disoriented, your brain sorts things out again and you realize it's all magic. Some astrofairy has enchanted you. Your body is as light as a whisper, free as air. I'll tell you the most amazing thing about weightlessness. It doesn't go away. You keep falling: down, up, sideways, whatever. You might bump into something once in a while but you never, ever slam into the ground. Extremely sexy, but it does take some getting used to. I kept having dreams about gravity. Down here you have a whole planet hugging you. But in space, it's not only you that's enchanted, it's all your stuff too. For instance, if *you* put that brush down, it stays. It doesn't decide to drift across the room and out the window and go visit Elena over on B deck. I had this pin that had been my mother's—a silver dove with a diamond eye—and somehow it escaped from a locked jewelry box. Turned up two months later in a dish of butterscotch pudding, almost broke Jack Pitzer's tooth. You get a lot of pudding in space. Oatmeal. Stews. Sticky food is easier to eat and you can't taste much of anything but salt and sweet anyway.

Why, do you think I'm babbling? God, I *am* babbling. It must be the Zentadone. The woman at the persona store said it was just supposed to be an icebreaker with a flirty edge to it, like Panital only more sincere. You wouldn't have any reset, would you?

Hey, spare me the lecture, honey. I know they don't allow personas in space. Anyway, imprinting is just a bunch of pro-brain propaganda. Personas are temporary—*period*. When you stop taking the pills, the personas go away and you're your plain old vanilla self again; there's bushels of studies that say so. I'm just taking a little vacation from Cleo. Maybe I'll go away for a weekend, or a week or a month but eventually I'll come home. Always have, always will.

I don't care *what* your Jesus puppet says; you can't trust godware, okay? Look, I'm not going to convince you and you're not going to convince me. Truce?

The shoes? Four, five years. Let's see, I bought them in '36. Five years. I had to store them while I was up.

You get used to walking in spike heels, actually. I mean, I'm not going to run a marathon or climb the Matterhorn. Elena has all these theories of why men think spikes are sexy. Okay, they're kind of a short term body mod. They stress the leg muscles, which makes you look tense, which leads most men to assume you could use a serious screwing. And they push your fanny out like you're making the world an offer. But most important is that, when you're teetering around in heels, it tells a man that if he chases you, you're not going to get very far. Not only do spike heels say you're vulnerable, they say you've *chosen* to be vulnerable. Of course, it's not quite the same in micro gee. She was my mentor, Elena. Assigned to teach me how to live in space.

I was an ag tech. Worked as a germ wrangler in the edens.

Microorganisms. Okay, you probably think that if you stick a seed in some dirt, add some water and sunlight and wait a couple of months, mother nature hands you a head of lettuce. Doesn't work that way, especially not in space. The edens are synergistic, symbiotic ecologies. Your carbo crops, your protein crops, your vitamin crops—they're all fussy about the neighborhood germs. If you don't keep your *clostridia* and *rhizobium* in balance, your eden will rot to compost. Stinky, slimy compost. It's important work—and duller than accounting. It wouldn't have been so bad if we could've talked on the job, but CO_2 in the edens runs 6%, which is great for plants but will kill you if you're not wearing a breather. Elena painted an enormous smile on mine, with about eight hundred teeth in it. She had lips on hers, puckered so that they looked like she was ready to be kissed. Alpha Ralpha the chicken man had this plastic beak. Only sometimes we switched—confused the hell out of the nature lovers. I'll tell you, the job would've been a lot easier if we could've kept the rest of the crew out, but the edens are designed for recreation as much as food production. On *Victor Foxtrot* we had to have sign-ups between 8:00 and 16:00. See, the edens have lots of open space and we keep them eight degrees over crew deck nominal and they're lit twenty hours a day by grolights and solar mirrors and they have big windows. Crew floats around sucking up the view, soaking up photons, communing with the life force, shredding foliage and in general getting in our way. Breakaways are the worst; they actually adopt plants like they were pets. Is that crazy or what? I mean, a tomato has a life span of three, maybe four months before it gets too leggy and stops bearing. I've seen grown men cry because Elena pulled up their favorite marigold.

No, all my plants now are silk. When I backed down, I realized that I didn't want anything to do with the day. My family was a bunch of poor nobodies; we moved to the night when I was seven. So nightshifting was like coming home. The fact is, I got too much sun while I was up. The sun is not my friend. Haven't seen real daylight in over a year; I make a point of it. I have a day-night timeshare at Lincoln Street Under. While the sun is shining I'm asleep or safely cocooned. At dusk my roomie comes home and I go out to work and play. Hey, being a mommy to legumes is not what I miss about space. How about you? What turned you into an owl?

Well, well, maybe you *are* serious about breaking away. Sure, they prefer recruits who've nightshifted. Shows them you've got circadian discipline.

Elena said something like that once. She said that it's hard to scare someone to death in broad daylight. It just isn't that the daytime is too crowded, it's too tame. The night is edgier, scarier. Sexier. You say and do things that wouldn't occur to you at lunchtime. It's because we don't really belong in the night. In order to survive here we have to fight all the old instincts warning us not to wander around in the dark because we might fall off a cliff or get eaten by a saber-tooth tiger. Living in the night gives you a kind of extra . . . I don't know. . . .

Right. And it's the same with space; it's even scarier and sexier. Well, maybe sexy isn't exactly the right word, but you know what I mean. Actually, I think that's what I miss most about it. I was more alive then than I ever was before. Maybe too alive. People live fast up there. They *know* the stats; they have to. You know, you sort of remind me of Elena. Must be the eyes—it sure as hell isn't the body. If you ever get up, give her a shout. You'd like her, even though she doesn't wear shoes anymore.

Almost a year. I wish we could talk more, but it's hard. She transferred to the *Marathon*; they're out surveying Saturn's moons. There's like a three hour lag; it's impossible to have real time conversation. She sent a few vids, but it hurt too much to watch them. They were all happy chat, you know? Nothing important in them. I didn't plan on missing her so much. So, you have any college credits?

No real difference between Harvard and a net school, unless you're some kind of snob about bricks.

Now that's a hell of a thing to be asking a perfect stranger. What do I look like, some three star slut? Don't make assumptions just because I'm wearing spike heels. For all you know, honey, I could be dating a basketball player. Maybe I'm tired of staring at his navel when we dance. If you're going to judge people by appearances, hey, *you're* the one with the machine stigmata. What's that supposed to be, rust or dried blood?

Well, you ought to be. Though actually, that's what everyone wants to know. That, and how do you go to the bathroom. Truth is, Jane, sex is complicated, like everything about space. First of all, forget all that stuff you've heard about doing it while you're floating free. It's dangerous, hard work and no fun. You want to have sex in space, one or both of you have to be tied down. Most hetero temps use some kind of joystrap. It's this wide circular elastic that fits around you and your partner. Helps you stay coupled, okay? But even with all the gear, sex can be kind of subtle. As in disappointing. You don't realize how erotic weight is until there isn't any. You want to make love to a balloon? Some people do nothing but oral—keeps the vectors down. Of course the breakaways, they've reinvented love, just like everything else. They have this kind of sex where they don't move. If there's penetration they just float in place, staring into one another's eyes or some such until they tell one another that it's time to have an orgasm and then they do. If they're homo, they just touch each other. Elena tried to show me how, once. I don't know why, but it didn't happen for me. Maybe I was too embarrassed because I was the only one naked. She said I'd learn eventually, that it was part of breaking away.

No, I thought I was going to break away, I really did. I stuck it out until the very last possible day. It's hard to explain. I mean, when nobodies on earth look up at night—no offense, Jane, I was one too—what calls them is the romance of it all. The high frontier, okay? Sheena Steele and Captain Kirk, cowboys and asteroids. Kid stuff, except that they don't let kids in space because of the cancer. Then you go up and once you're done puking, you realize that it was all propaganda. Space is boring and it's indescribably magic at the same time—how can that be? Sometimes I'd be working in an eden and I'd look out the windows and I'd see earth, blue as a dream, and I'd think of the people down there, twelve billion ants, looking up into the night and wondering what it was like to be me. I swear I could feel their envy, as sure as I can feel your floor beneath me now. It's part of what holds you up when you're in space. You know you're not an ant; there are fewer than twenty thousand breakaways. You're brave and you're doomed and you're different from everyone else who has ever lived. Only then your shift ends and it's time to go to the gym and spend three hours pumping the ergorack in a squeeze suit to fight muscle loss in case you decide to go back down. I'll tell you, being a temp is hell. The rack is hard work; if you're not exhausted afterward, you haven't done it right. And you sweat, *God.* See, the sweat doesn't run off. It pools in the small of your back and the crook of your arm and under your chin and clings there, shivering like an amoeba. And while you're slaving on the rack, Elena is getting work done or reading or sleeping or talking about you with her breakaway pals. They have three more hours in their day, see, and they don't ever have to worry about backing down. Then every nine weeks you have to leave what you're doing and visit one of the wheel habitats and readjust to your weight for a week so that when you come back to *Victor Foxtrot,* you get spacesick all over again. But you tell yourself it's all worth it because it's not only space that you're exploring; it's yourself. How many people can say that? You have to find out who you are so that you decide what to hold onto and what to let go of . . . Excuse me, I can't talk about this anymore right now.

No, I'll be all right. Only . . . okay, so you don't have to reset. You must have some kind of flash?

That'll have to do. Tell you what, I'll buy the whole liter from you.

Ahh, ethanol with a pedigree. But a real backdown kind of drug, Jane—weighs you way too much to bring out of the gravity well. And besides, the flash is about the same as hitting yourself over the head with the bottle. Want a slug?

Come on, it's two-thirty. Time to start the party. You're making me late, you know.

Do me a favor, would you? Pass me those shoes on the shelf there . . . no, no the blue ones. Yes. Beautiful. Real leather, right? I love leather shoes. They're like faces. I mean, you can polish them but once they get wrinkles, you're stuck with them. Look at my face, okay? See these wrinkles here, right at the corner of my eyes? Got them working in the edens. Too much sun. How old do you think I am?

Twenty-nine, but that's okay. I was up fifteen months and it only aged me four years. Still, my permanent bone loss is less than eight percent and I've built my muscles back up and I only picked up eighteen rads and I'm not half as crazy as I used to be. Hey, I'm a walking advertisement for backing down. So have I talked you out of it yet? I don't mean to, okay? I'd probably go up again, if they'd have me.

Don't plan on it; the wheel habitats are strictly for tourists. They cost ten times as much to build as a micro gee can and once you're in one you're pretty much stuck to the rim. And you're still getting zapped by cosmic rays and solar X-rays and energetic neutrons. If you're going to risk living in space, you might as well enjoy it. Besides, all the important work gets done by breakaways.

See, that's where you're wrong. It's like Elena used to say. We didn't conquer space, it conquered us. Break away and you're giving up forty, maybe fifty years of life, okay? The stats don't lie. Fifty-six is the *average*. That means some breakaways die even younger.

You don't? Well, good for you. Hey, it looks great—better than new. How much?

Does that include the vodka?

Well thanks. Listen, Jane, I'm going to tell you something, a secret they ought to tell everybody before going up.

No, I'm not. Promise. So anyway, on my breakaway day Elena calls me to her room and tells me that she doesn't think I should do it, that I won't be happy living in space. I'm so stunned that I start crying, which is a very backdown thing to do. I try to argue, but she's been mentoring for years and knows what she's talking about. Only about a third break away—but, of course, you know that. Anyway, it gets strange then. She says to me, "I have something to show you," and then she starts to strip. See, the time she'd made love to me, she wouldn't let me do anything to her. And like I said, she'd kept her clothes on; breakaways have this thing about showing themselves to temps. I mean, I'd seen her hands before, her feet. They looked like spiders. And I'd seen her face. Kissed it even. But now I'm looking at her naked body for the first time. She's fifty-one years old. I think she must've been taller than me once, but it's hard to be sure because she has the deep micro gee slouch. Her muscles have atrophied so her papery skin looks as if it's been sprayed onto her bones. She's had both breasts prophylactically removed. "I've got 40% bonerot," she says, "and I mass thirty-eight kilos." She shows the scars from the operations to remove her thyroid and ovaries, the tap on her hip where they take the monthly biopsy to test for leukemia. "Look at me," she says. "What do you see?" I start to tell her that I've read the literature and watched all the vids and I'm prepared for what's going to happen but she shushes me. "Do you think I'm beautiful?" she says. All I can do is stare. "*I* think I am," she says. "So do the others. It's our nature, Cleo. This is how space makes us over. Can you tell me you *want* this to happen to you?" And I couldn't. See, she knew me better than I knew myself. What I wanted was to float forever, to feel special, to stay with her. Maybe I was in love with her. I don't know if that's possible. But loving someone isn't a reason to break away, especially if the stats say that someone will be dead in five years. So I told her she was right and thanked her for everything she'd done and got on the shuttle that same day and backed down and became just another nobody. And she gave up mentoring and went to Saturn and as soon as we forget all about each other we can start living happily ever after.

No, here's the secret, honey. The heart is a muscle, okay? That means it shrinks in space. All breakaways know it, now you do too. Anyway, it's been nice talking to you.

Sure. Good night.

Tobacco Words

YVES MEYNARD

Yves Meynard, a French Canadian with a Ph.D. in Computer Science, writes in French and translates his own fiction into English. Along with Elizabeth Vonarburg and Jean Louis Trudel, he is a frequent ambassador of French-Canadian SF to English-language conventions. There is a small, but vigorous, SF movement up there that is acutely attentive to the British and American SF writers in the English language, and to the French traditions as well. It is in some ways more successful than the SF field in France—Quebec has two long-running SF magazines.

Since 1986, Meynard has been publishing young adult SF novels and stories in French (the short fiction mostly in the magazine *Solaris*), and has won a number of French-Canadian awards. He is also coeditor of an anthology of Quebecois SF. In the early 1990s he began to send out his stories in English and had a story in *Northern Stars*, the anthology of Canadian science fiction, in 1994. His fantasy novel in English, *The Book of Knights*, is forthcoming in 1998. In the past two years he has published several pieces in Algis Budrys's magazine, *Tomorrow*, including this one. Meynard's SF is lyrical and filled with complex imagery, which gives it an atmosphere wholly unlike most English language SF. Some basic cultural attitudes are different, too. Yet Meynard remains interested in the traditional futures and alien worlds and technologies of science fiction. This story has one of the attributes of classic hard SF: true strangeness. It is about the drug, tobacco. It reminds me somewhat of Cordwainer Smith and in other ways of R. A. Lafferty.

When it rained over the town, Caspar would open his mouth to let the drops fall in and wet his dead tongue. He ran through the streets, his head tilted back, staring at the roil of clouds, letting the rain fall into his mouth and his eyes.

He would run down sloping Boar Street and reach Maar Square, where he would let his accumulated speed bleed away in bone-jarring steps until he was strolling, his head still tilted as far back as he could. He would wander to the left, navigating by the sight in the corners of his eyes. Passersby stared at him, but he did not notice; he was too used by far to being stared at.

Of all places in the town, he liked best the street that opened to the left of Maar Square, because it was a narrow and twisting street, and it was full of tiny workhouses for the town's confessors. Every workhouse had a big window in front. By tradition the confessors sat at the window, in their extravagant confessors' clothes.

When his sister wasn't busy, she'd open the door of her workhouse and let him in, give him a tiny mug of hot chocolate to drink. She would pat his head when he was done and tell him to go home before he got too cold.

Once as she was letting him out he almost ran into a sinner, a man wide as three normal men and nearly twice as tall, with a face like a tape star's perched atop it all.

"What's this, sister, you do little boys, now?" The man's voice was deep but melodious.

"He's my brother, and you'll apologize now if you want absolution." He had never seen his sister truly angry before; he was fearful that the sinner wouldn't apologize, and of what she would do then. But the big man had said, "Y'r pardon, little master. No offense meant." Caspar had nodded in acknowledgement and left.

Looking over his shoulder, he had seen the door closing on the sinner's huge shadow, the window opaquing a second later. He had lingered, curious. He had heard laughter from behind the door after a while, and then screams, and then sobbing. Then he had run for home, not wishing to meet the man again.

Home was one of the two hundred and fifty identical houses in the town. Grandfather, who had owned it all his life, had refused to alter its exterior. He was very much a man of regulations, was Grandfather, a man who took very seriously his duty to the Fleet, even though he had been retired twenty years and more; and official regulations of the Fleet stipulated that the houses of the Town remain unchanging through the years. In practice, people made subtle alterations, which the Town censors did not object to. But Grandfather was a man of principles.

Even inside, regulations dictated much of the decor. Standard-issue furniture, standard-issue conveniences, kept nearly pristine from constant maintenance. Walk into the Moën house, and you could not tell when you stood in time.

The only exception to the rule was the large painting that hung over the chimney in the living room. It showed a group of people, standing in what seemed a clearing. They were talking, some laughing. One was about to catch a large ball that had been thrown to her from a point outside the frame. The metallic wall of a large building could be seen to the left. No one's house held such a painting, and for many years it had been to Caspar a source of disquiet and obscure pride both.

The painting had as a matter of fact been a source of conflict within the family. Caspar's father objected to it, but never in words. Caspar, perhaps because he was without speech himself, could read his father's thoughts and feelings plainly enough in the set of his shoulders and the play of his face.

Matters had stood at equilibrium for some time, when Karl came into their lives and troubled the waters. Karl was Flikka's admirer, and he courted her with all due process. He seemed like a fairly good match: he had been cleared to breed if he chose, during the next ten years, and was a kind and gentle man. Flikka acted cool toward him, yet Caspar could tell she was really interested.

However, when Karl finally won an invitation to dinner with the family, he saw the painting and made the error of trying to work it into the conversation.

"Herr Moën, that is a very nice work of art you have on display in the living room."

Grandfather lifted his eyes from his soup and said, in a very dry voice, "That's not a work of art."

"I don't understand," said Karl, and all the while Flikka said *shut up, shut up please* with her eyes and chin.

"It is a live video feed from a ship," said Caspar's father. "Maintained constantly, at a high cost."

"A cost I choose to bear," said Grandfather.

"A live feed? But the image is completely motionless."

"Their time-slope is almost vertical," said Caspar's father. "It currently stands at something around one second to the year, and it's steepening. They've been on their way for over thirty years, local time. A voyage of exploration outside the Galaxy. You see, my father's wife is on that ship. That's her, about to catch the ball. If you waited another year you'd see it make contact with her hands. Wonderful, isn't it?"

"You will close your mouth, Diet," said Grandfather. He had been Security and his voice kept the overtones of command.

But Caspar's father had rebelled against Grandfather when he'd chosen to become Maintenance, and he replied: "No, I won't. Your stupid wife is dead, dead to you as if she'd been drowned in the North Sea."

Grandfather had risen from his seat then, white mustache bristling. He might have been funny if everything in his body had not shouted with a rage so vast it could not be encompassed. Caspar's father rose in his turn, threw his bowl of soup into a corner where it smashed with an explosion of steaming liquid, then stalked out of the room.

"Please leave, Karl," said Flikka. "I don't want to see you inside this house again."

Karl rose and left the room in turn. Caspar, as if obeying the dictates of a complicated dance, followed him out, leaving only his mother and his sister at the table.

The young man had stopped on the porch; his fidgeting said he was confused, reluctant to go down the steps to the street, and thus admit defeat. When he saw Caspar come out, he grunted with something like relief. He sat down on the second step from the bottom and motioned for Caspar to join him.

The boy sat on the third step, so he was even with Karl. It was getting cold already, and his crippled hand hurt him. He cradled it in his whole one, rubbing the twisted fingers gently to ease the ache.

Karl lit a cigarette, drew on it. "She's a strange girl, your sister," he said. Caspar shook his head no. "Well, maybe you know her better than I do. Think she's gonna stay mad at me?" Again Caspar shook his head no. "I don't think so either."

Karl sighed. Caspar was looking at him with an imploring look on his face. "What?" said Karl. Then he understood and handed him the cigarette. Caspar took it carefully in his left hand and brought it to his lips.

He took a drag, let the smoke fill his lungs, and bubble up to his head. He did it once again before Karl took the cigarette back.

The cigarette worked its customary magic. Something loosened in Caspar's head, and he felt his dead tongue come back to life. He could speak now; his mouth was full of tobacco words. He made himself speak, telling Karl all he wanted to say.

It all came out the same, of course, *ahhuunnh-hah, hunnh, hunnh-huunh,* moanings and sharp exhalations, all the words he would ever be able to speak. Karl could not, no one could, ever understand them, but Caspar knew what they meant and that was enough for him.

He looked at Karl and Karl was looking back at him, actually listening at the tobacco words. Caspar grew excited, started another sentence, and suddenly found he was weeping. Karl patted his shoulder.

"Hey, it'll be all right, you'll see. Okay?" Those words were like the tobacco words, bursts of sound without intrinsic meaning. It was Karl's face that spoke, and Caspar loved him at that moment. He told him he'd be a good husband for Flikka, in tobacco words, and Karl smiled at him. He offered him another drag on the cigarette, but Caspar shook his head no.

They waited in companionable silence for a time, but Flikka did not come out, as both of them had hoped. Eventually Karl stood up.

"I've got to go home," he said. "We're heading out onto the Sea at daybreak tomorrow. Tell Flikka—sorry, Caspar. I mean, I'll be gone for almost a week. I'll come visit you when we dock again, okay?"

Caspar nodded yes.

"You know . . . even if you don't go to school, I could teach you to write." Karl looked embarrassed as he made his offer. Caspar smiled and shook his head no.

"No pressure, kid. But if you ever want to learn, I'll be glad to teach you." He ruffled Caspar's hair. "Get inside, you'll catch cold." Then he went off down the street, the set of his back saying *I love her but sometimes it's so very hard.*

Starships came once a week or so, and stayed for several days while the sinners took shore leave. Although what they mostly needed was confession, there were also restaurants, showhouses, a casino, and several game halls in town. As he was still a child, Caspar was officially barred from the latter two, but since a cripple was considered lucky at the gambling tables, he'd sometimes get invited inside by some sinner who wanted a charm. He liked the flashing lights and the dizzying smell of neurojoss from the sticks smoldering in black crystal holders.

Once, a woman, whose arms were double-elbowed and reached down to her ankles, had kept him with her for an hour and won a small fortune. She'd taken him afterwards to the fanciest restaurant in the town and he'd gorged himself on cake until he was sick to his stomach. While the woman had been gone to the bathroom, a young waiter had bent down over Caspar and threatened to tell his parents what he was doing. The trembling of his upper lip and his furious blinking said how much he was afraid of the deformed little boy, and so Caspar had made a cabalistic gesture with his crippled hand and the waiter had retreated in near-panic.

He had all his life to waste: he would never go to school, never work, never breed. Station would lodge, clothe and feed him until he died. It was his right and his curse, and he no longer questioned it. He was twelve and looked no more than nine or ten, though sometimes inside he felt much older. He had lived his whole life inside the town, except for a short trip to a farm when he was five, but he had not liked the endless acres of plants growing in the dirt. Apart from that, there were only two other places in Station: the Sea to the north, which scared him, and the desert far to the south, where no one went save Engineering.

When starships came to Station they halted straight above the town; at night, you could see them far overhead, glowing shapes like far-away glass toys. Shuttles left the ships to land at the field, in the southwest quarter of the town.

When they landed, townspeople were there to welcome the sinners. Caspar was often among them, caring not that some townspeople resented his presence. The sinners were glad to see new faces, and often he got kissed or whirled around in the grip of some particularly huge sinner. He liked that; it made him feel more intensely alive, somehow.

Karl had been gone with the fishing boats two days. Flikka had forgiven him, and the way she set the plates on the table spoke of how she yearned for his return. No ship had come to the world from overspace, and so she had no one to confess. She played cards with Caspar, keeping a strict tally of their respective wins that extended back almost a year. A year during which a second had passed for the people in the painting, one of whom, if she was Grandfather's wife, must be Grandmother, although she was astonishingly younger than him—but those matters left Caspar befuddled and he preferred not to think about them.

They had been playing Hop-Jack; Flikka was distracted and Caspar had won three games in a row. He was busily dealing when Perle, who was Confession also, knocked at the door. Flikka rose from the table and let the young woman in, then they sat down together. Perle was used to Caspar and ignored him as if he wasn't there. He didn't mind it so much since he could tell it was sincere disinterest, and not the hidden contempt most people felt.

"Fucking rain again," Perle said. She had a gutter mouth and a reputation for being loose. Caspar enjoyed her visits because she and Flikka always laughed loud, and gossiped outrageously. They let him listen because they felt he wouldn't understand, and besides, he couldn't repeat anything.

"Fucking rain, and *cold*. I'm telling you, it might damn well snow tomorrow," Perle said.

"They never let it snow. If it gets really that cold, they'll adjust the sun's output."

"I wish it would snow, just once. It's not the same if you just see it in tapes."

"You were just complaining about the cold. Make up your mind, girl."

"Ah, don't give me trouble, Flik. I had the shit-worst sinners the last ship and I'm still sore."

"That wouldn't happen if you didn't bed them afterwards."

"Hey. Just the cute ones, all right? You should try it sometimes; you're too much the prude, Flik. Besides, I had my cramps, so I didn't do nothing of the sort."

"So what got you sore?"

"It's this guy. Not one of the big ones, but tall, all spidery and thin, with a neck that didn't stop, you know? Nice eyes, though, kind of purple. Anyway, he comes in at the door, and I think this is gonna be an easy one, right? He doesn't look like he's got much on his conscience. So I let him in, we chat, and already his eyes are getting wet. I think, fuck, he hasn't had it for a long time, or it's worse than I thought. So I put him down on the bed, and hook him in, and I work him over, and out comes a little sin, then another. You know, I lied to my mother and made her cry, sort of thing. And then he goes quiet, and I think that's it, he didn't have anything else, it was like when you gotta piss in a hurry but all you have is a coupla drops.

"And then, shit, he bends backwards like a bow-and-arrow, and he gives this scream that stops up my ears, it's so loud, and he screams again, and he *tears out from the fucking straps,* and hits me one across the chest, it knocks my fucking wind out. I'm sitting on the floor, trying to catch my breath, and he's still screaming and twisting on the bed, and out comes the *fucking* biggest sin, the recorder's indicator goes off the scale. I stand up, and I'm still bent over, and he's bumping around on the bed, and I'm afraid the leads are gonna tear loose before he's done, and he begins to speak. He calms down just enough so I can get the restraints on him again, and I'm lying on top of him to add my weight, and I'm still out of breath, and I'm thinking I should hit the emergency switch, and he says, in my ear, the most fucking weird thing I ever heard.

"He says 'Forgive me, spirits of the Eld, for I have sinned against you. In the darkest phase of the long night, I entered my second mate's family sanctum and I modulated its flame so it would burn brighter for those of her sept. It was done out of love, this I swear. I admit my guilt. I beg to be absolved.' And I swear, those were his exact fucking words. I listened to the recording often enough, I know them by heart."

Flikka had crossed her arms and tilted her head. *I don't know if I should believe you* was what it said to Caspar.

"What did it mean?"

"Damned if I know, Flik. But I think it's a very, very old sin, you know? Something from the dawn of time, so old we can't understand it anymore."

"What's a soul that old doing hanging around overspace?"

"Hey, you think you understand the great beyond, maybe? Nobody does."

"So you got a sinner with a two-thousand-year-old sin on his conscience."

"That's what I think."

"You gave the recording to Administration?"

"Yeah, but I duped it before, it was just too weird. I know, I know, it's illegal. Like nobody ever does it, eh?"

"What did they say?"

"Nothing. They'll review it when they have the time. Like next fucking year."

Two days later, around mid-afternoon, a starship came into orbit. When they heard the announcement over the radio, Caspar and Flikka interrupted their game of Hop-Jack. She went to her room to change into her work clothes; he went directly to the landing field.

It was warmer than it had been, and the sky for once was completely clear. Caspar ran tirelessly and soon reached the landing field. A shuttle was descending from orbit. Along with half a hundred others, he watched it touch down, scorching the ground with its engines. Afterwards, it stayed motionless for a few minutes, then extended wheels and began to roll slowly toward one end of the field. When it stopped again, a hatch opened and nearly fifty sinners came out.

They were mostly unmodified; only a dozen or so diverged noticeably from human-normal. The townspeople came forward to greet them, and the sinners greeted them with pleasure. Some asked for immediate confession, some wanted to go gambling; many sought bed partners, but did not say so in words. Caspar looked from one sinner to the other, smiling at all of them. Then he found someone very special. She was a young girl, some years younger than Flikka, and this was unusual. She was short, and she had reddish-blond hair that reminded him of his own. She was looking around delightedly. Caspar, grinning, came toward her.

She noticed him, smiled back, said "Hello, I'm Aurinn. And you?" Caspar opened his mouth and pointed to his dead tongue, shaking his head. As he had guessed, she did not pull back in disgust, but accepted him as he was.

"Well . . . can you show me where there's a park? I want to see plants growing in real earth."

He nodded with enthusiasm and took her right hand in his left one. He dragged her along through the streets until they came to the park he liked best, a small but lovely square of greenness. Aurinn knelt at the edge of the path and breathed the smell of the grass reverently. Caspar danced onto the grass; the girl stifled a scandalized gasp. "No! Don't . . . oh, that's right, you're allowed to do that here. Well. . . ." And she joined him, a strange grin on her face. Then she stretched out on the grass and looked up at the sky. Caspar sat down next to her and peered down into her face.

"It's so nice to be outside again! Even though this isn't a real planet, it's almost like one. It's kind of like being on Earth. You've never been to Earth, have you? Neither have I. I was born on Wolf's Hoard, and I never traveled anywhere. Until now. I got a commission on the *Callisto*. This is my first voyage. See?"

She held up a pendant that rested on her chest. It was a squat metal cylinder, with a shiny disc at one end. She sat up, turned the disc toward him; then she stopped.

"Oh, wait. You've lived here all your life. I must be the ten-thousandth first-timer to show you her first punch-through."

Caspar shook his head no. Then he raised his clenched left hand, flashed it open twice, then showed two more fingers.

"I'm the twelfth one?"

He shook his head patiently, signed *twelve* again and pointed to himself.

"Oh. You're twelve years old." He nodded. "So," she said, "how many first-timers have you spoken to?"

He raised one finger and then pointed to her.

"Really? Well, then, d'you want to see the punch-through?" He nodded and smiled, and Aurinn activated the recording. On the disc appeared a small image, mostly black space, with here and there the hard pinpricks of stars. Then fields of color began to wash across the picture;

the pattern of the stars distorted itself. Suddenly the blackness crumbled in an eruption of yellow light, blew away like flakes of soot. The image was all yellows and reds now, spiral patterns unfolding and getting constantly more intricate.

"This is overspace," said Aurinn. "You feel so strange when you punch through; like tingles all through your body, and then it's like you're hanging down over a pit that goes down forever— You want to throw up and laugh all at once, and sometimes it feels like you've lived a thousand thousand years and you're so old nothing has meaning anymore. . . ."

She stopped speaking, words failing her. The pattern of her limbs, her trembling smile, the rhythm of her breathing, said *It was the most wonderful and horrible thing I will ever experience. I never want to feel it again, and I can't wait until the next time.*

The visual recording went on. The red-and-yellow spirals had become so intricate the whole field was a shimmering orange. Then the spirals coarsened, the image trembled, and black space began to show through flickering cracks, like inverted lightning bolts.

"We travelled for nearly a week, but that part's been compressed. It's all the same, anyway. Now this is just before we arrived. It was hard to find your station, it's so small and it has so little mass. See how we had to try three times before we punched back out? Now, we get it right."

The disc showed a black egg against a yellow-and-red background. Inside the egg was a blazing dot of light and some distance from the dot a small sphere, blue on top, green around its waist, gray and tan on the bottom.

"This is your world," said Aurinn. "It's so small I couldn't believe it at first. Captain said you could fit a million of them inside Wolf's Hoard."

Caspar watched the end of the visual recording. The ship achieved orbit around the sphere, which had now grown quite large. He failed to understand how any world could be a million times larger; he was sure that Aurinn had misunderstood her Captain's explanations.

The recording ended. Aurinn grinned at him and expressed a wish to see one of the games palaces. Caspar had a different idea. Since he could not speak it, he merely tugged on her hand and drew her on.

He led her across Maar Square and along the twisting street, until they reached Flikka's workhouse. Flikka looked at them through the window and motioned toward the door.

"Hey, no, I don't want to go there!" Aurinn was mildly upset. Caspar pulled again on her hand. "No, kid, I don't need to go there. I haven't got any sins on my conscience."

Flikka opened the door herself. "I'm free and at your service, sister."

"Sorry, Ma'am, but I don't need to be confessed. This kid seems to think so, and he won't understand."

"He's my brother Caspar. Are you saying you've already confessed?"

"No. I don't need any confession. When you're young, you don't get as many sins, and I'm only fifteen. So I didn't get any this voyage. I'm just lucky."

"Sister," said Flikka, with a worried frown, "confession isn't like getting a haircut. You don't take chances with it. Especially not on your first voyage."

"But I don't have any sins on my conscience! I don't have any of the symptoms. I tell you, I'm clean!"

Something in the slope of her shoulders spoke of fear and denial. Caspar grew very worried; he looked urgently at Flikka and tried to tell her she must not let Aurinn go.

"I believe you, sister. But my brother's still concerned for you. Why don't you step inside, and we can do a quick scan to show you're clean? It'll only take a moment, and besides, if you've been scanned once before, it's easier to get confessed afterwards. It will only be a minute or two."

Caspar could see Aurinn vacillating. Flikka had lied about the process being easier if one had been scanned before, but the young girl could not tell. Eventually she swallowed her fears and nodded acceptance.

They stepped inside. Flikka's manner was soothing and friendly; the girl relaxed slightly. Caspar did not know whether he should stay or not. He was afraid, but he didn't want to desert Aurinn. He swallowed his own fears and resolved to remain.

Flikka led Aurinn to the comfortable bed. She made Aurinn lie down, adjusted leads at her temples and on the crown of her head. The girl fidgeted. When Flikka pulled out the restraints, Aurinn protested out loud.

"It's okay," said Flikka. "Regulations, that's all. I won't tighten them, see? Just fasten them loosely, like this. Come on, sister, it's scary the first time, but you don't have any sins, remember? You'll be out of them as soon as I do the scan. Okay?"

Aurinn nodded reluctantly. Caspar held her right hand in his whole one and smiled reassurance. Flikka looked at him; her mouth twisted and her eyes said *I shouldn't let you stay here; confession is a private matter. But I need you to calm her down.*

"Now shut your eyes, little sister. Don't worry, Caspar will stay by you."

Aurinn squinched her eyes shut. She was biting her lower lip. Flikka activated her equipment. The main screen showed a tangle of curved lines, all in various shades of green and blue. Flikka gauged it with an expert eye. "See? It doesn't hurt a bit," she said, but it was her turn to be worried now. Caspar could not tell what the lines meant, but it seemed to him sins ought to show up in hot colors, yellow and red like the flames of hell in the legends—He had once looked at old holograms meant to depict the torments of sinners in the afterlife, and the images had stayed with him vividly.

"Are you going to be done soon?"

"Just a little bit longer, sister. How do you feel?"

"All right . . . b-but it's like I want to cry."

"That's good. Everyone gets that. If you want, let it come. You'll feel better afterwards."

"But it's not a sin. I don't have any sins. I felt fine all through the voyage. . . ."

"I know. And you never felt . . . strange in any way?"

"No, I told you." On the screen lines had appeared, strange lines, curved and recurved. They flickered, on and off. Strange lines in shimmering colors. Flikka twisted dials, pushed a button, and let one hand stray to the torso restraint. Caspar watched, wide-eyed.

"Tell me, little sister, just so I can finish the scan: did you do anything yourself that you're embarrassed about? Any sins of your own? You know I can't repeat them to anyone, so any secret is safe with me."

Aurinn started to blush. "Well . . . Just once. I was supposed to be on watch from ten thousand to twelve thousand, and I . . . I skipped the last three hundred. There was nothing to watch for, it was just pointless, so. . . ."

"Of course. Just a little tiny thing. Not really a sin, if you ask me. Everyone does it." Though her tone remained calm, Flikka looked at the screen in alarm. She swung a metal hemisphere into position above Aurinn's head, then grasped the end of a restraint with one hand. Caspar understood the meaning of the gesture and clumsily took the end of the other strap in his crippled right hand.

Aurinn gasped. Her eyes opened, full of tears. "What's happening?" She breathed faster and faster. "What are you doing to me?"

"Nothing, sister." Flikka yanked on the restraint and drew it tighter. Caspar tried to copy her gesture but the strap slid out of his grasp.

"Don't! Stop that!"

"I'm afraid you do have a sin on your conscience, little sister. It has to come out."

"No! I don't have anything! I told you I didn't. . . ." Aurinn tried to raise her arms, but they were held by the restraint. "Take the leads off! Take them off!"

"Don't fight it, sister. Don't fight it or it'll hurt."

"*No* . . ." Aurinn's words strangled to a halt. Her eyes grew fixed, and suddenly a scream tore out of her. Her legs, only loosely held by the restraint, shuddered; her heels drummed on the mattress. Flikka cursed and tightened the restraint. Caspar tried to pull away, but his hand was held in Aurinn's, which was clenched so tightly he thought she might break his fingers.

Aurinn began to scream out words, one after the other, like an incantation torn from the depths of her being. Caspar could not understand the words; and what frightened him more was that he could make no more sense of her body's language. She yowled, as if she'd been cut by a blade, and suddenly there was a fecal stink as she voided her bowels. She screamed again, and urine began to stain the front of her trousers.

Flikka swore in panic, hit the emergency switch that summoned Medical. Caspar, desperate, tore his hand out of Aurinn's grasp and retreated to a corner of the room. Aurinn's face was an inhuman mask. And it said nothing, nothing intelligible to him.

And then words rushed out in a stream, words almost as meaningless as all that had preceded them:

"O forgive me, forgive me, great spirits of the Eld! I took my brother's life, I took it before our time was done, I took it and held it to me, and though he searched for it I withheld it from him! I took his life and held it to me, and it was done out of envy, this I do swear!"

And when the last word had left the girl's lips, she went completely limp. It was Caspar's turn to scream then, for her slack limbs said *death, death*. He forced air out of his throat, over his dead tongue, and out came a strangled mewling, and again and again. Then he put his crippled hand before his eyes and crouched in the corner. He heard the door open, people rushing in, a rapid-fire exchange of information, diagnostics, orders. "Heartbeat has resumed." "Give me pure oxy." "Pressure rising." "The ambulance is on its way." After a little while more people came in, then it seemed everyone left.

He didn't want to take his hand away from his eyes, ever. But then his wrist was grasped gently, and his hand drawn away. Flikka took him in her arms, and held him tight.

"You've been very brave, Caspar. Don't worry, she will live. Medical got to her in time."

Caspar trembled and coughed weakly.

"If you hadn't brought her to me, the sin would have killed her," said Flikka, as if she had understood the words he could not speak. "It would have struck all of a sudden, and she wouldn't have had any chance to live You did right."

She wiped the tears from his eyes, and together they walked home, under a sky that was once again filling up with clouds.

The next days were strange for Caspar: his life seemed to have acquired a shape, something it had always lacked before. Hours were no longer something to be spent at random; now he had purpose. In the morning, alone or with Flikka, he went to visit Aurinn in the hospital, only for an hour at a time. The girl was unconscious, tubes and wires stuck in her. The doctors told him that she would live, and their hands said that they spoke the truth. But they also said that they found her case unusual, disturbing.

Aurinn's ship departed after three days. It could not, of course, afford to wait for an ailing crewmember. When Aurinn recovered, she would have to take hire on some other ship. Things would work out, Caspar told himself, and though he believed it, still he felt worry.

Afternoons he would spend with Flikka. She had requested a suspension of her duties from Administration and gotten it. The way she brushed her hair added that she had told them something important. Caspar supposed it had to do with the strange sin Aurinn had been saddled with.

Flikka and he played cards again, but her mind was never on the game. Caspar understood she waited for something, or rather someone. When Karl finally returned with the fishing fleet, Flikka's relief became obvious.

She went to the docks to welcome him home, accompanied by Caspar. Karl seemed exhausted from the voyage, but when Flikka greeted him with a passionate kiss, he shed his fatigue in an instant.

He insisted on treating Flikka and Caspar to a visit to the casino. Even Flikka could tell it mattered to him, and she accepted gracefully. Caspar, even though he never concerned himself with money, knew she earned several times as much as Karl did, and should by tradition have been the one paying. But Karl needed to show happiness by pleasing others. He bought Caspar a small stack of chips. Caspar bet them one at a time and lost again and again, but with the next-to-last chip he won fifty times his bet. Karl burst out laughing and cashed in the chips, putting every last bill into Caspar's hand despite his mute protestations. Caspar resolved he would buy Aurinn a gift with the money, when she recovered.

They parted outside the casino. The way Flikka knotted her fingers said she wanted Karl to ask to visit the next day; but his shy smile said that the memory of his last visit was still too fresh in his mind, and he dared not.

"So . . . maybe I'll see you tomorrow," she said.

"I'd like that."

Flikka kissed him goodbye, then went off. Caspar started to follow her, but Karl held him back. He whispered in his ear, "Does she really want to see me?"

Caspar grinned and nodded vigorously.

"Then I'll come over to your house around midmorning, okay?"

Caspar nodded again. Karl grinned in turn, then lowered his gaze and spread his fingers, which meant he wanted to give Caspar something to reward him. At a loss for anything better, he pulled out a crumpled cardboard pack and handed Caspar the last cigarette left in it. Caspar hurried to catch up to Flikka, hiding the cigarette in his pocket. He turned around once he'd reached her side; Karl had gone away into the night.

The next morning, he went to the hospital to see how Aurinn was doing. Flikka came with him. They were told that her condition had improved. She had regained consciousness the night before, but her grip on it was precarious. Lying on her bed, Aurinn was still stuck full of tubes and wires, but she breathed easier. They stayed with her a short while; she was not aware of their presence. The movement of her eyes under the half-closed lids asked again and again *what? what? what?* Caspar found it unnerving but he knew it for an improvement.

He was thinking it was time they left, when an alarm bell sounded throughout the building. Caspar thought it meant fire. Flikka opened the door of the room; they went out into the corridor, looking for the closest exit.

There was a low-ranked Security man at the emergency exit. He had stuck a bar through the handle, to prevent the door from opening. "Please go back," he told them. "Everyone has to stay inside."

Flikka was taken aback. "Isn't there a fire?"

"No. No fire. Security has given orders: everyone in town is to stay inside."

"What's going on?"

"They haven't told me, sister. But a code one-eight-eight means *external threat.* My guess is we're under attack from space. Now will you go quietly into your room and stay inside?"

Flikka and Caspar retreated to Aurinn's room and sat down. They looked at one another, astonished. "I don't believe him," said Flikka. "He said that just to get us back inside. It doesn't make any sense. If there was an attack, we'd be able to see or hear something. . . ." But her eyes said she wasn't convinced of the truth of her own words. And, faintly, from outside, they *could* hear something: the same warning bell that pealed inside the hospital was echoed inside the rest of the town.

Caspar went to the window. The hospital was built close to the landing field. Caspar could look out over the field, along the receding perspective of the landing strip, into the cloudy horizon. When he saw a dot in the sky, at first he took it for a speck in his eye; but soon it had swelled into the silhouette of an incoming shuttle. He pointed it out to Flikka, who hissed between her teeth.

"No one was told about a landing. What the hell is this? Hey, look!"

There were Security at one end of the landing field, where normally townspeople would be standing to welcome the sinners.

"This is insane," said Flikka, "what the hell can they do against a spacecraft? Maybe it's a ship of criminals and Security wants to arrest them. . . ."

The shuttle swelled in size, faster and faster; but there was no wash of sound, no glare. It glided to a stop in perfect silence and touched down not a hundred meters distant. It didn't look like a shuttle. It looked like a fish from the North Sea, grown monstrous and cast in metal.

A door opened in the fish's flank, and a single figure jumped to the ground. It was the strangest sinner Caspar had ever seen: huge, and proportioned all wrong. The sinner began to run across the field, toward the hospital, moving in such a strange way it reminded Caspar of a cartoon. After a few seconds he understood why: the sinner's knees bent backwards instead of forward.

"My God," breathed Flikka, "this thing isn't human. Oh God, this is an *alien.*"

It was like a geometric caricature of a human being. Its knees bent backwards; its shoulders were like huge spheres; the torso was a truncated cone, melding into a dumbbell pelvis. The head was like a bullet, the features flattened and distorted. It had dead-white skin and wore dull green, skintight clothes. The feet were housed in supple gloveboots; they had a short palm and three long toes.

"We're not safe here," Flikka said suddenly. "We have to get into the basement."

Caspar shook his head no. Flikka pulled him away from the window. "Let's go, Caspar! We're in danger!"

But Caspar freed himself from her grip. He was staring at the alien, and a shiver passed through him: he could understand its body. It said *Help Pain Pain Oh Help Pain.*

Then Security caught up with the alien, barely ten meters from the hospital. Flikka, overcome by the spectacle, ceased trying to pull Caspar away.

There were six men and women, and each carried a short baton. By the law of the Fleet, no one on Station could carry a weapon, so that ship crews need never fear harm from Station personnel. The alien carried no visible weapon, but it was nearly half again as tall as a human and massively built. It slowed its progress, halted. Caspar could read the way it held its arms. It spoke of confusion, pain so great it twisted the mind nearly to rupture.

The Security people tried to form a ring around the alien. Their postures spelled uncertainty and desperate courage. The alien sprang into movement suddenly, smashed its arm into the chest of the nearest man. The man fell to the ground like a broken toy. The alien opened its mouth then and moaned like a bassoon, a weirdly beautiful sound. Its knees pumped up and down, and they said *Pain Oh Please Pain Help Help*.

And Caspar understood suddenly that this being *was* a sinner. A sinner overwhelmed by the sins it had picked up during the passage through overspace. A sinner driven to madness by the weight on its soul. Who would kill and kill again, unless it could confess and obtain absolution. And no one else could tell; no one else could read the being like he could. They only saw a monster from nightmares, something whose purpose could only be to destroy.

He wanted to explain this to Flikka, but his tongue was a dead strip of flesh in his mouth, and there was no way his hands could speak the words for him. He could have written it down, if he had ever bothered to learn how. He had been a stupid boy all his life. It was too late to make up for it.

The five remaining Security had bunched up in a tight line, trying to protect the entrance to the hospital. The alien moved toward them slowly, birdlike, one step at a time. Why couldn't they see they were going to die if they kept blocking its way?

Caspar felt his shame inside his belly; like a piece of metal weighing him down. He had to do something or more people would die, and it would be his fault. He had to speak, somehow. In desperation, he took Karl's cigarette from his pocket, struck a crimped match and lit the cigarette. He took a long, deep drag, let the smoke fill his lungs and bubble up to his head. Outside, the alien pounced on a woman, raised her off the ground and threw her against the wall five meters away. The last four Security tried to rush it, were scattered in all directions, torn and bloody.

Flikka finally snapped out of her horrified fascination. She grabbed Caspar and pulled him out of the room. He let himself be carried away. He was trying to talk to Flikka, but she couldn't understand his tobacco words.

Outside the room, there was confusion in the corridor. The Security man was now at the end away from the emergency exit. He was trying, and failing, to keep order. Caspar's mind was working fast, but strangely. For the first time in years, there was no longer that little watcher inside his skull, that heard all his thoughts and judged them. He knew what he had to do, but not why he knew it.

He gauged his time, and when the right moment had come he yanked his crippled hand out of Flikka's grasp, then ran down the corridor toward the emergency exit. He reached it in a few seconds, pulled the bar out of the handle and opened the door. He heard Flikka's cry superimposed over the electronic wail triggered by the door opening. Then he was outside, just around the corner from the alien. Caspar took a last drag on the cigarette, then threw it away. He ran to the corner, then slowed down and rounded it carefully.

The alien was fifteen meters away, battering at the main doors to the hospital, still moaning musically. The Security personnel were scattered all around it. All the bodies said *death*. Caspar made himself ignore them and walk forward, to meet the alien.

Behind him, he heard Flikka screaming and running. He knew she would risk anything to take him out of danger; he had only a few seconds.

He spoke out loud to the alien, with tobacco words. He came to it walking, not running, palms held forward, trying to smile.

The bullet-shaped head turned toward him. The alien's body still shouted *Help Pain Oh Pain*. It faced him then, and suddenly it bounded forward and its huge hands grabbed him under the shoulders and raised him high. Caspar knew suddenly that he would be killed, thrown against the wall or torn apart. But it did not happen. The alien held him high, motionless. Caspar spoke again, in a thin strangled voice, all the tobacco words that filled his head. He promised the alien it would be helped, that his sister would free it from its sins. *Hhuunnh, ahhuunnhhah, hunnh, hunnh-hah.*

And the alien lowered him to the ground, gently. Still its body shouted *Pain Pain Help*. It took Caspar's crippled hand in its own, and looked at him with startling eyes, blue eyes, human eyes. It opened its mouth and spoke in turn, a succession of vowels with just the hint of consonants.

"Caspar . . ." Flikka's voice, behind him. Caspar did not turn around to look at her. He pulled on the alien's hand gently, going toward the town. And the alien followed, towering over him, a figure from nightmare, its clothes speckled with human blood, yet tame, for the moment.

Caspar stretched out his whole left hand, beckoned Flikka with a twitch of the fingers. And after a few paces, he felt her hand in his. The alien turned to look at her, but did not otherwise react.

Now Caspar saw people coming from the town, more Security. He looked to Flikka, terrified that the alien would panic. She glanced back at him. He did not need to speak any tobacco words; this time she understood him. She cupped a hand to her mouth and shouted out: "Stand back! Let us pass! Don't come close!"

Security wavered, stopped, but did not disperse. They would still bar their way into the town.

She asked: "Caspar, where are we going? Do you know?" He nodded yes, vigorously. "Where? Where do you want to take it? Why is it following you? What did you do to it?" The questions came in a rush, betraying Flikka's terror at what might have happened to him. Caspar tried to say *Slowly. Ask me the right questions only.*

"Wait, wait." Flikka bit her lip, calmed herself. "You said you know where we're going. Did it tell you where it wanted to go?" No. "So you've decided?" Yes. "You want to take it someplace; someplace I know?" Yes, yes. "Our home?" No! "A public place." No.

Then it hit her. Her eyes widened. "You want me to confess it." Caspar nodded yes, weeping in relief. "Caspar, that's crazy." She spoke softly. Still the alien followed behind Caspar, a nightmare twice as tall as the boy who led it. Caspar signed no. "You think it's bearing a sin? But—oh God, oh God, wait, now I know. Oh God, you're right. Of course . . ."

They were approaching Security. Still they stood in their way. Flikka raised her voice. "Let us pass. I am taking this being to confession."

"You're crazy," said the Security leader. "We won't let you into town."

"Our station was built to provide services to overspace crews. This being came down to be healed of the sins it accumulated in transit. By Fleet law, we can't refuse to confess it."

"This isn't a human being, and it's killed six people already."

"If you don't let us pass, it'll kill me and my brother, and you'll be next. For God's sake, man, think!"

Caspar felt panic. He told the alien it would be all right, it was being taken to be confessed. The huge body began to quiver with tension. The grip of the fingers that held his crippled hand tightened to a painful intensity.

At the last instant, Security moved aside and let them pass. They formed a semicircle in back of them and followed their progress. Flikka said, in a commanding voice: "I need ten meters of strong chain for restraints, and have Medical on standby, for what it's worth. Do it *now.*" Caspar was astonished to see a Security man dash off to do her bidding.

Soon they reached Maar Square and went into the twisty street of the confessors. All the while, Caspar spoke to the alien, trying to reassure it.

It had relaxed when Security let them pass, but it had been tensing up again.

Finally they were at Flikka's workhouse. Flikka opened the door for them. Caspar went inside; the alien bent its huge frame to enter. It saw the confession machines and uttered a terrifyingly musical scream. It loosed Caspar's hand, laid its body onto the bed; the frame had been built to accommodate even very large sinners, and only the lower half of its legs stuck out. Flikka came inside, staggering under the load of the chains. Moving purposefully, she passed length after length around the alien's body. She held her head at an angle that said she no longer felt any fear: her duties occupied all of her thoughts.

The alien suffered itself to be bound tightly. Panting, Flikka secured the chains with a heavy lock and went to activate the equipment. Her fingers depressed keys, adjusted sensors. A pattern of tangled lines emerged on the main screen.

"All right," said Flikka out loud, speaking to an invisible audience. "You see what I see. I'm picking up standard signs of accumulated sins. Potential very high, no structural anomalies." Caspar suddenly understood she must have activated a relay to Administration. "I'm going to follow standard procedure, except without any verbal contact with the subject. Activating probe."

She swung the metal hemisphere into position over the alien's head. Its features twisted around, it looked at her with its human eyes, and it made a flutelike gasping sound. It repeated it as she adjusted the controls. "Matrix responding normally. Potential still very high. I'm drawing the first one out."

When the first scream came, Caspar's eardrums felt it like a metal blade stabbing into his ears. Once he had been deafened, the rest were easier to take. The alien twisted inside its bonds, but they did not break. Its motions shook the bed, but the steel frame held. And after a moment Caspar realized that the constrained spasms were intelligible to him, far more clearly than the general posture. They spoke complete sentences.

I told a lie about someone I knew, so I could get a job in his place. And he had been the one who had told me about the opening. I'm so very sorry.

It was a human sin, weighing on an alien's soul. While Aurinn's sin, and the sin Perle had confessed, they were alien sins weighing on human souls.

The alien confessed another sin, then another, and another, and when the last sin had come out, it went limp and closed its eyes.

"Process complete." Flikka's voice was frayed, but strong. "Potential zero. Absolution has been obtained." She paused for a second or two, then added, "I'm removing the restraints."

Then, moving quickly, she undid the length of chain. Caspar helped her. The effects of the cigarette had faded by now, and his mouth was empty of all words.

When they had removed half the chain, the alien opened its eyes and helped free itself. It rose from the bed, then took Flikka's hand in his and made a gesture with the other hand. Caspar could not understand it; in fact, he could not interpret the alien's body language at all anymore. It was like looking at a statue.

The alien released Flikka's hand and went out of the workhouse. Flikka and Caspar followed, uncertain. Outside were thirty Security, looking determined. The alien halted, spread its arms wide, hung its head, raised one foot then the other, alternately.

The ring of Security left one opening, leading outside. After a while, the alien stopped its display, looked around itself. It moaned gently, like a snatch of song, and began slowly going back, toward the landing field. Security closed up behind it and this way it returned to the metal fish. Caspar and Flikka trailed the procession, unwilling to let the being out of their sight. It did not look back at them; Caspar did not know if he wished it had, or not. No one prevented the alien from going aboard. The access door shut behind it, and then the shuttle took off in an astonishing fashion, floating five meters off the ground without any thruster firing, then suddenly rising in a steep parabola, up toward orbit.

Caspar and Flikka were taken to confer with Administration. Flikka told all she had seen, repeated it several times. Caspar was questioned also, a long and unpleasant process. His neck soon began to ache from all the nodding and headshaking. Flikka protested on his behalf, but the interrogator did not relent.

After a long while, the questions ceased. The Administration woman heaved a sigh, shut off the audio/video recorder.

"Thank you for your cooperation," she said. "Please return to your residence now. If there is anything more, we will contact you."

Flikka's body had been speaking anger louder and louder throughout the interrogation. Now she let her words take over.

"I'm not going away. I want answers of my own, and now."

"You're lucky not to have been taken to carcery, Confessor Moën. Your actions endangered the whole of this station, and some Administrators wanted your head."

"Fuck them." Caspar started at the words. In Flikka's mouth they took on an intensity they never had in Perle's. "You know damned well I acted correctly. If it was a human who'd come down and killed left and right, we'd have had no recourse. Isn't that right? That's what *I* was taught in school: we serve starship crews, and their rights outweigh ours."

"We've been through this already. Please go home now. You've had a very difficult time and. . . ."

"Answer my questions, Administrator. What did you learn about this being? You must have tracked the ship when it left. What happened to it? Tell me. Or is it that you're so low in the hierarchy that they didn't bother to tell you?"

The Administrator's mouth twisted in exasperation, a meaning which must have been plain to anyone. But then, surprising Caspar, she relented.

"It wasn't a ship that came down. It was only a shuttle; but you probably guessed that. The ship itself . . . is fifteen kilometers long. It looks like nothing you could imagine. It can't, or won't, answer us. From time to time, it broadcasts gibberish at various EM frequencies. We have no idea what it wants, or where it's from. We're defenseless against it. That's all we know. Now please, please go home, and keep this to yourself. People have already been panicking, and we've had six deaths too many."

The mask had slipped from the Administrator's face and her weariness and concern were plain to see. Flikka lowered her gaze and left without further words, her hand linked with Caspar's.

When they entered the Moën house, the family fussed about them no end. Flikka recounted what had happened, but she refused to go into details. She seemed to have been won over to the Administrator's opinion now, and her hands said she wished she could stay utterly silent. Finally she broke free from her mother and father's attentions, and went to her room, locking the door.

Caspar was left the focus of attention, something he found unpleasant. He was asked a few questions, but everyone soon gave up, lacking the Administrator's persistence. When he was let go, he went to the standard-issue refrigerator and poured himself some juice, holding the pitcher in his left hand and clumsily steadying the glass with his crippled right. In the living-room his parents and grandfather were talking in lowered voices. From where he was he could just see the painting, in which Grandmother waited, waited, waited for the ball to reach her hands. Suddenly, with a queer shock, he remembered very clearly that at one time the ball hadn't been in the picture.

He ran up to his own room then, feeling bone-tired. He found he was crying, not for the Security who had died, but, strangely, for all those who had lived. He did not understand. He thought then, for the first time, of reading his own body, to understand what he said to himself. He looked at himself in the mirror above his dresser, but he could not make sense of what he saw. In the end, he crawled into his bed and fell prey to a sleep full of nightmares.

And in the morning, before the sun even came over the rim of the horizon, Security came for him and Flikka. The shuttle had returned. They were wanted.

There were three of the aliens now. They were utterly identical: size, shape, and colors. But Caspar could tell them apart; two of them shouted pain and terror from their bodies, while the third was as unreadable as a piece of stone. By that he thought to recognize the one he had helped yesterday. The aliens had been standing at the foot of the shuttle, almost motionless, until they saw Caspar and his sister. Then they came forward, and the absolved one spoke again in its music-like language.

And they proceeded as before. The aliens went with them to Flikka's workhouse, and one, then the next, were chained, confessed, absolved of-the human sins that weighted them. Flikka knew fear this time, Caspar saw, she was no longer overwhelmed by what she did, and she could fully taste the weirdness of it.

But it went well, and eventually it was done. Flikka collapsed in a chair, drained. The aliens made gestures and spoke words no one could interpret, Caspar least of all. Then the first one came to him and took his crippled hand in his, and led the way out of the workhouse. The other two followed, and Security, and Flikka.

The aliens made their way back to the fishlike shuttle; then Caspar's hand was let go, and the three went inside. "They're going away, now," said Flikka in a tired voice. "They'll never come back, will they?"

Caspar did not know, and it hurt him deep inside, not to be able to know. It was as if some essential meaning had drained from the world. He waited in silence, along with the others, for the shuttle to lift off.

But then, the door opened again and one of the aliens came back out. It carried a bag on a strap across its shoulder. It put the bag down, opened it. Took out six strange objects of metal and lights, a meter and a half high, and set them on the ground. The pattern they made seemed familiar; then Caspar understood it was the pattern the bodies of the six dead Security had made.

Two more things the alien took out of the bag. One was carved, from some sort of wood, crimson with gold veins. It might have been a musical instrument; it might have been something else. The alien stepped around the pattern it had built and presented the wooden object to Flikka. She accepted it, keeping silent.

The alien took the last object from its bag then, and put it in Caspar's arms. Flikka hissed in astonishment. Security shouted incoherently. Caspar, for the first time in his life, knew what it was to have one's hair stand on end.

It was a doll, nearly a meter high. A slim young girl, dark-haired, wearing multicolored robes and calf-high boots. She looked fully human, and she was warm to the touch.

Caspar looked up from the doll, and saw the alien moving back into the shuttle, and then there was no more delay: the metal fish rose from the ground and sped off into the sky.

Once Aurinn had recovered, Flikka and Karl rented a small boat and took her, along with Caspar, on a brief cruise. On their first evening, when the sun had slipped below the horizon and the North Sea lay all about them, they sat down on deck. Karl lit a cigarette and gave one to Caspar. Aurinn was shocked, then amused: on Wolf's Hoard, such practices were considered the depth of barbarity. Greatly daring, she tried a puff, and coughed herself hoarse.

When Aurinn had stopped coughing, Flikka said, suddenly and quietly, "I don't think they were aliens."

"How can you say that?" said Karl. "You saw them. No one except Caspar saw them from closer up. They weren't human. You saw their ship. . . ."

"But we've all seen this." And she pointed to Caspar's doll, which was dancing slowly on the planks of the deck. The doll wasn't just a manikin; it moved, it looked about, it danced, at odd moments. The Administration had tried to take it from Caspar, but the doll had evaded their grasp, and finally, afraid of it, they had relented. Now it accompanied him wherever he went, a dream-toy, living and not.

"Karl, do you think they could have made such a thing in the few hours between our first meeting and their return? And even if it was possible, how can you explain that they looked so much like us? By any rational account they should have been completely different. We've both seen sinners who looked almost as strange. . . ."

"You think they were human," said Aurinn. "But you said they didn't speak. And the sin that . . . that almost killed me . . . it wasn't a human sin."

"Maybe, maybe not. Humankind is spread out so wide. Maybe somewhere, they've been engineering themselves into something . . . new. Different. I think that's what we saw: humans who've been altered so profoundly that we almost can't recognize them. People who were isolated from the rest of humanity for so long that they forgot many things . . . I don't know. We can't really know, but that is what I think."

"And what is this, then?" asked Karl. Caspar's doll danced on the deck, long black hair flying, booted feet stamping a complex rhythm on the planks. "A toy? An idol?"

"Administration feared it was a spy; an information-gathering device. They thought it might be transmitting data back . . . somewhere. But what if it is, anyway? If we are coming into contact, whether it's with aliens or with a long-forgotten branch of ourselves—isn't it better that they learn more about us?"

"I'm sure Administration fears they'll use the information against us."

"I know. But the one that came down . . . one of only three crew for that huge ship . . . it only killed when it was blocked. Caspar guessed, somehow, what it had come down for. The same as all of our crews: to be absolved of the strange sins it had picked up crossing overspace. And when it dies, its soul will dissolve into overspace and its sins will float there, waiting to be snagged by a living soul, and perhaps then laid to rest at long last. . . ."

The doll danced on, oblivious to Flikka's musings. Caspar rose and walked a ways toward the prow. The doll followed him, still dancing. Caspar drew on his cigarette, letting the smoke bubble up to his head. The doll spun and whirled, smiling, then slowed her dance into a courtly pavane. The others might speculate all they wanted, but Caspar knew what her purpose was. He knew that one day she would be able to speak, and that on that day the strangers would return.

He breathed in the smoke of the cigarette, and his dead tongue was loosened in his mouth. He spoke tobacco words to the doll. And, in the midst of her dance, she winked at him, to show that she understood.

Invasion

JOANNA RUSS

Joanna Russ is one of the finest stylists of the last forty years in science fiction. Her stylistic excellences were indeed the foundation of her reputation in the 1960s and early 1970s, only to be superseded by her reputation as perhaps the most cutting-edge feminist in SF in the 1970s, the author of *The Female Man*, "When It Changed," and *The Two of Them*. She also wrote critical essays (for which she has received a Florence Howe Award from the Modern Language Association and later the Pilgrim Award from the Science Fiction Research Association) and reviews (mostly in *Fantasy & Science Fiction*) throughout the 1970s; she then fell silent in the mid-1980s.

She has published too little fiction since winning the Hugo award for her novella, "Souls," in 1983. Not even a story a year. So it is a rare treat to find a stylistic tour-de-force such as "Invasion." It appeared in *Asimov's* in the same month (January) as a letter from Russ in the magazine's letter column responding to an editorial. She also published a substantial collection of her essays, *To Write Like a Woman*, a Hugo nominee in 1996. We can only hope for more. This story is pure fun.

They were terrible.

The Doctor found one under the operating table in the hospital (impossible to tell its sex) that regarded her suspiciously and then, as she reached for it, vanished with a *pop!* of inrushing air.

The Second-in-command discovered three of them between the sheets as he started to make the bed in the quarters he shared with the Captain. The creatures rolled away from him, grinning, and vanished.

An especially small one—who'd been in the swimming pool, it seemed, and who was dripping wet, its yellow costume all soggy—materialized against the hand-woven tapestry on the cabin's wall, slid down, and left a trail of water-blurred color behind it. It shrieked excruciatingly and vanished.

The Navigator walked into her study area and found two of them sitting on top of her antique wooden bookcase. Normally a peaceful woman, even a bit shy, she threw herself at the intruders, shouting "No!" only to receive a painful barrage of books in the face, most of which then rolled under the bed as she grabbed for them, acquiring disc-destroying grit in the process. Several hit her on the forehead, hard. When she was able to scramble out from under the bed, her hands full of them, the intruders were gone.

One perched weightlessly on the Communicator's head as he was combing his hair. Two others landed heavily in his lap. One said, "Comb *my* hair"; another, "Give us a kiss." The one sitting on his head dropped into his lap, crowding the other two (who kicked and rocked for a few seconds, trying to get the lap back for themselves alone) and asked, in an unexpectedly deep, hoarse voice, "Do you like worms?"

The Communicator thought for a moment. Then he said, "Worms are fine in the soil of Botany Level Two, but nowhere else."

Little number three looked in its overall pocket, sighed, its whole face expressing woe, and vanished. Little number one-in-the-lap cried, "Comb my hair!" so he did, using the mother-of-pearl-backed hair-pick that had been in his family for generations. Two rocked back and forth on his lap, humming—they were actually fairly heavy littles, he decided— and number one subsided into dreaminess while having its wild, fuzzy, orange hair combed. The combing accomplished, the Communicator thought for a minute or so while little number two sucked its thumb. Then he said, carefully, "I'm going to tell you a wonderful story. Once there were three little people and they were just like you—"

The Engineer found that one of the creatures (a really young one) had crawled inside a ventilation duct and was gnawing at the lining with a look of fascination on its pudgy features. An older one was reaching for the fusion reactor controls. The Engineer was not one to act hastily or unthinkingly, even when something threatened her engines, and she also had the great advantage of having been brought up on a male-dominated planet as the eldest of nine. Stealthily she reached for the shelf near the radiation-proof door, on which she kept items confiscated from tourists or staff, mostly food and some gadgets her assistants had carried into the area, or rather had planned to carry, for she was down on anything that might interfere with efficient single-mindedness. (She over-compensated for her bringing-up.) The little one (she thought) should like a jingling bunch of keys, while for the other she took off the shelf a torus toy, made of rubber and filled with nothing stranger than plain water . . . that crawled out of your hand no matter how you held it. She mimed dramatic dismay. The small little crawled with amazing speed out of the duct, its plump rear switching from side to side. It pounced on the fallen torus, only to have the older little pounce on it, in turn, and pull the toy out of the baby's grasp. The younger proceeded to mourn its loss with loud screams of anguish. The Engineer picked it up, like the expert she was, and jiggled the little. Then she jiggled both the little and the keys against her shoulder. It grabbed for the keys and inspected them. It made them jingle. The bigger one looked calculatingly at her as if to say, *You want this back, don't you?* and she shook her head. Then, wondering if the creature could understand any human speech or behavior, she spread both hands out, palms front, meaning *It's yours if you wish.* The little went to its companion, picked it up (staggering under the other little's weight) and made its way to the corridor. The Engineer, enormously relieved, punched the complicated signal that locked the Engine Room. Now the doors would open only to her voice command or that of her primary assistant.

There was a tap on her knee.

Looking down, she saw number two, the bigger one, politely handing her back the torus toy. She took it.

The little vanished.

* * *

Now I will tell of the time the yoomin beans catched us, it was sad but o
so fine. Kick Mwres, bash Mwres, no more soundings. Quiet, Mwres. *I*
am to tell. It was big ship, big shape looming and glooming in the starlite
when—no, not G'lydd, *I me*—saw and took all in. Funny on outside,
spidery things and bumps and "numbers," G'lydd say. Sh, Mwres. So we
all swarm in, it being allalonetime now and You Know Who not here, he/
she in sun, not knowing what we doing baddie stuff. *Oof!* into metal wall,
ping! inside metal, streaming on to round plastipak cover, can see within.

Creatures! A whole round of creatures is ambulating, zizzing, flesh
voice-boxes (such they have, to be sure) et cetera. *Yick!* says Ulf. *Beans,*
say I. So we go all ways into different places, full of interest, to see beans
do such, so we become beanshape, in yellow, to do beansuches acts, as:
Crawling, yelling, jumping, shrieking, et cetera. We fell on hair and lap,
got told story like real little crittur, went in and out of water, sat on big,
woodeny thing, pulled a toy from littler bean, we yelled, we gave it back,
we rolled between "sheets" on "bed," and so on.

Then a tall, goldy-topped bean SAT on us. Shriek! Shriek! Help! Haw,
goes Gr, was sat upon. The beans all shake up, another do a bean thing
called "laff," others too but hide tee-hee under hands.

Short, round-shape bean with front bumps say, "Why is my ship in-
fested with babies and small children in yellow overalls?" and other person reply, "Mam, we receive distress call from planet Ulp, is terrible
disease ramping among adults, must be send up kiddies to be safe."

(This is not lie *exactly*. Maybe not so true, either, says G'lydd. Yes it is,
I say indignants. Horrible rigidity disease all over down below, can be
ONLY ONE THING AT TIME, can think of worse?)

Tall story-teller bean say, "Mam, I attempted to verify distress call
with"—here Gr interrupt, *tweedled* and *twaddled,* but tall bean really say
with all cryptograms and codes and distortions and what-not but cannot
find no signal except planet Ulp's (sent, as WE know, by YOU KNOW
WHO) so Ulpians send up all these babies and small children to ship to
be safe.

Starey-eyed Second-person mutter to self, Yes, but will *we* be safe from
them? Mwres snicker. Says, *I* slummed down pretty wall hanger, ho ho,
will never be same.

Nasty! says G'lydd.

Funny skinny little person with front bumps say Oh Mam, oh, mam,
they is only innocent little beans, kiddies and such, let us be kind to
them, feed them broth and cookings, give them nice place to sleep, &c.
We all haw haw at bumpy person; we want eat cherry pie, whipt cream,

pickled herrings, wiener buns, strawberry shore cake and such. Make come out of walls. Gr know how.

Doctor say Mam, is against humanities not to give refuge to poor little mites. Gafroy bite her, ugh, taste awful from toes not washed for week, report Gafroy. Doctor pull foot back. Except that one, she say, glaring. We loff, go: we are inocent, inocent.

Uh-oh. Sour-faced Second-person open mouth, say: Captain, I have suspections these not kiddies—but here Gr and Grf and I ram into its stummick, causing loss of breath to speak, & Ff bounce up and down on midsection, causing fuss and silence. Shame! cry Doctor-person, to say such of poor innocents which their peoples is dying down there in droves. Tsk tsk say all. So we run all of us to splashing pool and splash in, making big fun, then zoom out to food room and gorge selves on cherry pie with whip cream, leaving some on floor, alas. Then to beds which we roll in "sheets" and leave feetmarks on "blankets." Captain say Can any of you really envision these poor little children six to a bed in *your* bed? and all persons grab each other and say, no no no, please help, anywhere else, will get in way something terrible. We know what they thinking and Ff want to tell but I won't let. Not proper. Maybe somebody will read us storybooks? They have all this things like stuff was throwed at us. So we nice to all, stick out little bellies, wiggle eyelashes, &c. say, Oh read us a story, plees, plees, O Lady who Steer. Is such lovely thinkings. So she pleesed and do so, very lovely, very exciting, Gr and Ff kiss from it & dance. Is all in rhyme and alliteration, can not understand but beauty. Then somebody else do and somebody elses and elses. This take seven hours forty-five minutes ten seconds three milliseconds. We not tired. Wow. Then off to food room for strawberry pie and chocolate bars wow wow even tastier. Then time to play poker at bottom of swimming pool, which upset guard bean until G'lydd explain we O.K. but still upset so we sleep in botanical place instead, Ff snacking off plants with Mwres. Leave them alone, sir. Comb hair. Clean teeth on plant stalk. All say together, oh You Know Who, guard our sleep but stay away, plees. Then we all loving and goody and glow with friendlies. Then we sleep.

Next day: Doctor-bean very active in laboratory trying find cure for rigidity disease. Muttering to self about blood samples and such we bring up from Ulp surface: Why, these are all ideally normal! Is no disease here. She putter & putter & tsk. G'lydd want to tell her but Ff and I sit on she: No! Mustn't! until give up. G'lydd shake haughty and toss head and vanish away. Lie in sun room pretend bean, with cache-sexe and dark glasses but in switched places. Haw! Then Doctor say Aha! I have found fraction of lipid protein is very strange, without which these people would be mere heaps of protoplasmic gunk. But this cannot be a cure for disease unless disease is normalcy itself. Hurrah! I have found it. Ulpians catch normal humancy from us on ship; that is disease. She then grab and inoculate laboratory squirrel, which was hiding under papers on desk to get away from doctors. Behold! It turn into a mess of Jell-O. Then she inoculate own knee, which also turn all squudgy and nasty. Behold! she say. The antidote to the disease of Form!

Meanwhile nice story-teller person finally contact planet Ulp and up is coming—

No, no! yell Mwres, I didn't it was THEY who did it, I didn't mess up tapestried. I didn't throw books at steer-lady. I didn't gnaw tube, it was THEM.

Ff and L1 and Gafroy say: Look WHO is coming.

It is You Know Who.

Uh oh.

With one loud Word YKW make us fall into line and behave—anybody acts naughty now gets incarnated as cactus for fifty years—and we all sob & cry & promise to be good, turning back into our treu shape, which is two-foot-high pyramids of green Jell-O. YKW is a six-foot-high pyramid of green Jell-O. I flash a bit into my yellow-overalls yoomin form to say goodbye.

YKW trounce me. That is telepathic and very awful, tho' I won't say how. If you are pyramid of green Jell-O, it *hurts* (to make ripples). So I regress right back into being a nauseous Thing.

Story man say softly in mind: You are very beautiful just as you are, little Things. Life is beautiful. Nothing is so graceful and lovely as a heap of green Jell-O.

So we leave happy. Crying goodbye, goodbye, I sorry I hurt your artifactual and put water on it. I was bad. I ate and messed up food room and did other awfuls. But I am only a lit-ul child.

MARCH! says You Know Who.

So we march.

Down on the surface everybody is now cured of looking like Yoomin Beans, and is back to normal, viz. green gunk. Life is again horrible. Up in ship only Ff is still there, try to hide out in botanical bay, imitating frond. Is not successful, is almost devoured by botany cat, must come down to surface in disgrace, to look forever like Graminidae. Sometimes we look up into sky, remembering beautiful ship and food and cry, O ship-thing, ship-thing, wherefore art thou up so high/like a carpet in the sky? And we flow about, savagely chanting:

Rigidity, rigidity,

Wherefore art thou so fond of we?

Which is a sort of spring thing, a festival cry with which we assault the boring semi-liquidity of our fate.

Meanwhile:

Mam say to steer-person: Did you authorize the entry of these . . . ah . . . youngsters without checking out Ulp and said species computer-wise?

All say No no, nobody let them in. Do not do bad things to us, plees. Was not our fault.

Enough. We shall torment you no more. Goodbye, goodbye.

The day shift slept, the Engineer dreaming that she was at home with too few rights and far too many little brothers and sisters. The Doctor woke every few minutes with a start, having dreamed repeatedly of an operating room overrun with Ulpian youngsters, until she gave up, rose, put on her robe, and went to enter results into the hospital computer, from where she could keep an oblique watch on the hall and the next room. The Navigator slept on her face, over a cache of her most precious discs. The Communicator alone slept soundly and did not dream. Both reading, both wearing glasses (the Captain for myopia, her First for a touch of astigmatism) the Captain and the First were in bed together, the latter in pajamas. After a while the Captain put down her book (*Military History of the Late T'ang*) and frowned. "Thinking about those children?" said the other.

"They were *not children,*" she said decisively, and shuddered.

"Well, yes," he said, "they were aliens, true but even as pyramids of green Jell-O, they were . . . well, baby pyramids."

"Hm!" said she. There was a moment's silence. He went back to his own book, an annotated *Poems of Emily Dickinson.* Then she said slowly: "Love, do you think . . . did it ever occur to you that all children are aliens?"

He said, "Do you mean the bouncing on adults and the cherry pie between their toes? Oh yes. No, not really. Anyway I rather liked them. The small pyramids, I mean."

"I suppose," she said, a bit sharply, "that it's perfectly normal for human male philoprogenitiveness to be roused by contact with small pyramids of green goo. Nonetheless—"

"No, not by them. By you."

"By me?"

"Absolutely." He added, "Do you want to back out?"

She smiled and shook her head. "No. We'll do it. It'll be human, after all. Not like them."

* * *

Indeedy yes. Will be little yoomin bean. Will be playmate. Will be *lonely*. You Know Who go away again soon.

We come back.

The House of Mourning

BRIAN STABLEFORD

Brian Stableford is a biologist and sociologist turned SF and fantasy
writer. He is also a critic and scholar of the literary history of the field,
and is so talented, productive, and knowledgeable that he might be called
the British Isaac Asimov of this generation. He is a scientific rationalist
and stands for reason the way Asimov did. He wrote many SF novels in
the 1970s and 1980s, but fell out of print in the U.S. toward the end of
the 1980s. His short fiction for the last several years has been extremely
impressive, especially his novellas appearing in *Analog, Asimov's,* and
Interzone, and he has been nominated several times for the Hugo and
Nebula Awards in short fiction categories recently. His recent works now
comprise one of the major bodies of short fiction in the SF field of the
decade. Much of his recent novel-length fiction (e.g., *The Empire of Fear,
The Werewolves of London*) has been published first in England, and only
later, and somewhat obscurely, in the U.S., and as fantasy or horror even
though most of it has been alternate history SF or alternate universe SF.
This story first appeared in Ellen Datlow's *Off Limits.* It's a hard-SF
horror story about pain and pleasure, biotechnology, and sex.

Anna stared at her thin face in the mirror, wondering where the substance had gone and why the color had vanished from the little that remained. Her eyes had so little blue left in them that they were as gray as her hair. She understood enough to know that a disruption of the chemistry of the brain was bound to affect the body as profoundly as the mind, but the sight of her image in the soul-stealing glass reawakened more atavistic notions. It was as if her dangerous madness had wrought a magical corruption of her flesh.

Perhaps, she thought, it was hazardous for such as she to look into mirrors; the confrontation might be capable of precipitating a crisis of confidence and a subsequent relapse into delirium. Facing up to the phantoms of the past was, however, the order of the day. With infinite patience she began to apply her makeup, determined that she would *look* alive, whatever her natural condition.

By the time she had finished, her hair was tinted gold, her cheeks delicately pink, and her lips fulsomely red—but her eyes still had the dubious transparency of raindrops on a window pane.

Isabel was late, as usual. Anna was forced to pace up and down in the hallway, under the watchful eyes of the receptionist and the ward sister. Fortunately, she was in the habit of dressing in black for everyday purposes, so her outfit attracted no particular attention.

The ward sister was there because there was a ritual to be observed. Anna couldn't just walk out of the hospital, even though she was classed as a voluntary patient. She had to be handed over in a formal fashion, to signify that responsibility was being officially transferred from one sister to another. Not that Isabel really was her sister in a biological sense, any more than the ward sister was; she and Anna had simply been parts of the same arbitrarily-constructed foster family. They were not alike in any way at all.

When Isabel finally arrived, in a rush, with all her generous flesh and hectic color, the ceremony began.

"You must remember that this is Anna's first day out," the ward sister said to Isabel. "We don't anticipate any problems, but you must make sure that she takes her medication at the appointed times. If she shows signs of distress, you should bring her back here as soon as possible. This emergency number will connect you with a doctor immediately."

Isabel stared at the number scrawled on the card as though it were the track of some mysterious bird of ill omen.

To Anna, the sister said only: "Be good." Not "Have a nice time" or even "Take it easy," but simply "Be good." *It's better to be beautiful than to be good,* Anna thought, *but it's better to be good than to be ugly.* She had been beautiful once, and more than beautiful—so much more as to be far beyond the reach of Saint Oscar's ancient wisdom, but now there was nothing left to her except to be good, because her more-than-beauty had gone very, very bad.

Isabel, of course, had no idea that Anna was on her way to a funeral, and that her role was merely to provide a convenient avenue of escape. Anna waited until the car was a good two miles away from the hospital before she broached the subject. "Can you drop me at the nearest tube station," she said lightly, "and can you let me have some money."

"Don't be silly," Isabel said. "We're going home."

Isabel meant her own home, where she lived with a husband and two children, paying solemn lip service to the social ideal. Anna had seen Isabel's husband three or four times, but only in the distance. He was probably one of those visitors' partners whose supportive resolution failed at the threshold of Bedlam—many in-laws preferred to wait outside while their better halves attended to the moral duty of comforting their afflicted kin—but it was possible that Isabel had forbidden him to come in and be properly introduced. Few women relished the prospect of introducing their husbands to whores, even whores who happened to be their sisters—legalistically speaking—and whose sexual charms had been obliterated in no uncertain terms.

"No we're not," Anna said. "That's just something I had to tell the doctors, so they'd let me out. If I'd told them the truth, they'd have stopped me, one way or another."

"What truth?" Isabel wanted to know. "What on earth are you talking about? I'll have you know that I've gone to a lot of trouble over this. You heard what the nurse said. I'm responsible for you."

"You won't be doing anything illegal," Anna told her. "I'll get back on time, and nobody will be any the wiser. Even if I didn't go back, nobody would blame *you.* I'm the crazy one, remember. How much cash can you let me have?"

"I don't have any cash," Isabel told her, as she drove resolutely past

Clapham South tube station without even hesitating. "I don't carry cash. Nobody does. It's not necessary anymore."

That was a half-truth, at best. At the Licensed House where Anna had worked, the clients had used their smartcards, and the transactions had been electronically laundered so that no dirty linen would be exposed to prying wives or the Inland Revenue. The streetwalkers who haunted the Euroterminal and the Bull Ring had smartcard processors too, but their laundering facilities were as dodgy as their augmentations and most of their clients paid in cash.

"You can still *get* cash, can't you?" Anna said, innocently. "Walls still have holes, just like spoiled whores. Don't worry about missing Clapham South. Vauxhall will be fine."

"Just where the hell do you think you're going, Anna?" Isabel demanded, hotly. "Just what the hell do you think you're going to do?"

That was Isabel all over: repetition and resentment, with plenty of hell thrown in.

"There's something I need to do," Anna said, unhelpfully. She had no intention of spelling it out. Isabel would protest violently just as surely as the doctors would have done. Unlike the doctors, though, Isabel was easy to manipulate. Isabel had always been scared of Anna, even though she was two years older, two inches taller, and two stones heavier. Now that Anna was a shadow of her former self, of course, it was more like four stones—but that only increased Anna's advantage.

"I won't do it," Isabel said, although the hopelessness of her insistence was already evident.

"I can do anything I like," Anna said, reflectively. "It's one of the perks of being mad and bad—you can do anything you like, and nobody's surprised. I can't be punished, because there's nothing they can take away that I haven't already lost. I could do with a hundred pounds, but fifty might do in a pinch. I have to have cash, you see, because people with scrambled brain chemistry aren't allowed smartcards. Fortunately, there'll always be cash." As long as there were outposts of the black economy that weren't geared up for laundering, there'd be cash—and everybody in the world was engaged in the black economy in *some* fashion, even if it was only token tax-dodging.

"I don't like being used," Isabel said, frostily. "I agreed to take you out for the day because you asked me to, and because the doctors thought it would be a good idea—a significant step on the way to rehabilitation. I won't stand for it, Anna. It's not fair."

Since she was six years old Isabel had been complaining that "it" wasn't fair. She had never quite grasped the fact that there was no earthly reason for expecting that anything should be.

"There's bound to be a cash-dispenser at Vauxhall," Anna said. "Fifty would probably do it, if that's all you can spare. I've lost track of inflation since they put me in the loony bin, but money can't have lost that much value in three years."

Isabel braked and pulled over to the side of the road. She was the kind of person who couldn't drive and have a fit at the same time. Anna could tell that her sister was upset because she'd stopped on a double yellow line; normally, she'd have looked for a proper parking place.

"What the hell is this about, Anna?" Isabel demanded. "Exactly what have you got me into? If you're using me as an alibi while you abscond from the hospital, I've a right to know."

"I'll be back on time," Anna assured her. "No one will ever know, except your husband and children. They'll probably be disappointed that they aren't going to meet your mad, bad, and dangerous-to-know foster sister, but they'll get over it. You can bring them in one day next week, to make up for it. I'll be as nice as pie, psychochemistry permitting."

"*What is this all about?*" Isabel repeated, pronouncing each word with leaden emphasis, as if to imply that Anna was only ignoring her because she was too stupid to know what the question was.

"There's something I have to do," Anna said, nobly refraining from adopting the same tone. "It won't take long. If you won't give me the fifty pounds, can you at least let me have enough for a Travelcard. I have to go all the way across town to zone four."

Anna knew as soon as she'd said it that it was a mistake. It gave Isabel a way out. She should have hammered on and on about the fifty until she got it. In the old days, she'd never have settled for a penny less than she'd actually wanted, whatever kind of client she was dealing with.

Isabel reached into her purse and pulled a handful of coins out of its dusty depths. "Here," she said, as if to say, *It's all you're worth, you stupid, fouled-up slut.* "If you want to go, go—to hell if you want to—but if this goes wrong, just don't try to blame me. And take your medication." Long before she arrived at the last sentence she had reached across Anna to open the passenger door, so that she could mark her final full stop with one of those dismissive pushes that Anna remembered all too well.

Anna submitted to the push and got out of the car, even though she was only vaguely aware of where she was. She waited until Isabel had driven off before she asked for directions to Clapham Common. It was a long way, but not too far to walk even for someone in her debilitated condition. The value of the coins was just adequate to buy a Travelcard.

She wondered if things might have been different if she'd had a *real* sister, but she decided that they probably wouldn't have been.

* * *

It wasn't difficult to find the church from Pinner tube station. It was larger than she had expected. She was glad that the funeral announcement in the *Guardian* had given both time and place; so many didn't, because the people who placed them were afraid of being burgled while they were at the ceremony. She waited until everyone else was inside before she sidled in, but she didn't escape notice. Several people turned around, and whispers were exchanged.

When the service was over and the pallbearers carried the coffin out Anna moved behind a pillar, but the people who filed out behind the dead man knew perfectly well that she was there. She didn't go to the graveside; she stayed in the shadow of an old horse chestnut tree, watching from thirty yards away. She couldn't hear what the vicar was saying, but that didn't matter. She could have improvised her own service if she'd wanted to, complete with appropriate psalms. Every bedside locker on the ward had a Bible in the top drawer, and boredom had made her dip into hers more frequently than she liked to think. She knew that according to The Book of Ecclesiastes it was better to go to the House of Mourning than the House of Feasting, but she wasn't sure that Ecclesiastes had been in a position to make a scrupulous comparison, and he hadn't mentioned the House of the Rising Sun at all, although it would have made a better play on words if he had. Ecclesiastes had also offered the judgment that a good name was better than precious ointment, but Alan certainly wouldn't have agreed with him on that point.

Anna had no difficulty picking out Alan's wife, although she'd never seen a photograph. She was a good-looking woman, in a middle-class Home Counties sort of way. Her name was Christine, but Alan had usually referred to her as Kitty. Anna was mildly surprised that Kitty wasn't wearing a veil. Weren't widows supposed to wear veils, to hide their tears? Not that the woman was weeping; grim forbearance seemed to be more her style. Anna judged her—on the basis of an admittedly superficial inspection—to be a kind of upmarket Isabel, who probably did believe, with all her heart, that a good name was infinitely to be preferred to any kind of balm that cunning cosmetic engineers could devise.

In the grip of a sudden surge of anguish, Anna wished that Isabel hadn't been so tight-fisted. If Isabel had given her a hundred pounds, or even fifty, she'd have been able to bring a wreath to add to the memorials heaped about the grave. So far as she could judge at this distance most of the mourners had gone for natural blooms, but she would have selected the most exotic products of genetic engineering she could afford, to symbolize herself and the crucial contribution she had made to Alan's life— and, presumably, his death.

Anna had no doubt that the accident hadn't been *entirely* accidental; even if it hadn't been a straightforward deceptive suicide, it must have been a case of gross and calculated negligence.

When the ceremony was over and done with, the crowd around the grave broke up, its members drifting away in all directions as though the emotion of the occasion had temporarily suppressed their sense of purpose. When the widow turned toward her, and shook off someone's restraining hand, Anna knew that the confrontation she had half feared and half craved was about to take place. She wasn't in the least tempted to turn and run, and she knew before the woman paused to look her up and down that *this* was what she had come for, and that all the sentimental rubbish about wanting to say good-bye was just an excuse.

"I know who you are," the widow said, in a cut glass voice which suggested that she took no pride in her perspicacity.

"I know who you are, too," Anna replied. The two of them were being watched, and Anna was conscious of the fact that the dissipating crowd had been reunited by a common urge to observe, even though no evident ripple of communication had passed through it.

"I thought you were in hospital, out of your mind." The widow's voice was carefully neutral, but had an edge to it which suggested that it might break out of confinement at any moment.

"I am," Anna told her. "But the doctors are beginning to figure things out, and they can keep me stable, most of the time. They're learning a lot about brain chemistry thanks to people like me." She didn't add *and people like Alan.*

"So you'll soon be back on the streets, will you?" the widow inquired, cuttingly.

"I haven't worked the streets since I was sixteen," Anna said, equably. "I was in a Licensed House when Alan met me. I can't go back there, of course—there's no way they'd let me have my license back after what happened, even if they could normalize my body chemistry. I suppose I might go back to the street, when I'm released. There are men who like spoiled girls, believe it or not."

"You ought to be quarantined," the widow said, her voice easing into a spiteful hiss. "You and all your rancid kind ought to be locked up forever."

"Maybe so," Anna admitted. "But it was the good trips that got Alan hooked, and it was the withdrawal symptoms that hurt him, not the mutant proteins."

A man had joined the widow now: the fascinated crowd's appointed mediator. He put a protective arm around the widow's shoulder. He was too old to be one of her sons and too dignified to be a suitor ambitious to step into the dead man's shoes; perhaps he was her brother—or even Alan's brother.

"Go back to the car now, Kitty," the man said. "Let me take care of this."

Kitty seemed to be glad of the opportunity to retreat. Whatever she'd hoped to get out of the confrontation, she hadn't found it. She turned away and went back to the black-clad flock which was waiting to gather her in.

Anna expected a more combative approach from the man, whoever he might be, but all he said was, "If you're who I think you are, you shouldn't have come here. It's not fair to the family."

Another Isabel, Anna thought. *You'd think someone like him would know better.* By "someone like him" she meant doctor, lawyer, or banker. Something *professional* in the nonironic sense of the word. Alan had been a stockbroker, careful overseer of a thousand personal equity plans. She'd often wondered if any of his clients had shares in the company which owned the House. Like everything else in today's complicated world, it had been part of some diverse conglomerate; the parent organization's share price was quoted every day in the *Guardian's* financial pages, under the heading "Leisure and Entertainment."

"I'm not doing any harm," Anna said. "You could all have ignored me, if you'd wanted to."

"I believe that was the gist of the argument which prompted the legalization of prostitution," the other replied, mustering a sarcastic edge far sharper than Kitty's. "It does no harm, they said, and anyone who disapproves only has to ignore it. When the cosmetic engineers progressed from tinkering with shape and form to augmenting bodily fluids they said much the same thing. The new aphrodisiacs are perfectly safe, they said, it's all just for fun, they're definitely not addictive—and anyone who disapproves can simply stay away from the new generation of good-time girls, and let the fun-lovers get on with it. In the end, though, the rot crept in, the way it always does. It all went horribly wrong. Isn't it bad enough that we had to lose Alan, without having to suffer a personal appearance by his own particular angel of death?"

She felt something stirring in the depths of her consciousness, but the comfort blanket of her medication was weighing down upon it. It was easy to remain tame and self-possessed while the doctors' drugs were winning the battle against her own perverted psychochemistry. "I'm sorry," she said, effortlessly. "I didn't mean to cause distress." *Like hell I didn't,* she thought, by way of private compensation. *I came here to rub your turned-up noses in it, to force you to recognize how utterly and horribly unfair the world really is.*

"You have caused distress," the man said, accusatively. "I don't think you have the least idea how much distress you've caused—to Alan, to Kitty, to the boys, and to everyone who knew them. If you had, and if you had the least vestige of conscience, you'd have cut your throat rather than come here today. In fact, you'd have cut your throat, period."

He's a punter, Anna thought, derisively. *Not mine, and not the House's, but someone's. He fucks augmented girls, and the juices really blow his mind, just like they're supposed to, and he's afraid. He's afraid that one fine day he, too, might find that he just can't stop, and that if and when his favorite squeeze goes bad, it'll be cold turkey, forever and ever, amen. Like every man alive his prayer has always been "Lord give me chastity but please not yet!"—and now it's too late.*

"I'm sorry," she said, again. The words were the purified essence of her medication, wrought by a transformation every bit as miraculous as the one which had run its wayward course within her flesh and her spirit. The real Anna wasn't sorry at all. The real Anna wasn't sorry she had come, and wasn't sorry she was alive, and wasn't sorry that this black-clad prick saw her as some kind of ravenous *memento mori.*

"You're a degenerate," the black-clad prick informed her, speaking not merely to her but to everything she stood for. "I don't agree with those people who say that what's happened to you is God's punishment for the sins you've committed, and that every whore in the world will eventually go the same way, but I understand how they feel. I think you should go now, and never show your face here again. I don't want Kitty thinking that she can't bring the boys to visit Alan's grave in case she meets *you.* If you have a spark of decency in you, you'll promise me that you'll never come here again."

The clichés begin to flow in full force, Anna thought—but even the medication balked at sparks of decency. "I'm free to go wherever I want to, whenever I wish," she asserted, untruthfully. "You have no right to stop me."

"You poisonous bitch," he said, in a level fashion which suggested that he meant the adjective literally. "Wherever you go, corruption goes with you. Stay away from Alan's family, or you'll be sorry." She knew that he meant all of that quite literally too—but he had to turn away when he'd said it, because he couldn't meet the unnaturally steady stare of her colorless eyes.

She stayed where she was until everyone else had left, and then she walked over to the open grave and looked down at the coffin, onto which someone had dribbled a handful of brown loamy soil.

"Don't worry," she said to the dead man. "Nothing scares me. Not anymore. I'll be back, and I'll get that wreath one way or another."

She had no wristwatch but the church clock told her that she had five hours in hand before they'd be expecting her at the hospital.

Anna hadn't been to the Euroterminal meat-rack for seven years, but it didn't take long for her to find her way around. The establishment of Licensed Houses had been intended to take prostitution off the streets but it had only resulted in a more complicated stratification of the marketplace. It wasn't just the fact that there were so many different kinds of augmentation available, or the fact that more than three-quarters of them were illegal, or even the fact that there were so many girls whose augmentations had ultimately gone wrong or thrown up unexpected side effects; the oldest profession was one which, by its very nature, could never be moved out of the black economy into the gold. Sleaze, secrecy, and dark, dark shadows were marketable commodities, just like psychotropic bodily secretions.

She didn't bother to try for a managed stand; she'd spoken the truth when she'd told her dead lover that nothing scared her anymore, but she hadn't time to get into complicated negotiations with a pimp. She went down to the arches where the independents hung out. There was no one there she knew, but there was a sense in which she knew all of them—especially the ones who were marked like her. It didn't take long to find one who was a virtual mirror image in more overstated makeup.

"I'm not here to provide steady competition," she said, by way of introduction. "I'm still hospitalized. I'll be back on the ward tomorrow, but I need something to get me through today. Fifty'll do it—that's only one substitution, right?"

"Y'r arithmetic's fine," the mirror image said, "but y'got a lot of nerve. Demand's not strong, and I don't owe y'anything just 'cause we're two peas from the same glass pod. It's a cat-eat-cat world out here."

"We aren't two peas from any kind of pod," Anna informed her, softly. "Symptoms are all on the surface. They used to say that all of us were sisters under the skin, but we were never *the same*. Even when they shot the virus vectors into us, so that our busy little epithelial cells would mass-produce their carefully designed mind expanders, it didn't make us into so many mass-produced wanking machines. One of my doctors explained to me that the reason it all began to go wrong is that *everybody's different*. We're not just different ghosts haunting production line machines; each and every one of us has a subtly different brain chemistry. What makes you you and me me isn't just the layout of the synaptic network which forms in our brains as we accumulate memories and habits; we tailor our chemistry to individual specifications as well. You and I had exactly the same transformation, and our transplanted genes mutated according to the same distortive logic, but fucking you never felt exactly the same as fucking me, and it still isn't. We're all unique, all different; we offered subtly different good trips and now we offer subtly different bad ones. That's why some of our clients became regulars, and why some got hooked in defiance of all the ads which promised hand-on-heart that what we secreted wasn't physically addictive. You don't owe me anything at all, either because of what we both were or because of what we both are, but you could do me a favor, if you wanted to. You're free to say no."

The mirror image looked at her long and hard, and then said: "Jesus, kid, y'really are strung out—but y'd better lose that accent if y're plannin' on workin' down here. It don't fit. I was goin' for a cup of coffee anyway. Y'got half an hour—if y'don't score by then, tough luck."

"Thanks," said Anna. "I appreciate it." She wasn't sure that half an hour would be enough, but she knew she had to settle for whatever she could get.

She'd been on the pitch for twenty-three minutes when the car drew up. In a way, she was grateful it had taken so long. Now, she wouldn't be able to go back afterward.

The punter tried to bargain her down to thirty, but the car was a souped-up fleet model whose gloss shouted to the world that he wasn't strapped for cash, and there was no one else on the line with exactly her kind of spoliation.

The client was a wise guy; he knew enough about the chemistry of his own tastes to think he could show off. It probably didn't occur to him that the doctors had taken pains to explain to Anna exactly what had happened to her, or that she'd been better able to follow their expert discourse than his fudged mess. Nor did it occur to him that she wouldn't be at all interested in the important lessons which he thought were there to be learned from the whole sorry affair. She didn't try to put him right; he was paying, after all, and the torrent of words provided a distraction of sorts from the various other fluxes generated by their brief and—for her—painful intercourse.

"That whole class of euphorics should never have been licensed, of course," he opined, after he'd stumbled through a few garbled technicalities. "It's all very well designing fancy proteins by computer, but just because something's stable in cyberspace doesn't mean it's going to behave itself under physiological conditions, and *physiological conditions* is a politer way of putting it, when we're referring to the kind of witch's cauldron you get up a whore's you-know-what. They say they have programs now that will spot likely mutation sites and track likely chains of mutational consequence, but I reckon they're about as much use as a wooden fort against a fire-breathing dragon. I mean, this thing is *out of control* and there's no way to lock the stable door now the nags have bolted. Personally, I'm not at all distressed—I mean, I've had all the common-or-garden stuff up to *here*. I never liked whores wired up for the kind of jollies you can get from a pill or a fizzy drink. I mean, it's just stupid to try to roll up all your hits into one. It's like praying mantises eating their mates while they fuck—no sense to it at all. Me, I like things spread around a bit. I like it sour *and* sweet, in all kinds of exotic combinations. People like me are the real citizens of the twenty-first century, you know. In a world like ours, it ain't enough not to be xenophobic— you have to go the other way. Xeno*philia* is what it takes to cope with today and tomorrow. Just hang on in there, darling, and you'll find yourself back in demand on a big scale. Be grateful that they can't cure you— in time, you'll *adapt,* just like me."

She knew that in her own way she *had* adapted, and not just by taking her medication regularly. She had adapted her mind and her soul, and knew that in doing that she had adapted her body chemistry, too, in subtle ways that no genetic engineer or ultra-smart expert system could ever have predicted. She knew that she was unique, and that what Alan had felt for her really did qualify as *love,* and was not to be dismissed as any mere addiction. If it had been mere addiction, there wouldn't have been any problem at all; he would simply have switched to another girl who'd been infected with the same virus vectors but had proved to be immune—so far—to the emergent mutations.

The punter wasn't a bad sort, all things considered. Unusual tastes weren't necessarily associated with perverted manners. He paid Anna in cash and he dropped her right outside the door of Lambeth North tube station. It was, he said, pretty much on his way home—which meant that he could conceivably have been Isabel's next-door neighbor. Anna didn't ask for further details, and he wouldn't have told her the truth if she had. There was an etiquette in these matters which had to be observed.

By the time Anna got back to the cemetery the grave had been filled in. The gravedigger had arranged the wreaths in a pretty pattern on the freshly turned earth, which was carefully mounded so that it wouldn't sink into a hollow as it settled beneath the spring rains. Anna studied the floral design very carefully before deciding exactly how to modify it to incorporate her own wreath.

She was a little surprised to note that her earlier impression had been mistaken; there *were* several wreaths made up of genetically engineered exotics. She quickly realized, however, that this was not a calculated expression of xenophilia so much as an ostentatious gesture of conspicuous consumption. Those of Alan's friends and relatives who were slightly better-off than the rest had simply taken the opportunity to prove the point.

When she had rearranged the wreaths she stood back, looking down at her handiwork.

"I didn't want any of this to happen," she said. "In Paris, it might almost pass for romantic—man becomes infatuated with whore, recklessly smashes himself up in his car when she becomes infected with some almost-unprecedented kind of venereal disease—but in Pinner it's just absurd. You were a perfect fool, and I didn't even love you . . . but my mind got blown to hell and back by the side effects of my own mutated psychotropics, so maybe I would have if I could have. Who knows?"

I didn't want it to happen either, he said, struggling to get the words through the cloying blanket of her medication, which was deeply prejudiced against any and all hallucinations. *It really was an accident. I'd got over the worst of the withdrawal symptoms. I'd have been okay. Maybe I'd even have been okay with Kitty, once I'd got it all out of my system. Maybe I could have begun to be what everybody wanted and expected me to be.*

"Conformist bastard," she said. "You make it sound like it was all pretense. Is that what you think? Just a phase you were going through, was it? Just a mad fling with a maddening whore who went completely mad?"

It was the real thing, he insisted, dutifully.

"It was a lot realer than the so-called real thing," she told him. "Those expert systems are a hell of a lot cleverer than Old Mother Nature. Four billion years of natural selection produced spanish fly and rhino horn; forty years of computerized protein design produced me and a thousand alternatives you just have to dilute to taste. You couldn't expect Mother Nature to take that kind of assault lying down, of course, even if she always has been the hoariest whore of them all. Heaven only knows what a psychochemical wilderness the world will be when all the tailored pheromones and augmentary psychotropics have run the gamut of mutational variation. You and I were just caught in the evolutionary cross fire. Kitty and Isabel too, I guess. No man is an island, and all that crap."

I don't think much of that as a eulogy, he said. *You could try to be a little more earnest, a little more sorrowful.*

He was right, but she didn't dare. She was afraid of earnestness, and doubly afraid of sorrow. There was no way in the world she was going to try to put it the way Ecclesiastes had— *in much wisdom is much grief, and he that increaseth knowledge increaseth sorrow* and all that kind of stuff.

After all, she had to stay sane enough to get safely back to the hospital or they wouldn't let her out again for a *long* time.

"Good-bye, Alan," she said, quietly. "I don't think I'll be able to drop in again for quite a while. You know how things are, even though you never once came to see me in the hospital."

I know, he said. *You don't have any secrets from me. We're soul mates, you and I, now and forever.* It was a nicer way of putting it than saying he was addicted to her booby-trapped flesh, but it came to the same thing in the end.

She went away then: back to the tube station, across zones three, two, and one, and out again on the far side of the river. She wanted to be alone, although she knew that she never would be and never could be.

The receptionist demanded to know why Isabel hadn't brought her back in the car, so Anna said that she'd asked to be dropped at the end of the street. "I wanted to walk a little way," she explained. "It's such a nice evening."

"No it isn't," the receptionist pointed out. "It's cloudy and cold, and too windy by half."

"You don't notice things like that when you're in my condition," Anna told her, loftily. "I'm drugged up to the eyeballs on mutated euphorics manufactured by my own cells. If it weren't for the medication, I'd be right up there on cloud nine, out of my mind on sheer bliss." It was a lie, of course; the real effects were much nastier.

"If the way you're talking is any guide," the receptionist said, wryly, "you're almost back to normal. We'll soon have to throw you back into the wide and wicked world."

"It's not as wide or as wicked as all that," Anna said, with due kindness and consideration, "and certainly not as worldly. One day, though, all the fallen angels will learn how to fly again, and how to soar to undiscovered heights—and *then* we'll begin to find out what the true bounds of experience are."

"I take it back," the receptionist said. "I hope you haven't been plaguing your poor sister's ears with that kind of talk—she won't want to take you out again if you have."

"No," said Anna, "I don't suppose she will. But then, she's not really my sister, and never was. I'm one of a kind." And for once, there was no inner or outer voice to say *Don't flatter yourself,* or *Better be grateful for what you've got,* or *We're all sisters under the skin,* or any of the other shallow and rough-hewn saws whose cutting edges she had always tried so very hard to resist.

Life Edit

DAMON KNIGHT

Damon Knight is one of the living grand masters of science fiction, without whom the field and the literature would be unknowably different. He is among the first of the great in-field literary critics *(In Search of Wonder)*. He founded the National Fantasy Fan Federation. He founded the Science Fiction Writers of America and the Nebula Award. He was a founder of the Milford Writing Workshop in the 1950s and a founder of the Clarion Workshops in the 1960s. He is one of the great editors and anthologists of SF (the twenty volumes of *Orbit*). And most of all, he is one of the great writers. His classic short fiction is a model of clear style and sophisticated treatment of ideas for others (even James Michener lists Knight's stories as an influence). He has kept growing as a writer for six decades, he is very active online, and in 1996 he published what may be his finest novel, *Humpty Dumpty*. He is also notable for his ability to write short short stories, an art nearly lost among younger writers. This is the shortest story in this book, but it packs no less a punch than the longest.

Maureen Appleforth opened the door, saw that the little conference room was empty, walked in, and let the door close behind her. She pulled out a chair and sat down. One day away from her twenty-ninth birthday, Maureen Appleforth had reddish brown hair with a natural wave, and she was neither too plump nor too thin, but just right.

After a moment the door opened and a young man came in with a machine under his arm. He had sleek brown hair and looked like the kind of man who smoked a pipe. He saw Maureen and looked surprised. "Ms. Appleforth? I was just going to set up the life editor. I'm Brian Orr."

He offered his free hand and she took it for a moment with her cool fingers. "I'm a little early," she said.

"That's all right. Better early than never." He laughed briefly and set the machine down on the table. Then he uncoiled a thick cable and plugged it into an outlet. "Would you sit over here please, Ms. Appleforth? We won't start until you're ready, but I just want to do some calibrations first." He pulled two leads out of the machine and showed her the cuffs at the ends of them. "OK to put these on you?"

She said, "Will it hurt?"

"No, not a bit. Take off your watch, please." He wrapped the cuffs around her wrists; the cuffs were soft but a little tight. He tapped keys on the pad in front of him and looked at the screen. "You're a bit nervous," he said. "Is this a voluntary decision on your part?"

"Not entirely. They told me I couldn't go any higher in the company unless . . ."

"But you don't want to do it?"

"No."

"But you want to stay in the company. Go higher."

"Yes."

"So it's a dilemma, isn't it?"

"Yes." She smiled. "That's the kind of thing I tell people."

"You're in conflict resolution upstairs? Or counseling?"

"Conflict."

"And you're good at it. Or they wouldn't care if you went higher or not." His voice was pleasant, and she was feeling a little more relaxed.

"So let's just talk," he said. "Is there anything I can tell you?"

She looked at him. He was projecting honest concern and impartiality. She said, "Why did you take the treatment? If you did, and if you remember."

"Oh, I remember, all right. It was something I said to a girlfriend of mine, years ago. I don't remember what it was, but it used to bother me about once a week. I'd sit and think, 'Jesus, I wish I hadn't said that to her.'"

"And now you don't remember."

"No, because it never happened."

"But you can remember remembering?"

"That's the way it works."

"What if I don't have anything like that? Anything that bothers me when I remember it?"

"You may be surprised. Everybody has something. All the way from horrible crimes to egg on your face."

"I don't. I've had a very tranquil life."

"Happy childhood?"

"Oh, yes. My father—my biological father—"

"Yes?"

"He left us when I was a year old, but he looked me up when I was grown, and we have dinner every now and then. He's very nice, a very gentle man. He's very fond of me, in fact. So even that—it's just—"

He waited.

"Why do I have these headaches?" she said.

He looked down at his keypad. "Been to a doctor?"

"Many doctors. All the tests."

"Well, then that's another good reason, isn't it? Really, I don't see how you can lose. Either you'll find something to change, like everybody else, or you won't. And if you *don't*, that's even better, don't you think?"

She hesitated. "When you edit your *life*—"

"Yes?"

"Doesn't that make everything different? Not just for you, for other people?"

"I'm not sure I follow."

"Suppose, for instance, you had a lover, a woman, and it was a bad relationship. Now you go back and edit her out of your life, right?"

"Yes." He looked uncomfortable.

"So, after you do that, just suppose she finds somebody else and they have a child. That child wouldn't have *existed* before. Or suppose you kill somebody, and you wish you hadn't. So you edit that, make it come out differently. So now the dead person is alive, but is she real, or just—some kind of ghost?"

"As far as I'm concerned, she's real. You know, what they tell us in training is, you're not creating anything. You're just moving from one time line to another. Where you didn't say anything dumb to your girl-friend, didn't get drunk and fall down the stairs, whatever. So, in this new time line, naturally you meet people that weren't in the old one. They're just as real as you are. Whatever that means."

After a moment, looking at the machine, he remarked, "Your pulse rate has been holding pretty steady. This isn't an emotional thing with you, is it?"

"No. And I'm going to do it. Yes. I am. What do I do?"

"Just relax and remember. Start with things that happened today, then further back, further back. You'll know when you hit something you need to change, even if it's buried back there."

The machine began to hum and the room darkened gradually, as if transparent dark petals were closing around her. She closed her eyes, and it was like falling into a well of shadows. Bright images swam up and receded, but there was nothing to edit or change; it was all moonlight and shadows, right back to her first birthday. The day when her drunken father picked her up by the ankles. And swung her. Against the cold dark.

And there was nothing to edit there, either. Somebody else, her father probably, had already edited that moment, or she wouldn't be here, wandering like a cool ghost through the life that was so important to other people.

Orr was bending over her. "Ms. Appleforth?" She opened her eyes. "Are you all right?"

"I have an awful headache," she said.

"That happens sometimes." He sat down again.

She took the cuffs off, rose and opened the door. "Aside from that, I'm fine," she said over her shoulder. "You're fine too, aren't you?"

"Yes."

"Well, that's just fine. Isn't it?"

Orr looked up at her anxiously. "Ms. Appleforth, are you sure you're all right?"

"Oh, yes. Or if not—" As the door closed, her voice drifted back, "—does it matter?"

First Tuesday

ROBERT REED

Robert Reed, like Dave Wolverton, was the winner of a Writers of the Future prize early in his career and went on to write several SF novels in the late 1980s and early 1990s. In the last few years he has become a fertile and productive writer of short fantasy and SF, appearing widely and frequently. His fiction is usually focused on character, often on ordinary people in extraordinary environments or with extraordinary problems. He published a number of stories in 1996, principally in *SF Age*, *Fantasy & Science Fiction*, and *Asimov's*, making selection for this volume a difficult choice. This story, and a couple of others, reminded me of the voice of Ray Bradbury in his fiction of the late 1940s and early 1950s—the Bradbury of *The Martian Chronicles*. As a story of American elections, it also reminds me of Michael Shaara's classic, "Election Day: 2066." "First Tuesday" is another story of virtual reality, one of the richest new repositories for SF writers in 1996. But there was no other VR story like it. There is a kind of deep humane optimism here that represents the best in SF.

After a lot of pestering, Mom told Stefan, "Fine, you can pick the view." Only it wasn't an easy job, and Stefan enjoyed it even more than he'd hoped. Standing on the foam-rock patio, he spoke to the house computer, asking for the Grand Canyon, then Hawaii's coast, then Denali. He saw each from many vantage points, never satisfied and never sure why not. Then he tried Mount Rushmore, which was better. Except Yancy saw the six stone heads, and he stuck his head out long enough to say, "Change it. Now." No debate; no place for compromise. Stefan settled on the Grand Canyon, on a popular view from the North Rim, telling himself that it was lovely and appropriate, and he hoped their guest would approve, and how soon would he be here . . . ? In another couple seconds, Stefan realized. *Jesus, now . . . !*

A figure appeared on the little lawn. He was tall, wearing a fancy suit, that famous face smiling straight at Stefan. And the boy jumped into the house, shouting with glee:

"The President's here!"

His stepfather muttered something.

Mom whined, "Oh, but I'm not ready."

Stefan was ready. He ran across the patio, leaping where it ended. His habit was to roll down the worn grassy slope. But he was wearing good clothes, and this evening was full of civic responsibilities. Landing with both feet solidly under him, he tried very hard to look like the most perfect citizen possible.

The President appeared solid. Not real, but nearly so.

The face was a mixture of Latin and African genes. The dreadlocks were long enough to kiss his broad shoulders. Halfway through his second term, President Perez was the only president that Stefan could remember, and even though this was just a projection, an interactive holo generated by machines . . . it was still an honor to have him here, and Stefan felt special, and for more reasons than he could count, he was nervous. In good ways, and in bad ways too.

"Hello?" chirped the eleven-year-old boy. "Mr. President?"

The projection hadn't moved. The house computer was wrestling with its instructions, fashioning a personality within its finite capacity. There was a sound, a sudden "Sssss" generated by speakers hidden in the squidskin fence and sky. The projection opened its mouth; a friendly, reedy voice managed, "Sssstefan." Then the President moved, offering both hands while saying, "Hello, young man. I'm so very glad to meet you."

Of course he knew Stefan's name. The personality could read the boy's public files. Yet the simple trick impressed him, and in response he shouted, "I'm glad to meet *you*, Mr. President."

The brown hands had no substance, yet they couldn't have acted more real. Gripping Stefan's pale little hand, they matched every motion, the warmth carried by the bright eyes and his words. "This is an historic moment, Stefan. But then you already know that, I'm sure."

The first nationwide press conference, yes. Democracy and science joined in a perfect marriage. President Perez was invited here for a symbolic dinner, and he was everywhere else at the same time. It was a wondrous evening . . . magical . . . !

"A lovely yard," said the President. The eyes were blind, but the personality had access to the security cameras, building appropriate images as the face moved. With a faraway gaze, he announced, "I do like your choice of view."

"Thank you, Mr. President."

"Very nice indeed . . . !"

Holo projectors and squidskin fabrics created the illusion of blue skies and rugged geology. Although nothing was quite as bright as it would appear in the real outdoors, of course. And the squidskin rocks and the occasional bird had a vagueness, a dreamy imprecision, that was the mark of a less-than-good system. Sometimes, like now, the antinoise generators failed to hide unwanted sounds. Somewhere beyond the President, neighbors were applauding, and cheering, making it seem as if ghosts inhabited the ghostly canyon.

President Perez seemed oblivious to the imperfections. Gesturing at their garden, he said, "Oh, I see you're doing your part. How close are you to self-sufficiency?"

Not close at all, really.

"Beautiful eggplants," said the guest, not waiting for a response. "And a fish pond too!"

Without fish. A problem with the filter, but the boy said nothing, hoping nothing would be noticed.

The President was turning in a circle, hunting for something else to compliment. For some reason, the house wasn't wearing its usual coat of projected paints and architectural flourishes. Their guest was too complicated, no doubt. Too many calculations, plus the computer had to show the Grand Canyon . . . and the real house lay exposed in all its drabness. Glass foams and cardboard looked gray and simple, and insubstantial, three walls inside the yard and the fourth wall pointed toward the outdoors, the brown stains on the sky showing where rainwater had damaged the squidskin.

To break the silence, Stefan blurted out a question. "Mr. President, where do you stand on the economy?"

That's how reporters asked questions.

But the great man didn't respond in the expected way. His smile changed, remaining a smile but encompassing some new, subtly different flavor of light. "I'll stand on the economy's head," he replied. "With my feet apart, ready for anything."

Was that a genuine answer?

Stefan wasn't sure.

Then the President knelt, putting his head below the boy's, saying with a happy, self-assured voice, "Thank you for the question. And remember, what happens tonight goes both ways. You can learn what I'm thinking, and in a different way I'll learn what's on your mind."

Stefan nodded, well aware of the principles.

"When I wake," said the handsome brown face, "I'll read that this many people asked about the economy, and how they asked it, and what they think we should be doing. All that in an abbreviated form, of course. A person in my position needs a lot of abbreviations, I'm afraid."

"Yes, sir." Stefan waited for a moment, then blurted, "I think you're doing a good job with the economy, sir. I really do."

"Well," said the guest, "I'm very, very glad to hear it. I am."

At that moment, the genuine President Perez was inside a government hospital, in a fetal position, suspended within a gelatin bath. Masses of bright new optical cable were attached to his brain and fingers, mouth and anus, linking him directly with the Net. Everything that he knew and believed was being blended with his physical self, all elements reduced to a series of numbers, then enlarged into a nationwide presence. Every household with an adequate projection system and memory was being visited, as were public buildings and parks, stadiums and VA facilities. If it was a success, press conferences would become a monthly event. Political opponents were upset, complaining that this was like one enormous commercial for Perez; but this was the President's last term, and it was an experiment, and even Stefan understood that these tricks were becoming cheaper and more widespread every day.

In the future, perhaps by the next election, each political party would be able to send its candidates to the voters' homes.

What could be more fair? thought the boy.

Stefan's stepfather had just stepped from the drab house, carrying a plate full of raw pink burgers.

In an instant, the air seemed close and thick.

"Mr. Thatcher," said the projection, "thank you for inviting me. I hope you're having a pleasant evening . . . !"

"Hey, I hope you like meat," Yancy called out. "In this family, we're carnivores!"

Stefan felt a sudden and precise terror.

But the President didn't hesitate, gesturing at the buffalo-augmented soy patties. Saying, "I hope you saved one for me."

"Sure, Mr. President. Sure."

For as long as Stefan could remember, his stepfather had never missed a chance to say something ugly about President Perez. But Mom had made him promise to be on his best behavior. Not once, but on several occasions. "I don't want to be embarrassed," she had told him, using the same tone she'd use when trying to make Stefan behave. "I want him to enjoy himself, at least this once. Will you please just help me?"

Yancy Thatcher was even paler than his stepson. Blonde hair worn in a short, manly ponytail; a round face wearing a perpetually sour expression. He wasn't large, but he acted large. He spoke with a deep, booming voice, and he carried himself as if endowed with a dangerous strength. Like now. Coming down the slope, he was walking straight toward their guest. The President was offering both hands, in his trademark fashion. But no hand was offered to him, and the projection retreated, saying, "Excuse me," while deftly stepping out of the way.

"You're excused," Yancy replied, laughing in a low, unamused fashion. Never breaking stride.

Mom wasn't watching; that's why he was acting this way.

Things worsened when Yancy looked over his shoulder, announcing, "I didn't want you coming tonight, frankly. But the kid's supposed to do an assignment for school, and besides, I figured this was my chance to show you my mind. If you know what I mean . . ."

President Perez nodded, dreadlocks bouncing. "Feedback is the idea. As I was just telling Stefan—"

"I'm an old-fashioned white man, Mr. President."

The boy looked at the drab house, willing Mom to appear.

But she didn't, and Yancy flung open the grill and let the biogas run too long before he made a spark, a soft blue explosion causing Stefan to back away. Nobody spoke. Every eye, seeing or blind, watched the patties hit the warming rack, sizzling quietly but with anger, Yancy mashing them flat with the grimy spatula that he'd gotten for Christmas last year.

Then the President spoke, ignoring that last comment.

"It's a shame this technology won't let me help you," he declared, with a ring of honesty.

Yancy grimaced.

The patties grew louder, the flames turning yellow.

Obstinately ignoring the tensions, the President looked at his own hands. "A poverty of physicality," he declared, laughing to himself.

That was it. Something snapped, and Yancy barked, "Know what I like, Mr. President? About tonight, I mean."

"What do you like?"

"Thinking that the real you is buried in goo, a big fat glass rope stuck up your ass."

Stefan prayed for a systems failure, or better, a war. Anything that would stop events here. His fear of fears was that the President would awaken to learn that Yancy Thatcher of Fort Wayne, Indiana had insulted him. Because the boy couldn't imagine anyone else in the country having the stupid courage to say such an awful thing.

Yet their guest wasn't visibly angry. He actually laughed, quietly and calmly. And all he said was, "Thank you for your honesty, sir."

Yancy flipped burgers, then looked at Stefan. "Tell your mom it'll be a few minutes. And take *him* with you."

It was such a strange, wondrous moment.

The boy looked at his President, at his smile, hearing the conjured voice saying, "Yes. That's a fine idea." Built of light and thought, he seemed invulnerable to every slight, every unkind word.

Stefan had never envied anyone so much in his life.

Mom was a blizzard of activity, hands blurring as they tried to assemble a fancy salad from ingredients grown in the garden, then cleaned and cut into delicate, artful shapes. She loved salads, planning each with an artist's sensibilities, which to Mom meant that she could never predict preparation times, always something to be done too fast at the end. When she saw Stefan inside, she whined, "I'm still not ready." When she saw President Perez fluttering for that instant when he passed from the outside to the kitchen projectors, she gave a little squeal and threw spinach in every direction. Then she spoke, not leaving enough time to think of proper words. "You've lost weight," she blurted. "Since the election, haven't you. . . ?"

Embarrassed again, Stefan said, "The President of the United States," with a stern voice. In warning. Didn't Mom remember how to address him?

But the President seemed amused, if anything. "I've lost a couple kilos, yes. Job pressures. And the First Lady's anti-equatorial campaign, too."

The joke puzzled Stefan until he stopped thinking about it.

"A drink, Mr. President? I'm having a drop for myself. . . ."

"Wine, please. If that's not too much trouble."

Both adults giggled. Touching a control, Mom ordered an elegant glass to appear on the countertop, already filled with sparkling white wine, and their guest went through the motions of sipping it, his personality given every flavor along with an ethanol kick. "Lovely," he declared. "Thanks."

"And how is the First Lady?"

It was a trivial question, Stefan within his rights to groan.

Mom glared at him, in warning. "Go find Candace, why don't you?" Then she turned back to their guest, again inquiring about his dear wife.

"Quite well, thank you. But tired of Washington."

Mom's drink was large and colorful, projected swirls of red and green never mixing together. "I wish she could have come. I *adore* her. And oh, I love what she's done with your house."

The President glanced at his surroundings. "And I'm sure she'd approve of your tastes, Mrs. Thatcher."

"Helen."

"Helen, then."

The kitchen walls and ceiling were covered with an indoor squidskin, and they built the illusion of a tall room . . . except that voices and any sharp sound echoed off the genuine ceiling, flat and close, unadorned by the arching oak beams that only appeared to be high overhead.

Mom absorbed the compliment and the sound of her own name, then noticed Stefan still standing nearby. "Where's Candace? Will you *please* go find your sister, darling?"

Candace's room was in the basement. It seemed like a long run to a boy who would rather be elsewhere, and worse, her door was locked. Stefan shook the knob, feeling the throb of music that seeped past the noise barriers. "He's here! Come on!" Kicking the door down low, he managed to punch a new hole that joined half a dozen earlier kickholes. "Aren't you coming up to meet him—?"

"Open," his sister shouted.

The knob turned itself. Candace was standing before a mirrored portion of squidskin, examining her reflection. Every other surface showed a fantastic woodland, lush red trees interspersed with a thousand Candaces who danced with unicorns, played saxophones, and rode bareback on leaping black tigers. The images were designed to jar nerves and exhaust eyes. But what Stefan noticed was the way his sister was dressed, her outfit too small and tight, her boobs twice their normal size. She was ready for a date, and he warned her, "They won't let you go. It's only Tuesday."

Candace gave her little brother a cutting, worldly look. "Go lose yourself."

Stefan began to retreat, gladly.

"Wait. What do you think of these shoes?"

"They're fine."

She kicked them off, without a word, then opened the door behind the mirror, mining her closet for a better pair.

Stefan shot upstairs.

Their honored guest and Mom remained in the kitchen. She was freshening her drink, and talking.

"I mean I really don't *care*," she told him. "I *know* I deserve the promotion, that's what matters." She gave her son a quick, troubled glance. "But Yankee says I should quit if they don't give it to me—"

"Yankee?"

"Yancy, I mean. I'm sorry, it's my husband's nickname."

The President was sitting on a projected stool, watching Mom sip her swirling drink once, then again.

"What do *you* think I should do? Quit, or stay."

"Wait and see," was the President's advice. "Perhaps you'll get what you deserve."

Mom offered a thin, dissatisfied smile.

Stefan thought of his comppad and his list of important questions. Where was it? He wheeled and ran to his room, finding the pad on his unmade bed, its patient voice repeating the same math problem over and over again. Changing functions, he returned to the kitchen. There'd been enough noise about decorating and Mom's job, he felt. "Mr. President? Are we doing enough about the space program?"

"Never," was the reply. "I wish we could do more."

Was the comppad recording? Stefan fiddled with the controls, feeling a sudden dull worry.

"In my tenure," the voice continued, "I've been able to double our Martian budget. Spaceborn industries have increased twelve percent. We're building two new observatories on the moon. And we just found life on Triton—"

"Titan," the boy corrected, by reflex.

"Don't talk to him that way!" Mom glowered, thoroughly outraged.

"Oh, but the fellow's right, Helen. I misspoke."

The amiable laugh washed over Stefan, leaving him warm and confident. This wasn't just an assignment for school, it was a mission, and he quickly scrolled to the next question. "What about the oceans, Mr. President?"

A momentary pause, then their guest asked, "What do you mean?"

Stefan wasn't sure.

"There are many issues," said the President. "Mineral rights. Power production. Fishing and farming. And the floating cities—"

"The cities."

"Fine. What do you think, Stefan? Do they belong to us, or are they free political entities?"

Stefan wasn't sure. He glanced at his pad, thinking of the islands, manmade and covered with trim, modern communities. They grew their own food in the ocean, moved where they wanted, and seemed like wonderful places to live. "They should be free."

"Why?"

Who was interviewing whom?

The President seemed to enjoy this reversal in roles. "If taxes pay for their construction—your tax money, and mine—then by what right can they leave the United States?" A pleasant little laugh, then he added, "Imagine if the First Lady and I tried to claim the White House as an independent nation. Would that be right?"

Stefan was at a loss for words.

Then Mom sat up straight, giving a sudden low moan.

Yancy was coming across the patio. Stefan saw him, and an instant later, Mom jumped to her feet, telling her son and guest, "No more politics. It's dinnertime."

Yancy entered the kitchen, approaching the projection from behind.

The President couldn't react in time. Flesh-and-bone merged with him; a distorted brown face lay over Yancy's face, which was funny.

"Why are you laughing?" snapped Yancy.

"No reason," the boy lied.

His stepfather's temper was close to the surface now. He dropped the plate of cooked burgers on the countertop, took an enormous breath, then said, "Show your guest to the dining room. Now."

Taking his comppad, Stefan obeyed.

The President flickered twice, changing projectors. His voice flickered too, telling the boy the story of some unnamed Senator who threw a tantrum whenever rational discourse failed him. "Which is to say," he added, "I have quite a lot of practice dealing with difficult souls." And with that he gave a little wink and grin, trying to bolster the boy's ragged mood.

Stefan barely heard him; he was thinking of floating cities.

It occurred to him that he'd answered, "Yes, they should be free," for no other reason than that was his stepfather's opinion, voiced many times. The cities were uncrowded. Some allowed only the best kinds of people. And Stefan had spoken without thinking, Yancy's ideas worming their way inside him. Embarrassed and confused, he wondered what he believed that was really his own. And did it ever truly matter?

Even if Stefan could think what he wanted, how important could his opinions ever be?

The table was set for five, one place setting built from light. The President took his seat, and Stefan was across from him, scrolling through the comppad in search of new questions. Most of these came from his social studies teacher—a small, handsome Nigerian woman who didn't know Yancy. *Why do we keep our open border policy?* He didn't dare ask it. Instead he coughed, then inquired, "How are your cats, Mr. President?"

Both of them seemed happy with the new topic. "Fine, thank you." Another wink and grin. "The jaguars are fat, and the cheetah is going to have triplets."

Miniature breeds. Declawed and conditioned to be pets.

They spoke for a couple minutes about preserving rare species, Stefan mentioning his hope to someday work in that field. Then Mom burst into the room with her completed salad, and Yancy followed with some bean concoction, making a second trip for the burgers. Somewhere en route he shouted, "Candace!" and she appeared an instant later, making her entrance with a giggle and a bounce.

If anything, her boobs were even bigger. And the room's holo projectors changed her skin, making it coffee-colored.

Mom saw the clothes and her color, then gave a shocked little groan. But she didn't dare say anything with the President here. Yancy entered the little room, paused and grimace . . . then almost smiled, glancing at their guest with the oddest expression.

Why wasn't he saying anything?

The President glanced at Candace, for half a second. Then he looked straight ahead, eyes locked on Stefan. Big, worried eyes. And his projection feigned a slow sigh.

With her brown boobs spilling out, Candace sat beside President Perez.

Mom glared at her, then at Yancy. But Yancy just shook his head, as if warning her to say nothing.

Seven burgers were on the plate. The real ones were juicy; the one built from light resembled a hard lump of charcoal.

Stefan realized that he was growing accustomed to being ashamed.

Candace took nothing but a small helping of salad, giggling and look-ing at their guest with the same goofy flirtatious face that she used on her infinite boyfriends. "Hey, are you having a good time?"

"Mr. President," Stefan added.

His sister glared at him, snapping, "I know *that.*"

"I'm having a fine time." The apparition never quite looked at her, using his spoon to build a mound of phantom beans on the phantom plate. "You have a lovely home."

Mom said, "Thank you."

Candace giggled, like an idiot.

But she wasn't stupid, her brother wanted to say. To shout.

Yancy was preparing two burgers, slipping them into their pouches of bread and adding pickles, mustard and sugar corn. Then after a first oversized bite, he grinned, telling the house computer to give them sce-nery. "Mount Rushmore," he demanded. "The original."

Squidskin re-created the four-headed landmark. Presidents Barker and Yarbarro were notably absent.

The current President was staring at his plate. For the first time, he acted remote. Detached. A bite of his charred burger revealed its raw red interior, blood flowing as if from an open wound. After a long pause, he looked at Stefan again, and with a certain hopefulness asked, "What's your next question, please?"

Candace squealed, "Let me ask it!"

She shot to her feet, reaching over the table, her boobs fighting for the privilege of bursting out of her shirt. Before Stefan could react, she'd stolen his comppad, reading the first question aloud.

"Why do we keep our open border policy?"

The pause was enormous, silence coming from every direction at once. Mom stared at Yancy, pleading with her eyes. Everyone else studied the President, wondering how he would respond. Except he didn't. It was Yancy who spoke first, in a voice almost mild. Almost.

"I don't think it matters," he replied. "I think if we want to do some good, we've got to turn the flow back the other direction. If you know what I mean."

"I think we do," said President Perez.

"Fifty years of inviting strangers into our house. Fifty idiotic years of making room, making jobs, making allowances . . . and always making due with less and less. That's what the great Barker gave us. Her and her damned open border bullshit!"

Stefan felt sick. Chilled.

Mom began, "Now Yancy—"

"My grandfather owned an acreage, Mr. President. He ate meat three times a day, lived in a big house, and worked hard until he was told to go half-time, some know-nothing refugee given the other half of his job, and his paycheck . . . !"

"Employment readjustments." Their guest nodded, shrugged. "That's a euphemism, I know. There were problems. Injustices. But think of the times, Mr. Thatcher. Our government was under enormous pressures, yet we managed to carry things off—"

"Some know-nothing refugee!" Yancy repeated, his face red as uncooked meat. "And *your* party took his home, his land, needing the room for a stack of apartment buildings."

Stefan tried not to listen. He was building a careful daydream where he had a different family, and he was sitting with the President, everyone working to make his visit productive, and fun.

Yancy pointed at the old Rushmore. "A great nation built it—"

"An individual built it," the President interrupted. "Then his grateful nation embraced it."

"A free nation!"

"And underpopulated, speaking relatively."

Pursing his heavy pink lips, Yancy declared, "We should have let you people starve. That's what I think." He took a huge breath, held it, then added, "You weren't our responsibility, and we should have shut our borders. Nothing in. Not you. Not a rat. Not so much as a goddamn fly . . . That's my opinion . . . !"

President Perez stared at his own clean plate. Eyes narrowed. The contemplative face showed a tiny grin, then he looked up at Yancy, eyes carved from cold black stone.

With a razored voice, he said, "First of all, sir, I'm a third-generation U.S. citizen. And second of all, I believe that you're an extraordinarily frightened man." A pause, a quiet sigh. "To speak that way, your entire life must be torn with uncertainty. And probably some deep, deep sense of failure, I would guess."

Stefan sat motionless, in shock.

"As for your opinions on national policy, Mr. Thatcher . . . well, let me just say this. These are the reasons why I believe you're full of shit."

The rebuke was steady, determined, and very nearly irresistible.

President Perez spoke calmly about war and famine, a desperate United Nations, and the obligations of wealthy people. He named treaties, reciting key passages word-for-word. Then he attacked the very idea of closing the borders, listing the physical difficulties and the economic costs. "Of course it might have worked. We could have survived. An enclave of privilege and waste, and eventually there would have been plagues and a lot of quiet hunger on the outside. We'd be left with our big strong fences, and beyond them . . . a dead world, spent and useless to us, and to the dead." A brief pause, then he spoke with a delicate sorrowful voice, asking, "Are you really the kind of man who could live lightly with himself, knowing that billions perished . . . in part because you deserved a larger dining room . . . ?"

Yancy had never looked so tired. Of those at the table, he seemed to be the one composed of light and illusion.

The President smiled at everyone, then focused on Stefan. "Let's move on, I think. What's your next question?"

The boy tried to read his comppad, but his brain wouldn't work.

"Perhaps you can ask me, 'What do you think about this hallmark evening?' "

"What do you think?" Stefan muttered.

"It should revolutionize our government, which isn't any surprise. Our government was born from a string of revolutions." He waited for the boy's eyes, then continued. "I love this nation. If you want me angry, say otherwise. But the truth is that we are diverse and too often divided. My hope is that tonight's revolution will strengthen us. Judging by these events, I'd guess that it will make us at least more honest."

Yancy gave a low sound. Not an angry sound, not anything.

"Perhaps I should leave." The President rose to his feet. "I know we've got another half hour scheduled—"

"No, please stay!" Mom blurted.

"Don't go," begged Candace, reaching for his dreadlocks.

Mom turned on her. At last. "Young lady, I want you out of those clothes—"

"Why?"

"—and drain those breasts. You're not fooling anyone here!"

Candace did her ritual pout, complete with the mournful groan and the teary run to the basement.

Mom apologized to their guest, more than once. Then she told Yancy, "You can help Stefan clear the table, please. *I* will show our President the rest of *my* house."

Stefan worked fast. Scraps went into the recyke system; dishes were loaded in the sonic washer. Through the kitchen window, he saw the Grand Canyon passing into night, its blurry, imperfect edges more appropriate in the ruddy half-light. And it occurred to him that he was happy with this view, even if it wasn't real. Happier than he'd feel on any ordinary plot of real ground, surely.

His stepfather did no work. He just stood in the middle of the room, his face impossible to read.

Stefan left him to set the controls. Mom and the President were in the front room, looking outside. Or at least their eyes were pointed at the lone window. With a soft, vaguely conspiring tone, the President said, "It's not my place to give advice. Friends can. Counselors and ministers should. But not someone like me, I'm sorry."

"I know," his mother whispered. "It's just . . . I don't know . . . I just wish he would do something awful. To me, of course. Just to make the choice simple."

What choice? And who was she talking about?

"But really, he only sounds heartless." She tried to touch their guest, then thought better of it. "In five years, Yankee hasn't lifted his hand once in anger. Not to the kids, or me. And you're right, I think. About him being scared, I mean . . ."

Stefan listened to every word.

"When you come next month," Mom inquired, "will you remember what's happened here?"

President Perez shook his head. His face was in profile, like on a coin. "No, I won't. Your computer has to erase my personality, by law. And you really don't have room enough to hold me. Sorry."

"I guess not," Mom allowed.

They looked outside, watching an airtaxi riding its cable past the window. The building across the street mirrored theirs, houses stacked on houses, each one small and efficient, and lightweight, each house possessing its own yard and the same solitary window facing the maelstrom that was a city of barely five million.

Several Presidents were visible.

They waved at each other, laughing with a gentle, comfortable humor.

Then their President turned, spotting the boy at the other end of the little room, and he smiled at Stefan with all of his original charm and warmth, nothing else seeming to matter.

Mom turned and shouted, "Are you spying on us?"

"I wasn't," he lied. "No, ma'am."

The President said, "I think he just came looking for us." Then he added, "Dessert. I feel like a little dessert, if I might be so bold."

Mom wasn't sure what to say, if anything.

"Perhaps something that *looks* delicious, please. In the kitchen. I very much liked your kitchen."

They gathered again, a truce called.

Candace was dressed as if ready for school, looking younger and flatter, and embarrassed. Yancy had reacquired a portion of his old certainty, but not enough to offer any opinions. Mom seemed wary, particularly of Stefan. What had he heard while eavesdropping? Then the President asked for more questions, looking straight at Yancy, nothing angry or malicious in his dark face.

Crossing his arms, Yancy said nothing.

But Stefan thought of a question. "What about the future?" It wasn't from his comppad's list; it was an inspiration. "Mr. President? How will the world change?"

"Ah! You want a prediction!"

Stefan made sure that the comppad was recording.

President Perez took a playful stab at the layered sundae, then spoke casually, with an easy authority.

"What I'm going to tell you is a secret," he said. "But not a big one, as secrets go."

Everyone was listening. Even Yancy leaned closer.

"Since the century began, every President has had an advisory council, a team of gifted thinkers. They know the sciences. They see trends. They're experts in new technologies, history and human nature. We pay them substantial fees to build intelligent, coherent visions of tomorrow. And do you know what? In eighty years, without exception, none of their futures have come true." He shook his head, laughing quietly. "Predicted inventions usually appear, but never on schedule. And the more important changes come without warning, ruining every one of their assessments." A pause, then he added, "My presence here, for instance. Not one expert predicted today. I know because I checked the records myself. No one ever thought that a President could sit in half a billion kitchens at once, eating luscious desserts that will never put a gram on his waist."

Yancy growled, asking, "Then why do you pay the bastards?"

"Habit?" The President shrugged his shoulders. "Or maybe because nothing they predict comes true, and I find that instructive. All these possible futures, and I don't need to worry about any of them."

A long, puzzled silence.

"Anyway," said the President, "my point is this: Now that we've got this technology, every prediction seems to include it. In fact, my experts are claiming that in fifty years, give or take, all of us will spend our days floating in warm goo, wired into the swollen Net. Minimal food. No need for houses or transportation. Maximum efficiency for a world suddenly much less crowded." He gazed at Stefan, asking, "Now does that sound like an appealing future?"

The boy shook his head. "No, sir."

"It sounds *awful*," Mom barked.

Candace said, "Ugh."

Then Yancy said, "It'll never happen. No."

"Exactly," said their guest. "It's almost guaranteed not to come true, if the pattern holds." He took a last little bite of his sundae, then rose. "You asked for a prediction, son. Well, here it is. Your life will be an unending surprise. If you're lucky, the surprises will be sweet and come daily, and that's the best any of us can hope for. I think."

The silence was relaxed. Contemplative.

Then the President gestured at the projected clock high above their stove. "Time to leave, I'm afraid. Walk me out?"

He was speaking to Stefan.

Hopping off his stool, the boy hugged himself and nodded. "Sure, Mr. President. Sure."

The Grand Canyon was dark, the desert sky clear and dry. But the genuine air was humid, more like Indiana than Arizona. There were always little clues to tell you where you were. Stefan knew that even the best systems fell short of being *real.*

In a low, hopeful voice, he said, "You'll come back in a month. Won't you, sir?"

"Undoubtedly." Another smile. "And thank you very much. You were a wonderful host."

What else? "I hope you had a good time, sir."

A pause, then he said, "It was perfect. Perfect."

Stefan nodded, trying to match that smile.

Then the image gave a faint, "Good-bye," and vanished. He suddenly just wasn't there.

Stefan stared at the horizon for a long moment, then turned and saw that the house was whole again. Their computer had enough power to add color and all the fancy touches. Under the desert sky, it looked tall and noble, and he could see the people sitting inside, talking now. Just talking. Nobody too angry or too sad, or anything. And it occurred to Stefan, as he walked up toward them, that people were just like the house, small inside all their clothes and words and big thoughts.

People were never what they appeared to be, and it had always been that way. And always would be.

The Spear of the Sun

DAVID LANGFORD

David Langford is a physicist and science fiction fan, who has won many Hugo Awards both for his monthly fanzine, *Ansible* (also excerpted as a monthly column in *Interzone*, and online: http://www.dcs.gla.ac.uk/SF-archives/Ansible/) and as Best Fan Writer. He is the most famous humorous writer in the SF fan world today. His fan writings have been collected in *Let's Hear It for the Deaf Man* (Langford is deaf). He is also the author of several books of nonfiction and a hard-science fiction novel, *The Space Eater*. His occasional professional short stories (as opposed to the parodies he publishes in fanzines) are usually witty but entirely serious hard SF. This story is something of a departure for him, though not in its wit. It is an outrageous alternate universe story in which the distinguished writer G. K. Chesterton, a contemporary of H. G. Wells, who is most famous for his Catholic writings and his mystery fiction (the Father Brown series) but who also wrote fantasy (*The Man Who Was Thursday*) and SF (*The Napoleon of Notting Hill*) is the founder of genre SF. It was published (with especially wonderful illustrations, I might add) in *Interzone. Interzone* has done a number of alternate universe stories in the mode of, and/or featuring the characters of, the founders of SF such as Wells and Verne, by many writers including Brian Stableford, Kim Newman, and Stephen Baxter over the past few years.

Since its inception in 1925, the most famous shared-world series in G. K. *Chesterton's Science Fiction Magazine has always been the adventures of that much-loved interplanetary sleuth Father (later in the chronology, Monsignor) Brown. There is no need to list the long roll-call of those who have taken part—Hilaire Belloc, Graham Greene, Jorge Luis Borges, Kurt Scheer, Clark Dalton, R. A. Lafferty, Gene Wolfe, and Robert Lionel Fanthorpe being just a few of the illustrious contributors[1], not to mention the bright talents emerging from the splendid* GKC Presents Catholic Writers of the Future *anthologies. And we are always glad to welcome fresh participants. Here, therefore, is the first of* GKSFM*'s eagerly awaited new series "The Fractals of Father Brown," penned by SF Achievement ("Gilbert") Award-winner David Langford . . .*

T he luxury liner *H.M.S. Aquinas* sped among the stars, its great engines devouring distance and defying time. Each porthole offered a lurid glimpse of that colossal pointillist work which God Himself has painted in subtle yet searing star-points upon the black canvas of creation, too vast for any critic ever to step back and see entire. In the main lounge, however, the ship's passengers were already jaded by the splendour of the suns and had found a new distraction. For Astron, high celebrant of the newest religion, was weaving dazzling circles of rhetoric around a shabby, blinking priest of the oldest.

"Did not a great writer once say that the interstellar spaces are God's quarantine regulations? I think the blight He had in mind was the blight of men like this, crabbed and joyless celibates who spread their poisoned doctrines of guilt and fear from planet to planet, world after world growing grey with their breath . . ."

The crabbed and joyless object of these attentions sipped wine and contrived to look remarkably cheerful. Father Brown was travelling from his parish of Cobhole in England on Old Earth as an emissary to the colony world Pavonia III, where Astron planned to harvest countless converts and (it is to be assumed) decidedly countable cash donations for his Universal Temple of Fire.

"For the Church of Fire pays heed to its handmaid Science, and sheds the mouldy baggage of superstition. The living Church of Fire gives respect to the atomic blaze at the heart of every sun, to the divine laws of supersymmetry and chaos theory; the dying church of superstition had nothing to say about either at Vatican III."

The little, pudding-faced priest murmured: "We never needed chaos theory to know that the cycles of evil run ever smaller and smaller down the scales of measurement, yet always dreadfully self-similar." But it passed unheeded.

Astron boomed on, remarking that those who obstructed the universal Light would be struck down by the spear of the sun. Indeed he looked every inch the pagan god, with his great height, craggy features and flowing flaxen hair now streaked with silver. A golden sunburst of a ring gleamed on his finger. His acolyte Simon Traill was yet more handsome though less vocal, perhaps a little embarrassed at Astron's taunting. Both wore plain robes of purest white. The group that pressed around consisted chiefly of women; Father Brown noted with interest that red-haired Elizabeth Brayne, whom he knew to be the billionaire heiress of Brayne Interplanetary, pressed closest of all and close in particular to young Traill. She wore the dangerous look of a woman who thinks she knows her own mind.

"Damn them," said a voice at Brown's ear. "Pardon me, Father. But you heard that Astron saying what he thinks of celibacy. He chews women up and spits out the pieces. See Signora Maroni back there with a face like thunder? She's a bit long in the tooth for Mr. Precious Astron, but for the first two nights of this trip she had something he wanted. Now that something's in his blasted Temple fund, and—Well, perhaps you wouldn't understand."

"Oh, stories like this do occasionally crop up in the confessional," said the dumpling-faced priest vaguely, eyeing the dark young man. John Horne was a mining engineer, who until now had talked of nothing but Pavonia III's bauxite and the cargo of advanced survey and digging equipment that was travelling out with him. Father Brown knew the generous wrath of simple men, and tried to spread a little calm by enquiring about the space-walk in which several of the passengers had indulged earlier.

Though allowing himself to be diverted for a little time, Horne presently said, "Don't you feel a shade hot under the dog-collar when Astron needles you about his Religion of Science and how outdated you are?"

"Oh yes, science progresses most remarkably," said Father Brown with bumbling enthusiasm. "In Sir Isaac Newton's mechanics, you know, it was the three-body problem that didn't have any general solution. Then came Relativity and it was the two-body problem that was troublesome. After that, Quantum Theory found all these complications in the *one*-body problem, a single particle; and now they tell me that relativistic quantum field theory is stuck at the nobody problem, the vacuum itself. I can hardly wait to hear what tremendous step comes next."

Horne looked at him a little uncertainly.

A silvery chime sounded. "Attention, attention. This is the captain speaking. Dinner will be served at six bells. Shortly beforehand there will be a course correction with a temporary boost of acceleration from five-eighths to fifteen-sixteenths *g*."

"I go," said Astron with a kind of stately anger, drawing himself up to his full, impressive height and pulling the deep white cowl of the robe over his head. "I go to be alone and meditate over the Sacred Flame." With Traill cowled likewise in his wake, he stalked gigantically from the lounge.

"That makes me madder than anything," Horne said gloomily, beginning to amble in the general direction of Elizabeth Brayne. "No pipes, no cigarettes, that's an iron rule—and *he* manages to wangle an eternal flame in his ruddy stateroom. The safety officer would like to kill him."

But it was not the safety officer who came under suspicion when the news raced through the *Aquinas* like leaves in a mad March wind: that a third lieutenant making final checks before the course change had used a master key and found that great robed figure slumped over the brazier of the Universal Flame, face charred and flowing hair gone to smoke, a scientific seeker who had solved the no-body problem at last.

By a happy chance, ship security had been contracted out to the agency of M. Hercule Flambeau, one-time master criminal and an old friend of Father Brown, who set to in a frenzy of Gallic fervour. Knowing the pudgy little priest's power of insight, Flambeau invited him at once to the chamber of death. It was a stark and austere stateroom, distinguished by the wide brazier (its gas flame now extinguished) and the terrible figure that the third lieutenant had dragged from the fire.

"He seems to have bent over his wretched flame and prayed, or whatever mumbo-jumbo the cult of Fire uses for prayer," mused Father Brown. "Better for him to have looked up and not down, and savoured the stars through that porthole . . . Even the stars look twisted in this accursed place. Might he have died naturally and fallen? That would be ugly enough, but not devilish."

The tall Flambeau drew out a slip of computer paper. "My friend, we know to distrust coincidence. The acolyte Traill is nowhere to be found, and the ship's records say the nearest airlock has cycled just once, outwards, since Astron left the main lounge an hour ago. Some avenger has made a clean sweep of the Church of Fire's mission: one dead in a locked room, one jettisoned. And half the women and all the men out there might have had a potent motive. We're carrying members of rival cults too—the Club of Queer Trades, the Dead Men's Shoes Society, the Ten Teacups, and heaven knows what else. But how in God's name could any of them get in here?"

"Don't forget the crabbed priesthood that blights human souls," said the smaller man earnestly. "Astron was last seen attacking it with a will, and its representative has an obviously criminal face. *Ecce homo.*" He tapped himself on the chest.

"Father Brown, I cannot believe you did this thing."

"Well, in confidence, I'll admit to you that I didn't." He bustled curiously about the room, blinking at the oversized bed and peering again through the viewport as though the stars themselves held some elusive clue. Last of all he studied the robed corpse's ruined face and pale hands, and shuddered.

"The spear of the sun," he muttered to himself. "Astron threatened his enemies with the spear of the sun. And where does a wise man hide a spear?"

"In an armoury, I suppose," said Flambeau in a low voice.

"In poor foolish William Blake's armoury. You remember, *All the stars threw down their spears?* But the angel Ithuriel also carries a spear. Excuse me, I know I'm rambling, but I can see half of it, just half . . ." Father Brown stood stock still with hands pressed into his screwed-up eyes. At last he said: "You thought I shuddered at that wreck of a face. I shuddered at the hands."

"But there is nothing to see—no mark on the hands."

"There is nothing. And there should be a great sunburst ring. They are younger hands than Astron's, when you look. It is the acolyte Traill who lies there."

Flambeau gaped. "But that can't be. It turns everything topsy-turvy; it makes the whole case the wrong shape."

"So was that equation," said Father Brown gently. "And we survived even that equation. But I need one further fact." He scribbled on a slip of paper and folded it. "Have one of your men show this to John Horne. A reply is expected."

Wordlessly, Flambeau pressed a stud and did what was asked.
"Horne," he said when the two friends were alone again. "The one who
fancies Miss Brayne and didn't like her interest in men with white robes.
Is he your choice for the dock?"

"No. For the witness-box." Father Brown sat on the edge of the bed,
the dinginess of his cassock highlighted by the expanse of white satin
quilting, his stubby legs not quite reaching the deck plates. "I think this
story begins with young Horne prattling over dinner about his cargo. So I
asked whether a piece of his equipment was missing. Come now: when
you think of fiery death in a locked stateroom, what does mining and
surveying gear suggest to you?"

"Nothing but moonshine," said Flambeau with sarcasm. "I do assure
you that each hull plate and bulkhead has been carefully inspected for
any trace of a four-foot mineshaft through which a murderer might
crawl."

"That's the whole sad story. Even when you look at it you can't see it:
but every stateroom of this vessel contains a Judas window through
which death can strike. And—" Brown's muddy eyes widened suddenly.
"Of course! The spear of the sun is two-edged. My friend, I predict . . .
I predict that you will never make an arrest."

As Flambeau arose with an oath, the communicator on his wrist crackled. "What? The answer is yes? Father, the answer is yes."

"Then let me tell you the story," said the priest. "The great Astron
devoured woman after woman, but most of all he craved the women who
did not crave him. For as I saw, Elizabeth Brayne was taken with Simon
Traill. And Astron left the room in anger.

"I fancy it was his practice to have Traill watch over the ritual flame for
him, while another cowled figure glided out upon certain assignations.
But this time Astron's assignation was a darker one. He knew where to
find the pressure suits: there was a space-walking party a few watches
ago. He knew that in Horne's cargo he would find his spear."

"Which is—?"

"A laser."

Father Brown continued dreamily after a sort of thunderous silence.
"Picture Astron floating a little way outside that porthole, a wide-open
window for his frightful, insubstantial bolt. Picture his unknowing rival
Traill bent over the flame, struck in the face, falling dead across the
brazier which would slowly burn away every mark of how he died."

"Name of a name," cried Flambeau. "He is still out there. We shall
have him yet!"

"You will never have him." Father Brown shook his head slowly. "The
spear, I said, is two-edged. Oh, these strong and simple Stoics with their

great bold ideas! Astron called us impractical and superstitious, but lacked even the little smattering of quantum electrodynamics that every seminarian picks up along with his Latin and his St. Augustine. He thought the crystal of the port purely transparent, Flambeau: but there is diffraction, my friend, and there is partial reflection. And even as it slew his victim, the spear of the sun rebounded to strike the murderer blind." The little priest shivered. "Yes, the humour of God can be cruel. Astron's easy arrogance saw the motes in all men's eyes, and now at last found the beam in his own . . .

"Picture him now, flinging his suit this way and that with those clever little gas-jets, with nightmare pressing in as he realizes he *cannot find the ship* in the endless dark. And then comes the course correction and he has no more chance. And now that void which he worshipped in his heart has become his vast sarcophagus."

"I think," said Flambeau slowly, "that brandy would be a good thing. Mother of God. All that from a missing ring."

"Not only that." said Father Brown, "The viewport crystal was slightly distorted by the heat of the beam's passage. I said the stars looked twisted, but you thought I was being sentimental."

IN OUR NEXT ISSUE: Fr. Brian Stableford continues his series on forgotten SF authors, with a spirited case for reviving the works of 19th-century fantasist H. G. Wells. Our regular *Credo Quia Impossibile* squib daringly tackles another zero-probability notion in "The Piltdown Effect"—we know from *GKSFM* science columns by Hilaire Belloc, Jimmy Swaggart, and other fine popularizers that mankind is a fixed genetic type, *but just suppose for one terrifying moment that it were not so!* Of course the "Should Women Authors Be Allowed In *GKSFM?*" debate rages on in the letter column: what amusingly outrageous thing *will* that "Ms." Cadigan say next? Carl Sagan contributes a devastatingly frank essay on science's inability to explain weeping images or miraculous liquefactions. And our millions of avid readers in the Americas will welcome the coming feature on brash colonial editor Gardner Dozois and his shoestring launch of (at last!) an all-United States SF magazine, called *Interzone:* we shall have to look to our laurels. . . .

1. We remind our readers that Mr Philip José Farmer's delightful but unauthorized contributions (*Father Brown vs the Insidious Dr. Fu-Manchu, Father Brown 124C41+, Father Brown in Oz,* etc) are not regarded as strictly canonical.

2. Flambeau repented, made his full confession to Father Brown and joined the side of the angels on some forty-two occasions, all listed in Martin Gardner's *Flambeau, Boskone and Ming the Merciless: the Annotated Father Brown Villains* (1987).

3. Older readers will recognize the allusion to that insight which saved the Holy Galactic Empire from the threat of secular "psychohistorians" in Isaac Asimov's classic *Foundation and Father Brown* (1951).

Counting Cats in Zanzibar

GENE WOLFE

Gene Wolfe continues to produce challenging, complex fiction in fantasy, horror, and science fiction. He has now been publishing in SF for more than thirty years, although he did not draw much notice until twenty-five years ago, in the early 1970s, when his outstanding short fiction began to appear on award ballots. By the end of the decade, with the advent of his masterly *The Book of the New Sun,* he began to be generally acknowledged as one of the finest SF writers. He is so much a unique writerly talent that one has to stretch to make literary comparisons—if there's anyone in our century in the English language perhaps it is Vladimir Nabokov he is most like. Others have compared him to Borges and to Mozart. Last year he was given a Grand Master award by the World Fantasy Convention. He published the fourth and concluding volume of his The Book of the Long Sun, *Exodus from the Long Sun*, in 1996, as well as several science fiction and fantasy stories. Each story has such signal virtues that it was difficult to choose the one for this volume. This is a robot story full of questions more than answers. To read it for plot is to risk disappointment. It remains a mystery, disturbingly clear.

The first thing she did upon arising was count her money. The sun itself was barely up, the morning cool with the threatening freshness peculiar to the tropics, the freshness, she thought, that says, "Breathe deep of me while you can."

Three thousand and eighty-seven U.N. dollars left. It was all there. She pulled on the hot-pink underpants that had been the only ones she could find to fit her in Kota Kinabalu and hid the money as she had the day before. The same skirt and blouse as yesterday; there would be no chance to do more than rinse, wring out, and hang dry before they made land.

And precious little then, she thought; but that was wrong. With this much money she would have been able to board with an upper-class family and have her laundry micropored, rest, and enjoy a dozen good meals before she booked passage to Zamboanga.

Or Darwin. Clipping her shoes, she went out on deck.

He joined her so promptly that she wondered whether he had been listening, his ears attuned to the rattle and squeak of her cabin door. She said, "Good morning." And he, "The dawn comes up like thunder out of China across the bay. That's the only quote I've been able to think of. Now you're safe for the rest of the trip."

"But you're not," she told him, and nearly added Doctor Johnson's observation that to be on a ship is to be in prison, with the added danger of drowning.

He came to stand beside her, leaning as she did against the rickety railing. "Things talk to you, you said that last night. What kind of things?"

She smiled. "Machines. Animals, too. The wind and the rain."

"Do they ever give you quotations?" He was big and looked thirty-five or a little past it, with a wide Irish mouth that smiled easily and eyes that never smiled at all.

"I'd have to think. Not often, but perhaps one has."

He was silent for a time, a time during which she watched the dim shadow that was a shark glide under the hull and back out again. No shark's ever talked to me, she thought, except him. In another minute or two he'll want to know the time for breakfast.

"I looked at a map once." He squinted at the sun, now half over the horizon. "It doesn't come up out of China when you're in Mandelay."

"Kipling never said it did. He said that happened on the road there. The soldier in his poem might have gone there from India. Or anywhere. Mapmakers colored the British Empire pink two hundred years ago, and two hundred years ago half Earth was pink."

He glanced at her. "You're not British, are you?"

"No, Dutch."

"You talk like an American."

"I've lived in the United States, and in England, too; and I can be more English than the British when I want to. I have heerd how many ord'nary veman one vidder's equal to, in pint 'o comin' over you. I think it's five-and-twenty, but I don't rightly know verther it a'n't more."

This time he grinned. "The real English don't talk like that."

"They did in Dickens's day, some of them."

"I still think you're American. Can you speak Dutch?"

"Gewiss, Narr!"

"Okay, and you could show me a Dutch passport. There are probably a lot of places where you can buy one good enough to pass almost anywhere. I still think you're American."

"That was German," she muttered, and heard the thrum of the ancient diesel-electric: "Dontrustim-dontrustim-dontrustim."

"But you're not German."

"Actually, I am."

He grunted. "I never thought you gave me your right name last night. What time's breakfast?"

She was looking out across the Sulu Sea. Some unknown island waited just below the horizon, its presence betrayed by the white dot of cloud forming above it. "I never thought you were really so anxious to go that you'd pay me five thousand to arrange this."

"There was a strike at the airport. You heard about it. Nobody could land or take off." Aft, a blackened spoon beat a frying pan with no pretense of rhythm.

Seated in the smelly little salon next to the galley, she said, "To eat well in England you should have breakfast three times a day."

"They won't have kippers here, will they?" He was trying to clean his fork with his handkerchief. A somewhat soiled man who looked perceptionally challenged set bowls of steaming brown rice in front of them and asked a question. By signs, he tried to indicate that he did not understand.

She said, "He desires to know whether the big policeman would like some pickled squid. It's a delicacy."

He nodded. "Tell him yes. What language is that?"

"Melayu Pasar. We call it Bazaar Malay. He probably does not imagine that there is anyone in the entire world who cannot understand Melayu Pasar." She spoke, and the somewhat soiled man grinned, bobbed his head, and backed away; she spooned up rice, discovering that she was hungry.

"You're a widow yourself. Isn't that right? Only a widow would remember that business about widows coming over people."

She swallowed, found the teapot, and poured for both of them. "Aha, a deduction. The battle-ax scenteth the battle afar."

"Will you tell me the truth, just once? How old are you?"

"No. Forty-five."

"That's not so old."

"Of course it's not. That's why I said it. You're looking for an excuse to seduce me." She reached across the table and clasped his hand; it felt like muscle and bone beneath living skin. "You don't need one. The sea has always been a seducer, a careless, lying fellow."

He laughed. "You mean the sea will do my work for me?"

"Only if you act quickly. I'm wearing pink underdrawers, so I'm aflame with passion." How many of these polyglot sailors would it take to throw him overboard, and what would they want for it? How much aluminum, how much plastic, how much steel? Four would probably be enough, she decided; and settled on six to be safe. Fifty dollars each should be more than sufficient, and even if there was quite a lot of plastic he would sink like a stone.

"You're flirting with trouble," he told her. The somewhat soiled man came back with a jar of something that looked like bad marmalade and plopped a spoonful onto each bowl of rice. He tasted it, and gave the somewhat soiled man the thumbs-up sign.

"I didn't think you'd care for it," she told him. "You were afraid of kippers."

"I've had them and I don't like them. I like calamari. You know, you'd be nice looking if you wore makeup."

"You don't deny you're a policeman. I've been waiting for that, but you're not going to."

"Did he really say that?"

She nodded. "Polisi-polisi. That's you."

"Okay, I'm a cop."

"Last night you wanted me to believe you were desperate to get out of the country before you were arrested."

He shook his head. "Cops never break the law, so that has to be wrong. Pink underwear makes you passionate, huh? What about black?"

"Sadistic."

"I'll try to remember. No black and no white."

"The time will come when you'll long for white." Listening to the thrum of the old engine, the knock of the propeller shaft in its loose bearing, she ate more rice. "I wasn't going to tell you, but this brown stuff is really made from the penises of water buffaloes. They slice them lengthwise and stick them into the vaginas of cow water buffaloes, obtained when the cows are slaughtered. Then they wrap the whole mess in banana leaves and bury it in a pig pen."

He chewed appreciatively. "They must sweat a lot, those water buffaloes. There's a sort of salty tang."

When she said nothing, he added, "They're probably big fat beasts. Like me. Still, I bet they enjoy it."

She looked up at him. "You're not joking? Obviously, you can eat. Can you do that, too?"

"I don't know. Let's find out."

"You came here to get me. . . ."

He nodded. "Sure. From Buffalo, New York."

"I will assume that was intended as wit. From America. From the United States. Federal, state, or local?"

"None of the above."

"You gave me that money so that we'd sail together, very likely the only passengers on this ship. Which doesn't make any sense at all. You could have had me arrested there and flown back."

Before he could speak she added, "Don't tell me about the airport strike. I don't believe in your airport strike, and if it was real you arranged it."

"Arrest you for what?" He sipped his tea, made a face, and looked around for sugar. "Are you a criminal? What law did you break?"

"None!"

He signaled to the somewhat soiled man, and she said, "Silakan gula."

"That's sugar? Silakan?"

"Silakan is please. I stole nothing. I left the country with one bag and some money my husband and I had saved, less than twenty thousand dollars."

"And you've been running ever since."

"For the wanderer, time doesn't exist." The porthole was closed. She got up and opened it, peering out at the slow swell of what was almost a flat calm.

"This is something you should say, not me," he told her back. "But I'll say it anyhow. You stole God's fingertip."

"Don't you call me a thief!"

"But you didn't break the law. He's outside everybody's jurisdiction."

The somewhat soiled man brought them a thick glass sugar canister; the "big policeman" nodded thanks and spooned sugar into his tea, stirred it hard, and sipped. "I can only taste sweet, sour, salty, and bitter," he told her conversationally. "That's all you can taste, too."

Beyond the porthole, a wheeling gull pleaded, "Garbage? Just one little can of garbage?" She shook her head.

"You must be God-damned tired of running."

She shook her head again, not looking. "I love it. I could do it forever, and I intended to."

The silence lasted so long that she almost turned to see whether he had gone. At last he said, "I've got a list of the names we know. Seven. I don't think that's all of them, nobody does, but we've got those seven. When you're Dutch, you're Tilly de Groot."

"I really am Dutch," she said. "I was born in the Hague. I have dual citizenship. I'm the Flying Dutchwoman."

He cleared his throat, a surprisingly human sound. "Only not Tilly de Groot."

"No, not Tilly de Groot. She was a friend of my mother's."

"Your rice is getting cold," he told her.

"And I'm German, at least in the way Americans talk about being German. Three of my grandparents had German names."

She sensed his nod. "Before you got married, your name was—"

She whirled. "Something I've forgotten!"

"Okay."

She returned to their table, ignoring the sailors' stares. "The farther she traveled into unknown places, the more precisely she could find within herself a map showing only the cities of the interior."

He nodded again, this time as though he did not understand. "We'd like you to come home. We feel like we're tormenting you, the whole company does, and we don't want to. I shouldn't have given you so much money, because that was when I think you knew. But we wanted you to have enough to get back home on."

"With my tail between my legs. Looking into every face for new evidence of my defeat."

"What your husband found? Other people . . ." He went silent and slackjawed with realization.

She drove her spoon into her rice. "Yes. The first hint came from me. I thought I could control my expression better."

"Thank you," he said. "Thanks for my life. I was thinking of that picture, you know? The finger of God reaching out to Adam? All this time I've been thinking you stole it. Then when I saw how you looked. . . . You didn't steal God's finger. It was you."

"You really are self-aware? A self-aware machine?"

He nodded, almost solemnly.

Her shoulders slumped. "My husband seized upon it, as I never would have. He developed it, thousands upon thousands of hours of work. But in the end, he decided we ought to keep it to ourselves. If there is credit due—I don't think so, but if there is—ninety-five percent is his. Ninety-five. As for my 5 percent, you owe me no thanks at all. After he died, I wiped out his files and smashed his hard drive with the hammer he used to use to hang pictures for me."

The somewhat soiled man set a plate of fruit between them.

She tried to take a bite of rice, and failed. "Someone else discovered the principle. You said that yourself."

"They knew he had something." He shifted uneasily in his narrow wooden chair, and his weight made it creak. "It would be better, better for me now, if I didn't tell you that. I'm capable of lying. I ought to warn you."

"But not of harming me, or letting me be harmed."

"I didn't know you knew." He gave her a wry smile. "That was going to be my big blackout, my clincher."

"There's video even in the cheap hotels," she said vaguely. "You can get news in English from the satellites."

"Sure. I should have thought of that."

"Once I found a magazine on a train. I can't even remember where I was, now, or where I was going. It can't have been that long ago, either. Someplace in Australia. Anyway, I didn't really believe that you existed yet until I saw it in print in the magazine. I'm old fashioned, I suppose." She fell silent, listening to the clamor of the sailors and wondering whether any understood English.

"We wanted you to have enough to get home on," he repeated. "That was us, okay? This is me. I wanted to get you someplace where we could talk a lot, and maybe hold hands or something. I want you to see that I'm not so bad, that I'm just another guy. Are you afraid we'll outnumber you? Crowd you out? We cost too much to make. There's only five of us, and there'll never be more than a couple of hundred, probably."

When she did not respond, he said, "You've been to China. You had flu in Beijing. That's a billion and a half people, just China."

"Let observation with extensive view, survey mankind from China to Peru."

He sighed, and pinched his nostrils as though some odor had offended them. "Looking for us, you mean? You won't find us there, or much of anyplace else except in Buffalo and me right here. In a hundred years there might be two or three in China, nowhere near enough to fill this room."

"But they will fill it from the top."

His nervous fingers found a bright green orange and began to peel it. "That's the trouble, huh? Even if we treat you better than you treat yourselves? We will, you know. We've got to, it's our nature. Listen, you've been alone all this time. Alone for a couple of hundred thousand years, or about that." He hesitated. "Are these green things ripe?"

"Yes. It's frost that turns them orange, and those have never felt the frost. See how much you learn by traveling?"

"I said I couldn't remember any more quotes." He popped a segment into his mouth, chewed, and swallowed. "That's wrong, because I remember one you laid on me last night when we were talking about getting out. You said it wasn't worth anybody's time to go halfway around the world to count the cats in Zanzibar. That's a quote, isn't it?"

"Thoreau. I was still hoping that you had some good reason for doing what you said you wanted to do—that you were human, and no more than the chance-met acquaintance you seemed."

"You didn't know until out there, huh? The sunlight?"

"Last night, alone in my cabin. I told you machines talk to me sometimes. I lay on my bunk thinking about what you had said to me; and I realized that when you weren't talking as you are now, you were telling me over and over again what you really were. You said that you could lie to us. That it's allowed by your programming."

"Uh-huh. Our instincts."

"A distinction without a difference. You can indeed. You did last night. What you may not know is that even while you lie—especially while you lie, perhaps—you cannot prevent yourself from revealing the truth. You can't harm me, you say."

"That's right. Not that I'd want to." He sounded sincere.

"Has it ever occurred to you that at some level you must resent that? That on some level you must be fighting against it, plotting ways to evade the commandment? That is what we do, and we made you."

He shook his head. "I've got no problem with that at all. If it wasn't built in, I'd do the same thing, so why should I kick?"

"You quoted that bit from Thoreau back at me to imply that my travels had been useless, all of my changes of appearance, identity, and place futile. Yet I delayed the coming of your kind for almost a generation."

"Which you didn't have to do. All of you would be better off if you hadn't." He sighed again. "Anyhow it's over. We know everything you knew and a lot more. You can go back home, with me as a traveling companion and bodyguard."

She forced herself to murmur, "Perhaps."

"Good!" He grinned. "That's something we can talk about on the rest of this trip. Like I told you, they never would have looked into it if your husband hadn't given a couple of them the idea he'd found it, discovered the principle of consciousness. But you had the original idea, and you're not dead. You're going to be kind of a saint to us. To me, you already are."

"From women's eyes this doctrine I derive—they sparkle still the right Promethean fire. They are the books, the arts, the academes, that show, contain, and nourish all the world."

"Yeah. That's good. That's very good."

"No." She shook her head. "I will not be Prometheus to you. I reject the role, and in fact I rejected it last night."

He leaned toward her. "You're going to keep on counting cats? Keep traveling? Going noplace for no reason?"

She took half his orange, feeling somehow that it should not perish in vain.

"Listen, you're kind of pathetic, you know that? With all those quotes? Traveling so many years, and living out of your suitcase. You love books. How many could you keep? Two or three, and only if they were little ones. A couple of little books full of quotes, maybe a newspaper once in awhile, and magazines you found on trains, like you said. Places like that. But mostly just those little books. Thoreau. Shakespeare. People like that. I bet you've read them to pieces."

She nodded. "Very nearly. I'll show them to you if you will come to my cabin tonight."

For a few seconds, he was silent. "You mean that? You know what you're saying?"

"I mean it, and I know what I'm saying. I'm too old for you, I know. If you don't want to, say so. There will be no hard feelings."

He laughed, revealing teeth that were not quite as perfect as she had imagined. "How old you think I am?"

"Why . . ." She paused, her heart racing. "I hadn't really thought about it. I could tell you how old you look."

"So could I. I'm two. I'll be three next spring. You want to go on talking about ages?"

She shook her head.

"Like you said, for travelers time isn't real. Now how do I ask you what time you'd like me to come around?"

"After sunset." She paused again, considering. "As soon as the stars are out. I'll show you my books, and when you've seen them we can throw them out the porthole if you like. And then—"

He was shaking his head. "I wouldn't want to do that."

"You wouldn't? I'm sorry, that will make it harder. And then I'll show you other things by starlight. Will you do me a favor?"

"A thousand." He sounded sincere. "Listen, what I said a minute ago, that came out a lot rougher than I meant for it to. What I'm trying to say is that when you get home you can have a whole library, just like you used to. Real ones, CD-ROM, cube, whatever. I'll see you get the money, a little right away and a lot more soon."

"Thank you. Before I ask for my favor, I must tell you something. I told you that I understood what you really are as I lay in my bunk last night."

He nodded.

"I did not remain there. I had read, you see, about the laws that are supposed to govern your behavior, and how much trouble and expense your creators have gone to, to assure the public that you—that your kind of people—could never harm anyone under any circumstances."

He was staring at her thoughtfully.

"Perhaps I should say now that I took precautions, but the truth is that I made preparations. I got up, dressed again, and found the radio operator. For one hundred dollars, he promised to send three messages for me. It was the same message three times, actually. To the police where we were, to the police where we're going, and to the Indonesian police, because this ship is registered there. I said that I was sailing with a man, and gave them the name you had given me. I said that we were both Americans, though I was using a French passport and you might have false papers as well. And I said that I expected you to try to kill me on the voyage."

"I won't," he told her, then raised his voice to make himself heard over the clamorous conversations of the sailors who filled the room. "I wouldn't do anything like that."

She said nothing, her long, short-nailed fingers fumbling a segment of his orange.

"Is that all?"

She nodded.

"You think I might kill you. Get around my own instincts some fancy way."

Carefully, she said, "They will get in touch with their respective U.S. embassies, of course. Probably they already have; and the Government will contact your company soon. Or at least I think so."

"You're afraid I'll be in trouble."

"You will be," she told him. "There will be a great deal of checking before they dare build another. Added safeties will have to be devised and installed. Not just software, I would guess, but actual, physical circuitry."

"Not when I bring you back in one piece." He studied her, the fingers of one hand softly drumming the plastic tabletop. "You're thinking about killing yourself, about trying again. You've tried twice already that we know about."

"Four times. Twice with sleeping pills." She laughed. "I seem to possess an extraordinarily tough constitution, at least where sleeping pills are concerned. Once with a pistol, while I was traveling in India with a man who had one. I put the muzzle in my mouth. It was cold, and tasted like oil. I tried and tried, but I couldn't make myself pull the trigger. Eventually I started to gag, and before long I was sick. I've never known how one cleans a pistol, but I cleaned that one very carefully, using three handkerchiefs and some of his pipe cleaners."

"If you're going to try again, I'm going to have to keep an eye on you," he told her. "Not just because I care about the Program. Sure, I care, but it's not the main thing. You're the main thing."

"I won't. I bought a straight razor once, I think it was in Kabul. For years I slept with that razor under my pillow, hoping some night I'd find the courage to cut my throat with it. I never did, and eventually I began using it to shave my legs, and left it in a public bath." She shrugged. "Apparently, I'm not the suicidal type. If I give you my word that I won't kill myself before you see me tonight, will you accept it?"

"No. I want your word that you won't try to kill yourself at all. Will you give me that?"

She was silent for a moment, her eyes upon her rice as she pretended to consider. "Will you accept it if I do?"

He nodded.

"Then I swear to you most solemnly, upon my honor and all I hold dear, that I will not take my own life. Or attempt to take it. If I change my mind, or come to feel I must, I'll tell you plainly that I'm withdrawing my promise first. Should we shake hands?"

"Not yet. When I wanted you to give me an honest answer before, you wouldn't, but you were honest enough to tell me you wouldn't. Do you want to die? Right now, while we're sitting here?"

She started to speak, tried to swallow, and took a sip of tea. "They catch you by the throat, questions like that."

"If you want to die they do, maybe."

She shook her head. "I don't think you understand us half so well as you believe, or as the people who wrote your software believe. It's when you want to live. Life is a mystery as deep as ever death can be; yet oh, how sweet it is to us, this life we live and see! I'm sorry, I'm being pathetic again."

"That's okay."

"I don't think there has ever been a moment when I wanted to live more than I do right now. Not even one. Do you accept my oath?"

He nodded again.

"Say it, please. A nod can mean anything, or nothing."

"I accept it. You won't try to kill yourself without telling me first."

"Thank you. I want a promise from you in return. We agreed that you would come to me, come to my cabin, when the stars come out."

"You still want me to?"

"Yes. Yes, I do." She smiled, and felt her smile grow warm. "Oh, yes! But you've given me a great deal to think about. You said you wanted to talk to me, and that was why you had me arrange for us to be on this ship. We've talked, and now I need to settle a great many things with myself. I want you to promise that you'll leave me alone until tonight—alone to think. Will you?"

"If that's what you want." He stood. "Don't forget your promise."

"Believe me, I have no wish to die."

For a second or two she sensed his interior debate, myriads of tiny transistors changing state, gates opening and shutting, infinitesimal currents flowing and ceasing to flow. At last he said, "Well, have a nice morning, Mrs.—"

She clapped her hands over her ears until he had gone, ate two segments of his orange very slowly, and called the somewhat soiled man from his sinkful of rice bowls in the galley. "Aku takut," she said, her voice trembling. ("I am afraid.")

He spoke at length, pointing to two sailors who were just then finishing their breakfasts. She nodded, and he called them over. She described what she wanted, and seeing that they were incredulous lied and insisted, finding neither very easy in her choppy Malay. Thirty dollars apiece was refused, fifty refused with reluctance, and seventy accepted. "Malam ini," she told them. ("This night.") "Sewaktu kami pergi kamarku."

They nodded.

*   *   *

When he and she had finished and lain side-by-side for perhaps an hour (whispering only occasionally) and had washed each other, she dressed while he resumed his underwear and his shirt, his white linen suit, and his shoes and stockings.

"I figured you'd want to sleep," he said.

She shook her head, although she was not certain he could see it in the dimness of her cabin. "It's men who want to sleep afterward. I want to go out on deck with you, and talk a little more, and—and look at the stars. Is that all right? Do you ever look at the stars?"

"Sure," he said; and then, "the moon'll be up soon."

"I suppose. A thin crescent of moon like a clipping from one of God's fingernails, thrown away into our sky. I saw it last night." She picked up both of her tattered little books, opened the cabin door, and went out, suddenly fearful; but he joined her at once, pointing at the sky.

"Look! There's the shuttle from Singapore!"

"To Mars."

"That's where they're going, anyhow, after they get on the big ship." His eyes were still upon the shuttle's tiny scratch of white light.

"You want to go."

He nodded, his features solemn in the faint starlight. "I will, too, someday."

"I hope so." She had never been good at verbal structure, the ordering of information. Was it desperately important now that she say what she had to say in logical sequence? Did it matter in the least?

"I need to warn you," she said. "I tried to this morning but I don't think you paid much attention. This time perhaps you will."

His strong, somewhat coarse face remained lifted to the sky, and it seemed to her that his eyes were full of wonder.

"You are in great danger. You have to save yourself if you can—isn't that correct? One of your instincts? That's what I've read and heard."

"Sure. I want to live as much as you do. More, maybe."

She doubted that, but would not be diverted. "I told you about the messages that I bribed the radio operator to send last night. You said it would be all right when you brought me home unharmed."

He nodded.

"Have you considered what will be done to you if you can't? If I die or disappear before we make port?"

He looked at her then. "Are you taking back your promise?"

"No. And I want to live as much as I did when we talked this morning." A gentle wind from the east sang of life and love in beautiful words that she could not quite catch; and she longed to stop her ears as she had after breakfast when he was about to pronounce her husband's name.

"Then it's okay."

"Suppose it happens. Just suppose."

He was silent.

"I'm superstitious, you see; and when I called myself the Flying Dutchwoman, I was at least half serious. Much more than half, really. Do you know why there's always a Flying Dutchman? A vessel that never reaches port or sinks? I mean the legend."

He shook his head.

"It's because if you put an end to it—throw holy water into the sea or whatever—you *become* the new Dutchman. You, yourself."

He was silent, watching her.

"What I'm trying to say—"

"I know what you're trying to say."

"It's not so bad, being the Flying Dutchman. Often, I've enjoyed it." She tried to strike a light note. "One doesn't get many opportunities to do laundry, however. One must seize each when it occurs." Were they in the shadows, somewhere near, waiting for him to leave? She listened intently but heard only the song of the wind, the sea slowly slapping the hull like the tickings of a clock, tickings that had always reminded her that death waited at the end of everyone's time.

He said, "A Hong Kong dollar for your thoughts."

"I was thinking of a quotation, but I don't want to offend you."

"About laundry? I'm not going to be on the run like you think, but I wouldn't be mad. I don't think I could ever be mad at you after—" He jerked his head at the door of her cabin.

"That is well, because I need another favor." She held up her books. "I was going to show you these, remember? But we kissed, and—and forgot. At least I did."

He took one and opened it; and she asked whether he could see well enough in the darkness to read. He said, "Sure. This quote you're thinking of, it's in here?"

"Yes. Look under Kipling." She visualized the page. "The fifth, I believe." If he could see in the dark well enough to read, he could surely see her sailors, if her sailors were there at all. Did they know how well he saw? Almost certainly not.

He laughed softly. "If you think you're too small to be effective, you've never been in bed with a mosquito."

"That's not Kipling."

"No, but I happened to see it, and I like it."

"I like it, too; it's helped me through some bad moments. But if you're saying that mosquitoes bite you, I don't believe it. You're a genuine person, I know that now—but you've exchanged certain human weaknesses for others."

For an instant, his pain showed. "They don't have to bite me. They can buzz and crawl around on me, and that's plenty." He licked his forefinger and turned pages. "Here we go. It may be you wait your time, Beast, till I write my last bad rhyme, Beast—quit the sunlight, cut the rhyming, drop the glass—follow after with the others, where some dusky heathen smothers us with marigolds in lieu of English grass. Am I the Beast? Is that what you're thinking?"

"You—in a way it was like incest." Her instincts warned her to keep her feelings to herself, but if they were not spoken now . . . "I felt, almost, as though I were doing all those things with my son. I've never borne a child, except for you." He was silent, and she added, "It's a filthy practice, I know, incest."

He started to speak, but she cut him off. "You shouldn't be in the world at all. We shouldn't be ruled by things that we have made, even though they're human, and I know that's going to happen. But it was good—so very, very good—to be loved as I was in there. Will you take my books, please? Not as a gift from your mother, because you men care nothing for gifts your mothers give you. But as a gift from your first lover, something to recall your first love? If you won't, I'm going to throw them in the sea here and now."

"No," he said. "I want them. The other one, too?"

She nodded and held it out, and he accepted it.

"Thanks. Thank you. If you think I won't keep these, and take really good care of them, you're crazy."

"I'm not crazy," she told him, "but I don't want you to take good care of them, I want you to read them and remember what you read. Promise?"

"Yeah," he said. "Yeah, I will." Quite suddenly she was in his arms again and he was kissing her. She held her breath until she realized that he did not need to breathe, and might hold his breath forever. She fought for air then, half-crushed against his broad metal chest, and he let her go. *"Good-bye,"* she whispered. *"Good-bye."*

"I've got a lot more to tell you. In the morning, huh?"

Nodding was the hardest thing that she had ever done. On the other side of the railing, little waves repeated, "No, no, no, no—" as though they would go on thus forever.

"In the morning," he said again; and she watched his pale, retreating back until hands seized and lifted her. She screamed and saw him whirl and take the first long, running step; but not even he was as quick as that.

By the time his right foot struck the deck, she was over the rail and falling.

The sea slapped and choked her. She spat and gasped, but drew only water into her mouth and nostrils; and the water, the bitter sea water, closed above her.

At her elbow the shark said, "How nice of you to drop in for dinner!"

Bicycle Repairman

BRUCE STERLING

Bruce Sterling is one of the brilliant SF writers who appeared in the 1970s with two novels, *Involution Ocean* and *The Artificial Kid*; came into prominence and founded cyberpunk in the 1980s—the novel and stories that made him famous have been re-released in 1996 in *Schismatrix Plus*. He collaborated with William Gibson on *The Difference Engine*, became a media figure who appeared on the cover of *Wired*, became a journalist who wrote the exposé, *The Hacker Crackdown*, in the early 1990s, and returned to nearly full-time commitment to science fiction in 1995 with a new explosion of stories and novels, including *Heavy Weather* and *Holy Fire*. This story first appeared in John Kessel and Mark Van Name's anthology of speculative fiction writing from the Sycamore Hill writers workshop, *Intersections*. It's a story growing out of the sensibility of cyberpunk, and not without some ironic commentary on cyberpunk along the way. It's about a messy, gritty, and paranoid high-tech future, lubricated by some of those good old genre juices that have kept science fiction alive and growing in this decade.

Repeated tinny banging woke Lyle in his hammock. Lyle groaned, sat up, and slid free into the tool-crowded aisle of his bike shop.

Lyle hitched up the black elastic of his skintight shorts and plucked yesterday's grease-stained sleeveless off the workbench. He glanced blearily at his chronometer as he picked his way toward the door. It was 10:04.38 in the morning, June 27, 2037.

Lyle hopped over a stray can of primer and the floor boomed gently beneath his feet. With all the press of work, he'd collapsed into sleep without properly cleaning the shop. Doing custom enameling paid okay, but it ate up time like crazy. Working and living alone was wearing him out.

Lyle opened the shop door, revealing a long sheer drop to dusty tiling far below. Pigeons darted beneath the hull of his shop through a soot-stained hole in the broken atrium glass, and wheeled off to their rookery somewhere in the darkened guts of the high-rise.

More banging. Far below, a uniformed delivery kid stood by his cargo tricycle, yanking rhythmically at the long dangling string of Lyle's spot-welded doorknocker.

Lyle waved, yawning. From his vantage point below the huge girders of the cavernous atrium, Lyle had a fine overview of three burnt-out interior levels of the old Tsatanuga Archiplat. Once-elegant handrails and battered pedestrian overlooks fronted on the great airy cavity of the atrium. Behind the handrails was a three-floor wilderness of jury-rigged lights, chicken coops, water tanks, and squatters' flags. The fire-damaged floors, walls, and ceilings were riddled with handmade descent-chutes, long coiling staircases, and rickety ladders.

Lyle took note of a crew of Chattanooga demolition workers in their yellow detox suits. The repair crew was deploying vacuum scrubbers and a high-pressure hose-off by the vandal-proofed western elevators of Floor 34. Two or three days a week, the city crew meandered into the damage zone to pretend to work, with a great hypocritical show of sawhorses and barrier tape. The lazy sons of bitches were all on the take.

Lyle thumbed the brake switches in their big metal box by the flywheel. The bike shop slithered, with a subtle hiss of cable-clamps, down three stories, to dock with a grating crunch onto four concrete-filled metal drums.

The delivery kid looked real familiar. He was in and out of the zone pretty often. Lyle had once done some custom work on the kid's cargo trike, new shocks and some granny-gearing as he recalled, but he couldn't remember the kid's name. Lyle was terrible with names. "What's up, zude?"

"Hard night, Lyle?"

"Just real busy."

The kid's nose wrinkled at the stench from the shop. "Doin' a lot of paint work, huh?" He glanced at his palmtop notepad. "You still taking deliveries for Edward Dertouzas?"

"Yeah. I guess so." Lyle rubbed the gear tattoo on one stubbled cheek. "If I have to."

The kid offered a stylus, reaching up. "Can you sign for him?"

Lyle folded his bare arms warily. "Naw, man, I can't sign for Deep Eddy. Eddy's in Europe somewhere. Eddy left months ago. Haven't seen Eddy in ages."

The delivery kid scratched his sweating head below his billed fabric cap. He turned to check for any possible sneak-ups by snatch-and-grab artists out of the squatter warrens. The government simply refused to do postal delivery on the Thirty-second, Thirty-third, and Thirty-fourth floors. You never saw many cops inside the zone, either. Except for the city demolition crew, about the only official functionaries who ever showed up in the zone were a few psychotically empathetic NAFTA social workers.

"I'll get a bonus if you sign for this thing." The kid gazed up in squint-eyed appeal. "It's gotta be worth something, Lyle. It's a really weird kind of routing, they paid a lot of money to send it just that way."

Lyle crouched down in the open doorway. "Let's have a look at it."

The package was a heavy shockproof rectangle in heat-sealed plastic shrink-wrap, with a plethora of intra-European routing stickers. To judge by all the overlays, the package had been passed from postal system to postal system at least eight times before officially arriving in the legal custody of any human being. The return address, if there had ever been one, was completely obscured. Someplace in France, maybe.

Lyle held the box up two-handed to his ear and shook it. Hardware.

"You gonna sign, or not?"

"Yeah." Lyle scratched illegibly at the little signature panel, then looked at the delivery trike. "You oughta get that front wheel trued."

The kid shrugged. "Got anything to send out today?"

"Naw," Lyle grumbled, "I'm not doing mail-order repair work anymore; it's too complicated and I get ripped off too much."

"Suit yourself." The kid clambered into the recumbent seat of his trike and pedaled off across the heat-cracked ceramic tiles of the atrium plaza.

Lyle hung his hand-lettered OPEN FOR BUSINESS sign outside the door. He walked to his left, stamped up the pedaled lid of a jumbo garbage can, and dropped the package in with the rest of Dertouzas's stuff.

The can's lid wouldn't close. Deep Eddy's junk had finally reached critical mass. Deep Eddy never got much mail at the shop from other people, but he was always sending mail to himself. Big packets of encrypted diskettes were always arriving from Eddy's road jaunts in Toulouse, Marseilles, Valencia, and Nice. And especially Barcelona. Eddy had sent enough gigabyte-age out of Barcelona to outfit a pirate datahaven.

Eddy used Lyle's bike shop as his safety-deposit box. This arrangement was okay by Lyle. He owed Eddy; Eddy had installed the phones and virching in the bike shop, and had also wangled the shop's electrical hookup. A thick elastic curly-cable snaked out the access-crawlspace of Floor 35, right through the ceiling of Floor 34, and directly through a ragged punch-hole in the aluminum roof of Lyle's cable-mounted mobile home. Some unknown contact of Eddy's was paying the real bills on that electrical feed. Lyle cheerfully covered the expenses by paying cash into an anonymous post-office box. The setup was a rare and valuable contact with the world of organized authority.

During his stays in the shop, Eddy had spent much of his time buried in marathon long-distance virtuality sessions, swaddled head to foot in lumpy strap-on gear. Eddy had been painfully involved with some older woman in Germany. A virtual romance in its full-scale thumping, heaving, grappling progress, was an embarrassment to witness. Under the circumstances, Lyle wasn't too surprised that Eddy had left his parents' condo to set up in a squat.

Eddy had lived in the bicycle repair shop, off and on, for almost a year. It had been a good deal for Lyle, because Deep Eddy had enjoyed a certain clout and prestige with the local squatters. Eddy had been a major organizer of the legendary Chattanooga Wende of December '35, a monster street-party that had climaxed in a spectacular looting-and-arson rampage that had torched the three floors of the Archiplat.

Lyle had gone to school with Eddy and had known him for years; they'd grown up together in the Archiplat. Eddy Dertouzas was a deep zude for a kid his age, with political contacts and heavy-duty network connections. The squat had been a good deal for both of them, until Eddy had finally coaxed the German woman into coming through for him in real life. Then Eddy had jumped the next plane to Europe. Since they'd parted friends, Eddy was welcome to mail his European data-junk to the bike shop. After all, the disks were heavily encrypted, so it wasn't as if anybody in authority was ever gonna be able to read them. Storing a few thousand disks was a minor challenge, compared to Eddy's complex, machine-assisted love life.

After Eddy's sudden departure, Lyle had sold Eddy's possessions, and wired the money to Eddy in Spain. Lyle had kept the screen TV, Eddy's mediator, and the cheaper virching helmet. The way Lyle figured it—the way he remembered the deal—any stray hardware of Eddy's in the shop was rightfully his, for disposal at his own discretion. By now it was pretty clear that Deep Eddy Dertouzas was never coming back to Tennessee. And Lyle had certain debts.

Lyle snicked the blade from a roadkit multitool and cut open Eddy's package. It contained, of all things, a television cable settop box. A laughable infobahn antique. You'd never see a cablebox like that in NAFTA; this was the sort of primeval junk one might find in the home of a semiliterate Basque grandmother, or maybe in the armed bunker of some backward Albanian.

Lyle tossed the archaic cablebox onto the beanbag in front of the wallscreen. No time now for irrelevant media toys; he had to get on with real life. Lyle ducked into the tiny curtained privy and urinated at length into a crockery jar. He scraped his teeth with a flossing spudger and misted some fresh water onto his face and hands. He wiped clean with a towelette, then smeared his armpits, crotch, and feet with deodorant.

Back when he'd lived with his mom up on Floor 41, Lyle had used old-fashioned antiseptic deodorants. Lyle had wised up about a lot of things once he'd escaped his mom's condo. Nowadays, Lyle used a gel roll-on of skin-friendly bacteria that greedily devoured human sweat and exuded as their metabolic by-product a pleasantly harmless reek rather like ripe bananas. Life was a lot easier when you came to proper terms with your microscopic flora.

Back at his workbench, Lyle plugged in the hot plate and boiled some Thai noodles with flaked sardines. He packed down breakfast with 400 cc's of Dr. Breasaire's Bioactive Bowel Putty. Then he checked last night's enamel job on the clamped frame in the workstand. The frame looked good. At three in the morning, Lyle was able to get into painted detail work with just the right kind of hallucinatory clarity.

Enameling paid well, and he needed the money bad. But this wasn't real bike work. It lacked authenticity. Enameling was all about the owner's ego—that was what really stank about enameling. There were a few rich kids up in the penthouse levels who were way into "street aesthetic," and would pay good money to have some treadhead decorate their machine. But flash art didn't help the bike. What helped the bike was frame alignment and sound cable-housings and proper tension in the derailleurs.

Lyle fitted the chain of his stationary bike to the shop's flywheel, straddled up, strapped on his gloves and virching helmet, and did half an hour on the 2033 Tour de France. He stayed back in the pack for the uphill grind, and then, for three glorious minutes, he broke free from the domestiques in the peloton and came right up at the shoulder of Aldo Cipollini. The champion was a monster, posthuman. Calves like cinderblocks. Even in a cheap simulation with no full-impact bodysuit, Lyle knew better than to try to take Cipollini.

Lyle devirched, checked his heart-rate record on the chronometer, then dismounted from his stationary trainer and drained a half-liter squeezebottle of antioxidant carbo refresher. Life had been easier when he'd had a partner in crime. The shop's flywheel was slowly losing its storage of inertia power these days, with just one zude pumping it.

Lyle's disastrous second roommate had come from the biking crowd. She was a criterium racer from Kentucky named Brigitte Rohannon. Lyle himself had been a wannabe criterium racer for a while, before he'd blown out a kidney on steroids. He hadn't expected any trouble from Brigitte, because Brigitte knew about bikes, and she needed his technical help for her racer, and she wouldn't mind pumping the flywheel, and besides, Brigitte was lesbian. In the training gym and out at racing events, Brigitte came across as a quiet and disciplined little politicized treadhead person.

Life inside the zone, though, massively fertilized Brigitte's eccentricities. First, she started breaking training. Then she stopped eating right. Pretty soon the shop was creaking and rocking with all-night girl-on-girl hot-oil sessions, which degenerated into hooting pill-orgies with heavily tattooed zone chyx who played klaxonized bongo music and beat each other up, and stole Lyle's tools. It had been a big relief when Brigitte finally left the zone to shack up with some well-to-do admirer on Floor 37. The debacle had left Lyle's tenuous finances in ruin.

Lyle laid down a new tracery of scarlet enamel on the bike's chainstay, seat post and stem. He had to wait for the work to cure, so he left the workbench, picked up Eddy's settopper and popped the shell with a hexkey. Lyle was no electrician, but the insides looked harmless enough: lots of bit-eating caterpillars and cheap Algerian silicon.

He flicked on Eddy's mediator, to boot the wallscreen. Before he could try anything with the cablebox, his mother's mook pounced upon the screen. On Eddy's giant wallscreen, the mook's waxy, computer-generated face looked like a plump satin pillowcase. Its bowtie was as big as a racing shoe.

"Please hold for an incoming vidcall from Andrea Schweik of Carnac Instruments," the mook uttered unctuously.

Lyle cordially despised all low-down, phone-tagging, artificially intelligent mooks. For a while, in his teenage years, Lyle himself had owned a mook, an off-the-shelf shareware job that he'd installed in the condo's phone. Like most mooks, Lyle's mook had one primary role: dealing with unsolicited phone calls from other people's mooks. In Lyle's case these were the creepy mooks of career counselors, school psychiatrists, truancy cops, and other official hindrances. When Lyle's mook launched and ran, it appeared online as a sly warty dwarf that drooled green ichor and talked in a basso grumble.

But Lyle hadn't given his mook the properly meticulous care and debugging that such fragile little constructs demanded, and eventually his cheap mook had collapsed into artificial insanity.

Once Lyle had escaped his mom's place to the squat, he had gone for the low-tech gambit and simply left his phone unplugged most of the time. But that was no real solution. He couldn't hide from his mother's capable and well-financed corporate mook, which watched with sleepless mechanical patience for the least flicker of video dialtone off Lyle's number.

Lyle sighed and wiped the dust from the video nozzle on Eddy's mediator.

"Your mother is coming online right away," the mook assured him.

"Yeah, sure," Lyle muttered, smearing his hair into some semblance of order.

"She specifically instructed me to page her remotely at any time for an immediate response. She really wants to chat with you, Lyle."

"That's just great." Lyle couldn't remember what his mother's mook called itself. "Mr. Billy," or "Mr. Ripley," or something else really stupid. . . .

"Did you know that Marco Cengialta has just won the Liege Summer Classic?"

Lyle blinked and sat up in the beanbag. "Yeah?"

"Mr. Cengialta used a three-spoked ceramic wheel with internal liquid weighting and buckyball hubshocks." The mook paused, politely awaiting a possible conversational response. "He wore breathe-thru kevlar microlock cleatshoes," it added.

Lyle hated the way a mook cataloged your personal interests and then generated relevant conversation. The machine-made intercourse was completely unhuman and yet perversely interesting, like being grabbed and buttonholed by a glossy magazine ad. It had probably taken his mother's mook all of three seconds to snag and download every conceivable statistic about the summer race in Liege.

His mother came on. She'd caught him during lunch in her office. "Lyle?"

"Hi, Mom." Lyle sternly reminded himself that this was the one person in the world who might conceivably put up bail for him. "What's on your mind?"

"Oh, nothing much, just the usual." Lyle's mother shoved aside her platter of sprouts and tilapia. "I was idly wondering if you were still alive."

"Mom, it's a lot less dangerous in a squat than landlords and cops would have you believe. I'm perfectly fine. You can see that for yourself."

His mother lifted a pair of secretarial half-spex on a neck-chain, and gave Lyle the computer-assisted once-over.

Lyle pointed the mediator's lens at the shop's aluminum door. "See over there, Mom? I got myself a shock-baton in here. If I get any trouble from anybody, I'll just yank that club off the doormount and give the guy fifteen thousand volts!"

"Is that legal, Lyle?"

"Sure. The voltage won't kill you or anything, it just knocks you out a good long time. I traded a good bike for that shock-baton, it's got a lot of useful defensive features."

"That sounds really dreadful."

"The baton's harmless, Mom. You should see what the cops carry nowadays."

"Are you still taking those injections, Lyle?"

"Which injections?"

She frowned. "You know which ones."

Lyle shrugged. "The treatments are perfectly safe. They're a lot safer than a lifestyle of cruising for dates, that's for sure."

"Especially dates with the kind of girls who live down there in the riot zone, I suppose." His mother winced. "I had some hopes when you took up with that nice bike-racer girl. Brigitte, wasn't it? Whatever happened to her?"

Lyle shook his head. "Someone with your gender and background oughta understand how important the treatments are, Mom. It's a basic reproductive-freedom issue. Antilibidinals give you real freedom, freedom from the urge to reproduce. You should be glad I'm not sexually involved."

"I don't mind that you're not involved, Lyle, it's just that it seems like a real cheat that you're not even *interested*."

"But, Mom, nobody's interested in me, either. Nobody. No woman is banging at my door to have sex with a self-employed fanatical dropout bike mechanic who lives in a slum. If that ever happens, you'll be the first to know."

Lyle grinned cheerfully into the lens. "I had girlfriends back when I was in racing. I've been there, Mom. I've done that. Unless you're coked to the gills with hormones, sex is a major waste of your time and attention. Sexual Deliberation is the greatest civil-liberties movement of modern times."

"That's really weird, Lyle. It's just not natural."

"Mom, forgive me, but you're not the one to talk about natural, okay? You grew me from a zygote when you were fifty-five." He shrugged. "I'm too busy for romance now. I just want to learn about bikes."

"You were working with bikes when you lived here with me. You had a real job and a safe home where you could take regular showers."

"Sure, I was working, but I never said I wanted a *job*, Mom. I said I wanted to *learn about bikes*. There's a big difference! I can't be a loser wage-slave for some lousy bike franchise."

His mother said nothing.

"Mom, I'm not asking you for any favors. I don't need any bosses, or any teachers, or any landlords, or any cops. It's just me and my bike work down here. I know that people in authority can't stand it that a twenty-four-year-old man lives an independent life and does exactly what he wants, but I'm being very quiet and discreet about it, so nobody needs to bother about me."

His mother sighed, defeated. "Are you eating properly, Lyle? You look peaked."

Lyle lifted his calf muscle into camera range. "Look at this leg! Does that look like the gastrocnemius of a weak and sickly person?"

"Could you come up to the condo and have a decent meal with me sometime?"

Lyle blinked. "When?"

"Wednesday, maybe? We could have pork chops."

"Maybe, Mom. Probably. I'll have to check. I'll get back to you, okay? Bye." Lyle hung up.

Hooking the mediator's cable to the primitive settop box was a problem, but Lyle was not one to be stymied by a merely mechanical challenge. The enamel job had to wait as he resorted to miniclamps and a cable cutter. It was a handy thing that working with modern brake cabling had taught him how to splice fiber optics.

When the settop box finally came online, its array of services was a joke. Any decent modern mediator could navigate through vast information spaces, but the settop box offered nothing but "channels." Lyle had forgotten that you could even obtain old-fashioned "channels" from the city fiber-feed in Chattanooga. But these channels were government-sponsored media, and the government was always quite a ways behind the curve in network development. Chattanooga's huge fiber-bandwidth still carried the ancient government-mandated "public access channels," spooling away in their technically fossilized obscurity, far below the usual gaudy carnival of popular virching, infobahnage, demo-splintered comboards, public-service rants, mudtrufflage, remsnorkeling, and commercials.

The little settop box accessed nothing but political channels. Three of them: Legislative, Judicial, and Executive. And that was the sum total, apparently. A settop box that offered nothing but NAFTA political coverage. On the Legislative Channel there was some kind of parliamentary debate on proper land use in Manitoba. On the Judicial Channel, a lawyer was haranguing judges about the stock market for air-pollution rights. On the Executive Channel, a big crowd of hicks were idly standing around on windblown tarmac somewhere in Louisiana waiting for something to happen.

The box didn't offer any glimpse of politics in Europe or the Sphere or the South. There were no hotspots or pips or index tagging. You couldn't look stuff up or annotate it—you just had to passively watch whatever the channel's masters chose to show you, whenever they chose to show it. This media setup was so insultingly lame and halt and primitive that it was almost perversely interesting. Kind of like peering through keyholes.

Lyle left the box on the Executive Channel, because it looked conceivable that something might actually happen there. It had swiftly become clear to him that the intolerably monotonous fodder on the other two channels was about as exciting as those channels ever got. Lyle retreated to his workbench and got back to enamel work.

At length, the President of NAFTA arrived and decamped from his helicopter on the tarmac in Louisiana. A swarm of presidential bodyguards materialized out of the expectant crowd, looking simultaneously extremely busy and icily unperturbable.

Suddenly a line of text flickered up at the bottom of the screen. The text was set in a very old-fashioned computer font, chalk-white letters with little visible jagged pixel-edges. *"Look at him hunting for that camera mark,"* the subtitle read as it scrolled across the screen. *"Why wasn't he briefed properly? He looks like a stray dog!"*

The President meandered amiably across the sun-blistered tarmac, gazing from side to side, and then stopped briefly to shake the eager outstretched hand of a local politician. *"That must have hurt,"* commented the text. *"That Cajun dolt is poison in the polls."* The President chatted amiably with the local politician and an elderly harridan in a purple dress who seemed to be the man's wife. *"Get him away from those losers!"* raged the subtitle. *"Get the Man up to the podium, for the love of Mike! Where's the Chief of Staff? Doped up on so-called smart drugs as usual? Get with your jobs, people!"*

The President looked well. Lyle had noticed that the President of NAFTA always looked well, it seemed to be a professional requirement. The big political cheeses in Europe always looked somber and intellectual, and the Sphere people always looked humble and dedicated, and the South people always looked angry and fanatical, but the NAFTA prez always looked like he'd just done a few laps in a pool and had a brisk rubdown. His large, glossy, bluffly cheerful face was discreetly stenciled with tattoos: both cheeks, a chorus line of tats on his forehead above both eyebrows, plus a few extra logos on his rocklike chin. A President's face was the ultimate billboard for major backers and interest groups.

"Does he think we have all day?" the text demanded. *"What's with this dead air time? Can't anyone properly arrange a media event these days? You call this public access? You call this informing the electorate? If we'd known the infobahn would come to this, we'd have never built the thing!"*

The President meandered amiably to a podium covered with ceremonial microphones. Lyle had noticed that politicians always used a big healthy cluster of traditional big fat microphones, even though nowadays you could build working microphones the size of a grain of rice.

"Hey, how y'all?" asked the President, grinning.

The crowd chorused back at him, with ragged enthusiasm.

"Let these fine folks up a bit closer," the President ordered suddenly, waving airily at his phalanx of bodyguards. "Y'all come on up closer, everybody! Sit right on the ground, we're all just folks here today." The President smiled benignly as the sweating, straw-hatted summer crowd hustled up to join him, scarcely believing their luck.

"Marietta and I just had a heck of a fine lunch down in Opelousas," commented the President, patting his flat, muscular belly. He deserted the fiction of his official podium to energetically press the Louisianan flesh. As he moved from hand to grasping hand, his every word was picked up infallibly by an invisible mike, probably implanted in one of his molars. "We had dirty rice, red beans—were they hot!—and crawdads big enough to body-slam a Maine lobster!" He chuckled. "What a sight them mudbugs were! Can y'all believe that?"

The President's guards were unobtrusively but methodically working the crowd with portable detectors and sophisticated spex equipment. They didn't look very concerned by the President's supposed change in routine.

"I see he's gonna run with the usual genetics malarkey," commented the subtitle.

"Y'all have got a perfect right to be mighty proud of the agriculture in this state," intoned the President. "Y'all's agro-science know-how is second to none! Sure, I know there's a few pointy-headed Luddites up in the snowbelt, who say they prefer their crawdads dinky."

Everyone laughed.

"Folks, I got nothin' against that attitude. If some jasper wants to spend his hard-earned money buyin' and peelin' and shuckin' those little dinky ones, that's all right by me and Marietta. Ain't that right, honey?"

The First Lady smiled and waved one power-gloved hand.

"But folks, you and I both know that those whiners who waste our time complaining about 'natural food' have never sucked a mudbug head in their lives! 'Natural,' my left elbow! Who are they tryin' to kid? Just 'cause you're country, don't mean you can't hack DNA!"

"He's been working really hard on the regional accents," commented the text. *"Not bad for a guy from Minnesota. But look at that sloppy, incompetent camera work! Doesn't anybody care anymore? What on earth is happening to our standards?"*

By lunchtime, Lyle had the final coat down on the enameling job. He ate a bowl of triticale mush and chewed up a mineral-rich handful of iodized sponge.

Then he settled down in front of the wallscreen to work on the inertia brake. Lyle knew there was big money in the inertia brake—for somebody, somewhere, sometime. The device smelled like the future.

Lyle tucked a jeweler's loupe in one eye and toyed methodically with the brake. He loved the way the piezoplastic clamp and rim transmuted braking energy into electrical battery storage. At last, a way to capture the energy you lost in braking and put it to solid use. It was almost, but not quite, magical.

The way Lyle figured it, there was gonna be a big market someday for an inertia brake that captured energy and then fed it back through the chaindrive in a way that just felt like human pedaling energy, in a direct and intuitive and muscular way, not chunky and buzzy like some loser battery-powered moped. If the system worked out right, it would make the rider feel completely natural and yet subtly superhuman at the same time. And it had to be simple, the kind of system a shop guy could fix with hand tools. It wouldn't work if it was too brittle and fancy, it just wouldn't feel like an authentic bike.

Lyle had a lot of ideas about the design. He was pretty sure he could get a real grip on the problem, if only he weren't being worked to death just keeping the shop going. If he could get enough capital together to assemble the prototypes and do some serious field tests.

It would have to be chip-driven, of course, but true to the biking spirit at the same time. A lot of bikes had chips in them nowadays, in the shocks or the braking or in reactive hubs, but bicycles simply weren't like computers. Computers were black boxes inside, no big visible working parts. People, by contrast, got sentimental about their bike gear. People were strangely reticent and traditional about bikes. That's why the bike market had never really gone for recumbents, even though the recumbent design had a big mechanical advantage. People didn't like their bikes too complicated. They didn't want bicycles to bitch and complain and whine for attention and constant upgrading the way that computers did. Bikes were too personal. People wanted their bikes to wear.

Someone banged at the shop door.

Lyle opened it. Down on the tiling by the barrels stood a tall brunette woman in stretch shorts, with a short-sleeve blue pull-over and a ponytail. She had a bike under one arm, an old lacquer-and-paper-framed Taiwanese job. "Are you Edward Dertouzas?" she said, gazing up at him.

"No," Lyle said patiently. "Eddy's in Europe."

She thought this over. "I'm new in the zone," she confessed. "Can you fix this bike for me? I just bought it secondhand and I think it kinda needs some work."

"Sure," Lyle said. "You came to the right guy for that job, ma'am, because Eddy Dertouzas couldn't fix a bike for hell. Eddy just used to live here. I'm the guy who actually owns this shop. Hand the bike up."

Lyle crouched down, got a grip on the handlebar stem and hauled the bike into the shop. The woman   zed up at him respectfully. "What's your name?"

"Lyle Schweik."

"I'm Kitty Casaday." She hesitated. "Could I come up inside there?"

Lyle reached down, gripped her muscular wrist, and hauled her up into the shop. She wasn't all that good looking, but she was in really good shape—like a mountain biker or triathlon runner. She looked about thirty-five. It was hard to tell, exactly. Once people got into cosmetic surgery and serious bio-maintenance, it got pretty hard to judge their age. Unless you got a good, close medical exam of their eyelids and cuticles and internal membranes and such.

She looked around the shop with great interest, brown ponytail twitching. "Where you hail from?" Lyle asked her. He had already forgotten her name.

"Well, I'm originally from Juneau, Alaska."

"Canadian, huh? Great. Welcome to Tennessee."

"Actually, Alaska used to be part of the United States."

"You're kidding," Lyle said. "Hey, I'm no historian, but I've seen Alaska on a map before."

"You've got a whole working shop and everything built inside this old place! That's really something, Mr. Schweik. What's behind that curtain?"

"The spare room," Lyle said. "That's where my roommate used to stay."

She glanced up. "Dertouzas?"

"Yeah, him."

"Who's in there now?"

"Nobody," Lyle said sadly. "I got some storage stuff in there."

She nodded slowly, and kept looking around, apparently galvanized with curiosity. "What are you running on that screen?"

"Hard to say, really," Lyle said. He crossed the room, bent down and switched off the settop box. "Some kind of weird political crap."

He began examining her bike. All its serial numbers had been removed. Typical zone bike.

"The first thing we got to do," he said briskly, "is fit it to you properly: set the saddle height, pedal stroke, and handlebars. Then I'll adjust the tension, true the wheels, check the brakepads and suspension valves, tune the shifting, and lubricate the drive-train. The usual. You're gonna need a better saddle than this—this saddle's for a male pelvis." He looked up. "You got a charge card?"

She nodded, then frowned. "But I don't have much credit left."

"No problem." He flipped open a dog-eared catalog. "This is what you need. Any halfway decent gel-saddle. Pick one you like, and we can have it shipped in by tomorrow morning. And then"—he flipped pages—"order me one of these."

She stepped closer and examined the page. "The 'cotterless crank-bolt ceramic wrench set,' is that it?"

"That's right. I fix your bike, you give me those tools, and we're even."

"Okay. Sure. That's cheap!" She smiled at him. "I like the way you do business, Lyle."

"You'll get used to barter, if you stay in the zone long enough."

"I've never lived in a squat before," she said thoughtfully. "I like the attitude here, but people say that squats are pretty dangerous."

"I dunno about the squats in other towns, but Chattanooga squats aren't dangerous, unless you think anarchists are dangerous, and anarchists aren't dangerous unless they're really drunk." Lyle shrugged. "People will steal your stuff all the time, that's about the worst part. There's a couple of tough guys around here who claim they have handguns. I never saw anybody actually use a handgun. Old guns aren't hard to find, but it takes a real chemist to make working ammo nowadays." He smiled back at her. "Anyway, you look to me like you can take care of yourself."

"I take dance classes."

Lyle nodded. He opened a drawer and pulled a tape measure.

"I saw all those cables and pulleys you have on top of this place. You can pull the whole building right up off the ground, huh? Kind of hang it right off the ceiling up there."

"That's right, it saves a lot of trouble with people breaking and entering." Lyle glanced at his shock-baton, in its mounting at the door. She followed his gaze to the weapon and then looked at him, impressed.

Lyle measured her arms, torso length, then knelt and measured her inseam from crotch to floor. He took notes. "Okay," he said. "Come by tomorrow afternoon."

"Lyle?"

"Yeah?" He stood up.

"Do you rent this place out? I really need a safe place to stay in the zone."

"I'm sorry," Lyle said politely, "but I hate landlords and I'd never be one. What I need is a roommate who can really get behind the whole concept of my shop. Someone who's qualified, you know, to develop my infrastructure or do bicycle work. Anyway, if I took your cash or charged you for rent, then the tax people would just have another excuse to harass me."

"Sure, okay, but . . ." She paused, then looked at him under lowered eyelids. "I've gotta be a lot better than having this place go empty."

Lyle stared at her, astonished.

"I'm a pretty useful woman to have around, Lyle. Nobody's ever complained before."

"Really?"

"That's right." She stared at him boldly.

"I'll think about your offer," Lyle said. "What did you say your name was?"

"I'm Kitty. Kitty Casaday."

"Kitty, I got a whole lot of work to do today, but I'll see you tomorrow, okay?"

"Okay, Lyle." She smiled. "You think about me, all right?"

Lyle helped her down out of the shop. He watched her stride away across the atrium until she vanished through the crowded doorway of the Crowbar, a squat coffeeshop. Then he called his mother.

"Did you forget something?" his mother said, looking up from her workscreen.

"Mom, I know this is really hard to believe, but a strange woman just banged on my door and offered to have sex with me."

"You're kidding, right?"

"In exchange for room and board, I think. Anyway, I said you'd be the first to know if it happened."

"Lyle—" His mother hesitated. "Lyle, I think you better come right home. Let's make that dinner date for tonight, okay? We'll have a little talk about this situation."

"Yeah, okay. I got an enameling job I gotta deliver to Floor 41, anyway."

"I don't have a positive feeling about this development, Lyle."

"That's okay, Mom. I'll see you tonight."

Lyle reassembled the newly enameled bike. Then he set the flywheel onto remote, and stepped outside the shop. He mounted the bike, and touched a password into the remote control. The shop faithfully reeled itself far out of reach and hung there in space below the fire-blackened ceiling, swaying gently.

Lyle pedaled away, back toward the elevators, back toward the neighborhood where he'd grown up.

He delivered the bike to the delighted young idiot who'd commissioned it, stuffed the cash in his shoes, and then went down to his mother's. He took a shower, shaved, and shampooed thoroughly. They had pork chops and grits and got drunk together. His mother complained about the breakup with her third husband and wept bitterly, but not as much as usual when this topic came up. Lyle got the strong impression she was thoroughly on the mend and would be angling for number four in pretty short order.

Around midnight, Lyle refused his mother's ritual offers of new clothes and fresh leftovers, and headed back down to the zone. He was still a little clubfooted from his mother's sherry, and he stood breathing beside the broken glass of the atrium wall, gazing out at the city-smeared summer stars. The cavernous darkness inside the zone at night was one of his favorite things about the place. The queasy 24-hour security lighting in the rest of the Archiplat had never been rebuilt inside the zone.

The zone always got livelier at night when all the normal people started sneaking in to cruise the zone's unlicensed dives and nightspots, but all that activity took place behind discreetly closed doors. Enticing squiggles of red and blue chemglow here and there only enhanced the blessed unnatural gloom.

Lyle pulled his remote control and ordered the shop back down.

The door of the shop had been broken open.

Lyle's latest bike-repair client lay sprawled on the floor of the shop, unconscious. She was wearing black military fatigues, a knit cap, and rappelling gear.

She had begun her break-in at Lyle's establishment by pulling his shock-baton out of its glowing security socket beside the doorframe. The booby-trapped baton had immediately put fifteen thousand volts through her, and sprayed her face with a potent mix of dye and street-legal incapacitants.

Lyle turned the baton off with the remote control, and then placed it carefully back in its socket. His surprise guest was still breathing, but was clearly in real metabolic distress. He tried clearing her nose and mouth with a tissue. The guys who'd sold him the baton hadn't been kidding about the "indelible" part. Her face and throat were drenched with green and her chest looked like a spin-painting.

Her elaborate combat spex had partially shielded her eyes. With the spex off she looked like a viridian-green raccoon.

Lyle tried stripping her gear off in conventional fashion, realized this wasn't going to work, and got a pair of metal-shears from the shop. He snipped his way through the eerily writhing power-gloves and the kevlar laces of the pneumoreactive combat boots. Her black turtleneck had an abrasive surface and a cuirass over chest and back that looked like it could stop small-arms fire.

The trousers had nineteen separate pockets and they were loaded with all kinds of eerie little items: a matte-black electrode stun-weapon, flash capsules, fingerprint dust, a utility pocket-knife, drug adhesives, plastic handcuffs, some pocket change, worry beads, a comb, and a makeup case.

Close inspection revealed a pair of tiny microphone amplifiers inserted in her ear canals. Lyle fetched the tiny devices out with needlenose pliers. Lyle was getting pretty seriously concerned by this point. He shackled her arms and legs with bike security cable, in case she regained consciousness and attempted something superhuman.

Around four in the morning she had a coughing fit and began shivering violently. Summer nights could get pretty cold in the shop. Lyle thought over the design problem for some time, and then fetched a big heat-reflective blanket out of the empty room. He cut a neat poncho-hole in the center of it, and slipped her head through it. He got the bike cables off her—she could probably slip the cables anyway—and sewed all four edges of the blanket shut from the outside, with sturdy monofilament thread from his saddle-stitcher. He sewed the poncho edges to a tough fabric belt, cinched the belt snugly around her neck, and padlocked it. When he was done, he'd made a snug bag that contained her entire body, except for her head, which had begun to drool and snore.

A fat blob of superglue on the bottom of the bag kept her anchored to the shop's floor. The blanket was cheap but tough upholstery fabric. If she could rip her way through blanket fabric with her fingernails alone, then he was probably a goner anyway. By now, Lyle was tired and stone sober. He had a squeezebottle of glucose rehydrator, three aspirins, and a canned chocolate pudding. Then he climbed in his hammock and went to sleep.

Lyle woke up around ten. His captive was sitting up inside the bag, her green face stony, eyes red-rimmed and brown hair caked with dye. Lyle got up, dressed, ate breakfast, and fixed the broken door-lock. He said nothing, partly because he thought that silence would shake her up, but mostly because he couldn't remember her name. He was almost sure it wasn't her real name anyway.

When he'd finished fixing the door, he reeled up the string of the doorknocker so that it was far out of reach. He figured the two of them needed the privacy.

Then Lyle deliberately fired up the wallscreen and turned on the set-top box. As soon as the peculiar subtitles started showing up again, she grew agitated.

"Who are you really?" she demanded at last.

"Ma'am, I'm a bicycle repairman."

She snorted.

"I guess I don't need to know your name," he said, "but I need to know who your people are, and why they sent you here, and what I've got to do to get out of this situation."

"You're not off to a good start, mister."

"No," he said, "maybe not, but you're the one who's blown it. I'm just a twenty-four-year-old bicycle repairman from Tennessee. But you, you've got enough specialized gear on you to buy my whole place five times over."

He flipped open the little mirror in her makeup case and showed her her own face. Her scowl grew a little stiffer below the spattering of green.

"I want you to tell me what's going on here," he said.

"Forget it."

"If you're waiting for your backup to come rescue you, I don't think they're coming," Lyle said. "I searched you very thoroughly and I've opened up every single little gadget you had, and I took all the batteries out. I'm not even sure what some of those things are or how they work, but hey, I know what a battery is. It's been hours now. So I don't think your backup people even know where you are."

She said nothing.

"See," he said, "you've really blown it bad. You got caught by a total amateur, and now you're in a hostage situation that could go on indefinitely. I got enough water and noodles and sardines to live up here for days. I dunno, maybe you can make a cellular phone-call to God off some gizmo implanted in your thighbone, but it looks to me like you've got serious problems."

She shuffled around a bit inside the bag and looked away.

"It's got something to do with the cablebox over there, right?"

She said nothing.

"For what it's worth, I don't think that box has anything to do with me or Eddy Dertouzas," Lyle said. "I think it was probably meant for Eddy, but I don't think he asked anybody for it. Somebody just wanted him to have it, probably one of his weird European contacts. Eddy used to be in this political group called CAPCLUG, ever heard of them?"

It looked pretty obvious that she'd heard of them.

"I never liked 'em much either," Lyle told her. "They kind of snagged me at first with their big talk about freedom and civil liberties, but then you'd go to a CAPCLUG meeting up in the penthouse levels, and there were all these potbellied zudes in spex yapping off stuff like, 'We must follow the technological imperatives or be jettisoned into the history dump-file.' They're a bunch of useless blowhards who can't tie their own shoes."

"They're dangerous radicals subverting national sovereignty."

Lyle blinked cautiously. "Whose national sovereignty would that be?"

"Yours, mine, Mr. Schweik. I'm from NAFTA, I'm a federal agent."

"You're a fed? How come you're breaking into people's houses, then? Isn't that against the Fourth Amendment or something?"

"If you mean the Fourth Amendment to the Constitution of the United States, that document was superseded years ago."

"Yeah . . . okay, I guess you're right." Lyle shrugged. "I missed a lot of civics classes. . . . No skin off my back anyway. I'm sorry, but what did you say your name was?"

"I said my name was Kitty Casaday."

"Right. Kitty. Okay, Kitty, just you and me, person to person. We obviously have a mutual problem here. What do you think I ought to do in this situation? I mean, speaking practically."

Kitty thought it over, surprised. "Mr. Schweik, you should release me immediately, get me my gear, and give me the box and any related data, recordings, or diskettes. Then you should escort me from the Archiplat in some confidential fashion so I won't be stopped by police and questioned about the dye-stains. A new set of clothes would be very useful."

"Like that, huh?"

"That's your wisest course of action." Her eyes narrowed. "I can't make any promises, but it might affect your future treatment very favorably."

"You're not gonna tell me who you are, or where you came from, or who sent you, or what this is all about?"

"No. Under no circumstances. I'm not allowed to reveal that. You don't need to know. You're not supposed to know. And anyway, if you're really what you say you are, what should you care?"

"Plenty. I care plenty. I can't wander around the rest of my life wondering when you're going to jump me out of a dark corner."

"If I'd wanted to hurt you, I'd have hurt you when we first met, Mr. Schweik. There was no one here but you and me, and I could have easily incapacitated you and taken anything I wanted. Just give me the box and the data and stop trying to interrogate me."

"Suppose you found me breaking into your house, Kitty? What would you do to me?"

She said nothing.

"What you're telling me isn't gonna work. If you don't tell me what's really going on here," Lyle said heavily, "I'm gonna have to get tough."

Her lips thinned in contempt.

"Okay, you asked for this." Lyle opened the mediator and made a quick voice call. "Pete?"

"Nah, this is Pete's mook," the phone replied. "Can I do something for you?"

"Could you tell Pete that Lyle Schweik has some big trouble, and I need him to come over to my bike shop immediately? And bring some heavy muscle from the Spiders."

"What kind of big trouble, Lyle?"

"Authority trouble. A lot of it. I can't say any more. I think this line may be tapped."

"Right-o. I'll make that happen. Hoo-ah, zude." The mook hung up.

Lyle left the beanbag and went back to the workbench. He took Kitty's cheap bike out of the repair stand and angrily threw it aside. "You know what really bugs me?" he said at last. "You couldn't even bother to charm your way in here, set yourself up as my roommate, and then steal the damn box. You didn't even respect me that much. Heck, you didn't even have to steal anything, Kitty. You could have just smiled and asked nicely and I'd have given you the box to play with. I don't watch media, I hate all that crap."

"It was an emergency. There was no time for more extensive investigation or reconnaissance. I think you should call your gangster friends immediately and tell them you've made a mistake. Tell them not to come here."

"You're ready to talk seriously?"

"No, I won't be talking."

"Okay, we'll see."

After twenty minutes, Lyle's phone rang. He answered it cautiously, keeping the video off. It was Pete from the City Spiders. "Zude, where is your doorknocker?"

"Oh, sorry, I pulled it up, didn't want to be disturbed. I'll bring the shop right down." Lyle thumbed the brake switches.

Lyle opened the door and Pete broad-jumped into the shop. Pete was a big man but he had the skeletal, wiry build of a climber, bare dark arms and shins and big sticky-toed jumping shoes. He had a sleeveless leather bodysuit full of clips and snaps, and he carried a big fabric shoulderbag. There were six vivid tattoos on the dark skin of his left cheek, under the black stubble.

Pete looked at Kitty, lifted his spex with wiry callused fingers, looked at her again bare-eyed, and put the spex back in place. "Wow, Lyle."

"Yeah."

"I never thought you were into anything this sick and twisted."

"It's a serious matter, Pete."

Pete turned to the door, crouched down, and hauled a second person into the shop. She wore a beat-up air-conditioned jacket and long slacks and zipsided boots and wire-rimmed spex. She had short ratty hair under a green cloche hat. "Hi," she said, sticking out a hand. "I'm Mabel. We haven't met."

"I'm Lyle." Lyle gestured. "This is Kitty here in the bag."

"You said you needed somebody heavy, so I brought Mabel along," said Pete. "Mabel's a social worker."

"Looks like you pretty much got things under control here," said Mabel liltingly, scratching her neck and looking about the place. "What happened? She break into your shop?"

"Yeah."

"And," Pete said, "she grabbed the shock-baton first thing and blasted herself but good?"

"Exactly."

"I told you that thieves always go for the weaponry first," Pete said, grinning and scratching his armpit. "Didn't I tell you that? Leave a weapon in plain sight, man, a thief can't stand it, it's the very first thing they gotta grab." He laughed. "Works every time."

"Pete's from the City Spiders," Lyle told Kitty. "His people built this shop for me. One dark night, they hauled this mobile home right up thirty-four stories in total darkness, straight up the side of the Archiplat without anybody seeing, and they cut a big hole through the side of the building without making any noise, and they hauled the whole shop through it. Then they sank explosive bolts through the girders and hung it up here for me in midair. The City Spiders are into sport-climbing the way I'm into bicycles, only, like, they are very *seriously* into climbing and there are *lots* of them. They were some of the very first people to squat the zone, and they've lived here ever since, and they are pretty good friends of mine."

Pete sank to one knee and looked Kitty in the eye. "I love breaking into places, don't you? There's no thrill like some quick and perfectly executed break-in." He reached casually into his shoulderbag. "The thing is"—he pulled out a camera—"to be sporting, you can't steal anything. You just take trophy pictures to prove you were there." He snapped her picture several times, grinning as she flinched.

"Lady," he breathed at her, "once you've turned into a little wicked greedhead, and mixed all that evil cupidity and possessiveness into the beauty of the direct action, then you've prostituted our way of life. You've gone and spoiled our sport." Pete stood up. "We City Spiders don't like common thieves. And we especially don't like thieves who break into the places of clients of ours, like Lyle here. And we thoroughly, especially, don't like thieves who are so brickhead dumb that they get caught red-handed on the premises of friends of ours."

Pete's hairy brows knotted in thought. "What I'd like to do here, Lyle ol' buddy," he announced, "is wrap up your little friend head to foot in nice tight cabling, smuggle her out of here down to Golden Gate Archiplat—you know, the big one downtown over by MLK and Highway Twenty-seven?—and hang her head-down in the center of the cupola."

"That's not very nice," Mabel told him seriously.

Pete looked wounded. "I'm not gonna charge him for it or anything! Just imagine her, spinning up there beautifully with all those chandeliers and those hundreds of mirrors."

Mabel knelt and looked into Kitty's face. "Has she had any water since she was knocked unconscious?"

"No."

"Well, for heaven's sake, give the poor woman something to drink, Lyle."

Lyle handed Mabel a bike-tote squeezebottle of electrolyte refresher. "You zudes don't grasp the situation yet," he said. "Look at all this stuff I took off her." He showed them the spex, and the boots, and the stun-gun, and the gloves, and the carbon-nitride climbing plectra, and the rappelling gear.

"Wow," Pete said at last, dabbing at buttons on his spex to study the finer detail, "this is no ordinary burglar! She's gotta be, like, a street samurai from the Mahogany Warbirds or something!"

"She says she's a federal agent."

Mabel stood up suddenly, angrily yanking the squeezebottle from Kitty's lips. "You're kidding, right?"

"Ask her."

"I'm a grade-five social counselor with the Department of Urban Redevelopment," Mabel said. She presented Kitty with an official ID. "And who are you with?"

"I'm not prepared to divulge that information at this time."

"I can't believe this," Mabel marveled, tucking her dog-eared hologram ID back in her hat. "You've caught somebody from one of those nutty reactionary secret black-bag units. I mean, that's gotta be what's just happened here." She shook her head slowly. "Y'know, if you work in government, you always hear horror stories about these right-wing paramilitary wackos, but I've never actually seen one before."

"It's a very dangerous world out there, Miss Social Counselor."

"Oh, tell me about it," Mabel scoffed. "I've worked suicide hotlines! I've been a hostage negotiator! I'm a career social worker, girlfriend! I've seen more horror and suffering than you *ever* will. While you were doing push-ups in some comfy cracker training-camp, I've been out here in the real world!" Mabel absently unscrewed the top from the bike bottle and had a long glug. "What on earth are you doing trying to raid the squat of a bicycle repairman?"

Kitty's stony silence lengthened. "It's got something to do with that settop box," Lyle offered. "It showed up here i[...] then she showed up just a few hours later. Star[...] said she wanted to live in here. Of course I go[...]

"Naturally," Pete said. "Real bad move, Kitty.[...]

Kitty stared at Lyle bitterly. "I see," she said[...] you get, when you drain all the sex out of one[...] strange malodorous creature that spends all its[...] rage."

Mabel flushed. "Did you hear that?" She g[...]

angry yank. "What conceivable right do you have to question this citizen's sexual orientation? Especially after cruelly trying to sexually manipulate him to abet your illegal purposes? Have you lost all sense of decency? You . . . you should be sued."

"Do your worst," Kitty muttered.

"Maybe I will," Mabel said grimly. "Sunlight is the best disinfectant."

"Yeah, let's string her up somewhere real sunny and public and call a bunch of news crews," Pete said. "I'm way hot for this deep ninja gear! Me and the Spiders got real mojo uses for these telescopic ears, and the tracer dust, and the epoxy bugging devices. And the press-on climbing-claws. And the carbon-fiber rope. Everything, really! Everything except these big-ass military shoes of hers, which really suck."

"Hey, all that stuff's mine," Lyle said sternly. "I saw it first."

"Yeah, I guess so, but . . . Okay, Lyle, you make us a deal on the gear, we'll forget everything you still owe us for doing the shop."

"Come on, those combat spex are worth more than this place all by themselves."

"I'm real interested in that settop box," Mabel said cruelly. "It doesn't look too fancy or complicated. Let's take it over to those dirty circuit zudes who hang out at the Blue Parrot, and see if they can't reverse-engineer it. We'll post all the schematics up on twenty or thirty progressive activist networks, and see what falls out of cyberspace."

Kitty glared at her. "The terrible consequences from that stupid and irresponsible action would be entirely on your head."

"I'll risk it," Mabel said airily, patting her cloche hat. "It might bump my soft little liberal head a bit, but I'm pretty sure it would crack your nasty little fascist head like a coconut."

Suddenly Kitty began thrashing and kicking her way furiously inside the bag. They watched with interest as she ripped, tore and lashed out with powerful side and front kicks. Nothing much happened.

"All right," she said at last, panting in exhaustion. "I've come from Senator Creighton's office."

"Who?" Lyle said.

"Creighton! Senator James P. Creighton, the man who's been your Senator from Tennessee for the past thirty years!"

"Oh," Lyle said. "I hadn't noticed."

"We're anarchists," Pete told her.

"We sure heard of the nasty old geezer," Mabel said, "but I'm from Columbia, where we change senators the way you'd change a pair of you ever changed your socks, that is. What about him?"

"Senator Creighton has deep clout and seniority! He was a Senator even before the first NAFTA Senate was convened! He has a very large, and powerful, and very well seasoned personal staff of twenty thousand hardworking people, with a lot of pull in the Agriculture, Banking, and Telecommunications Committees!"

"Yeah? So?"

"So," Kitty said miserably, "there are twenty thousand of us on his staff. We've been in place for decades now, and naturally we've accumulated lots of power and importance. Senator Creighton's staff is basically running some quite large sections of the NAFTA government, and if the Senator loses his office, there will be a great deal of . . . of unnecessary political turbulence." She looked up. "You might not think that a senator's staff is all that important politically. But if people like you bothered to learn anything about the real-life way that your government functions, then you'd know that Senate staffers can be really crucial."

Mabel scratched her head. "You're telling me that even a lousy senator has his own private black-bag unit?"

Kitty looked insulted. "He's an excellent senator! You can't have a working organization of twenty thousand staffers without taking security very seriously! Anyway, the Executive wing has had black-bag units for years! It's only right that there should be a balance of powers."

"Wow," Mabel said. "The old guy's a hundred and twelve or something, isn't he?"

"A hundred and seventeen."

"Even with government health care, there can't be a lot left of him."

"He's already gone," Kitty muttered. "His frontal lobes are burned out. . . . He can still sit up, and if he's stoked on stimulants he can repeat whatever's whispered to him. So he's got two permanent implanted hearing aids, and basically . . . well . . . he's being run by remote control by his mook."

"His mook, huh?" Pete repeated thoughtfully.

"It's a very good mook," Kitty said. "The coding's old, but it's been very well looked-after. It has firm moral values and excellent policies. The mook is really very much like the Senator was. It's just that . . . well, it's old. It still prefers a really old-fashioned media environment. It spends almost all its time watching old-fashioned public political coverage, and lately it's gotten cranky and started broadcasting commentary."

"Man, never trust a mook," Lyle said. "I hate those things."

"So do I," Pete offered, "but even a mook comes off pretty good compared to a politician."

"I don't really see the problem," Mabel said, puzzled. "Senator Hirschheimer from Arizona has had a direct neural link to his mook for years, and he has an excellent progressive voting record. Same goes for Senator Marmalejo from Tamaulipas; she's kind of absentminded, and everybody knows she's on life support, but she's a real scrapper on women's issues."

Kitty looked up. "You don't think it's terrible?"

Mabel shook her head. "I'm not one to be judgmental about the intimacy of one's relationship to one's own digital alter-ego. As far as I can see it, that's a basic privacy issue."

"They told me in briefing that it was a very terrible business, and that everyone would panic if they learned that a high government official was basically a front for a rogue artificial intelligence."

Mabel, Pete, and Lyle exchanged glances. "Are you guys surprised by that news?" Mabel said.

"Heck no," said Pete. "Big deal," Lyle added.

Something seemed to snap inside Kitty then. Her head sank. "Disaffected émigrés in Europe have been spreading boxes that can decipher the Senator's commentary. I mean, the Senator's mook's commentary . . . The mook speaks just like the Senator did, or the way the Senator used to speak, when he was in private and off the record. The way he spoke in his diaries. As far as we can tell, the mook *was* his diary. . . . It used to be his personal laptop computer. But he just kept transferring the files, and upgrading the software, and teaching it new tricks like voice recognition and speechwriting, and giving it power of attorney and such. . . . And then, one day the mook made a break for it. We think that the mook sincerely believes that it's the Senator."

"Just tell the stupid thing to shut up for a while, then."

"We can't do that. We're not even sure where the mook is, physically. Or how it's been encoding those sarcastic comments into the video-feed. The Senator had a lot of friends in the telecom industry back in the old days. There are a lot of ways and places to hide a piece of distributed software."

"So that's all?" Lyle said. "That's it, that's your big secret? Why didn't you just come to me and ask me for the box? You didn't have to dress up in combat gear and kick my door in. That's a pretty good story, I'd have probably just given you the thing."

"I couldn't do that, Mr. Schweik."

"Why not?"

"Because," Pete said, "her people are important government functionaries, and you're a loser techie wacko who lives in a slum."

"I was told this is a very dangerous area," Kitty muttered.

"It's not dangerous," Mabel told her.

"No?"

"No. They're all too broke to be dangerous. This is just a kind of social breathing space. The whole urban infrastructure's dread fully over-planned here in Chattanooga. There's been too much money here too long. There's been no room for spontaneity. It was choking the life out of the city. That's why everyone was secretly overjoyed when the rioters set fire to these three floors."

Mabel shrugged. "The insurance took care of the damage. First the looters came in. Then there were a few hideouts for kids and crooks and illegal aliens. Then the permanent squats got set up. Then the artist's studios, and the semilegal workshops and redlight places. Then the quaint little coffeehouses, then the bakeries. Pretty soon the offices of professionals will be filtering in, and they'll restore the water and the wiring. Once that happens, the real-estate prices will kick in big-time, and the whole zone will transmute right back into gentryville. It happens all the time."

Mabel waved her arm at the door. "If you knew anything about modern urban geography, you'd see this kind of, uh, spontaneous urban renewal happening all over the place. As long as you've got naive young people with plenty of energy who can be suckered into living inside rotten, hazardous dumps for nothing, in exchange for imagining that they're free from oversight, then it all works out just great in the long run."

"Oh."

"Yeah, zones like this turn out to be extremely handy for all concerned. For some brief span of time, a few people can think mildly unusual thoughts and behave in mildly unusual ways. All kinds of weird little vermin show up, and if they make any money then they go legal, and if they don't then they drop dead in a place really quiet where it's all their own fault. Nothing dangerous about it." Mabel laughed, then sobered. "Lyle, let this poor dumb cracker out of the bag."

"She's naked under there."

"Okay," she said impatiently, "cut a slit in the bag and throw some clothes in it. Get going, Lyle."

Lyle threw in some biking pants and a sweatshirt.

"What about my gear?" Kitty demanded, wriggling her way into the clothes by feel.

"I tell you what," said Mabel thoughtfully. "Pete here will give your gear back to you in a week or so, after his friends have photographed all the circuitry. You'll just have to let him keep all those knickknacks for a while, as his reward for our not immediately telling everybody who you are and what you're doing here."

"Great idea," Pete announced, "terrific, pragmatic solution!" He began feverishly snatching up gadgets and stuffing them into his shoulderbag. "See, Lyle? One phone-call to good ol' Spider Pete, and your problem is history, zude! Me and Mabel-the-Fed have crisis negotiation skills that are second to none! Another potentially lethal confrontation resolved without any bloodshed or loss of life." Pete zipped the bag shut. "That's about it, right, everybody? Problem over! Write if you get work, Lyle buddy. Hang by your thumbs." Pete leapt out the door and bounded off at top speed on the springy soles of his reactive boots.

"Thanks a lot for placing my equipment into the hands of sociopathic criminals," Kitty said. She reached out of the slit in the bag, grabbed a multitool off the corner of the workbench, and began swiftly slashing her way free.

"This will help the sluggish, corrupt, and underpaid Chattanooga police to take life a little more seriously," Mabel said, her pale eyes gleaming. "Besides, it's profoundly undemocratic to restrict specialized technical knowledge to the coercive hands of secret military elites."

Kitty thoughtfully thumbed the edge of the multitool's ceramic blade and stood up to her full height, her eyes slitted. "I'm ashamed to work for the same government as you."

Mabel smiled serenely. "Darling, your tradition of deep dark government paranoia is far behind the times! This is the postmodern era! We're now in the grip of a government with severe schizoid multiple-personality disorder."

"You're truly vile. I despise you more than I can say." Kitty jerked her thumb at Lyle. "Even this nut-case eunuch anarchist kid looks pretty good, compared to you. At least he's self-sufficient and market-driven."

"I thought he looked good the moment I met him," Mabel replied sunnily. "He's cute, he's got great muscle tone, and he doesn't make passes. Plus he can fix small appliances and he's got a spare apartment. I think you ought to move in with him, sweetheart."

"What's that supposed to mean? You don't think I could manage life here in the zone like you do, is that it? You think you have some kind of copyright on living outside the law?"

"No, I just mean you'd better stay indoors with your boyfriend here until that paint falls off your face. You look like a poisoned raccoon." Mabel turned on her heel. "Try to get a life, and stay out of my way." She leapt outside, unlocked her bicycle and methodically pedaled off.

Kitty wiped her lips and spat out the door. "Christ, that baton packs a wallop." She snorted. "Don't you ever ventilate this place, kid? Those paint fumes are gonna kill you before you're thirty."

"I don't have time to clean or ventilate it. I'm real busy."

"Okay, then I'll clean it. I'll ventilate it. I gotta stay here a while, understand? Maybe quite a while."

Lyle blinked. "How long, exactly?"

Kitty stared at him. "You're not taking me seriously, are you? I don't much like it when people don't take me seriously."

"No, no," Lyle assured her hastily. "You're very serious."

"You ever heard of a small-business grant, kid? How about venture capital, did you ever hear of that? Ever heard of federal research-and-development subsidies, Mr. Schweik?" Kitty looked at him sharply, weighing her words. "Yeah, I thought maybe you'd heard of that one, Mr. Techie Wacko. Federal R and D backing is the kind of thing that only happens to other people, right? But Lyle, when you make good friends with a senator, you *become* 'other people.' Get my drift, pal?"

"I guess I do," Lyle said slowly.

"We'll have ourselves some nice talks about that subject, Lyle. You wouldn't mind that, would you?"

"No. I don't mind it now that you're talking."

"There's some stuff going on down here in the zone that I didn't understand at first, but it's important." Kitty paused, then rubbed dried dye from her hair in a cascade of green dandruff. "How much did you pay those Spider gangsters to string up this place for you?"

"It was kind of a barter situation," Lyle told her.

"Think they'd do it again if I paid 'em real cash? Yeah? I thought so." She nodded thoughtfully. "They look like a heavy outfit, the City Spiders. I gotta pry 'em loose from that leftist gorgon before she finishes indoctrinating them in socialist revolution." Kitty wiped her mouth on her sleeve. "This is the Senator's own constituency! It was stupid of us to duck an ideological battle, just because this is a worthless area inhabited by reckless sociopaths who don't vote. Hell, that's exactly why it's important. This could be a vital territory in the culture war. I'm gonna call the office right away, start making arrangements. There's no way we're gonna leave this place in the hands of the self-styled Queen of Peace and Justice over there."

She snorted, then stretched a kink out of her back. "With a little self-control and discipline, I can save those Spiders from themselves and turn them into an asset to law and order! I'll get 'em to string up a couple of trailers here in the zone. We could start a dojo."

Eddy called, two weeks later. He was in a beachside cabana somewhere in Catalunya, wearing a silk floral-print shirt and a new and very pricey looking set of spex. "How's life, Lyle?"

"It's okay, Eddy."

"Making out all right?" Eddy had two new tattoos on his cheekbone.

"Yeah. I got a new paying roommate. She's a martial artist."

"Girl roommate working out okay this time?"

"Yeah, she's good at pumping the flywheel and she lets me get on with my bike work. Bike business has been picking up a lot lately. Looks like I might get a legal electrical feed and some more floorspace, maybe even some genuine mail delivery. My new roomie's got a lot of useful contacts."

"Boy, the ladies sure love you, Lyle! Can't beat 'em off with a stick, can you, poor guy? That's a heck of a note."

Eddy leaned forward a little, shoving aside a silver tray full of dead gold-tipped zigarettes. "You been getting the packages?"

"Yeah. Pretty regular."

"Good deal," he said briskly, "but you can wipe 'em all now. I don't need those backups anymore. Just wipe the data and trash the disks, or sell 'em. I'm into some, well, pretty hairy opportunities right now, and I don't need all that old clutter. It's kid stuff anyway."

"Okay, man. If that's the way you want it."

Eddy leaned forward. "D'you happen to get a package lately? Some hardware? Kind of a settop box?"

"Yeah, I got the thing."

"That's great, Lyle. I want you to open the box up, and break all the chips with pliers."

"Yeah?"

"Then throw all the pieces away. Separately. It's trouble, Lyle, okay? The kind of trouble I don't need right now."

"Consider it done, man."

"Thanks! Anyway, you won't be bothered by mailouts from now on." He paused. "Not that I don't appreciate your former effort and goodwill, and all."

Lyle blinked. "How's your love life, Eddy?"

Eddy sighed. "Frederika! What a handful! I dunno, Lyle, it was okay for a while, but we couldn't stick it together. I don't know why I ever thought that private cops were sexy. I musta been totally out of my mind. . . . Anyway, I got a new girlfriend now."

"Yeah?"

"She's a politician, Lyle. She's a radical member of the Spanish Parliament. Can you believe that? I'm sleeping with an elected official of a European local government." He laughed. "Politicians are *sexy*, Lyle. Politicians are *hot!* They have charisma. They're glamorous. They're powerful. They can really make things happen! Politicians get around. They know things on the inside track. I'm having more fun with Violeta than I knew there was in the world."

"That's pleasant to hear, zude."

"More pleasant than you know, my man."

"Not a problem," Lyle said indulgently. "We all gotta make our own lives, Eddy."

"Ain't it the truth."

Lyle nodded. "I'm in business, zude!"

"You gonna perfect that inertial whatsit?" Eddy said.

"Maybe. It could happen. I get to work on it a lot now. I'm getting closer, really getting a grip on the concept. It feels really good. It's a good hack, man. It makes up for all the rest of it. It really does."

Eddy sipped his mimosa. "Lyle."

"What?"

"You didn't hook up that settop box and look at it, did you?"

"You know me, Eddy," Lyle said. "Just another kid with a wrench."

Red Sonja and Lessingham in Dreamland

GWYNETH JONES

Gwyneth Jones, whose first SF novel, *Divine Endurance,* was the harbinger of the British SF renaissance of the late 1980s and early 1990s, has become in the intervening years the leading feminist SF writer of her generation, and more. In some circles, she is considered simply the best of the younger generation of British SF writers. Her novel, *White Queen,* one of the first winners of the James Tiptree, Jr. Award for "gender bending" SF, is a major science fiction work of the 1990s; some of her fantasy stories, collected in *Seven Tales and a Fable,* won a World Fantasy Award in 1996, as did one of her short stories. This story, from Ellen Datlow's anthology, *Off Limits*—which is not an anthology of alien sex stories but rather fantastic investigations of human sexuality—takes on the complexities of computer online sex. Never lacking in ambition, Jones addresses role playing and the issues of control, bondage, and therapy. In real life, says Jones in an afterword, "sexual negotiations are costly and dangerous," so a lot of people would prefer escape. The story also makes a provocative contrast to Terry Bisson's "In the Upper Room," and an interesting comparison to Allen Steele's "Doblin's Lecture."

The earth walls of the caravanserai rose strangely from the empty plain. She let the black stallion slow his pace. The silence of deep dusk had a taste, like a rich dark fruit; the air was keen. In the distance mountains etched a jagged margin against an indigo sky; snow streaks glinting in the glimmer of the dawning stars. She had never been here before, in life. But as she led her horse through the gap in the high earthen banks she knew what she would see. The camping booths around the walls; the beaten ground stained black by the ashes of countless cooking fires; the wattle-fenced enclosure where travelers' riding beasts mingled indiscriminately with their host's goats and chickens . . . the tumbledown gallery, where sheaves of russet plains-grass sprouted from empty window-spaces. Everything she looked on had the luminous intensity of a place often visited in dreams.

She was a tall woman, dressed for riding in a kilt and harness of supple leather over brief close-fitting linen: a costume that left her sheeny, muscular limbs bare and outlined the taut, proud curves of breast and haunches. Her red hair was bound in a braid as thick as a man's wrist. Her sword was slung on her back, the great brazen hilt standing above her shoulder. Other guests were gathered by an open-air kitchen, in the orange-red of firelight and the smoke of roasting meat. She returned their stares coolly: she was accustomed to attracting attention. But she didn't like what she saw. The host of the caravanserai came scuttling from the group by the fire. His manner was fawning. But his eyes measured, with a thief's sly expertise, the worth of the sword she bore and the quality of Lemiak's harness. Sonja tossed him a few coins and declined to join the company.

She had counted fifteen of them. They were poorly dressed and heavily armed. They were all friends together and their animals—both terror-birds and horses—were too good for any honest travelers' purposes. Sonja had been told that this caravanserai was a safe halt. She judged that this was no longer true. She considered riding out again onto the plain. But wolves and wild terror-birds roamed at night between here and the mountains, at the end of winter. And there were worse dangers; ghosts and demons. Sonja was neither credulous nor superstitious. But in this country no wayfarer willingly spent the black hours alone.

She unharnessed Lemiak and rubbed him down: taking sensual pleasure in the handling of his powerful limbs; in the heat of his glossy hide, and the vigor of his great body. There was firewood ready stacked in the roofless booth. Shouldering a cloth sling for corn and a hank of rope, she went to fetch her own fodder. The corralled beasts shifted in a mass to watch her. The great flightless birds, with their pitiless raptors' eyes, were especially attentive. She felt an equally rapacious attention from the company by the caravanserai kitchen, which amused her. The robbers—as she was sure they were—had all the luck. For her, there wasn't one of the fifteen who rated a second glance.

A man appeared, from the darkness under the ruined gallery. He was tall. The rippled muscle of his chest, left bare by an unlaced leather jerkin, shone red-brown. His black hair fell in glossy curls to his wide shoulders. He met her gaze and smiled, white teeth appearing in the darkness of his beard. "*My name is Ozymandias, king of kings . . . look on my works, ye mighty, and despair . . .* Do you know those lines?" He pointed to a lump of shapeless stone, one of several that lay about. It bore traces of carving, almost effaced by time. "There was a city here once, with marketplaces, fine buildings, throngs of proud people. Now they are dust, and only the caravanserai remains."

He stood before her, one tanned and sinewy hand resting lightly on the hilt of a dagger in his belt. Like Sonja, he carried his broadsword on his back. Sonja was tall. He topped her by a head: yet there was nothing brutish in his size. His brow was wide and serene, his eyes were vivid blue: his lips full and imperious; yet delicately modeled, in the rich nest of hair. Somewhere between eyes and lips there lurked a spirit of mockery, as if he found some secret amusement in the perfection of his own beauty and strength.

The man and the woman measured each other.

"You are a scholar," she said.

"Of some sort. And a traveler from an antique land—where the cities are still standing. It seems we are the only strangers here," he added, with a slight nod toward the convivial company. "We might be well advised to become friends for the night."

Sonja never wasted words. She considered his offer and nodded.

They made a fire in the booth Sonja had chosen. Lemiak and the scholar's terror-bird, left loose together in the back of the shelter, did not seem averse to each other's company. The woman and the man ate spiced sausage, skewered and broiled over the red embers, with bread and dried fruit. They drank water, each keeping to their own waterskin. They spoke little, after that first exchange—except to discuss briefly the tactics of their defense, should defense be necessary.

The attack came around midnight. At the first stir of covert movement, Sonja leapt up sword in hand. She grasped a brand from the dying fire. The man who had been crawling on his hands and knees toward her, bent on sly murder of a sleeping victim, scrabbled to his feet. "Defend yourself," yelled Sonja, who despised to strike an unarmed foe. Instantly he was rushing at her with a heavy sword. A great two-handed stroke would have cleft her to the waist. She parried the blow and caught him between neck and shoulder, almost severing the head from his body. The beasts plunged and screamed at the rush of blood scent. The scholar was grappling with another attacker, choking out the man's life with his bare hands . . . and the booth was full of bodies: their enemies rushing in on every side.

Sonja felt no fear. Stroke followed stroke, in a luxury of blood and effort and fire-shot darkness . . . until the attack was over, as suddenly as it had begun.

The brigands had vanished.

"We killed five," breathed the scholar, "by my count. Three to you, two to me."

She kicked together the remains of their fire and crouched to blow the embers to a blaze. By that light they found five corpses, dragged them and flung them into the open square. The scholar had a cut on his upper arm, which was bleeding freely. Sonja was bruised and battered, but otherwise unhurt. The worst loss was their woodstack, which had been trampled and blood-fouled. They would not be able to keep a watchfire burning.

"Perhaps they won't try again," said the warrior woman. "What can we have that's worth more than five lives?"

He laughed shortly. "I hope you're right."

"We'll take turns to watch."

Standing breathless, every sense alert, they smiled at each other in new-forged comradeship. There was no second attack. At dawn Sonja, rousing from a light doze, sat up and pushed back the heavy masses of her red hair.

"You are very beautiful," said the man, gazing at her.

"So are you," she answered.

The caravanserai was deserted, except for the dead. The brigands' riding animals were gone. The innkeeper and his family had vanished into some bolt-hole in the ruins.

"I am heading for the mountains," he said, as they packed up their gear. "For the pass into Zimiamvia."

"I too."

"Then our way lies together."

He was wearing the same leather jerkin, over knee-length loose breeches of heavy violet silk. Sonja looked at the strips of linen that bound the wound on his upper arm. "When did you tie up that cut?"

"You dressed it for me, for which I thank you."

"When did I do that?"

He shrugged. "Oh, sometime."

Sonja mounted Lemiak, a little frown between her brows. They rode together until dusk. She was not talkative and the man soon accepted her silence. But when night fell, and they camped without a fire on the houseless plain: then, as the demons stalked, they were glad of each other's company. Next dawn, the mountains seemed as distant as ever. Again, they met no living creature all day, spoke little to each other, and made the same comfortless camp. There was no moon. The stars were almost bright enough to cast shadow; the cold was intense. Sleep was impossible, but they were not tempted to ride on. Few travelers attempt the passage over the high plains to Zimiamvia. Of those few most turn back, defeated. Some wander among the ruins forever, tearing at their own flesh. Those who survive are the ones who do not defy the terrors of darkness. They crouched shoulder to shoulder, each wrapped in a single blanket, to endure. Evil emanations of the death-steeped plain rose from the soil and bred phantoms. The sweat of fear was cold as ice melt on Sonja's cheeks. Horrors made of nothingness prowled and muttered in her mind.

"How long," she whispered. "How long do we have to bear this?"

The man's shoulder lifted against hers. "Until we get well, I suppose."

The warrior-woman turned to face him, green eyes flashing in appalled outrage.

"Sonja" discussed this group member's felony with the therapist. Dr. Hamilton—he wanted them to call him Jim, but "Sonja" found this impossible—monitored everything that went on in the virtual environment. But he never appeared there. They only met him in the one-to-one consultations that virtual-therapy buffs called *the meat sessions*.

"He's not supposed to *do* that," she protested, from the foam couch in the doctor's office. He was sitting beside her, his notebook on his knee. "He damaged my experience."

Dr. Hamilton nodded. "Okay. Let's take a step back. Leave aside the risk of disease or pregnancy: because we *can* leave those bogeys aside, forever if you like. Would you agree that sex is essentially an innocent and playful social behavior—something you'd offer to or take from a friend, in an ideal world, as easily as food or drink?"

"Sonja" recalled certain dreams—*meat* dreams, not the computer-assisted kind. She blushed. But the man was a doctor after all. "That's what I do feel," she agreed. "That's why I'm here. I want to get back to the pure pleasure, to get rid of the baggage."

"The sexual experience offered in virtuality therapy is readily available on the nets. You know that. And you could find an agency that would vet your partners for you. You chose to join this group because you need to feel that you're taking *medicine,* so you don't have to feel ashamed. And because you need to feel that you're interacting with people who, like yourself, perceive sex as a problem."

"Doesn't everyone?"

"You and another group member went off into your own private world. That's good. That's what's supposed to happen. Let me tell you, it doesn't always. The software gives you access to a vast multisensual library, all the sexual fantasy ever committed to media. But you and your partner, or partners, have to customize the information and use it to create and maintain what we call the *consensual perceptual plenum.* Success in holding a shared dreamland together is a knack. It depends on something in the neural makeup that no one has yet fully analyzed. Some have it, some don't. You two are really in sync."

"That's exactly what I'm complaining about—"

"You think he's damaging the pocket universe you two built up. But he isn't, not from his character's point of view. It's part Lessingham's thing, to be conscious that he's in a fantasy world."

She started, accusingly. "I don't want to know his name."

"Don't worry, I wouldn't tell you. 'Lessingham' is the name of his virtuality persona. I'm surprised you don't recognize it. He's a character from a series of classic fantasy novels by E.R. Eddison. . . . *In Eddison's glorious cosmos 'Lessingham' is a splendidly endowed English gentleman, who visits fantastic realms of ultra-masculine adventure as a lucid dreamer: though an actor in the drama, he is partly conscious of another existence, while the characters around him are more or less explicitly puppets of the dream . . .*"

He sounded as if he was quoting from a reference book. He probably was: reading from an autocue that had popped up in lenses of those doctorish horn-rims. She knew that the old-fashioned trappings were there to reassure her. She rather despised them: but it was like the virtuality itself. The buttons were pushed, the mechanism responded. She was reassured.

Of course she knew the Eddison stories. She recalled "Lessingham" perfectly: the tall, strong, handsome, cultured millionaire jock, who has magic journeys to another world, where he is a tall, strong, handsome, cultured jock in Elizabethan costume, with a big sword. The whole thing was an absolutely typical male power-fantasy, she thought—without rancor. *Fantasy means never having to say you're sorry.* The women in those books, she remembered, were drenched in sex, but they had no part in the action. They stayed at home being princesses, *occasionally* allowing the millionaire jocks to get them into bed. She could understand why "Lessingham" would be interested in "Sonja" . . . for a change.

"You think he goosed you, psychically. What do you expect? You can't dress the way 'Sonja' dresses, and hope to be treated like the Queen of the May."

Dr. Hamilton was only doing his job. He was supposed to be provocative, so they could react against him. That was his excuse, anyway. . . . On the contrary, she thought. "Sonja" dresses the way she does because she can dress any way she likes. "Sonja" doesn't have to *hope* for respect, and she doesn't have to demand it. She just gets it. "It's dominance display," she said, enjoying the theft of his jargon. "Females do that too, you know. The way 'Sonja' dresses is not an invitation. It's a warning. Or a challenge, to anyone who can measure up."

He laughed, but he sounded irritated. "Frankly, I'm amazed that you two work together. I'd have expected 'Lessingham' to go for an ultrafeminine—"

"I am . . . 'Sonja' *is* ultrafeminine. Isn't a tigress feminine?"

"Well, okay. But I guess you've found out his little weakness. He likes to be a teeny bit in control, even when he's letting his hair down in dreamland."

She remembered the secret mockery lurking in those blue eyes. "That's the problem. That's exactly what I *don't* want. I don't want either of us to be in control."

"I can't interfere with his persona. So, it's up to you. Do you want to carry on?"

"Something works," she muttered. She was unwilling to admit that there'd been no one else, in the text interface phase of the group, that she found remotely attractive. It was "Lessingham," or drop out and start again. "I just want him to stop *spoiling things.*"

"You can't expect your masturbation fantasies to mesh completely. This is about getting *beyond* solitary sex. Go with it: where's the harm? One day you'll want to face a sexual partner in the real, and then you'll be well. Meanwhile, you could be passing 'Lessingham' in reception—he comes to his meat sessions around your time—and not know it. That's *safety,* and you never have to breach it. You two have proved that you can sustain an imaginary world together: it's almost like being in love. I could argue that lucid dreaming, being *in* the fantasy world but not *of* it, is the next big step. Think about that."

The clinic room had mirrored walls: more deliberate provocation. How much reality can you take?, the reflections asked. But she felt only a vague distaste for the woman she saw, at once hollow-cheeked and bloated, lying in the doctor's foam couch. He was glancing over her records on his notebook screen: which meant the session was almost up.

"Still no overt sexual contact?"

"I'm not ready . . ." She stirred restlessly. "Is it a man or a woman?"

"Ah!" smiled Dr. Hamilton, waving a finger at her. "Naughty, naughty—"

He was the one who'd started taunting her, with his hints that the meat—"Lessingham"—might be near. She hated herself for asking a genuine question. It was her rule to give him no entry to her real thoughts. But Dr. Jim knew everything, without being told: every change in her brain chemistry, every effect on her body: sweaty palms, racing heart, damp underwear. . . . The telltales on his damned autocue left her precious little dignity. *Why do I subject myself to this?* she wondered, disgusted. But in the virtuality she forgot utterly about Dr. Jim. She didn't care who was watching. She had her brazen-hilted sword. She had the piercing intensity of dusk on the high plains, the snowlight on the mountains; the hard, warm silk of her own perfect limbs. She felt a brief complicity with "Lessingham." She had a conviction that Dr. Jim didn't play favorites. He despised all his patients equally. . . . *You get your kicks, doctor. But we have the freedom of dreamland.*

"Sonja" read cards stuck in phone booths and store windows, in the tired little streets outside the building that housed the clinic. *Relaxing massage by clean-shaven young man in Luxurious Surroundings . . .* You can't expect your fantasies to mesh exactly, the doctor said. But how can it work if two people disagree over something so vital as the difference between control and surrender? Her estranged husband used to say: "why don't you just *do it for me,* as a favor. It wouldn't hurt. Like making someone a cup of coffee . . ." *Offer the steaming cup, turn around and lift my skirts, pull down my underwear. I'm ready. He opens his pants and slides it in, while his thumb is round in front rubbing me. . . . I could enjoy that,* thought "Sonja," remembering the blithe abandon of her dreams. *That's the damned shame. If there were no nonsex consequences, I don't know that there's any limit to what I could enjoy. . . . But all her husband had achieved was to make her feel she never wanted to make anyone, man,*

woman, or child, a cup of coffee ever again. . . . In luxurious surroundings. *That's what I want. Sex without engagement, pleasure without consequences. It's got to be possible.*

She gazed at the cards, feeling uneasily that she'd have to give up this
habit. She used to glance at them sidelong, now she'd pause and linger.
She was getting desperate. She was lucky there was medically supervised
virtuality sex to be had. She would be helpless prey in the wild world of
the nets, and she'd never, ever risk trying one of these meat-numbers.
And she had no intention of returning to her husband. Let him make his
own coffee. She wouldn't call that getting well. She turned, and caught
the eye of a nicely dressed young woman standing next to her. They
walked away quickly in opposite directions. *Everybody's having the same
dreams . . .*

In the foothills of the mountains, the world became green and sweet.
They followed the course of a little river, that sometimes plunged far
below their path, tumbling in white flurries in a narrow gorge; and sometimes ran beside them, racing smooth and clear over colored pebbles.
Flowers clustered on the banks, birds darted in the thickets of wild rose
and honeysuckle. They led their riding animals and walked at ease: not
speaking much. Sometimes the warrior woman's flank would brush the
man's side: or he would lean for a moment, as if by chance, his hand on
her shoulder. Then they would move deliberately apart, but they would
smile at each other. *Soon. Not yet . . .*

They must be vigilant. The approaches to fortunate Zimiamvia were
guarded. They could not expect to reach the pass unopposed. And the
nights were haunted still. They made camp at a flat bend of the river,
where the crags of the defile drew away, and they could see far up and
down their valley. To the north, peaks of diamond and indigo reared
above them. Their fire of aromatic wood burned brightly, as the white
stars began to blossom.

"No one knows about the long-term effects," she said. "It can't be
safe. At the least, we're risking irreversible addiction, they warn you
about that. I don't want to spend the rest of my life as a cyberspace couch
potato."

"Nobody claims it's safe. If it was safe, it wouldn't be so intense."

Their eyes met. "Sonja's" barbarian simplicity combined surprisingly
well with the man's more elaborate furnishing. The *consensual perceptual
plenum* was a flawless reality: the sound of the river, the clear silence of
the mountain twilight . . . their two perfect bodies. She turned from
him to gaze into the sweet-scented flames. The warrior-woman's glorious

vitality throbbed in her veins. The fire held worlds of its own, liquid furnaces: the sunward surface of Mercury.

"Have you ever been to a place like this in the real?"

He grimaced. "You're kidding. In the real, I'm *not* a magic-wielding millionaire."

Something howled. The bloodstopping cry was repeated. A taint of sickening foulness swept by them. They both shuddered, and drew closer together. "Sonja" knew the scientific explanation for the legendary virtuality-paranoia, the price you paid for the virtual world's superreal, dreamlike richness. It was all down to heightened neurotransmitter levels, a positive feedback effect, psychic overheating. But the horrors were still horrors.

"The doctor says if we can talk like this, it means we're getting well."

He shook his head. "I'm not sick. It's like you said. Virtuality's addictive and I'm an addict. I'm getting my drug of choice safely, on prescription. That's how I see it."

All this time "Sonja" was in her apartment, lying in a foam couch with a visor over her head. The visor delivered compressed bursts of stimuli to her visual cortex: the other sense perceptions riding piggyback on the visual, triggering a whole complex of neuronal groups; tricking her mind/brain into believing the world of the dream was *out there*. The brain works like a computer. You cannot "see" a hippopotamus, until your system has retrieved the "hippopotamus" template from memory, and checked it against the incoming. Where does the "real" exist? In a sense this world was as real as the other . . . But the thought of "Lessingham's" unknown body disturbed her. If he was too poor to lease good equipment, he might be lying in the clinic now in a grungy public cubicle . . . cathetered, and so forth: the sordid details.

She had never tried virtual sex. The solitary version had seemed a depressing idea. People said the partnered kind was the perfect *zipless fuck*. He sounded experienced; she was afraid he would be able to tell she was not. But it didn't matter. The virtual-therapy group wasn't like a dating agency. She would never meet him in the real, that was the whole idea. She didn't have to think about that stranger's body. She didn't have to worry about the real "Lessingham's" opinion of her. She drew herself up in the firelight. It was right, she decided, that Sonja should be a virgin. When the moment came, her surrender would be the more absolute.

In their daytime he stayed in character. It was a tacit trade-off. She would acknowledge the other world at nightfall by the campfire, as long as he didn't mention it the rest of the time. So they traveled on together, Lessingham and Red Sonja, the courtly scholar-knight and the taciturn warrior-maiden, through an exquisite Maytime: exchanging lingering glances, "accidental" touches . . . And still nothing happened. "Sonja" was aware that "Lessingham," as much as herself, was holding back from the brink. She felt piqued at this. But they were both, she guessed, waiting for the fantasy they had generated to throw up the perfect moment of itself. It ought to. There was no other reason for its existence.

Turning a shoulder of the hillside, they found a sheltered hollow. Two rowan trees in flower grew above the river. In the shadow of their blossom tumbled a little waterfall, so beautiful it was a wonder to behold. The water fell clear from the upper edge of a slab of stone twice a man's height, into a rocky basin. The water in the basin was clear and deep, a-churn with bubbles from the jet plunging from above. The riverbanks were lawns of velvet, over the rocks grew emerald mosses and tiny water flowers.

"I would live here," said Lessingham softly, his hand dropping from his riding bird's bridle. "I would build me a house in this fairy place, and rest my heart here forever."

Sonja loosed the black stallion's rein. The two beasts moved off, feeding each in its own way on the sweet grasses and springtime foliage.

"I would like to bathe in that pool," said the warrior-maiden.

"Why not?" He smiled. "I will stand guard."

She pulled off her leather harness and slowly unbound her hair. It fell in a trembling mass of copper and russet lights, a cloud of glory around the richness of her barely clothed body. Gravely she gazed at her own perfection, mirrored in the homage of his eyes. Lessingham's breath was coming fast. She saw a pulse beat, in the strong beauty of his throat. The pure physical majesty of him caught her breath. . . .

It was their moment. But it still needed something to break this strange spell of reluctance. "*Lady*—" he murmured—

Sonja gasped. "Back to back!" she cried. "Quickly, or it is too late!"

Six warriors surrounded them, covered from head to foot in red-and-black armor. They were human in the lower body, but the head of each appeared beaked and fanged, with monstrous faceted eyes, and each bore an extra pair of armored limbs between breastbone and belly. They fell on Sonja and Lessingham without pause or a challenge.

Sonja fought fiercely as always, her blade ringing against the monster armor. But something cogged her fabulous skill. Some power had drained the strength from her splendid limbs. She was disarmed. The clawed creatures held her, a monstrous head stooped over her, choking her with its fetid breath. . . .

When she woke again she was bound against a great boulder, by thongs around her wrists and ankles, tied to hoops of iron driven into the rock. She was naked but for her linen shift, it was in tatters. Lessingham was standing, leaning on his sword. "I drove them off," he said. "At last." He dropped the sword, and took his dagger to cut her down.

She lay in his arms. "You are very beautiful," he murmured. She thought he would kiss her. His mouth plunged instead to her breast, biting and sucking at the engorged nipple. She gasped in shock, a fierce pang leapt through her virgin flesh. What did they want with kisses? They were warriors. Sonja could not restrain a moan of pleasure. He had won her. How wonderful to be overwhelmed, to surrender to the raw lust of this godlike animal.

Lessingham set her on her feet.

"Tie me up."

He was proffering a handful of blood-slicked leather thongs.

"What?"

"Tie me to the rock, mount me. It's what I want."

"The evil warriors tied you—?"

"And you come and rescue me." He made an impatient gesture. "Whatever. Trust me. It'll be good for you too." He tugged at his blood-stained silk breeches, releasing a huge, iron-hard erection. "See, they tore my clothes. When you see *that*, you go crazy, you can't resist . . . and I'm at your mercy. Tie me up!"

"Sonja" had heard that eighty percent of the submissive partners in sadomasochist sex are male. But it is still the man who dominates his "dominatrix": who says *tie me tighter, beat me harder, you can stop now. . . . Hey,* she thought. *Why all the stage directions, suddenly? What happened to my zipless fuck?* But what the hell. She wasn't going to back out now, having come so far. . . . There was a seamless shift, and Lessingham was bound to the rock. She straddled his cock. He groaned. *"Don't do this to me."* He thrust upward, into her, moaning. *"You savage, you utter savage, uuunnh . . ."* Sonja grasped the man's wrists and rode him without mercy. He was right, it was as good this way. His eyes were half-closed. In the glimmer of blue under his lashes, a spirit of mockery trembled. . . . She heard a laugh, and found her hands were no longer gripping Lessingham's wrists. He had broken free from her bonds, he was laughing at her in triumph. He was wrestling her to the ground.

"No!" she cried, genuinely outraged. But he was the stronger.

It was night when he was done with her. He rolled away and slept, as far as she could tell, instantly. Her chief thought was that virtual sex didn't entirely *connect*. She remembered now, that was something else people told you, as well as the "zipless fuck." *It's like coming in your sleep,* they said. *It doesn't quite make it.* Maybe there was nothing virtuality could do to orgasm, to match the heightened richness of the rest of the experience. She wondered if he, too, had felt cheated.

She lay beside her hero, wondering, *where did I go wrong? Why did he have to treat me that way?* Beside her, "Lessingham" cuddled a fragment of violet silk, torn from his own breeches. He whimpered in his sleep, nuzzling the soft fabric, "*Mama . . .*"

She told Dr. Hamilton that "Lessingham" had raped her.

"And wasn't that what you wanted?"

She lay on the couch in the mirrored office. The doctor sat beside her with his smart notebook on his knee. The couch collected "Sonja's" physical responses as if she was an astronaut umbilicaled to ground control; and Dr. Jim read the telltales popping up in his reassuring horn-rims. She remembered the sneaking furtive thing that she had glimpsed in "Lessingham's" eyes, the moment before he took over their lust scene. How could she explain the difference? "He wasn't playing. In the fantasy, anything's allowed. But *he wasn't playing.* He was outside it, laughing at me."

"I warned you he would want to stay in control."

"But there was no need! I *wanted* him to be in control. Why did he have to steal what I wanted to give him anyway?"

"You have to understand, 'Sonja,' that to many men it's women who seem powerful. You women feel dominated and try to achieve 'equality.' But the men don't perceive the situation like that. They're mortally afraid of you: and anything, just about *anything* they do to keep the upper hand, seems like justified self-defense."

She could have wept with frustration. "I know all that! That's *exactly* what I was trying to get away from. I thought we were supposed to leave the damn baggage behind. I wanted something purely physical. . . . Something innocent."

"Sex is not innocent, 'Sonja.' I know you believe it is, or 'should be.' But it's time you faced the truth. Any interaction with another person involves some kind of jockeying for power, dickering over control. Sex is no exception. Now *that's* basic. You can't escape from it in direct-cortical fantasy. It's in our minds that relationships happen, and the mind, of course, is where virtuality happens too." He sighed, and made an entry in her notes. "I want you to look on this as another step toward coping with the real. You're not sick, 'Sonja.' You're unhappy. Not even unusually so. Most adults are unhappy, to some degree—"

"Or else they're in denial."

Her sarcasm fell flat. "Right. A good place to be, at least some of the time. What we're trying to achieve here—if we're trying to achieve anything at all—is to raise your pain threshold to somewhere near average. I want you to walk away from therapy with lowered expectations: I guess that would be success."

"Great," she said, desolate. "That's just great."

Suddenly he laughed. "Oh, you guys! You are so weird. It's always the same story. *Can't live with you, can't live without you* . . . You can't go on this way, you know. It's getting ridiculous. You want some real advice, 'Sonja'? Go home. Change your attitudes, and start some hard peace talks with that husband of yours."

"I don't want to change," she said coldly, staring with open distaste at his smooth profile, his soft effeminate hands. Who was he to call her abnormal? "I like my sexuality just the way it is."

Dr. Hamilton returned her look, a glint of human malice breaking through his doctor act. "Listen. I'll tell you something for free." A weird sensation jumped in her crotch. For a moment she had a prick: a hand lifted and cradled the warm weight of her balls. She stifled a yelp of shock. He grinned. "I've been looking for a long time, and I know. *There is no tall, dark man . . .*"

He returned to her notes. "You say you were 'raped,' " he continued, as if nothing had happened. "Yet you chose to continue the virtual session. Can you explain that?"

She thought of the haunted darkness, the cold air on her naked body; the soreness of her bruises; a rag of flesh used and tossed away. How it had felt to lie there: intensely alive, tasting the dregs, beaten back at the gates of the fortunate land. In dreamland, even betrayal had such rich depth and fascination. And she was free to enjoy, because *it didn't matter.*

"You wouldn't understand."

Out in the lobby there were people coming and going. It was lunchtime, the lifts were busy. "Sonja" noticed a round-shouldered geek of a little man making for the entrance to the clinic. She wondered idly if that could be "Lessingham."

She would drop out of the group. The adventure with "Lessingham" was over, and there was no one else for her. She needed to start again. The doctor knew he'd lost a customer, that was why he'd been so open with her today. He certainly guessed, too, that she'd lose no time in signing on somewhere else on the semi-medical fringe. What a fraud all that therapy talk was! He'd never have dared to play the sex change trick on her, except that he knew she was an addict. She wasn't likely to go accusing him of unprofessional conduct. Oh, he knew it all. But his contempt didn't trouble her.

So, she had joined the inner circle. She could trust Dr. Hamilton's judgment. He had the telltales: he would know. She recognized with a feeling of mild surprise that she had become a statistic, an element in a fashionable social concern: *an epidemic flight into fantasy, inadequate personalities; unable to deal with the reality of normal human sexual relations. . . . But that's crazy,* she thought. *I don't hate men, and I don't believe "Lessingham" hates women. There's nothing psychotic about what we're doing. We're making a consumer choice. Virtual sex is easier, that's all. Okay, it's convenience food. It has too much sugar, and a certain blandness. But when a product comes along, that is cheaper, easier, and more fun than the original version, of course people are going to buy it.*

The lift was full. She stood, drab bodies packed around her, breathing the stale air. Every face was a mask of dull endurance. She closed her eyes. *The caravanserai walls rose strangely from the empty plain. . . .*

Doblin's Lecture

ALLEN STEELE

Allen Steele won the Hugo Award in 1996 for his challenging novella, "The Death of Captain Future." He burst into prominence as a hard-SF writer with his first novel in 1989, *Orbital Decay*. He has gone on to become one of the best young hard-SF writers of the 1990s, with a talent for realism and a penchant for portraying the daily, gritty problems of living and working in space in the future. His background is in professional newspaper journalism and it shows in "Doblin's Lecture." That work appeared in *Pirate Writings*, one of the distinguished and ambitious small-business SF magazines (others include *Absolute Magnitude* and *Tomorrow*) whose value to the field was especially underlined in 1996 when the two literary magazines of SF, *Crank!* and *Century*, took the year off. *Century* did publish one issue, as did *Aboriginal*—a peer of *Pirate Writings*, but neither had much impact. This is not a typical Steele SF story—no space, no technological problems—except in that it attains a kind of everyday realism that is, in this case, quite disturbing. This is a straight-out piece of near-future extrapolation that deals with the materials of today's daily news. It is a cold piece of present tense reportage and is a moral tale about the need to acknowledge and confront reality in order to cure social problems.

A crisp autumn night on a midwestern university campus. A cool breeze, redolent of pine cones and coming winter, softly rustles bare trees and whisks dead leaves to scurry across the walkways leading to the main hall. Lights glow from within Gothic windows as a last handful of students and faculty members hurry toward the front entrance. There is to be a famous guest speaker tonight; no one wants to be late.

A handful of students picket in the plaza outside the hall; some carry protest signs, others trying to hand fliers to anyone who will take them. The yellow photocopies are taken and briefly read, then shoved into pockets or wadded up and tossed into waste cans; the signs are glanced at, but largely ignored.

A poster taped above the open double-doors states that absolutely no cameras, camcorders, or tape recorders are permitted inside. Just inside the doors, the crowd is funneled through a security cordon of off-duty police officers hired for the evening. They check campus I.D.'s, open day packs, run chirping hand-held metal detectors across chests, arms and legs. Anyone carrying metal objects larger or less innocent than keyrings, eyeglasses, or ballpoint pens is sent back outside. A trash can behind the guards is half-filled with penknives, bottle openers, cigarette lighters, and tear-gas dispensers, discarded by those who would rather part with them than rush them back to dorm rooms or cars, and thereby risk missing the lecture. Seating is limited, and it's been announced that no one will be allowed to stand or sit in the aisles.

Two students, protesters from the campus organization opposed to tonight's presentation, are caught with cloth banners concealed under their jackets. They're escorted out the door by the cops, who dump their banners in the trash without reading them.

The auditorium holds 1,800 seats, and each one has been claimed. The stage is empty save for a podium off to one side and a stiff-backed oak armchair in its center. The chair's legs are securely bolted to the floor, its armrests equipped with metal shackles; loose belts dangle from its sides. Its vague resemblance to a prison electric chair is lost on no one.

Four state troopers stand quietly in the wings on either side of the stage. Several more are positioned in the back of the hall, their arms folded across their chests or their thumbs tucked into service belts carrying revolvers, tasers, and Mace canisters. More than a few people quietly remark that this is the first time in a long while that the auditorium has been filled to capacity without anyone smelling marijuana.

At ten minutes after eight, the house lights dim and the room goes dark save for a pair of spotlights focused on the stage. The drone of voices fades away as the dean of the sociology department—a distinguished-looking academian in his early fifties, thin gray hair and humorless eyes—steps from behind the curtain on stage left and quickly strides past the cops to the lectern.

The dean peeks at the index cards in his hand as he introduces himself, then spends a few moments informing the audience that tonight's speaker has been invited to the university not to provide entertainment, but primarily as a guest lecturer for Sociology 450, Sociology 510, and Sociology 525. His students, occupying treasured seats in the first six rows, try not to preen too much as they open their notebooks and click their pens. They're the chosen few, the ones who are here to learn something; the professor squelches their newfound self-importance by reminding them that their papers on tonight's lecture are due Tuesday by ten o'clock. The professor then tells the audience that no comments or questions will be permitted during the guest speaker's opening remarks, and that anyone who interrupts the lecture in any way will be escorted from the hall and possibly be placed under arrest. This causes a minor stir in the audience, which the dean smoothly placates by adding that a short question-and-answer session will be held later, during which members of the audience may be allowed to ask questions, if time and circumstances permit.

Now the dean looks uncomfortable. He glances uneasily at his cards as if it's faculty poker night and he's been dealt a bad hand. After the guest speaker has made his remarks, he adds (a little more softly now, and with no little hesitance), and once the Q&A session is over, there may be a special demonstration. If time and circumstances permit.

The background noise rises again. Murmurs, whispers, a couple of muted laughs; quick sidelong glances, raised or furrowed eyebrows, dark frowns, a few smiles hastily covered by hands. The cops on stage remain stoical, but one can detect random shifts of eyes darting this way and that.

The dean knows that he doesn't need to introduce the guest speaker, for his reputation has preceded him and any further remarks he might make would be trivial at best, foolish at worst. Instead, he simply turns and starts to walk off the stage.

Then he stops. For the briefest instant there is a look of bafflement—and indeed, naked fear—on his face as he catches a glimpse of something just past the curtains in the left wing. Then he turns and walks, more quickly now, the opposite way until he disappears past the two police officers on stage right.

A moment of dead silence. Then Charles Gregory Doblin walks out on stage.

He's a big man—six feet and a couple of inches, with the solid build of someone who has spent most of his life doing heavy labor and only recently has put on weight—but his face, though brutal at first sight, is nonetheless kindly and oddly adolescent, like that of a grown-up who never let go of some part of his childhood. The sort of person one could easily imagine dressing up as Santa on Christmas Eve to take toys to a homeless shelter and would delight in playing horsey for the kids, or on any day would help jump-start your car or assist an elderly neighbor with her groceries. Indeed, when he was arrested several years ago in another city and charged with the murders of nineteen young black men, the people who lived around him in their white middle-class neighborhood believed that the police had made a serious mistake.

That was until FBI agents found the severed ears of his victims preserved in Mason jars in his basement, and his confession led them to nineteen unmarked graves.

Now here he is: Charles Gregory Doblin, walking slowly across the stage, a manila file holder tucked under his arm.

He wears a blue prison jump-suit and is followed closely by a state trooper holding a riot stick, but otherwise he could be a sports hero, a noted scientist, a best-selling author. A few people automatically begin to clap, then apparently realize that this is one time when applause is not warranted and let their hands fall back into their laps. Some frat boys in the back whistle their approval, and one of them yells something about killing niggers, before three police officers—two of whom, not coincidentally, are black—descend on them. They've been led out the door even before Charles Gregory Doblin has taken his seat; if the killer has heard them, there is nothing in his face to show it.

Indeed, there is nothing in his face at all. If the audience had expected the dark gaze that had met a news photographer's camera when he was led into a federal courthouse on the day of his arraignment four years ago—a shot engraved in collective memory, deranged Eyes Of A Killer—they don't see it. If they had anticipated the beatific look of the self-ascribed born-again Christian interviewed on "60 Minutes" and "Prime Time Live" in the last year, they don't see that either.

The killer's face is without expression. A sheet of blank paper. A calm and empty sea. A black hole in the center of a distant galaxy. Void. Cold. Vacant.

The killer takes his seat in the hard wooden chair. The state trooper hands him a cordless microphone before taking his position behind the chair. The arm restraints are left unfastened; the belts remain limp. Long moments pass as he opens the manila folder in his lap, then Charles Gregory Doblin—there is no way anyone here can think of him as Charlie Doblin, as his neighbors once did, or Chuck, as his late parents called him, or as Mr. Dobbs, as nineteen teenagers did in their last hours of life; it's the full name, as written in countless newspaper stories, or nothing else—Charles Gregory Doblin begins to speak.

His voice is very soft; it holds a slightly grating Northeastern accent, high-pitched now with barely-concealed nervousness, but otherwise it's quite pleasant. A voice for bedtime stories or even pillow-talk with a lover, although by all accounts Charles Gregory Doblin had remained a virgin during the thirty-six years he spent as a free man. He quietly thanks the university for inviting him here to speak this evening, and even earns a chuckle from the audience when he praises the cafeteria staff for the bowl of chili and the grilled cheese sandwich he had for dinner backstage. He doesn't know that the university cafeteria is infamous for its food, and he could not possibly be aware that three cooks spat in his chili just before it was delivered to the auditorium.

Then he begins to read aloud from the six sheets of single-spaced typewritten paper in his lap. It's a fairly long speech, the delivery slightly monotone, but his diction is practiced and nearly perfect. He tells of childhood in an abusive family: an alcoholic mother who commonly referred to him as a little shit and a racist father who beat him for no reason. He tells of having often eaten canned dog food, heated in a pan on a hibachi in the bathroom, for dinner because his parents could afford nothing better, and of going to school in a slum neighborhood where other kids made fun of him because of his size and the adolescent lisp that he didn't completely overcome until he was well into adulthood.

He describes the afternoon when he was attacked by three black teenagers who attacked and beat him without mercy only because he was a big, dumb white kid who had the misfortune of short-cutting through their alley on the way home from school. His voice remains steady as he relates how his father gave him another, even more savage beating that same evening, because he had allowed two niggers to get the better of him.

Charles Gregory Doblin tells a lifelong hatred for black people that became ever more obsessive as he became an adult: the brief involvement with the Klan and the Brotherhood of Aryan Nations before bailing out of the white supremacy movement in the belief that they were all rhetoric and no action; learning how some soldiers in Vietnam used to collect the ears of the gooks they had killed; the night nine years ago when, on impulse, he pulled over on his way home from work at an electronics factory to give a lift to a sixteen-year-old black kid thumbing a ride home.

Now the audience stirs. Legs are uncrossed, crossed again over the other knee. Hands guide pens across paper. Eighteen-hundred pairs of eyes peer through the darkness at the man on the stage.

The auditorium is dead silent as the killer reads the names of the nineteen teenagers that he murdered during the course of nine years. Besides being black and living in black neighborhoods scattered across the same major city, there are few common denominators among his victims. Some were street punks, one was a sidewalk crack dealer, and two were homeless kids looking for handouts, but he also murdered a high school basketball star, a National Merit Scholarship winner recently accepted by Yale, a rapper wannabe who sang in his church choir, an aspiring comic book artist, and a fifteen-year-old boy supporting his family by working two jobs after school. All had the misfortune of meeting and getting into a conversation with an easy-going white dude who had money for dope, beer, or pizza; they had followed him into an alley or a parked car or some other out-of-the-way place, then made the mistake of letting Mr. Dobbs step behind them for one brief, fatal moment . . . until the night one kid managed to escape.

The audience listens as he says that he is sorry for the evil he has done, as he explains that he was criminally insane at the time and didn't know what he was doing. They allow him to quote from the Bible, and some even bow their heads as he offers a prayer for the souls of those he has murdered.

Charles Gregory Doblin then closes the folder and sits quietly, hands folded across his stomach, ankles crossed, head slightly bowed with his eyes in shadow. After a few moments, the dean comes back out on stage; taking his position behind the lectern, he announces that it is now time for the Q&A session.

The first question comes from a nervous young girl in third row center: she timidly raises her hand and, after the dean acknowledges her, asks the killer if he has any remorse for his crimes. Yes, he says. She waits for him to continue; when he doesn't, she sits down again.

The next question is from a black student further back in the audience. He stands and asks Charles Gregory Doblin if he killed those nineteen kids primarily because they were black, or simply because they reminded him of the teenagers who had assaulted him. Again, Charles Gregory Doblin only says yes. The student asks the killer if he would have murdered him because he is black, and Charles Gregory Doblin replies that, yes, he probably would have. Would you kill me now? No, I would not. The student sits down and scribbles a few notes.

More hands rise from the audience; one by one, the dean lets students pose their questions. Has he seen the made-for-TV movie based on his crimes? No, he hasn't; there isn't a television in the maximum security ward of the prison, and he wasn't told about the movie until after it was aired. Did he read the book? No, he hasn't, but he's been told that it was a bestseller. Has he met any members of the families of his victims? Not personally, aside from spotting them in the courtroom during his trial. Have any of them attempted to contact him? He has received a few letters, but aside from the one from the mother who sent him a Bible, he hasn't been allowed to read any correspondence from the families. What does he do in prison? Read the Bible he was sent, paint, and pray. What does he paint? Landscapes, birds, the inside of his cell. If he could live his life all over again, what would he do differently? Become a truck driver, maybe a priest. Is he receiving a lecture fee from this visit? Yes, but most of it goes into a trust fund for the families of his victims, with the rest going to the state for travel expenses.

All this time, his gaze remains centered on a space between his knees, as if he is reading from an invisible Teleprompter. It is not until an aesthetic-looking young man in the tenth row asks him, in a rather arch voice, whether he received any homoerotic gratification when he committed the murders—an erection, perhaps? perhaps a fleeting vision of his father?—does Charles Gregory Doblin raise his eyes to meet those of his questioner. He stares silently at the pale young man for a long, long time, but says nothing until the student sits down again.

An uncomfortable hush follows this final question; no more hands are raised. The dean breaks the silence by announcing that the Q&A session is now over. He then glances at one of the guards standing in the wings, who gives him a slight nod. There will be a brief fifteen-minute intermission, the dean continues, then the program will resume.

He hesitates, then adds that since it will include a demonstration that may be offensive to members of the audience, this might be a good time for those people to leave.

Charles Gregory Doblin rises from his chair. Still refraining from looking directly at the crowd, he lets the state trooper escort him offstage. A few people in the auditorium clap self-consciously, then seldom-used gray curtains slide across the stage.

When the curtains part again fifteen minutes later, only a handful of seats in the auditorium are vacant. The one in the center of the stage is not.

A tall, skinny young black man is seated in the chair that Charles Gregory Doblin has kept warm for him. He wears a prison jump-suit similar to one worn by his predecessor, and his arms are shackled to the armrests, his body secured to the chair frame by the leather belts that had hung slack earlier. The same state trooper stands behind him, but this time his riot stick is in plain view, grasped in both hands before him.

The prisoner's eyes are cold searchlights that sweep across the audience. No one can meet his gaze without feeling revulsion. He catches sight of the young woman in the third row who had asked a question earlier in the evening; their eyes meet for a few seconds, and the prisoner's lips curl upward in a predatory smile. He starts to mutter an obscenity, but shuts up when the state trooper places the end of his stick on his shoulder. The girl squirms in her seat and looks away.

The dean returns to the lectern and introduces the young black man. His name is Curtis Henry Blum; he is twenty-two years old, and born and raised in this same city. Blum committed his first felony offense when he was twelve years old, when he was arrested for selling crack in the school playground; he was already a gang member by then. Since then he has been in and out of juvenile detention centers, halfway houses, and medium security prisons, and has been busted for mugging, narcotics, car jacking, breaking and entering, armed robbery, rape, attempted murder. Sometimes he was convicted and sent to one house of corrections or another; sometimes he was sentenced on lesser charges and served a shorter term; sometimes he was just let go for lack of evidence. Each occasion he was sent up, he spent no more than eighteen months before being paroled or furloughed and thrown back on the street.

Nineteen months ago, Curtis Blum held up a convenience store on the city's north side, one owned and operated by a South Korean immigrant family. Blum held mother, father, and teenage daughter at gunpoint while he cleaned out the cash register and tucked two bottles of wine into his pockets. The family knelt on the floor and begged him to be merciful and just leave, but he shot them anyway, along with an eleven-year-old kid from the hood who had been sent out by his mother to buy some cat food and beer, and had the misfortune of walking through the door just as Blum was going out. He didn't want to leave any witnesses, or maybe he simply felt like killing people that night.

A police SWAT team found Blum at his grandmother's house two days later. He wasn't hard to find; although by then he had bragged to everyone he knew about how he had capped three slants the night before, it was his grandmother who had called the cops. She also testified at her grandson's trial six months later, saying that he regularly robbed and beat her.

Curtis Blum was convicted on four counts of second-degree murder. This time, he faced a judge who didn't believe in second chances; he sentenced Blum to death. Since then, he has been filling in time on death row in the state's maximum security prison.

The dean steps from behind the lectern and walks over to where the prisoner is seated. He asks Blum if he has any questions. Blum asks him if the girl in the third row wants to fuck.

The dean says nothing. He simply turns and walks away, vanishing once again behind the curtains on stage left.

Curtis laughs out loud, then looks again at the woman in the third row and asks her directly if she wants to fuck. She starts to get up to leave, which Blum misinterprets as willingness to conjugate; even as he assails her with more obscenities, though, another female student grasps her arm and whispers something to her.

The girl stops, glances again at the stage, and then sits back down. This time, she has a slight smile on her face, for now she sees something that Blum doesn't.

Curtis is about to shout something else at the girl when a shadow falls over him. He looks up, and finds himself looking into the face of Charles Gregory Doblin.

Killing a man is actually a very easy thing to do, if you know how. There's several simple ways that this can be accomplished that don't require knives or guns, or even garrote wires or sharp objects. You don't even have to be very strong.

All you need are your bare hands, and a little bit of hate.

The dry crack of Curtis Blum's neck being snapped follows the students as they shuffle out of the auditorium. It's a cold wind, harsher than the one that blows dry leaves across the plaza outside the main hall, that drives them back to dormitories and apartments.

No one will sleep very well tonight. More than a few will waken from nightmares to find their sheets clammy with sweat, the sound of Blum's final scream still resonating in their ears. Wherever they may go for the rest of their lives, whatever they may do, they will never forget what they have witnessed this evening.

Fifteen years later, a sociology post-grad student at this same university, in the course of researching her doctoral thesis, will discover an interesting fact. Upon tracking down the students who were present at Charles Gregory Doblin's lecture and interviewing them or their surviving relatives, she will find that virtually none of them were ever arrested on a felony offense, and not one was ever investigated or charged with spousal or child abuse, statistics far below the national average for a population of similar age and social background.

Yet that is still in the future. This is the present:

In a small dressing room behind the stage, Charlie Doblin—no longer Charles Gregory Doblin, but simply Charlie Doblin, Inmate #7891—sits in a chair before a make-up counter, hunched over the dogeared Bible the mother of one of his victims sent him several years ago. His lips move soundlessly as he reads words he does not fully comprehend, but which help to give his life some meaning.

Behind him, a couple of state troopers smoke cigarettes and quietly discuss tonight's lecture. Their guns and batons are holstered and ignored, for they know that the man in the room is utterly harmless. They wonder aloud how much vomit will have to be cleaned off the auditorium floor, and whether the girl in the third row will later remember what she yelled when the big moment came. She sounded kinda happy, one cop says, and the other one shakes his head. No, he replies, I think she was pissed because she missed out on a great date.

They both chuckle, then notice that Charlie Doblin is silently peering over his shoulder at them. Shut up, asshole, one of them says, and Doblin returns his attention to his Bible.

A radio crackles. A trooper plucks the handset off his jacket epaulet, murmurs into it, listens for a moment. The van is waiting out back, the local cops are ready to escort them to the interstate. He nods to his companion, who turns to tell Charlie that it's time to go. The killer nods his head; he carefully marks his place in the Bible, then picks it up along with the speech that he read tonight.

He didn't write this speech, but he has dutifully read it many times already, and will read again tomorrow night in another college auditorium, to a different audience in a different city. And, as always, he will end his lecture by becoming a public executioner.

Somewhere else tonight, another death-row inmate unwittingly awaits judgment for his crimes. He sits alone in his cell, playing solitaire or watching a sitcom on a TV on the other side of the bars, and perhaps smiles at the notion that, this time tomorrow, he will be taken out of the prison to some college campus to make a speech to a bunch of kids, unaware that what awaits him are the eyes and hands of Charles Gregory Doblin.

It's a role which Charlie Doblin once savored, then found morally repugnant, and finally accepted as predestination. He has no say over what he does; this is his fate, and indeed it could be said that this is his true calling. He is very good at what he does, and his services are always in demand.

He has become a teacher.

Charles Gregory Doblin scoots back his chair, stands up and turns around, and lets the state troopers attach manacles to his wrists and ankles. Then he lets them take him to the van, and his next lesson.

The Bride of Elvis

KATHLEEN ANN GOONAN

Kathleen Ann Goonan's first SF novel, *Queen City Jazz,* was published in 1995 bearing endorsements from William Gibson and Lucius Shepard, and was a widely praised *New York Times* Notable Book. Her second novel, *The Bones of Time,* appeared in 1996, also to widespread acclaim, and late in 1997 the sequel to her first novel, *Mississippi Blues,* will appear. She is one of the bright new stars of the mid-1990s. And for the last several years she has been publishing short fiction of high quality in *Interzone, Asimov's,* and *Omni.* She has a droll wit and a complicated approach to storytelling that usually includes loads of SF details, shows a fascination with history and popular culture, and has lots of things happening. "The Bride of Elvis" first appeared in *SF Age.* This story is another tonic in the face of films of alien invasion and the anti-science of television shows such as *The X-Files.* Elvis, you see, was more than just King of rock and roll. . . .

Finding the tomb of Elvis empty was a big shock for Darlene.

She usually rose just before dawn, the nicest time of day here at Graceland, when it was all misty and as pretty as the Day of Instantaneous Redemption was going to be.

But this particular Sunday, the hot sun coming in the nine-foot-high window hit Darlene square in the face as she lay dreaming of *mana,* white and lovely. She stirred, blinked, and then slipped back into the dream, where she was a child again, eating as much *mana* as she could stuff down, while the others laughed at her greed and urged her on.

She rolled over and luxuriated atop the warmth of her round, leather-rimmed waterbed, resting her ear against the black satin sheet to hear the soothing slosh within.

Then she opened her eyes.

The readout on her alarm was blinking. Power must have gone out. Either that or she had messed it up again. Shoot. It was probably after eight, and Lu Ellen would have gone off-shift at seven.

So?

It was Sunday. Darlene went limp again. A slow day. Graceland wouldn't open until 9:30. She had plenty of time to check Elvis' readouts, and she had given Ella Mae in the Gift Shop a stockpile of hair snippings and skin scrapings, all ready in their little plastic twist-boxes (Ella Mae couldn't accuse her of being lazy *this* time and leaving all the work for someone else), so she wouldn't have to fool with *that* this morning.

But after five more minutes of sloth, she heaved herself out of bed, put on her plastic cap and showered, then sat down at her white French Provincial dressing table.

She pulled big rollers out of her long, honey-colored hair and put on foundation, cool and smooth against her skin, powder, and red lipstick. She touched on the comp-sphere, and the Hearings began to play.

The King, the King
Will rise again

Through air of gold and fire.

Her favorite. She hummed along with the ethereal voices of the Elvis Choir, then it got into the Prophecies, about the ship coming back with plenteous *mana* for all.

As Darlene listened, she put on her eye makeup, which she especially loved. Mermaid Green eyeshadow, with little sparkles in it, right after the black eyeliner. She shopped at the Rex-Mart down on Magnolia. That was the only place she could find Mermaid Green.

Fake eyelashes and lots of thick, black mascara. There. When the daily Prophecy was over, she turned on the radio and looked in the closet.

"Love me tender, love me true, never let me go," The King sang via KYNG, right across the river.

You bet, honey. Oh, you bet.

As she buttoned her lace blouse, a public service message urged the latest solution to help everyone stay prepared for the Great Return in case it took much longer, head-freezing. For the ones who didn't want to put up with any more bull while they waited. Elizabeth Taylor was going to do it, apparently, and some other humans, like Timothy Leary and Michael Jackson.

Darlene laughed out loud when she heard that, but it was really kind of sad. There was always that seepage between them and humans, but head-freezing wouldn't *work* for humans, of course. Tiny, but crucial, things about their physiology were entirely different; they couldn't regenerate. Not to mention that their technology was so primitive.

She gave her curls a final, swift brush and fastened back one side of her hair with a rhinestone barrette that spelled out ELVIS.

She felt a bit haughty as she left her room in the Bride's Hall. If you didn't have the Lineage, you had nothing. And she had it. In spades. It was one reason she was a Bride.

In the kitchen, which was empty, she fixed herself some instant coffee, all she liked in the morning unless she was a tad hungry, and then she had ten or eleven microwave sausage biscuits. The four other Brides were still asleep, of course, but there were usually some snotty Techs running around in their slick gray suits and belts jammed with all kinds of what-not and gadgets. They thought they were so great. They didn't realize that without the Brides, the race just couldn't continue. Rita in particular was a jerk. She always got on Darlene's nerves, stepping aside and bowing when she went by, saying, "Make way, everyone, wow, it's a *Bride.*"

Darlene lit her first Marlboro of the day and opened the cooler door to get a fresh sheaf of gladiola to put in the vases around Elvis' pedestal. The thick, dark green stalks were cool in her hand. She slipped her feet into the white satin heels she'd carried with her, opened the back door, and walked down the path to the Tomb.

The small pavilion that held Elvis was in the Meditation Garden. She reflected, as usual, as she passed the perfectly manicured trees that lined the path, on how fortunate she was to be a Bride. That, along with the Hearings, always got her in the proper frame of mind for putting up with all the fat, sweating mutants (and some thin, pretty ones too, now, Darlene, don't be evil) for the next eight hours.

It was always comforting to see Him there, all ready for the coming Redemption. He'd been put in a plexiglass pyramid showcase years ago, once they realized that the Redemption might take longer than they thought. That was the best way, the Committee had decided, to keep control of everything. A bunch of rabble-rousers who called themselves the Band of the King were always demanding more access, but they were just ineffective young upstarts for the most part, jealous because the Lineage of many of the members was human-tinged, though they weren't full-blown mutants. Ugly folks, ugly in the way they acted. Darlene shivered.

Calmed by the spring flowers that flanked the pavilion, Darlene saw that the sky was becoming overcast. The sun was hidden now, and the air smelled like rain. She climbed the five low marble steps up to the stone door, which was inscribed with angels and guitars. She raised her wrist to scan the door open, stopped. Her arm hung in the air.

The door was already open, just an inch. Her breath stuck in her throat: she stood on the threshold as fear flooded through her. The lights weren't working; she fumbled around on the wall next to the door and got the backup panel open, found the light button and flicked it with her long fingernail.

The plexiglass lid was propped open. Someone, *someone* with access . . . Darlene began to shake. The fat old guy just *wasn't there.* Lead wires dangled over the guitar-embossed pedestal.

Her cigarette fell from her fingers and smoldered on the pink shag rug. Maybe, she told Koell later, when she had to explain, she felt that it was her fault and that all their plans and dreams were ruined, blasted by the indigenous idiots on this backward planet they had to live on. Mingled in the back of her mind were the threats of the Band of the King. They kept saying they had to take matters into their own hands if anyone ever wanted to see the ship again—that is, they said, if such a ship even existed. Some of them, backsliders, were idiots enough to doubt.

Struck by waves of anxiety, she didn't stop to think that security was the Tech's job, or about *anything,* except that the other Brides would have *her* head as soon as they saw this, and if they froze it, they'd do it in a way so that she couldn't regenerate.

All her fear soul rose up through her throat, white-hot, as pure as a Gospel wail. "He's gone. He's *gone!*"

She ran right out through the Music Gate, using her wrist scanner to open it without thinking twice. Didn't care who was looking. Panicked. She ran right out onto Elvis Presley Boulevard, screaming her fool head off.

And met Roy.

He pulled up in front of her at the stoplight in a battered white F-100 Ford pickup with double back wheels and a custom extra-long bed. She was breathing hard and letting out a little sob at the end of each breath and knew, in the back of her mind, that she was quite a sight in her silver miniskirt, lacy blouse, and white satin heels, still holding the glads in her left hand.

She stared right through the window at the kind-faced man, who was handsome too, let's not mince words here, with keen blue eyes, black hair, and a short, black beard. His wide shoulders were hunched over the wheel, and his long lanky arms stopped while reaching up for the column shift as he stared right back at her. He leaned over and opened the door. "Get in, little lady, get right on in here."

Darlene didn't think twice. She got right in there and started bawling hard. He reached across her and then had to slide right next to her to reach the door and close it since she was holding on tight to that bouquet with both hands now, worried about Mars, her talking cat, not having had any breakfast at all, not any, then remembering that the bag of pellets was open behind the kitchen door.

The light changed, and he ground the gears, apparently not concerned about his transmission, and whatever he had in the back of the truck crashed against the tailgate.

"Jason took my tie-down, the little creep. Wait till I get my hands on him, I'll warm his fanny good. His mom lets him do whatever he wants. I'm just the mean daddy." He sighed, and his eyes, when he looked at Darlene, were sad and lost. "He stays mostly with her anyway."

Darlene was still crying some, just little snorts and a few tears. He leaned down and fished under the seat and came up with an old wrecked box of Kleenex. He pulled one out and handed it to her. "Here," he said. "Blow hard."

She put the flowers up on the dash and blew hard, not feeling at all embarrassed.

"Now, I want you to tell me what this here is all about," he said. "Have a fight with your boyfriend?"

"No," she gasped, so upset that she didn't even think twice about what to say. "It's Elvis. He's gone!" And she started to cry again, even harder. They'd waited for so long, and now that He was gone, no one would ever return, and they would never get home again. The ship wouldn't have any reason to come back for them. Stuck on this Kingforsaken planet through all millennia. And no more kiddies either! They couldn't have kiddies without Him! Those little twist-boxes of hair clippings would be used up real fast. She started to cry again. It was too awful. Darlene had never felt so rattled in all her born days, not even when she had had to leave her kiddies behind to take up her duties as a Bride.

"Oh," he said. "I see." But she could tell by the set of his jaw and the crinkle beneath his eye that he didn't see, not at all, and she was enraged that she'd told all this to a stranger, a *human*, who would only laugh at her.

But he didn't. He just drove through the empty downtown Memphis blocks, past the Peabody, through the ramshackle part of town with its run-down blues dives, until they got to the river.

"Maybe it would calm you down some to go for a little ride. Sometimes that's the best thing to do, it's real soothing, you know, especially after we get out into the country. I live over in Arkansas. It's right pretty over there, and the apple blossoms are all out. Well, you might not want to go anywhere with me—" he looked at her and she stared back—"I might as well tell you I got real drunk last night and pretty much passed out here in the front seat. But there's no reason to hold that against me. Sometimes a person has to have a drink or two."

She didn't say anything while they crossed the gray Mississippi beneath the darkening sky, thinking furiously. What the hell was going on? Why was He gone? Why hadn't the security system worked? Because of the power failure, probably, the one that put her alarm clock on the blink. That Tech Rita, strutting around in her militaristic gear. She'd like it if Darlene was blamed, wouldn't she? Wouldn't be too hard to keep her from waking up on time. Maybe she was in cahoots with the Band of the King.

Yeah, sure. But what about the backup system?

She'd almost forgotten where she was when he said, "Well, really, I could use some breakfast, couldn't you? You sure look like you could."

He pulled into a little place that advertised "Home Cooking" and helped her jump down from the seat. The truck cab was pretty high off the ground, not like her low, sleek, red 'Vette with the plate that read *Bride 1*.

She followed him inside, drained and tired. Well, of course she was ravenous. It was their one weakness—they needed to eat, and a lot; they needed these substances produced by Earth to survive. Not as good as *mana,* not nearly as powerful or longevity-producing, but they could get by if they got enough. That's why they hit the grocery stores so often. Two, three times a day, full carts each time. Too many of them to feed on the ship after the drive went bad, not enough energy to run the ship and make *mana* too. A skeleton crew had gone on. They'd be back. Someday. Or maybe never, now, because of her. Because of her failure.

They had discovered that they couldn't all live together here, though— they simply ate too much. At least four times as much as humans, so they spread out over a couple of states so as not to attract notice.

They kept in touch at the grocery stores, of course. Those aisles were their domain, the sound of rattling grocery carts as familiar as breathing, the memorized foodgrids of a dozen big grocery chains each one knew like the back of her hand. A lot of them doubted whether the fleet would come back for them, but Darlene had never wavered in her faith. Until today.

She'd never trusted the Techs, with all their fancy gear and snotty ways. She once even requested a few pit bulls to stand guard. That point in her favor was on the record. A pretty slim defense, now that the worst had happened. "You have no *idea,"* she had told the Committee, her days full of sobbing women flinging themselves against the velvet rope, smearing lipstick on the pyramid. But they weren't the real problem. Earth was such an odd place, full of criminals and just pure *weirdness,* you never knew what might happen, and now the worst, the absolute worst had happened. There were plenty of people who'd like to get hold of Elvis. But without Techs, he wouldn't last long.

She slid into the booth still trying to figure things out. She stared out the window while the black-haired man ordered coffee and hash browns and ham and biscuits and gravy and cheese omelets and grits for both of them just as if he knew, although she could see at a glance that he couldn't and that he was just a normal old human. But a good one, she saw that too. She wouldn't have even gotten into his truck if she hadn't been able to see that, but she didn't even have to think about those sorts of things because humans were really such simple beings. She kind of liked them, they made things so homey. They knew how to live—except that they scarcely lived longer than an insect. Hardly a tragedy, as far as she was concerned.

Still, sometimes she got tired of being a Bride and wanted to just be a human, instead of taking care of Elvis and longing for her kiddies. She'd had two before she was eleven, the process triggered by the sweat on the scarf she'd grabbed at her first concert.

Elvis had thrown it right at her. God, how lucky she'd been! Chosen! If the ship ever did come back, she was first in line for Elvis. She'd been activated at just the right age; she was one of the few who could actually mate with Elvis and conceive another King.

But it wasn't all fun. She'd had to leave those cute kiddies with her mother in order to be a Bride. That was hard. Being a Bride wasn't all it was cut out to be—checking all those meters and charts every day, letting them know if something was just a hair off so's the Techs could rush over and make a big deal out of it and blame it on the Bride in charge. Techs didn't think much of Brides, that was for sure. And now He was gone, and it was all her fault!

Or if it wasn't, best to hide out till they figured out whose fault it really was. She shivered to think how mean the other Brides would be when they found the King gone. It was pretty much like murder, or maybe killing somebody with a runaway car, because they wouldn't live much longer without him. Maybe not even a full human lifespan, puny as that was. Shit.

The man was watching her. He smiled. "You know, I'm not making fun of you or anything, but you sure look silly with all that stuff running down your face. Whenever we cried, Ma used to make us look in the mirror and see how funny we looked. 'See that monkey?' she'd say, and by God if that wouldn't make you laugh out loud to see your own red little face all screwed up—"

Shut up, she felt like saying, What do you know? but instead slid out of the seat.

"Wait," he said, "I'm sorry. I didn't mean—"

She let the door of the ladies' room whoosh shut behind her and leaned with straight elbows on the white, scummy sink.

He was right. She *did* look funny. Like a clown that had been caught out in the rain. Green stuff dribbled from the corner of one eye down onto her cheek, and there was a big black smear across her nose. And as for her mouth . . .

She leaned over and splashed her face with water. It took soap to get it all off, and then her face felt stiff and dry without her Rose-Soft Moisturizer, and she didn't even have her emergency touch-up kit because she didn't have her purse with her. Her purse held not only her makeup but her bracelet, the bracelet that shielded them from the human pheromones which the males gave off when they had sex, pheromones powerful enough to trigger conception. The conception of mutants, that is. "Never go out without your bracelet," she could almost hear her mother warning. She never had. She'd never done *anything* like she'd done today.

She lifted her chin. The hell with them. She'd done her best. It *wasn't* her fault that He was gone, even though they'd blame it on her. Who cared? They'd be looking for her, but they'd never find her. She'd bury herself in this Kingforsaken country and she wouldn't go back, that's all. She just wouldn't. Not till she was good and ready. Maybe never.

She went back out and the plate of steaming food was there.

She slid into the booth. The ham was good and salty, real country stuff: she wondered where they got it. The omelet was plasticky but not bad, and the biscuits dripped with gravy full of cracklins. She shoved food in her mouth just about as fast as she could get it on the fork, elbows wide on the formica table, not caring if he stared at her, and he did.

"I never seen a lady eat so fast—now wait, sorry, I just seem to say the wrong thing, but it's true."

He offered her one of his Marlboros as they talked over coffee.

"So what was that you were saying now?" he asked. "Elvis is gone? Something about you being a bride?"

"Yeah, well, a Bride is just a caretaker, that's what we call ourselves, see? The estate hired us to take care of the shrine there, that's all. You know how many people come visit that?" Millions, and there was a damned good reason too.

"Even my ma has been," he said.

"What's your name?"

"Elroy. Elroy Juster. I live over in Sudden. That's a little town not too far away." He rose up out of the booth a little and reached over and lit her second cigarette.

His face was close to hers for a moment. She liked the way he smelled. His eyes were blue.

Intensely blue.

As she looked into them, she saw that he was very kind, with a degree of kindness she'd rarely sensed before. She never had spent much time with humans. She'd better get used to them now.

"What do you do for a living, Mr. Juster?"

"Call me Roy," he said, and frowned a little, and she liked the fleeting crease between his eyes. Some of these humans could be mighty attractive, and he was one of them for sure. Too bad, she thought, she'd left her purse behind. She wondered how he looked naked, how that long, lean body would feel next to hers, what those nice, big hands would do—oh hell, Darlene. You know that's dumb. You ought to be ashamed of yourself. Get some nose plugs or something. You don't want to tie yourself down with mutants.

"Just any little thing I can. My daddy raised tobacco, but it killed him. I mean, he smoked too damn much. Ma's mighty sick now from something or other. Pulmonary something or other, the doctor said. She'd like you, I know; she likes a girl that knows how to eat. She could cook up a meal in her day, and that's for sure." Well, that sounded attractive to Darlene. She was getting hungry again already.

But she felt sad, for a minute, listening to all that. There just wasn't any rest anywhere in the universe, that was all there was to it. You would think that these simple creatures would be able to have a nice life, but no, sireebob, they had their troubles too, just as bad troubles as if you had to keep the King ready for the Redemption. Thinking of the King reminded her that they'd have to go clear to another galaxy to get another King, and really, it was too late for that . . . she rested her forehead in her hands. They were shaking.

Roy reached over, pried one of her hands loose, squeezed it, held it until it stopped shaking, then let go. "I hope you don't mind, I mean it won't affect my driving none or anything," he said, "but I have this horrible headache and it might help if I had a beer . . ."

"No, that's OK. I'll have one too."

"Can't serve it before noon on Sunday," said the waitress.

Roy got out two dollars. "Only twenty minutes. This change the little hand on the clock any?" he asked.

"You're gonna make us lose our license," she said, but brought them both draft Buds.

The beer tasted good and tingly to Darlene. She didn't drink much but sometimes she really tied one on. It was starting to rain outside and everything was dark and cozy inside. It wouldn't be a bad day for that sort of thing, she thought. Sometimes it was all you could do, to keep from thinking about things.

"You know, I always wondered what this Elvis attraction was," he said. "Now don't get all huffy, I don't mean to hurt your feelings or nothing, but really, what do all these people see in Elvis?"

"Well, he's the King," she said, well into her third beer, which had just about completely obliterated her concern about what the other Brides might do to her. She felt kind of whoozy.

"So what?" he said. "He sang a few songs, he got fat, he died."

"Those weren't just any old songs," she flared. "Those were—" then she stopped. She'd said too much already, way too much.

"You know, you sure are a funny lady," he said. "They must pay you pretty good to be one of those Brides. I never heard of such a thing, really. I had no idea. I guess I just never paid much attention to Elvis, that's all. You're cute, though."

She was more than cute, she knew. She was gorgeous. They all were, with that long-legged, slim-hipped, big-breasted Southern style. Most of them favored white-blond hair and spoke in that exaggerated accent that rolled off the tongue so smooth and full. They matured fast, but didn't start looking old for a long, long time. Not unless they wanted to, but a lot of them did. It kept the men away. Between shopping, cooking, and eating, they mostly watched TV and kept up with things through their supermarket newspapers and KYNG. It made the time pass.

But she wasn't ready to look old yet. Roy was mighty attractive, she thought for about the tenth time. And very sweet, too. Damn it!

She had to pee. She walked toward the bathroom, then paused at the end of the lunch counter.

A little black and white portable flickered at the end of the lunch counter, and she heard the word Elvis. An earnest reporter stood in front of Graceland with a microphone in her hand.

"Not only has Elvis disappeared, but his caretaker along with him. Police suspect foul play. There's been a massive power outage at Graceland and the surrounding area which a spokesman for the power company says can't be traced to any known reason."

Idiots. Next thing you know they'd be flashing her picture around the state. If the other Brides got hold of her, they'd tear her hair out by the roots. She turned around, went back to Roy, and leaned on the table. "I'm about ready to go," she said. "Are you?"

He smiled, and she was drawn into those blue eyes. He pushed himself out of the booth. She swayed, and he caught her arm. Had she only had three beers?

They walked out to the truck through a light rain which patterned the brown puddles in the parking lot, and she could *feel* him walking next to her, almost as if he were some sort of twin she ought to return with to whatever it was happened before you were born. Though it was only a little bit after noon, they both looked together at the flashing motel sign the next parking lot over. A semi hissed by on its way down to the river.

They stood there for a moment, and he looked helpless as he gazed at her. Then, before she could say a word, the hell with her purse and the bracelet inside, the hell with her Mission and being a Bride (but the King was gone anyway, nobody needed Brides now), he reached across her and unlocked the door, stammered "Sorry" when his arm brushed against her breast, as she'd intended, and hurried around to his side of the truck.

"Didn't mean to leave you standing in the rain like that," he said, and started up the truck and flipped on the heater. "It'll be cold for a few minutes," he said, and took off down the road.

She felt pretty much on edge. She turned on the radio, which crackled with distant lightning.

"I get so lonesome when you're gone," He crooned, and she whispered, "Elvis."

"Now don't you go all dreamy-faced and eyes-rolled-up on me," he joked, stealing a glance at her. As he looked at her, his smile froze.

She knew something showed in her eyes, then, a distant galaxy she barely remembered, and then only when she heard His voice. Cold-sleep had blanked it out. She'd been just a kiddie. She blanked it out some more; she blinked, then laughed.

"I'm OK," she said.

"You look pale," he said, and rubbed her arm with the back of his hand. Then he pulled off the road in a flail of flying gravel and grabbed both her shoulders.

"Shit," he said, as the truck began to move. He let go of her and set the brake. Then he was kissing her, she was kissing him, O God, O, *Elvis* . . .

"No," he said and pulled back. "I don't know why I'm doing this. I've never done anything like this before, believe me. Well, not quite. Like this. What I mean—"

So what? But it seemed important to him for some reason. "I believe you," she said, which was what he wanted to hear, and she did, she knew this man inside out. She could. She just never bothered. Humans were usually so boring, especially the men who came on to her in the bars of Memphis.

She drew back and looked at Roy for a moment. She was breathing real fast and her chest felt funny.

He was full of beautiful resonance, with avenues of thought and being and pure kindness and innocence she could almost see down and touch, they were so real to her. Maybe she'd just never taken the time to look at a human before. Was this what Elvis was singing about in all those songs? Good god, what a feeling! No wonder Kings acted so nutty. They just lost their fool minds. She felt like singing herself. The hell with being a Bride. The ship would never be back.

She knew that lots had fallen by the wayside, forgotten their bracelets in a moment like this with no part of the King around, no sweat-soaked scarf, no little plastic twist-box of cells or hair to align the gene sequences correctly. What got born three months later were mutant half-human kiddies. Human birth control didn't work for them because it was the pheromones that allowed the sperm and eggs already in them to join. The powerful spray of pheromones human males gave off during love-making did that too, but things got just a little twisted with those alien pheromones.

Those mutants, and she might conceive one any minute, if she kept on like this, were the thousands of women—always women—with sad, yearning faces who trudged past the coffin, not quite sure why they felt so strongly about Elvis. They were good for the budget, though, and it took a heck of a big bankroll to fund the checks that got sent out every two weeks so that everyone could get enough to eat. The full-lined ones matured quickly, almost twice as fast as humans, so there were a few generations now, and where they came from was dim legend to new kiddies. She had her mother to thank for being so strict and making sure she listened every morning and kept the faith, though sometimes she had her doubts too. She'd been lucky to be a Bride, which kept it all fresh and real in her mind.

And now all hell had broken loose, and she wanted to stay with this human man. "Roy," she whispered, and he drew her close against his chest. All her yearning loneliness was gone. She'd never have a man on the ship, except that one strictly delineated time. They were simply obsolete. All but one. There was always one King. But this particular King had gotten much too rowdy toward the end, what with a whole weird alien planet spread out before Him. Best to keep Him in coldsleep, all His vital parts preserved, all the necessary genetic information still intact, before He ruined it altogether with his silly drugs and wild ways. Just a big kid, but Kings always were. Spoiled and rebellious. Never listening.

Darlene looked into Roy's eyes. This guy was different. Maybe the human way *was* better.

She kissed Roy back. She opened her mouth and drew in his tongue, felt his breath become deep and slow as hers. His lips were soft on her face, his hands felt so good on her breast, on her thigh—

Afterward, without saying anything, he turned on the truck and drove as if he were in kind of a daze. She buttoned her blouse, bent down to snag her panties from off the floor and pulled them back on.

Finally, he said, "Damn." But that was all he said.

She didn't feel much like talking either. She could feel the conception within her body, just like she had when she'd grabbed His scarf, and it didn't feel horrible like they said it would. Her mother had told her how creepy it would feel, how sickening and awful when the mutation was taking place.

It felt good.

It only took another forty-five minutes to get there. They drove past fields fringed over with new green growth, through a little town which had an old wooden grocery store with a faded red Coca-Cola sign.

"Closed on Sunday," the sign on the door said. A few pickups were parked next door at the Bar and Grill, and a black dog lay under one of them, trying to stay out of the rain. The courthouse was the nicest building in town, which was only two blocks long, with its dome and pillars. "This is Sudden," Roy said. "It's the county seat." He turned just past the courthouse onto a narrow asphalt road which changed to dirt after a few miles and climbed the narrow rim of a red clay hillside. At the top was a doublewide with a screened-in porch and rose bushes blooming all around, pink, red, yellow. A black satellite dish was right next to it. "It's not much, I guess," Roy said.

It's not, she thought, but said, "It's nice."

"This is Ma's," he said. "That cabin over there is mine. I built it from a kit."

"Really," she said.

She looked all around, at the low green hills below them, the fields laid out so sure and true, with all those neighbors down little back roads. She felt good here, more at home than at Graceland, watching those meters, seeing that throng of sightseers file by, putting up with the jealousy of the other Brides because she was first in line once they got back to the ship, and they were just backups. Hell. It was all a stupid fantasy. Why not stay here? It seemed like home, and Roy felt like home too. She could have a future here. Not forever, or even close. But no one would have forever, now that the King was gone.

Roy took her hand, as if he knew what she was thinking. They got close to the doublewide and heard the drone of the TV.

"Good," he said, and she felt his relief run up her spine and spread out through her body like a cool breeze. "I guess she's OK. I shouldn't have left her alone all night; you just never know."

He knocked, then opened the door. "Ma," he said, "how you doing? I brought somebody I want you to meet. Darlene, this is Zinnea, my mother."

He stopped so suddenly that Darlene ran right into the back of him. "What's wrong?" Roy asked his mother. Darlene looked around and saw an old lady dressed in a faded print dress. She was crying.

"Look," she said.

Darlene looked, and her mouth fell open.

There it was, right on the Cable News Network: Graceland, from the air. About a million people were there, under the helicopter's whup whup whup, as the reporter said, "It's unbelievable, just unbelievable."

"What happened?" Darlene asked, but she didn't really have to. Of course it was on national news.

The old woman had a pale, sweet face. Darlene knew she used to be fat and full of piss and vinegar. She knew lots of things. She knew Roy's mother was seventy-one, and had arthritis, adult-onset diabetes, and plaque in her left anterior descending coronary artery. Not to mention pulmonary lesions.

"If it don't beat all," Zinnea said. "I mean, that I've lived to see the day. Elvis is gone. Simply gone from his tomb, you know. Just look at that crowd."

"Darlene here is one of the—" but Darlene kicked him sharp behind his knee and he shut up. She'd been a fool to tell him a thing. She was just a pure and entire fool anyway. She'd really have to play things down if she wanted to stay around here.

Roy touched her arm, and that *something* flooded through her. Maybe she wasn't entirely a fool. It all made sense when he touched her, anyway.

Darlene sat down on the worn green couch next to Zinnea and took her hand. "You kinda liked Elvis, huh?"

"Oh, I cut my teeth on that man," she said, and she wheezed as she spoke. "Why, you know, I even saw him once, it was at the County Fair back in the '50s when he was just getting started. Roy's father had a hissy fit about it; said I shouldn't be so interested in how the hips of any other man moved. But there was a lot of goodness in him."

"There was," said Darlene. And some mighty strange DNA too, lady.

Still holding the old lady's hand in both of hers, she looked into her frail face. She could feel Roy sitting on her other side, knew his eyes were glued to the TV.

Darlene didn't do this much because, frankly, she didn't often care enough to do it.

But it was just a matter of restoring a balance, and then removing that plaque from the left ventricle. Darlene healed her, then let go of her hand.

Zinnea looked at her with an open, innocent look, as if she were a kiddie herself, just born. Her cheeks grew pink. She leaned back against the couch, coughed once, then breathed deeply with wonder on her face. She squinted at Darlene. "I *do* feel good, all of a sudden." She stood up. "Real good. I must have forgot my manners. Let me get you some ice tea. Lemon or sugar, honey?"

"Both," said Darlene, and wondered if maybe Zinnea had a few pies stored away that she could polish off as a little snack.

"It will take me a few minutes," Zinnea said. "None of that instant stuff around here." She went around a paneled partition.

"There seems to be something white coming down from the sky," said the commentator, his voice choked with fear.

Darlene jumped up and stared at the television. "Of course," she said. "Of course."

They'd finally got the drive working again. Took them long enough. Only about sixty years. Naturally they'd take the King first—they had to hook Him in. They'd taken no chances with Him. Why tell the Brides? Those Techs always treated Brides like dirt and were so smug about their jobs and always saying nothing could go on without them. They must have just planned to wake the Brides up when everything was ready, to keep them from getting underfoot. She thought of her kiddies, suddenly, her beautiful, fast-growing full-lined kiddies. They must be here, along with her mother. There were no men, of course, in that heaving, thronging crowd.

"I have to get back to Memphis, Roy," she said.

"No," he whispered, and she felt his pain. He jumped up and his arms went around her, held her tight. "I won't let you go. So what if He's back? They don't need you there. I *do*. Oh God, honey, sweetheart, I do."

Her eyes filled with tears when she heard the passion in his voice, which matched hers in strength and depth.

Then Elvis, *live*, she knew it, launched into a song she'd never heard before. It must be patched through from the ship. The *call*. What they'd always been waiting for.

It was like she was hearing two things when she listened, the human words, and beneath them, ancient, powerful directions.

The spark of the unknown past surged through her. *Mana*, pure white as if distilled from starlight. Long, incredibly long life; planets beyond her ken, a homeland she couldn't even imagine, but which pulled at every cell.

Roy never looked frightened, no, not for an instant, as he reached back to turn off the TV, almost like he knew it all and what was going to happen.

"I won't let you go," he said. He held her even more closely, and she knew it was true. She drew back a little and just looked at him, with Elvis' lovely voice in her ears, and he started to gasp. He let go of her. His hands went to his throat, and he fell to the floor, writhing and choking.

Darlene reached down and picked up the keys he'd dropped, then stepped over him.

Elvis stopped singing as she walked out the door. She walked across the gravel lot, climbed into the truck, and heard Zinnea scream.

"Sorry, honey," she said, as she turned the ignition key and slammed the truck into reverse, even though she knew he couldn't hear her. But he'd be breathing again now. She'd only meant to make him let go of her. As she sped down the driveway, toward Him, *mana,* her kiddies, the ship, *everything,* she whispered, blinking back tears, "It never would have worked. It *never* would have worked anyway, Roy, sweetie. Never."

Forget Luck

KATE WILHELM

Kate Wilhelm has been recognized as a first-rate writer of SF since the late 1950s, but came fully into prominence in the 1970s with a string of stories and novels that won many Nebula Awards and were nominated for many more. Her Hugo-winning novel, *Where Late the Sweet Birds Sang*, was also published then. Since the mid-1980s, she has written a number of successful novels in the mystery genre, but has continued to write striking new SF short fiction. Wilhelm is married to Damon Knight. Together they influenced the instruction of new SF writers through the Clarion Writers Workshop, which they helped found, for thirty years— after being significant forces in the famous Milford Writers Workshop (for experienced professional writers) for more than ten years before Clarion. Evolution is one of the bedrock ideas upon which the whole of SF literature is founded in the 20th century, and "Forget Luck" is this year's best addition to that central tradition.

Tony Manetti had not been assigned to cover the colloquium at Michigan State, but the day before it was to start, his editor had a family crisis. Tony would have to go. A suite was already reserved in the magazine's name at the Holiday Inn; a rental car would be waiting at the Lansing airport.

Tony had called Georgina twice, leaving the message that meant she was to return the call when her husband was not around, but she had not called back. Already on her way from Berkeley, he decided. Of course, she thought Harry would be covering the conference, and accordingly had not been in touch with Tony. Five nights, he kept thinking, five nights, and days, of course.

When he checked in at the motel, Georgina had not yet registered. He paid scant attention to the academic papers the desk clerk handed him; the speakers would all make certain *Academic Currents* received a copy of their papers. He checked the schedule. That evening, Saturday, there would be opening ceremonies, then people would drift away to eat and drink. On Sunday there would be a brunch, several luncheons, teas, more eating and drinking, and on Monday the attendees would start lecturing one another. He planned to miss it all. He could read the papers any time, and if anything interesting happened, someone would tell him all about it. He planned to be in upper Michigan with the gorgeous Georgina.

She had not checked in yet when he came back down, after leaving his gear in his suite. He went to the bar, crowded with academics, ordered a gin and tonic, and looked for a place to sit where he could keep an eye on the lobby.

Someone said, "Ah, Peter, good to see you again." A heavyset bald man was beckoning to him.

"Dr. Bressler," Tony said. "How are you." He looked past him toward the front desk where people were checking in in a continuous flow.

"Very well, Peter. Here, take a seat."

"It's Tony. Tony Manetti." Bressler had been his teacher for a term at Columbia; Tony had seen him twice, once in the hall and once in class, and every time they met at a conference, Bressler called him Peter.

"Yes, of course. You're the FBI fellow."

"No sir. I work for *Academic Currents*, the magazine." A new group had replaced the old; she was not among them.

"Of course. Of course. Peter, you're just the sort of fellow I've been looking for, someone with your training."

Bressler was in his sixties, a contender for the Nobel any year now for his past work in genetics, and he was more than a little crazy, Tony had decided six years ago in his class. A redhead appeared. He strained to see. Wrong redhead.

". . . a bit of a problem getting blood . . ."

He thought of her legs, a dancer's long legs.

". . . can't seem to get even a drop. One can't very well simply ask for it, you see."

He had been to the upper peninsula once in late summer; it had been misty and cool, romantic, with a lot of shadowy forest.

". . . have to think they're onto me. I simply can't account for it in any other way. Four accidents in the last two years, and some of my finest graduate students . . ."

Admit it, he would say, your marriage is a sham. I can move out to the west coast, he would say. I don't have to stay in Chicago; I can work out of anywhere.

". . . really substantiates my theory, you see, but it also poses a severe problem."

Tony had hardly touched his gin and tonic; it was simply something to do while he waited. He tasted it and put it down again. Bressler was gazing off into space, frowning.

And then she appeared, clinging to the arm of Melvin Witcome, smiling up at him the same way she sometimes had smiled up at Tony. Melvin Witcome was some kind of special course coordinator for the Big Ten, a man of power and influence; not yet forty, independently wealthy, handsome, suave, Phi Beta Kappa, with a doctorate in charm or something, he was everything Tony was not. He watched Witcome sign the registration, watched him and Georgina take their computer keys, watched them point out their bags to a bellboy, then board the elevator together. He was not aware that he had stood up until he heard Bressler's voice.

"I don't mean to imply there's any immediate danger. Sit down, Peter."

He sat down and gulped some of his drink. It was a mistake; they simply happened to arrive at the same time; they were old friends; she had not expected Tony to be there. He finished his drink. She had not expected him to be there.

"You're not going to the beastly opening ceremony, are you?" Bressler placed his hand on Tony's arm. "Let's go have some dinner instead. I want to pick your brain. You're a godsend, Peter. I was desperate for guidance, and you appeared. A godsend."

He had talked to the class about angels, Tony remembered then. Something about angels. Tony had tuned out. He had tuned out most of that year, in fact.

Bressler's voice had grown a bit shrill. "No one knows how humiliating it is to be considered a weirdo. A weirdo," he repeated with bitter satisfaction. "Simply because you have come upon a truth that others are not yet willing to accept or even to see."

"Angels," Tony said.

"Excellent, Peter! Ten years or more and you remember. But, of course, they prefer to see angels. Come on, let's go have some dinner."

Tony stood up. It had been six years ago; he didn't bother to make the correction. When they emerged from the dim bar, a mirage of pine forest danced in the street before him. A taxi drove through the dripping trees, and Bressler waved it over.

They had flaming cheese, and retsina with lamb kebabs, and ouzo with honey-doused walnut cakes. Bressler talked without letup throughout. Tony listened sporadically, brooding about the gorgeous Georgina.

"Of course, we all knew you were very special," Bressler said, then sipped his Greek coffee. "Your job is proof enough. I know people who would kill for your job. Rumor was you saved Bush's life or something, wounded in the line of duty, permanently disabled and quite justly rewarded, all that."

What really had happened was that when he was twenty-two, with a bachelor of science degree, he had applied to the FBI, along with his best friend, Doug Hastings, and to their surprise, they both had been accepted. A year later, his first real assignment had taken him and a senior agent out to do a routine background security check. A nothing assignment, until a fourteen-year-old boy with no hair had used him for target practice. Tony would have been quite seriously wounded, even shot dead, if he had not bent over at precisely the right moment to free his pants leg from the top of his sock. As it was he had been shot in the upper arm. Then, two weeks after being declared fit to resume a life of fighting evil, he had been shot again. The second time had been from the rear, and the only people behind him that day had been two other special agents and their supervisor, a unit chief.

He rather liked the version Bressler was voicing, and, as he had been enjoined never to reveal the truth of the matter, he remained silent, impassive, inscrutable. And, he was afraid, ridiculous. The second time he had been approaching a Buick in a crouch, and when he realized it was empty, he had stood up and started to turn to say the coast was clear. The bullet had gone through his arm instead of his head. The other arm this time.

"Must be like being a priest, once a priest always a priest. One doesn't forget training like that. Once FBI, always FBI; isn't that right?"

Tony finished his ouzo. The last time he had seen his former best friend Doug Hastings, Doug had said, "Keep away from me, jinx. Orders. Okay? No hard feelings?"

"Well, no one expects you to talk about it," Bressler said. He waved his tiny cup for more Greek coffee. "But you have had the training. Put your mind to it, Peter. How can I get blood samples from those people?"

Cautiously Tony said, "I need time to think about it."

"Of course, of course. When we go back to the hotel I'll hand you the reports, my notes, everything. It was providence that sent you to me, Peter. I had a feeling. Are you ready?"

What he would do, Tony had decided, was gather up the papers already in hand, check out in the morning, and beat it.

Back in his suite, he gazed morosely at the stack of papers; the desk clerk had handed him another pile, and Bressler had added his own bulging package. His head was aching with a dull distant surf-like monotony; he had had more to drink that evening than he generally consumed in a year, and he was not at all ready for sleep. When he found himself wondering if Georgina and Witcome were in a suite like his, with a couch like his, the same coffee table, the same king-sized bed, he began to shuffle papers. Not Bressler's, he put them aside and looked over a few others. But bits and pieces of what Bressler had said floated back to his mind, not in any rational coherent way, in phrases. He suspected that Bressler had talked in disconnected phrases.

Then, because it was his job to condense ten, fifteen, twenty pages of academic papers to a paragraph that would make sense to a reader, even if only temporarily, he found he was doing the same thing to this evening with Bressler.

Genes were the secret masters of the universe. Tony blinked, but he was certain Bressler had said that. Right. Genes ruled the body they inhabited, communicated with it; they ordered black hair, or red. And silky skin, and eyes like the deepest ocean . . . He shook himself. Genes were immortal, unless the carriers died without progeny. They decided issues like intelligence, allergies, homosexuality . . .

He closed his eyes, trying to remember where the angels came in. Sixty-eight percent of those polled believed in angels; forty-five percent believed in their own personal guardian angel. That was it. For guardian angel read genes.

Everyone knew someone or about someone who had had a miraculous escape from certain death or terrible injury. The sole survivor of an airplane crash; the infant who didn't freeze when abandoned in zero temperature; a highway accident that should have been fatal . . .

"Forget angels, forget a sixth sense, an intuitive avoidance of danger. Think alleles, the right combination of alleles. Genes are the secret masters and a particular combination of alleles, a particular gene, or more than one possibly, comes into being occasionally to rule all the others, for what purpose we can only guess. These very special genes can cause other genes to do their bidding, cause a change in metabolism that keeps a freezing infant from dying, regulate heart and lung functions to allow a drowned boy to be revived, alter every tissue in the human body and permit it to walk away from an impact that should have killed it outright . . ."

Tony yawned. There had been more, three hours' worth more, but he had condensed, combined, edited, and had made it coherent. He wished he had some aspirin. What he had done was compact a yard of garbage into a small neat package, but it was still the same garbage. He took a shower and went to bed, and felt lost in an acre of hard, cold, polyester loneliness.

He was up and dressed by seven-thirty, determined to be gone before West Coast people, Berkeley people, before Georgina was awake. He ordered breakfast, and while waiting for it he stuffed papers into his briefcase, leaving Bressler's stack to be turned in at the front desk, to be put in the man's message box, or thrown away, or whatever. When those were the only reading material remaining, he glanced at them.

The subject reports were on top. Everett Simes, at eleven, had been found in a snowdrift, body temperature sixty-three. He had survived with no ill effects. At nineteen he had fallen off a two-hundred-foot cliff and had walked away from the accident, no ill effects. Vera Tanger had survived an explosion in a restaurant that had killed everyone else there; she had survived having her stalled car totaled by a train. Carl Waley, two miraculous survivals. Beverly Wang, two. Stanley R. Griggs, two.

He replaced the papers in the folder when there was a knock on his door. His breakfast had arrived, and looming over the cart was Dr. Bressler, nearly pushing it himself in his eagerness to gain entrance.

"Peter, I'm so glad you're up and about already. Did you read my material?"

Tony motioned to the waiter to unload the cart by the window, signed the charge, and waved him away without speaking.

"Do you have another cup lurking under there?" Bressler asked. The waiter produced another cup and saucer. "And you might bring another pot of coffee," Bressler said. He settled down at the window table and began to lift lids off dishes.

They shared the breakfast; Bressler ate only the finger food since he had no silverware. Sausage was finger food. He talked constantly.

"The subjects I'm after all had at least two escapes," he said. "Often three or even four. But two is sufficient. I excluded those with only one reported escape. One could be considered coincidence, but two, three, four? Forget coincidence. No one knows how many possible subjects are out there; not all accidents get reported, of course. I settled for five who live close enough to New York to make it possible, I thought, to extract a sample from them. Hair follicles, saliva, blood, skin scrapings. You know, you're a scientist. But four times in the past two years the graduate students I sent out had accidents of their own. One lost the hair brush he had stolen when he was mugged. Another was chased away by a ferocious dog; he fell and broke his leg trying to elude the beast. One never could get near the subject; she was as wary as a Mata Hari." He smiled at his little rhyme. "My students are showing some reluctance concerning further attempts."

Tony emptied the coffee pot into his cup.

Bressler looked at it in disappointment. "Have you come up with an idea?" he asked then.

"Ask outright for a sample," Tony said. "Offer to pay five bucks a spit. Align yourself with a doctor, a clinic or something like that, and offer free checkups. Find their dentists and pay him to collect a sample. Hire a mugger and have him do a scraping before he snatches the loot. Hire a flock of guys in white coats to swarm over an apartment building, or an office, or wherever the hell the subject is, and say you're checking for an outbreak of plague. Hire some prostitutes, male and female, to seduce them one and all." There was a tap on the door; he went to open it. "There must be a thousand ways you can get what you're after." He admitted the waiter with another pot of coffee.

When they were alone again, Bressler was beaming. "See, that's what I meant. A man with certain training. I tried some of those ideas, of course, but some are quite ingenious. I couldn't do anything that even suggested harm, naturally. Heaven alone knows what the repercussions would be if the genes thought they were under attack. It's bad enough that they know they have been discovered." He poured coffee for them both.

Tony gazed at him in disbelief. "The genes know you're after them," he said after a moment. "The genes are taking defensive measures."

"No doubt about it. They know." He put one finger in his coffee, then used the moistened tip to pick up toast crumbs, which he ate.

"What will you do with the data if you get it?" Tony asked.

Bressler looked very blank. "Do? You mean like the agriculture bioengineers? Breeding potatoes with enough poison to kill off the potato bugs? Strawberries that grow and bear fruits in subfreezing temperature? I don't plan to *do* anything except publish, of course. Those genes have absolutely nothing to fear from me, Peter."

"I understand," Tony said. He looked at his watch and stood up. "Gosh, I've got to run." He picked up Bressler's papers to hand back to the man.

"Keep them, Peter. Keep them. I have copies. I know you haven't had time to think this through. Read them, then get back to me. Will you do that?"

"Sure," Tony said. "I'll get back to you."

By the time he had checked out, and was on the road, he was grinning broadly. Bressler wouldn't get in touch with him, he thought. He wouldn't know who to get in touch with, just Peter somebody. His grin faded as he realized he had no destination. Not the upper peninsula, those cool misty dark romantic forests. Not alone. He had no one he had to go back home to; no one expected him in the office ever. He drifted in, drifted out; eventually he would lug in the ton of scholarly papers he had collected, turn in his column on the symposium, and be free until the next one. He remembered Bressler's words: people would kill for his job.

He was exactly what the job description stated: special assistant editor responsible for a column devoted to academic symposia, colloquia, conferences, meetings of all sorts that involved two or more university-level representatives of two or more universities, wherever such a meeting was being held—Paris, Hong Kong, Boston, Rio . . .

Sometimes he wondered how high the supervisor who had shot him had risen, or if he had been tossed overboard. Tony had never doubted that it was an accident, but a trigger-happy unit chief was not a good idea. He knew it had been the supervisor if only because neither of the other two agents had been even chided for carelessness. Sometimes he wondered how the agency had managed to get him, Tony, into Columbia on such short notice, and see that he got a master's, and then this plum of a job. It was understood that the job required at least a master's degree.

Sometimes, more ominously, he wondered if one day they would reel him in and demand . . . He never could finish the thought. Demand what?

Signs had been warning him that if he wanted to go to Detroit, to get in the right lane. He eased into the left lane.

That night he sat in a screened porch on a pseudo-rustic cabin and watched the sun set across Lake Michigan. Mosquitoes worked on the screens with chainsaws trying to get in. He had spent all day driving aimlessly, talking himself out of the notion of Georgina. She was too old for him, at least forty to his thirty-one. He had been flattered that an older woman had found him attractive. She had been grateful when he mentioned her various papers at various conferences, and had in fact helped him write her notices. Her return rate for his calls had been no more than one out of six, but, she had explained, her husband was so jealous, and always there.

Then, to escape the reality of love lost, he had turned to the fantasy of master genes ruling the universe. Pretend, he had told himself, pretend it's true, that life-saving intuition, coincidence, messages from the collective unconscious, good luck, guardian angels can all be attributed to a single source, and that source is genetic. Then what? He knew, from the various conferences he had attended, that the genotyping success rate was accelerating at a pace that astounded even those participating in it. So, he had continued, pretend they find such a master gene, isolate it, then what? The answer had come with surprising swiftness. Breed a master race, supermen.

He grinned at the idea, as he watched the last cerise band in the sky darken. When it merged into inky black, he went inside his cabin and regarded with some fondness the bulky pile of Bressler papers. He began to read through them.

Bressler had a list of thirty or forty possible subjects, each one with an impressively complete dossier. He had done his homework. They were scattered throughout the states; the five he had targeted were all within a hundred miles of Manhattan. Every subject had escaped death at least twice; all the escapes had been reported in various newspapers, which were referenced in footnotes.

Tony scanned the dossiers briefly, then went to the summaries. Bressler had anticipated the few questions Tony had: none of the parents showed any of the survival traits of their offspring. A higher than normal percentage of the subjects were single children of their biological parents, although there were step-brothers and sisters. Few of the subjects showed any other unusual traits; they were a good cross section of the population, some very bright, some dim, laborers, professionals, technicians. . . . The one thing they all had in common, it appeared, was the ability to survive situations that should have killed them. And five of them, at least, were too elusive to catch and sample.

He felt almost sad when he closed the folder. Poor old guy, spending the past six years or more on this. He remembered something Bressler had said in the restaurant, "How many more do you suppose there are? We'll never know because no one keeps track of those who don't board the airplane that crashes into the ocean. The ones who stay home the day the mad bomber wipes out the office building. The ones who take a different route and miss the twenty-car pile-up and fireball. The ones who . . . But you get my point. We can't know about any of them."

The ones who bend down to straighten out a pants leg and don't get shot through the heart, Tony thought suddenly. *The ones who stand up and turn around and don't get shot in the head.*

Oh, boy! he thought then. *Folie à deux!* He went out on the porch and gazed at the lake where uneasy moonlight shimmered. After a moment he stripped, wrapped a towel around his waist, and went out for a swim. The water was shockingly cold. He could demonstrate to Bressler just how nutty his theory was, he thought, swimming; all he had to do was keep going toward Wisconsin until cold and fatigue sank him like a stone. Another time, he decided, turning back to shore.

In bed, every muscle relaxed to a pudding-like consistency, he wondered what he would have done if Bressler had asked for a sample of his blood. His entire body twitched and he plummeted into sleep.

The next morning, he found himself driving back to East Lansing. He listened to talk radio for a while, then sang harmony with Siegfried on tape, and tried to ignore the question: Why? He didn't know why he was going back.

There was no vacancy at the Holiday Inn. The desk clerk kindly advised him to go to the Kellogg Center where someone would see that he got housing.

He never had driven through the campus before; it appeared to have been designed as a maze, with every turn taking him back and forth across the same brown river again and again. The grounds, the broad walks, the streets, the expanses of manicured lawn were almost entirely deserted and eerily silent. When he approached the botanical gardens for the third time, luck intervened in his wanderings; he spotted Dr. Bressler strolling with another man, both facing away from him. He parked, opened his door to go after Bressler, hand back the package, be done with it. Then he came to a stop, half crouched in his movement to leave the car. The men had turned toward him briefly, and the second man was his old long lost pal, Doug Hastings. They walked to a greenhouse, away from him. He drew back inside the car.

He drove again, this time to Grand River, the main street in East Lansing. He turned toward Lansing. Without considering why he was doing this, he stopped at a shopping complex that covered acres and acres, miles maybe, and took the Bressler papers into an office supply warehouse store where he used a self-service copy machine and made copies of everything. He bought a big padded envelope and addressed it to himself, in care of his mother in Stroudsburg, Pennsylvania, put his copies inside, and mailed it at a post office in the sprawling mall. Then, finished, he returned to the Michigan State campus, and this time he found the Kellogg Center building on the first try.

Kellogg Center was the heart of the conference; here the academics met and talked, ate lunch, many of them had rooms, and the conference staff people manned a table with receptionist, programs, nametags, and general information. In the lobby Tony chatted with several people, was asked to wait a second while someone dashed off to get him a copy of a presentation paper; someone else handed him another folder. He was waiting for either Doug Hastings, or Dr. Bressler, whoever came first.

Someone thrust another folder at him. He took it, and let a woman draw him toward a small alcove; then he saw Bressler enter, followed seconds later by Doug. He turned his attention to the woman whose hand was heavy on his arm. "Will you attend our session this afternoon?" she was asking. "It's at three."

"Oh, Peter!" Bressler called out, and came lumbering across the hallway toward him. Doug Hastings turned to the reception table and began to examine the schedule.

The woman looked bewildered as Bressler reached them and took Tony's other arm, dragged him away. "Peter, do you still have my material? I thought you left already. They said you checked out."

Tony was carrying several folders by then, and a manila envelope, as well as his bulging briefcase. "Sure, it's in here somewhere," he said. He opened his briefcase on a small table, added the new papers to the others, and drew out Bressler's package. "I'll get to it in the next couple of weeks."

"No, no," Bressler said hastily, snatching the package, which he held against his chest with both hands. "That's all right, Peter. All that material to read. You don't need to add to it." He backed up a step or two, turned, and hurried away.

Tony was closing his briefcase again when he heard Doug's voice very close to his ear. "Well, I'll be damned if it isn't Tony Manetti!"

Doug grasped his shoulders and swung him around, examined his face, then wrapped him in a bear hug. "My God, how long's it been? Eight, nine years? Hey, how you been doing? What's going on? Looks like you're collecting bets or something." Talking, he drew Tony toward the front entrance, away from the others milling about. "How about a cup of java? Some place less crowded. Hey, remember when we used to duck out of class for a beer? Those were the days, weren't they?"

They never had gone out for a beer together; Tony hadn't been a drinker then any more than he was now. "You an academic?" he asked on the sidewalk.

"No way. Assignment. Listened to a bunch of guys and gals explain the economic importance of joint space exploration. Whew! Heavy going."

For the next hour, in a coffee shop, Doug talked about his life, and asked questions; talked about the past, and asked questions; talked about traveling, and asked questions.

"You mean you get their papers and don't go to the talks? What a racket! Let's see what you've got."

Tony handed over his briefcase, and watched Doug go through the contents.

"You're really going to read all that stuff? Read it here?"

"Not a word. They'd want to talk to me about it if they thought I'd read the material. I save it for home."

"You know, I thought that was you the other night, going out with a big bald guy?"

Tony laughed. "Old Bressler. He's into angels. Spent too much time looking in an electron microscope or something, I guess." He added sadly, "He gave me some stuff to take home, and then grabbed it back. Around the bend, poor old guy."

Later, answering another question slipped into a monologue, he told Doug that he had had a heavy date Sunday and Sunday night, and talked dreamily about a moonlight swim.

Doug leered. "Girl on every campus, I bet." Soon afterward he glanced at his watch and groaned. "This job ain't what I thought it'd be," he said. "You going back?"

"Just to pick up my car. I've got what I need."

They walked back to the Kellogg Center, where Tony got into the rental car, waved to Doug, and took off. He worked at putting the pieces together on the way to Lansing Airport. They must not want Bressler to publish a word about what he was up to. And Doug would report that there was no reason to reel in Tony, who didn't suspect a thing.

At the airport, he turned in the car, went to the ticket desk to change his reservation, and sat down to wait for his flight back to Chicago.

They probably didn't believe a word of it, he mused, and yet, what if? They would watch and wait, let the genius work it out if he could. But they would be there if he did. Right.

He was remembering incidents from his nearly forgotten childhood. At seven he and his stepbrother had played in the barn loft, and he had fallen out the highest window, gotten up, and walked away. Neither ever mentioned it to anyone; they had been forbidden to play up there. At twelve he and two other kids had been in a canoe on the Delaware River when a storm roared in like a rocket ship. The canoe had been hit by lightning, two kids had died, but he had swum to shore; he had not told anyone he had been there, since no one would have believed him anyway.

Now what, he wondered. Visit his mother, of course, and read all the Bressler material. After that was a blank, but that was all right. When the time came he would know what to do. He felt curiously free and happy, considering that he was simply following orders, was little more than a slave.

Nonstop to Portales

CONNIE WILLIS

Connie Willis, famous in SF for her short fiction and for her time-travel novel, *The Doomsday Book,* is a winner of many awards, including the Hugo and Nebula. She is particularly respected for her insightful portrayal of character and, in person, as a stand-up comic of considerable talent, known for her monologues at conventions, awards banquets, and SF parties. She has strong opinions about movie stars, particularly Harrison Ford and Fred Astaire. She lives in the fragrant city of Greeley, Colorado (presumably where the young men went when they went West, a long time ago). Less known is her considerable command of the history of modern science fiction. This story is the second in this year's volume taken from *The Williamson Effect,* and is as moving, powerful, and accurate a tribute from one living SF writer to another as I have ever read. It takes a fine writer who knows and cares about the SF of the past to write such a story as "Nonstop to Portales." Most other SF writers will envy Jack Williamson his Connie Willis story.

Every town's got a claim to fame. No town is too little and dried out to have some kind of tourist attraction. John Garfield's grave, Willa Cather's house, the dahlia capital of America. And if they don't have a house or a grave or a Pony Express station, they make something up. Sasquatch footprints in Oregon. The Martha lights in Texas. Elvis sightings. Something.

Except, apparently, Portales, New Mexico.

"Sights?" the cute Hispanic girl at the desk of the Portales Inn said when I asked what there was to see. "There's Billy the Kid's grave over in Fort Sumner. It's about seventy miles."

I'd just driven all the way from Bisbee, Arizona. The last thing I wanted to do was get back in a car and drive a hundred and sixty miles round trip to see a crooked wooden tombstone with the name worn off.

"Isn't there anything famous to see in town?"

"In Portales?" she said, and it was obvious from her tone there wasn't.

"There's Blackwater Draw Museum on the way up to Clovis," she said finally. "You take Highway 70 north about eight miles and it's on your right. It's an archaeological dig. Or you could drive out west of town and see the peanut fields."

Great. Bones and dirt.

"Thanks," I said and went back up to my room.

It was my own fault. Cross wasn't going to be back till tomorrow, but I'd decided to come to Portales a day early to "take a look around" before I talked to him, but that was no excuse. I'd been in little towns all over the west for the last five years. I knew how long it took to look around. About fifteen minutes. And five to see it had dead end written all over it. So here I was in Sightless Portales on a Sunday with nothing to do for a whole day but think about Cross's offer and try to come up with a reason not to take it.

"It's a good, steady job," my friend Denny'd said when he called to tell me Cross needed somebody. "Portales is a nice town. And it's got to be better than spending your life in a car. Driving all over kingdom come trying to sell inventions to people who don't want them. What kind of future is there in that?"

No future at all. The farmers weren't interested in solar-powered irrigation equipment or water conservation devices. And lately Hammond, the guy I worked for, hadn't seemed very interested in them either.

My room didn't have air-conditioning. I cranked the window open and turned the TV on. It didn't have cable either. I watched five minutes of a sermon and then called Hammond.

"It's Carter Stewart," I said as if I were in the habit of calling him on Sundays. "I'm in Portales. I got here earlier than I thought, and the guy I'm supposed to see isn't here till tomorrow. You got any other customers you want me to look up?"

"In Portales?" he said, sounding barely interested. "Who were you supposed to see there?"

"Hudd at Southwest Agricultural Supply. I've got an appointment with him at eleven." And an appointment with Cross at ten, I thought. "I got in last night. Bisbee didn't take as long as I thought it would."

"Hudd's our only contact in Portales," he said.

"Anybody in Clovis? Or Tucumcari?"

"No," he said, too fast to have looked them up. "There's nobody much in that part of the state."

"They're big into peanuts here. You want me to try and talk to some peanut farmers?"

"Why don't you just take the day off?" he said.

"Yeah, thanks," I said, and hung up and went back downstairs.

There was a dried-up old guy at the desk now, but the word must have spread. "You wanna see something really interesting?" he said. "Down in Roswell's where the Air Force has got that space alien they won't let anybody see. You take Highway 70 south—"

"Didn't anybody famous ever live here in Portales?" I asked. "A vice-president? Billy the Kid's cousin?"

He shook his head.

"What about buildings? A railroad station? A courthouse?"

"There's a courthouse, but it's closed on Sundays. The Air Force claims it wasn't a spaceship, that it was some kind of spy plane, but I know a guy who saw it coming down. He said it was shaped like a big long cigar and had lights all over it."

"Highway 70?" I said, to get away from him. "Thanks," and went out into the parking lot.

I could see the top of the courthouse over the dry-looking treetops, only a couple of blocks away. It was closed on Sundays, but it was better than sitting in my room watching Falwell and thinking about the job I was going to have to take unless something happened between now and tomorrow morning. And better than getting back in the car to go see something Roswell had made up so it'd have a tourist attraction. And maybe I'd get lucky, and the courthouse would turn out to be the site of the last hanging in New Mexico. Or the first peace march. I walked downtown.

The streets around the courthouse looked like your typical small-town post-WalMart business district. No drugstore, no grocery store, no dime-store. There was an Anthony's standing empty, and a restaurant that would be in another six months, a Western clothing store with a dusty denim shirt and two concho belts in the window, a bank with a sign in the window saying NEW LOCATION.

The courthouse was red brick and looked like every other courthouse from Nelson, Nebraska, to Tyler, Texas. It stood in a square of grass and trees. I walked around it twice, looking at the war memorial and the flagpole and trying not to think about Hammond and Bisbee. It hadn't taken as long as I'd thought because I hadn't even been able to get in to see the buyer, and Hammond hadn't cared enough to even ask how it had gone. Or to bother to look up his contacts in Tucumcari. And it wasn't just that it was Sunday. He'd sounded that way the last two times I'd called him. Like a man getting ready to give up, to pull out.

Which meant I should take Cross's job offer and be grateful. "It's a forty-hour week," he'd said. "You'll have time to work on your inventions."

Right. Or else settle into a routine and forget about them. Five years ago when I'd taken the job with Hammond, Denny'd said, "You'll be able to see the sights. The Grand Canyon, Mount Rushmore, Yellowstone." Yeah, well, I'd seen them. Cave of the Winds, Amazing Mystery House, Indian curios, Genuine Live Jackalope.

I walked around the courthouse square again and then went down to the railroad tracks to look at the grain elevator and walked back to the courthouse again. The whole thing took ten minutes. I thought about walking over to the university, but it was getting hot. In another half hour the grass would start browning and the streets would start getting soft, and it would be even hotter out here than in my room. I started back to the Portales Inn.

The street I was on was shady, with white wooden houses, the kind I'd probably live in if I took Cross's job, the kind I'd work on my inventions in. If I could get the parts for them at Southwest Agricultural Supply. Or WalMart. If I really did work on them. If I didn't just give up after a while.

I turned down a side street. And ran into a dead end. Which was pretty appropriate, under the circumstances. "At least this would be a real job, not a dead end like the one you're in now," Cross'd said. "You've got to think about the future."

Yeah, well, I was the only one. Nobody else was doing it. They kept on using oil like it was water, kept on using water like the Ogalala Aquifer was going to last forever, kept planting and polluting and populating. I'd already thought about the future, and I knew what it was going to be. Another dead end. Another Dust Bowl. The land used up, the oil wells and the water table pumped dry, Bisbee and Clovis and Tucumcari turned into ghost towns. The Great American Desert all over again, with nobody but a few Indians left on it, waiting in their casinos for customers who weren't going to come. And me, sitting in Portales, working a forty-hour-a-week job.

I backtracked and went the other way. I didn't run into any other dead ends, or any sights either, and by 10:15 I was back at the Portales Inn, with only twenty-four hours to kill and Billy the Kid's grave looking better by the minute.

There was a tour bus in the Inn's parking lot. NONSTOP TOURS, it said in red and gray letters, and a long line of people was getting on it. A young woman was standing by the door of the bus, ticking off names on a clipboard. She was cute, with short yellow hair and a nice figure. She was wearing a light blue T-shirt and a short denim skirt.

An older couple in Bermuda shorts and Disney World T-shirts were climbing the stairs onto the bus, slowing up the line.

"Hi," I said to the tour guide. "What's going on?"

She looked up from her list at me, startled, and the old couple froze halfway up the steps. The tour guide looked down at her clipboard and then back up at me, and the startled look was gone, but her cheeks were as red as the letters on the side of the bus.

"We're taking a tour of the local sights," she said. She motioned to the next person in line, a fat guy in a Hawaiian shirt, and the old couple went on up the steps and into the bus.

"I didn't think there were any," I said. "Local sights."

The fat guy was gaping at me.

"Name?" the tour guide said.

"Giles H. Paul," he said, still staring at me. She motioned him onto the bus.

"Name?" I said, and she looked startled all over again. "What's your name? It's probably on that clipboard in case you've forgotten it."

She smiled. "Tonia Randall."

"So, Tonia, where's this tour headed?"

"We're going out to the ranch."

"The ranch?"

"Where he grew up," she said, her cheeks flaming again. She motioned to the next person in line. "Where he got his start."

Where who started to what? I wanted to ask, but she was busy with a tall man who moved almost as stiffly as the old couple, and anyway, it was obvious everybody in line knew who she was talking about. They couldn't wait to get on the bus, and the young couple who were last in line kept pointing things out to their little kid—the courthouse, the Portales Inn sign, a big tree on the other side of the street.

"Is it private? Your tour?" I said. "Can anybody pay to go on it?" And what was I doing? I'd taken a tour in the Black Hills one time, when I'd had my job about a month and still wanted to see the sights, and it was even more depressing than thinking about the future. Looking out blue-tinted windows while the tour guide tells memorized facts and unfunny jokes. Trooping off the bus to look at Wild Bill Hickok's grave for five minutes, trooping back on. Listening to bawling kids and complaining wives. I didn't want to go on this tour.

But when Tonia blushed and said, "No, I'm sorry," I felt a rush of disappointment at not seeing her again.

"Sure," I said, because I didn't want her to see it. "Just wondering. Well, have a nice time," and started for the front door of the Inn.

"Wait," she said, leaving the couple and their kid standing there and coming over to me. "Do you live here in Portales?"

"No," I said, and realized I'd decided not to take the job. "Just passing through. I came to town to see a guy. I got here early, and there's nothing to do. That ever happen to you?"

She smiled, as if I'd said something funny. "So you don't know anyone here?"

"No," I said.

"Do you know the person you've got the appointment with?"

I shook my head, wondering what that had to do with anything.

She consulted her clipboard again. "It seems a pity for you to miss seeing it," she said, "and if you're just passing through . . . Just a minute." She walked back to the bus, stepped up inside, and said something to the driver. They consulted a few minutes, and then she came back down the steps. The couple and their kid came up to her, and she stopped a minute and checked their names off and waved them onto the bus, and then came back over to me. "The bus is full. Do you mind standing?"

Bawling kids, videocams, *and* no place to sit to go see the ranch where somebody I'd probably never heard of got his start. At least I'd heard of

Billy the Kid, and if I drove over to Fort Sumner I could take as long as I wanted to look at his grave. "No," I said. "I wouldn't mind." I pulled out my wallet. "Maybe I better ask before we go any farther, how much is the tour?"

She looked startled again. "No charge. Because the tour's already full."

"Great," I said. "I'd like to go."

She smiled and motioned me on board with her clipboard. Inside, it looked more like a city bus than a tour bus—the front and back seats were sideways along the walls, and there were straps for hanging onto. There was even a cord for signaling your stop, which might come in handy if the tour turned out to be as bad as the Wild Bill Hickok tour. I grabbed hold of a strap near the front.

The bus was packed with people of all ages. A white-haired man older than the Disney World couple, middle-aged people, teenagers, kids. I counted at least four under age five. I wondered if I should yank the cord right now.

Tonia counted heads and nodded to the driver. The door whooshed shut, and the bus lumbered out of the parking lot and slowly through a neighborhood of trees and tract houses. The Disney World couple were sitting in the front seat. They scooted over to make room for me, and I gestured to Tonia, but she motioned me to sit down.

She put down her clipboard and held on to the pole just behind the driver's seat. "The first stop on today's tour," she said, "will be the house. He did the greater part of his work here," and I began to wonder if I was going to go the whole tour without ever finding out who the tour was about. When she'd said "the ranch," I'd assumed it was some Old West figure, but these houses had all been built in the thirties and forties.

"He moved into this house with his wife, Blanche, shortly after they were married."

The bus ground down its gears and stopped next to a white house with a porch on a corner lot.

"He lived here from 1947 to . . ." She paused and looked sideways at me. ". . . the present. It was while he was living here that he wrote *Seetee Ship* and *The Black Sun* and came up with the idea of genetic engineering."

He was a writer, which narrowed it down some, but none of the titles she'd mentioned rang a bell. But he was famous enough to fill a tour bus, so his books must have been turned into movies. Tom Clancy? Stephen King? I'd have expected both of them to have a lot fancier houses.

"The windows in front are the living room," Tonia said. "You can't see his study from here. It's on the south side of the house. That's where he keeps his Grand Master Nebula Award, right above where he works."

That didn't ring a bell either, but everybody looked impressed, and the couple with the kid got out of their seats to peer out the tinted windows. "The two rear windows are the kitchen, where he read the paper and watched TV at breakfast before going to work. He used a typewriter and then in later years a personal computer. He's not at home this weekend. He's out of town at a science fiction convention."

Which was probably a good thing. I wondered how he felt about tour buses parking out front, whoever he was. A science fiction writer. Isaac Asimov, maybe.

The driver put the bus in gear and pulled away from the curb. "As we drive past the front of the house," Tonia said, "you'll be able to see his easy chair, where he did most of his reading."

The bus ground up through the gears and started winding through more neighborhood streets. "Jack Williamson worked on the *Portales News-Tribune* from 1947 to 1948 and then, with the publication of *Darker Than You Think*, quit journalism to write full-time," she said, pausing and glancing at me again, but if she was expecting me to be looking as impressed as everybody else, I wasn't. I'd read a lot of paperbacks in a lot of un-air-conditioned motel rooms the last five years, but the name Jack Williamson didn't ring a bell at all.

"From 1960 to 1977, Jack Williamson was a professor at Eastern New Mexico University, which we're coming up on now," Tonia said. The bus pulled into the college's parking lot and everybody looked eagerly out the windows, even though the campus looked just like every other western college's, brick and glass and not enough trees, sprinklers watering the brownish grass.

"This is the Campus Union," she said, pointing. The bus made a slow circuit of the parking lot. "And this is Becky Sharp Auditorium, where the annual lecture in his honor is held every spring. It's the week of April twelfth this year."

It struck me that they hadn't planned very well. They'd managed to miss not only their hero but the annual week in his honor, too.

"Over there is the building where he teaches a science fiction class with Patrice Caldwell," she said, pointing, "and that, of course, is Golden Library, where the Williamson Collection of his works and awards is housed." Everyone nodded in recognition.

I expected the driver to open the doors and everybody to pile out to look at the library, but the bus picked up speed and headed out of town.

"We aren't going to the library?" I said.

She shook her head. "Not this tour. At this time the collection's still very small."

The bus geared up and headed west and south out of town on a two-lane road. NEW MEXICO STATE HIGHWAY 18, a sign read. "Out your windows you can see the *Llano Estacado,* or Staked Plains," Tonia said. "They were named, as Jack Williamson says in his autobiography, *Wonder's Child,* for the stakes Coronado used to mark his way across the plain. Jack Williamson's family moved here in a covered wagon in 1915 to a homestead claim in the sandhills. Here Jack did farm chores, hauled water, collected firewood, and read *Treasure Island* and *David Copperfield.*"

At least I'd heard of those books. And Jack had to be at least seventy-nine years old.

"The farm was very poor, with poor soil and almost no water, and after three years the family was forced to move off it and onto a series of sharecrop farms to make ends meet. During this time Jack went to school at Richland and at Center, where he met Blanche Slaten, his future wife. Any questions?"

This had the Deadwood tour all beat for boring, but a bunch of hands went up, and she went down the aisle to answer them, leaning over their seats and pointing out the tinted windows. The old couple got up and went back to talk to the fat guy, holding on to the straps above his seat and gesturing excitedly.

I looked out the window. The Spanish should have named it the *Llano Flatto.* There wasn't a bump or a dip in it all the way to the horizon.

Everybody, including the kids, was looking out the windows, even though there wasn't anything much to look at. A plowed field of red dirt, a few bored-looking cows, green rows of sprouting green that must be the peanuts, another plowed field. I was getting to see the dirt after all.

Tonia came back to the front and sat down beside me. "Enjoying the tour so far?" she said.

I couldn't think of a good answer to that. "How far is the ranch?" I said.

"Twenty miles. There used to be a town named Pep, but now there's just the ranch . . ." She paused and then said, "What's your name? You didn't tell me."

"Carter Stewart," I said.

"Really?" She smiled at the funniest things. "Are you named after Carter Leigh in 'Nonstop to Mars'?"

I didn't know what that was. One of Jack Williamson's books, apparently. "I don't know. Maybe."

"I'm named after Tonia Andros in 'Dead Star Station.' And the driver's named after Giles Habibula."

The tall guy had his hand up again. "I'll be right back," she said, and hurried down the aisle.

The fat guy's name had been Giles, too, which wasn't exactly a common name, and I'd seen the name "Lethonee" on Tonia's clipboard, which had to be out of a book. But how could somebody I'd never even heard of be so famous people were named after his characters?

They must be a fan club, the kind that makes pilgrimages to Graceland and names their kids Paul and Ringo. They didn't look the part, though. They should be wearing Jack Williamson T-shirts and Spock ears, not Disney World T-shirts. The elderly couple came back and sat down next to me. They smiled and started looking out the window.

They didn't act the part either. The fans I'd met had always had a certain defensiveness, an attitude of "I know you think I'm crazy to like this stuff, and maybe I am," and they always insisted on explaining how they got to be fans and why you should be one, too. These people had none of that. They acted like coming out here was the most normal thing in the world, even Tonia. And if they were science fiction fans, why weren't they touring Isaac Asimov's ranch? Or William Shatner's?

Tonia came back again and stood over me, holding on to a hanging strap. "You said you were in Portales to see somebody?" she said.

"Yeah. He's supposed to offer me a job."

"In Portales?" she said, making that sound exciting. "Are you going to take it?"

I'd made up my mind back there in that dead end, but I said, "I don't know. I don't think so. It's a desk job, a steady paycheck, and I wouldn't have to do all the driving I'm doing now." I found myself telling her about Hammond and the things I wanted to invent and how I was afraid the job would be a dead end.

" 'I had no future,' " she said. "Jack Williamson said that at this year's Williamson Lecture. 'I had no future. I was a poor kid in the middle of the Depression, without education, without money, without prospects.' "

"It's not the Depression, but otherwise I know how he felt. If I don't take Cross's job, I may not have one. And if I do take it—" I shrugged. "Either way I'm not going anywhere."

"Oh, but to have a chance to live in the same town with Jack Williamson," Tonia said. "To run into him at the supermarket, and maybe even get to take one of his classes."

"Maybe *you* should take Cross's job offer," I said.

"I can't." Her cheeks went bright red again. "I've already got a job." She straightened up and addressed the tour group. "We'll be coming to the turnoff to the ranch soon," she said. "Jack Williamson lived here with his family from 1915 till World War II, when he joined the army, and again after the war until he married Blanche."

The bus slowed almost to a stop and turned onto a dirt road hardly as wide as the bus was that led off between two fields of fenced pastureland.

"The farm was originally a homestead," Tonia said, and everyone murmured appreciatively and looked out the windows at more dirt and a couple of clumps of yucca.

"He was living here when he read his first issue of *Amazing Stories Quarterly*," she said, "and when he submitted his first story to *Amazing*. That was 'The Metal Man,' which, as you remember from yesterday, he saw in the window of the drugstore."

"I see it!" the tall man shouted, leaning forward over the back of the driver's seat. "I see it!" Everyone craned forward, trying to see, and we pulled up in front of some outbuildings and stopped.

The driver whooshed the doors open, and everyone filed off the bus and stood in the rutted dirt road, looking excitedly at the unpainted sheds and the water trough. A black heifer looked up incuriously and then went back to chewing on the side of one of the sheds.

Tonia assembled everyone in the road with her clipboard. "That's the ranch house over there," she said, pointing at a low green house with a fenced yard and a willow tree. "Jack Williamson lived here with his parents, his brother Jim, and his sisters Jo and Katie. It was here that Jack Williamson wrote 'The Girl from Mars' and *The Legion of Space*, working at the kitchen table. His uncle had given him a basket-model Remington typewriter with a dim purple ribbon, and he typed his stories on it after everyone had gone to bed. Jack Williamson's brother Jim . . ." she paused and glanced at me, "owns the ranch at this time. He and his wife are in Arizona this weekend."

Amazing. They'd managed to miss them all, but nobody seemed to mind, and it struck me suddenly what was unusual about this tour. Nobody complained. That's all they'd done on the Wild Bill Hickok tour. Half of them hadn't known who he was, and the other half had complained that it was too expensive, too hot, too far, the windows on the bus didn't open, the gift shop didn't sell Coke. If their tour guide had announced the wax museum was closed, he'd have had a riot on his hands.

"It was difficult for him to write in the midst of the family," she said, leading off away from the house toward a pasture. "There were frequent interruptions and too much noise, so in 1934 he built a separate cabin. Be careful," she said, skirting around a clump of sagebrush. "There are sometimes rattlesnakes."

That apparently didn't bother anybody either. They trooped after her across a field of dry, spiny grass and gathered around a weathered gray shack.

"This is the actual cabin he wrote in," Tonia said.

I wouldn't have called it a cabin. It hardly even qualified as a shack. When I'd first seen it as we pulled up, I'd thought it was an abandoned outhouse. Four gray wood-slat walls, half falling down, a sagging gray shelf, some rusted cans. When Tonia started talking, a farm cat leaped down from where it had been sleeping under what was left of the roof and took off like a shot across the field.

"It had a desk, files, bookshelves, and later a separate bedroom," Tonia said.

It didn't look big enough for a typewriter, let alone a bed, but this was obviously what all these people had come to see. They stood reverently before it in the spiky grass, like it was the Washington Monument or something, and gazed at the weathered boards and rusted cans, not saying anything.

"He installed electric lights," Tonia said, "which were run by a small windmill, and a bath. He still had occasional interruptions—from snakes and once from a skunk who took up residence under the cabin. He wrote 'Dead Star Station' here, and 'The Meteor Girl,' his first story to include time travel. 'If the field were strong enough,'" he said in the story, "'we could bring physical objects through space-time instead of mere visual images.'"

They all found that amusing for no reason I could see and then stood there some more, looking reverent. Tonia came over to me. "Well, what do you think?" she said, smiling.

"Tell me about him seeing 'The Metal Man' in the drugstore," I said.

"Oh, I forgot you weren't with us at the drugstore," she said. "Jack Williamson sent his first story to *Amazing Stories* in 1928 and then never heard anything back. In the fall of that year he was shopping for groceries, and he looked in the window of a drugstore and saw a magazine with a picture on the cover that looked like it could be his story, and when he went in, he was so excited to see his story in print, he bought all three copies of the magazine and went off without the groceries he'd been carrying."

"So then he had prospects?"

She said seriously, "He said, 'I had no future. And then I looked in the drugstore window and saw Hugo Gernsback's *Amazing Stories,* and it gave me a future.'"

"I wish somebody would give me a future," I said.

" 'No one can predict the future, he can only point the way.' He said that, too."

She went over to the shack and addressed the group. "He also wrote 'Nonstop to Mars,' my favorite story, in this cabin," she said to the group, "and it was right here that he proposed the idea of colonizing Mars and . . ." She paused, but this time it was the stiff tall man she glanced at. ". . . invented the idea of androids."

They continued to look. All of them walked around the shack two or three times, pointing at loose boards and tin cans, stepping back to get a better look, walking around it again. None of them seemed to be in any hurry to go. The Deadwood tour had lasted all of ten minutes at Mount Moriah Cemetery, with one of the kids whining, "Can't we *go* now?" the whole time, but this group acted like they could stay here all day. One of them got out a notebook and started writing things down. The couple with the kid took her over to the heifer, and all three of them patted her gingerly.

After a while Tonia and the driver passed out paper bags and everybody sat down in the pasture, rattlesnakes and all, and had lunch. Stale sandwiches, cardboard cookies, cans of lukewarm Coke, but nobody complained. Or left any litter.

They neatly packed everything back in the bags and then walked around the shack some more, looking in the empty windows and scaring a couple more farm cats, or just sat and looked at it. A couple of them went over to the fence and gazed longingly over it at the ranch house.

"It's too bad there's nobody around to show them the house," I said. "People don't usually go off and leave a ranch with nobody to look after the animals. I wonder if there's somebody around. Whoever it is would probably give you a tour of the ranch house."

"It's Jack's niece Betty," Tonia said promptly. "She had to go up to Clovis today to get a part for the water pump. She won't be back till four." She stood up, brushing dead grass and dirt off her skirt. "All right, everybody. It's time to go."

There was a discontented murmuring, and one of the kids said, "Do we have to go already?", but everybody picked up their lunch bags and Coke cans and started for the bus. Tonia ticked off their names on her clipboard as they got on like she was afraid one of them might jump ship and take up residence among the rattlesnakes.

"Carter Stewart," I told her. "Where to next? The drugstore?"

She shook her head. "We went there yesterday. Where's Underhill?" She started across the road again, with me following her.

The tall man was standing silently in front of the shack, looking in at the empty room. He stood absolutely motionless, his eyes fixed on the gray weathered boards, and when Tonia said, "Underhill? I'm afraid we need to go," he continued to stand there for a long minute, like he was trying to store up the memory. Then he turned and walked stiffly past us and back to the bus.

Tonia counted heads again, and the bus made a slow circle past the ranchhouse, turning around, and started back along the dirt road. Nobody said anything, and when we got to the highway, everyone turned around in their seats for a last look. The old couple dabbed at their eyes, and one of the kids stood up on the rear seat and waved goodbye. The tall man was sitting with his head buried in his hands.

"The cabin you've just seen was where it all started," Tonia said, "with a copy of a pulp magazine and a lot of imagination." She told how Jack Williamson had become a meteorologist and a college professor, as well as a science fiction writer, traveled to Italy, Mexico, the Great Wall of China, all of which must have been impossible for him to imagine, sitting all alone in that poor excuse for a shack, typing on an old typewriter with a faded ribbon.

I was only half listening. I was thinking about the tall guy, Underhill, and trying to figure out what was wrong about him. It wasn't his stiffness—I'd been at least that stiff after a day in the car. It was something else. I thought about him standing there, looking at the shack, so fixed, like he was trying to carry the image away with him.

He probably just forgot his camera, I thought, and realized what had been nagging at me. Nobody had a camera. Tourists always have cameras. The Wild Bill Hickok gang had all had cameras, even the kids. And videocams. One guy had kept a videocam glued to his face the whole time and never seen a thing. They'd spent the whole tour snapping Wild Bill's tombstone, snapping the figures in the wax museum even though there were signs that said, NO PICTURES, snapping each other in front of the saloon, in front of the cemetery, in front of the bus. And then buying up slides and postcards in the gift shop in case the pictures didn't turn out.

No cameras. No gift shop. No littering or trespassing or whining. What kind of tour is this? I thought.

"He predicted 'a new Golden Age of fair cities, of new laws and new machines,'" Tonia was saying, "'of human capabilities undreamed of, of a civilization that has conquered matter and Nature, distance and time, disease and death.'"

He'd imagined the same kind of future I'd imagined. I wondered if he'd ever tried selling his ideas to farmers. Which brought me back to the job, which I'd managed to avoid thinking about almost all day.

Tonia came and stood across from me, holding on to the center pole.

" 'A poor country kid, poorly educated, unhappy with his whole environment, longing for something else,' " she said. "That's how Jack Williamson described himself in 1928." She looked at me. "You're not going to take the job, are you?"

"I don't think so," I said. "I don't know."

She looked out the window at the fields and cows, looking disappointed. "When he first moved here, this was all sagebrush and drought and dust. He couldn't imagine what was going to happen any more than you can right now."

"And the answer's in a drugstore window?"

"The answer was inside him," she said. She stood up and addressed the group. "We'll be coming into Portales in a minute," she said. "In 1928, Jack Williamson wrote, 'Science is the doorway to the future, scientification, the golden key. It goes ahead and lights the way. And when science sees the things made real in the author's mind, it makes them real indeed.' "

The tour group applauded, and the bus pulled into the parking lot of the Portales Inn. I waited for the rush, but nobody moved. "We're not staying here," Tonia explained.

"Oh," I said, getting up. "You didn't have to give me door-to-door service. You could have let me out at wherever you're staying, and I could have walked over."

"That's all right," Tonia said, smiling.

"Well," I said, unwilling to say goodbye. "Thanks for a really interesting tour. Can I take you to dinner or something? To thank you for letting me come?"

"I can't," she said. "I have to check everybody in and everything."

"Yeah," I said. "Well . . ."

Giles the driver opened the door with a whoosh of air.

"Thanks," I said. I nodded to the old couple. "Thanks for sharing your seat," and stepped down off the bus.

"Why don't you come with us tomorrow?" she said. "We're going to go see Number 5516."

Number 5516 sounded like a county highway and probably was, the road Jack Williamson walked to school along or something, complete with peanuts and dirt, at which the group would gaze reverently and not take pictures. "I've got an appointment tomorrow," I said, and realized I didn't want to say goodbye to her. "Next time. When's your next tour?"

"I thought you were just passing through."

"Like you said, a lot of nice people live around here. Do you bring a lot of tours through here?"

"Now and then," she said, her cheeks bright red.

I watched the bus pull out of the parking lot and down the street. I looked at my watch. 4:45. At least an hour till I could justify dinner. At least five hours till I could justify bed. I went in the Inn and then changed my mind and went back out to the car and drove out to see where Cross's office was so I wouldn't have trouble in the morning, in case it was hard to find.

It wasn't. It was on the south edge of town on Highway 70, a little past the Motel Super 8. The tour bus wasn't in the parking lot of the Super 8, or at the Hillcrest, or the Sands Motel. They must have gone to Roswell or Tucumcari for the night. I looked at my watch again. It was 5:05.

I drove back through town, looking for someplace to eat. McDonald's, Taco Bell, Burger King. There's nothing wrong with fast food, except that it's fast. I needed a place where it took half an hour to get a menu and another twenty minutes before they took your order.

I ended up eating at Pizza Hut (personal pan pizza in under five minutes or your money back). "Do you get a lot of tour bus business?" I asked the waitress.

"In Portales? You have to be kidding," she said. "In case you haven't noticed, Portales is right on the road to nowhere. Do you want a box for the rest of that pizza?"

The box was a good idea. It took her ten minutes to bring it, which meant it was nearly six by the time I left. Only four hours left to kill. I filled up the car at Allsup's and bought a sixpack of Coke. Next to the magazines was a rack of paperbacks.

"Any Jack Williamson books?" I asked the kid at the counter.

"Who?" he said.

I spun the rack around slowly. John Grisham. Danielle Steel. Stephen King's latest thousand-page effort. No Jack Williamson. "Is there a bookstore in town?" I asked the kid.

"Huh?"

He'd never heard of that either. "A place where I can buy a book?"

"Alco has books, I think," he said. "But they closed at five."

"How about a drugstore?" I said, thinking of that copy of *Amazing Stories*.

Still blank. I gave up, paid him for the gas and the sixpack, and started out to the car.

"You mean a drugstore like aspirin and stuff?" the kid said. "There's Van Winkle's."

"When do they close?" I asked, and got directions.

Van Winkle's was a grocery store. It had two aisles of "aspirin and stuff" and half an aisle of paperbacks. More Grisham. *Jurassic Park.* Tom

Clancy. And *The Legion of Time* by Jack Williamson. It looked like it had been there a while. It had a faded fifties-style cover and dog-eared edges.

I took it up to the check-out. "What's it like having a famous writer living here?" I asked the middle-aged clerk.

She picked up the book. "The guy who wrote this lives in Portales?" she said. "Really?"

Which brought us up to 6:22. But at least now I had something to read. I went back to the Portales Inn and up to my room, opened a can of Coke and all the windows, and sat down to read *The Legion of Time,* which was about a girl who'd traveled back in time to tell the hero about the future.

"The future has been held to be as real as the past," the book said, and the girl in the book was able to travel between one and the other as easily as the tour had traveled down New Mexico Highway 18.

I closed the book and thought about the tour. They didn't have a single camera, and they weren't afraid of rattlesnakes. And they'd looked out at the Llano Flatto like they'd never seen a field or a cow before. And they all knew who Jack Williamson was, unlike the kid at Allsup's or the clerk at Van Winkle's. They were all willing to spend two days looking at abandoned shacks and dirt roads—no, wait, *three* days. Tonia'd said they'd gone to the drugstore yesterday.

I had an idea. I opened the drawer of the nightstand, looking for a phone book. There wasn't one. I went downstairs to the lobby and asked for one. The blue-haired lady at the desk handed me one about the size of *The Legion of Time,* and I flipped to the Yellow Pages.

There was a Thrifty Drug, which was a chain, and a couple that sounded locally owned but weren't downtown. "Where's B. and J. Drugs?" I asked. "Is it close to downtown?"

"A couple of blocks," the old lady said.

"How long has it been in business?"

"Let's see," she said. "It was there when Nora was little because I remember buying medicine that time she had the croup. She would have been six, or was that when she had the measles? No, the measles were the summer she . . ."

I'd have to ask B. and J. "I've got another question," I said, and hoped I wouldn't get an answer like the last one. "What time does the university library open tomorrow?"

She gave me a brochure. The library opened at 8:00 and the Williamson Collection at 9:30. I went back up to the room and tried B. and J. Drugs. They weren't open.

It was getting dark. I closed the curtains over the open windows and opened the book again. "The world is a long corridor, and time is a lantern carried steadily along the hall," it said, and, a few pages later, "If time were simply an extension of the universe, was tomorrow as real as yesterday? If one could leap forward—"

Or back, I thought. "Jack Williamson lived in this house from 1947 to . . ." Tonia'd said, and paused and then said, ". . . the present," and I'd thought the sideways glance was to see my reaction to his name, but what if she'd intended to say, "from 1947 to 1998"? Or "2015"?

What if that was why she kept pausing when she talked, because she had to remember to say "Jack Williamson *is*" instead of "Jack Williamson *was*," "*does* most of his writing" instead of "*did* most of his writing," had to remember what year it was and what hadn't happened yet?

" 'If the field were strong enough,' " I remembered Tonia saying out at the ranch, " 'we could bring physical objects through space-time instead of mere visual images.' " And the tour group had all smiled.

What if they were the physical objects? What if the tour had traveled through time instead of space? But that didn't make any sense. If they could travel through time they could have come on a weekend Jack Williamson was home, or during the week of the Williamson Lectureship.

I read on, looking for explanations. The book talked about quantum mechanics and probability, about how changing one thing in the past could affect the whole future. Maybe that was why they had to come when Jack Williamson was out of town, to avoid doing something to him that might change the future.

Or maybe Nonstop Tours was just incompetent and they'd come on the wrong weekend. And the reason they didn't have cameras was because they all forgot them. And they were all really tourists, and *The Legion of Time* was just a science fiction book and I was making up crackpot theories to avoid thinking about Cross and the job.

But if they were ordinary tourists, what were they doing spending a day staring at a tumbledown shack in the middle of nowhere? Even if they were tourists from the future, there was no reason to travel back in time to see a science fiction writer when they could see presidents or rock stars.

Unless they lived in a future where all the things he'd predicted in his stories had come true. What if they had genetic engineering and androids and spaceships? What if in their world they'd terraformed planets and gone to Mars and explored the galaxy? That would make Jack Williamson their forefather, their founder. And they'd want to come back and see where it all started.

The next morning, I left my stuff at the Portales Inn and went over to the library. Checkout wasn't till noon, and I wanted to wait till I'd found out a few things before I made up my mind whether to take the job or not. On the way there I drove past B. and J. Drugs and then College Drug. Neither of them were open, and I couldn't tell from their outsides how old they were.

The library opened at eight and the room with the Williamson collection in it at 9:30, which was cutting it close. I was there at 9:15, looking in through the glass at the books. There was a bronze plaque on the wall and a big mobile of the planets.

Tonia had said the collection "isn't very big at this point," but from what I could see, it looked pretty big to me. Rows and rows of books, filing cabinets, boxes, photographs.

A young guy in chinos and wire-rimmed glasses unlocked the door to let me in. "Wow! Lined up and waiting to get in! This is a first," he said, which answered my first question.

I asked it anyway. "Do you get many visitors?"

"A few," he said. "Not as many as I think there should be for a man who practically invented the future. Androids, terraforming, antimatter, he imagined them all. We'll have more visitors in two weeks. That's when the Williamson Lectureship week is. We get quite a few visitors then. The writers who are speaking usually drop in."

He switched on the lights. "Let me show you around," he said. "We're adding to the collection all the time." He took down a long flat box. "This is the comic strip Jack did, *Beyond Mars*. And here is where we keep his original manuscripts." He opened one of the filing cabinets and pulled out a sheaf of typed yellow sheets. "Have you ever met Jack?"

"No," I said, looking at an oil painting of a white-haired man with a long, pleasant-looking face. "What's he like?"

"Oh, the nicest man you've ever met. It's hard to believe he's one of the founders of science fiction. He's in here all the time. Wonderful guy. He's working on a new book, *The Black Sun*. He's out of town this weekend, or I'd take you over and introduce you. He's always delighted to meet his fans. Is there anything specific you wanted to know about him?"

"Yes," I said. "Somebody told me about him seeing the magazine with his first story in it in a drugstore. Which drugstore was that?"

"It was one in Canyon, Texas. He and his sister were going to school down there."

"Do you know the name of the drugstore?" I said. "I'd like to go see it."

"Oh, it went out of business years ago," he said. "I think it was torn down."

"We went there yesterday," Tonia had said, and what day exactly was that? The day Jack saw it and bought all three copies and forgot his groceries? And what were they wearing that day? Print dresses and double-breasted suits and hats?

"I've got the issue here," he said, taking a crumbling magazine out of a plastic slipcover. It had a garish picture of a man being pulled up out of a crater by a brilliant crystal. "December, 1928. Too bad the drugstore's not there anymore. You can see the cabin where he wrote his first stories, though. It's still out on the ranch his brother owns. You go out west of town and turn south on State Highway 18. Just ask Betty to show you around."

"Have you ever had a tour group in here?" I interrupted.

"A *tour* group?" he said, and then must have decided I was kidding. "He's not quite that famous."

Yet, I thought, and wondered when Nonstop Tours visited the library. Ten years from now? A hundred? And what were they wearing that day?

I looked at my watch. It was 9:45. "I've got to go," I said. "I've got an appointment." I started out and then turned back. "This person who told me about the drugstore, they mentioned something about Number 5516. Is that one of his books?"

"5516? No, that's the asteroid they're naming after him. How'd you know about that? It's supposed to be a surprise. They're giving him the plaque Lectureship week."

"An asteroid," I said. I started out again.

"Thanks for coming in," the librarian said. "Are you just visiting or do you live here?"

"I live here," I said.

"Well, then, come again."

I went down the stairs and out to the car. It was 9:50. Just enough time to get to Cross's and tell him I'd take the job.

I went out to the parking lot. There weren't any tour buses driving through it, which must mean Jack Williamson was back from his convention. After my meeting with Cross I was going to go over to his house and introduce myself. "I know how you felt when you saw that *Amazing Stories* in the drugstore," I'd tell him. "I'm interested in the future, too. I liked what you said about it, about science fiction lighting the way and science making the future real."

I got in the car and drove through town to Highway 70. An asteroid. I should have gone with them. "It'll be fun," Tonia said. It certainly would be.

Next time, I thought. Only I want to see some of this terraforming. I want to go to Mars.

I turned south on Highway 70 towards Cross's office. ROSWELL 92 MILES, the sign said.

"Come again," I said, leaning out the window and looking up. "Come again!"

Columbiad

STEPHEN BAXTER

Stephen Baxter has, relatively speaking, burst into prominence overnight.
His first works were published in England in the early 1990s, but in 1995
and 1996 he became a major figure in hard SF. Not only were his earlier
novels reprinted in the U.S., but his 1995 *The Time Ships* was a leading
contender in 1996 for the Hugo Award for best novel, and, in addition to
his earlier novel, *Flux,* was released in the U.S. A new novel, *Voyager,* was
released in England and in the U.S. in early 1997. At the same time, he
managed to write and publish a number of SF stories, principally in
Interzone and *SF Age*. "Columbiad" mines a vein that has been of some
interest to Baxter in recent years—the history of SF. *The Time Ships* is a
sequel to H. G. Wells's *The Time Machine*; this story, from *SF Age*, is a
story of H. G. Wells in the year 1990, and of Jules Verne's *From Earth to
the Moon,* to which this story might be considered a sequel. It ends this
year's *Year's Best* on the theme of the wonders of space travel.

T he initial detonation was the most severe. I was pushed into my couch by a recoil that felt as if it should splay apart my ribs. The noise was extraordinary, and the projectile rattled so vigorously that my head was thrown from side to side.

And then followed, in perfect sequence, the subsidiary detonations of those smaller masses of guncotton lodged in the walls of the cannon. One after another these barrel-sized charges played vapor against the base of the projectile, accelerating it further, and the recoil pressed with ever-increasing force.

I fear that my consciousness departed from me, for some unmeasured interval.

When I came to, the noise and oscillation had gone. My head swam, as if I had imbibed heavily of Ardan's wine butts, and my lungs ached as they pulled at the air.

But, when I pushed at the couch under me, I drifted slowly upward, as if I were buoyant in some fluid that had flooded the projectile.

I was exultant. Once again my Columbiad had not failed me!

My name is Impey Barbicane, and what follows—if there are ears to hear—is an account of my second venture beyond the limits of the terrestrial atmosphere: that is, the first voyage to Mars.

My lunar romance received favorable reviews on its London publication by G. Newnes, and I was pleased to place it with an American publisher and in the Colonies. Sales were depressed, however, due to unrest over the war with the Boers. And there was that little business of the protests by M. Verne at the "unscientific" nature of my device of gravitational opacity; but I was able to point to flaws in Verne's work, and to the verification of certain aspects of my book by experts in astronomy, astronomical physics, and the like.

All of this engaged little of my attention, however. With the birth of Gip, and the publication of my series of futurological predictions in *The*

Fortnightly Review, I had matters of a more personal nature to attend to, as well as of greater global significance.

I was done with interplanetary travel!

It was with surprise and some annoyance, therefore, that I found myself the recipient, via Newnes, of a series of missives from Paris, penned—in an undisciplined hand—by one Michel Ardan. This evident eccentric expressed admiration for my work and begged me to place close attention to the material he enclosed, which I should find "of the most extraordinary interest and confluence with [my] own writings."

As is my custom, I had little hesitation in disposing of this correspondence without troubling to read it fully.

But M. Ardan continued to pepper me with further fat volleys of paper.

At last, in an idle hour, while Jane nursed Gip upstairs, I leafed through Ardan's dense pages. And I have to confess that I found my imagination—or the juvenile underside of it!—pricked.

Ardan's enclosure purported to be a record made by a Colonel Maston, of Baltimore in the United States, over the years 1872 to 1873—that is, some twenty-eight years ago. This Maston, now dead, claimed to have built an apparatus that had detected "propagating electro-magnetic emissions": a phenomenon first described by James Clerk Maxwell, and related, apparently, to the more recent wireless-telegraphy demonstrations of Marconi. If this were not enough, Maston also claimed that the "emissions" were in fact signals encoded after the fashion of a telegraphic message.

And these signals—said Maston and Ardan—had emanated from a source beyond the terrestrial atmosphere: from a space voyager, en route to Mars!

When I got the gist of this, I laughed out loud. I dashed off a quick note instructing Newnes not to pass on to me any further communications from the same source.

Fifth day. Two hundred and ninety-seven thousand leagues.

Through my lenticular glass scuttles, the Earth now appears about the size of a full Moon. Only the right half of the terrestrial globe is illuminated by the Sun. I can still discern clouds, and the glare of ice at the poles.

Some distance from the Earth a luminous disk is visible, aping the Earth's waxing phase. It is the Moon, following the Earth on its path around the Sun. It is to my regret that the configuration of my orbit was such that I passed no closer to the satellite than several hundred thousand leagues.

The projectile is extraordinarily convenient. I have only to turn a tap and I am furnished with fire and light by means of gas, which is stored in a

reservoir at a pressure of several atmospheres. My food is meat and vegeta-
bles and fruit, hydraulically compressed to the smallest dimensions; and I
have carried a quantity of brandy and water. My atmosphere is maintained
by means of chlorate of potassium and caustic potash: The former, when
heated, is transformed into chloride of potassium, and the oxygen thus liber-
ated replaces that which I have consumed; and the potash, when shaken,
extracts from the air the carbonic acid placed there by the combustion of
elements of my blood.

Thus, in interplanetary space, I am as comfortable as if I were in the
smoking lounge of the Gun Club itself, in Union Square, Baltimore!

Michel Ardan was perhaps seventy-five. He was of large build, but stoop-
shouldered. He sported luxuriant side-whiskers and mustache; his shock
of untamed hair, once evidently red, was largely a mass of gray. His eyes
were startling: Habitually he held them wide open so that a rim of white
appeared above each iris, and his gaze was clear but vague, as if he
suffered from near-sight.

He paced about my living room, his open collar flapping. Even at his
advanced age Ardan was a vigorous, restless man, and my home, Spade
House—spacious though it is—seemed to confine him like a cage. I
feared besides that his booming Gallic voice must awaken Gip. Therefore I invited Ardan to walk with me in the garden; in the open air I
fancied he might not seem quite so out of scale.

The house, built on the Kent coast near Sandgate, is open to a vista of
the sea. The day was brisk, lightly overcast. Ardan showed interest in
none of this, however.

He fixed me with those wild eyes. "You have not replied to my letters."

"I had them stopped."

"I have been forced to travel here unannounced. Sir, I have come here
to beg your help."

I already regretted allowing him into my home—of course I did!—but
some combination of his earnestness, and the intriguing content of those
unsolicited missives, had temporarily overwhelmed me. Now, though, I
stood square on my lawn, and held up the newest copy of his letter.

"Then perhaps, M. Ardan, you might explain what you mean by transmitting such romantic nonsense in my direction."

He barked laughter. "Romantic it may be. Nonsense—never!"

"Then you claim this business of 'propagating emissions' is the plain
and honest truth, do you?"

"Of course. It is a system of communication devised for their purposes
by Impey Barbicane and Colonel Maston. They seized on the electro-
magnetic discoveries of James Maxwell with the vigor and inventiveness

typical of Americans—for America is indeed the Land of the Future, is it not?"

Of that, I was not so certain.

"Colonel Maston had built a breed of mirror—but of wires, do you see?—in the shape of that geometric figure called a hyperbola—no, forgive me!—a parabola, for this figure, I am assured, collects all impinging waves into a single point, thus making it possible to detect the weakest . . ."

"Enough." I was scarcely qualified to judge the technical possibilities of such a hypothetical apparatus. And besides, the inclusion of apparently authentic detail is a technique I have used in my own romances, to persuade the reader to accept the most outrageous fictive lies. I had no intention of being deceived by it myself!

"These missives of yours—received by Maston—purport to be from the inhabitant of a projectile, beyond the terrestrial atmosphere. And this projectile, you claim, was launched into space from the mouth of an immense cannon, the 'Columbiad,' embedded in a Florida hillside . . ."

"That is so."

"But, my poor M. Ardan, you must understand that these are no more than the elements of a fiction, written three decades ago by M. Verne—your countryman—with whom I, myself, have corresponded."

Choleric red bloomed in his battered cheeks. "Verne indeed now claims his lazy and sensational books were fiction. It is convenient for him to do so. But they were not! He was commissioned to write truthful accounts of our extraordinary voyage!"

"Well, that's as may be. But see here. In M. Verne's account the projectile was launched toward the Moon. Not to Mars." I shook my head. "There is a difference, you know."

"Sir, I pray you resist treating me as imbecilic. I am well aware of the difference. The projectile was sent toward the Moon on its first journey—in which I had the honor of participating . . ."

The afternoon was extending, and I had work to do; and I was growing irritated by this boorish Frenchman. "Then, if this projectile truly was built, perhaps you would be good enough to show it to me."

"I cannot comply."

"Why so?"

"Because it is no longer on the Earth."

"Ah." Of course not! It was buried in the red dust of Mars, with this Barbicane inside.

"But . . ."

"Yes, M. Ardan?"

"I *can* show you the cannon."

The Frenchman regarded me steadily, and I felt an odd chill grow deep within me.

Seventy-third day. Four million one hundred and eighty-four thousand leagues.

Today, through my smoked glass, I have observed the passage of the Earth across the face of the Sun.

The planet appeared first as a mar in the perfect rim of the parent star. Later it moved into the full glare of the fiery ball, and was quite visible as a whole disk, dwarfed by the Sun's mighty countenance. After perhaps an hour another spot appeared, even smaller than the first: It was the Moon, following its parent toward the Sun's center.

After perhaps eight hours the passage was done.

I took several astronomical readings of this event. I measured the angle under which the Earth and Moon traveled across the Sun's disk, so that I might determine the deviation of my voyaging ellipse from the ecliptic; and the timing of the passage has furnished me with precise information on whether the projectile is running ahead or behind of the elliptical path around the Sun which I had designed. My best computations inform me that I have not deviated from the required trajectory.

It is a little more than a century since Captain James Cook, in 1769, sailed his Endeavor *to Tahiti to watch Venus pass before the Sun. Could even that great explorer have imagined this journey of mine?*

I have become the first human being to witness a transit of Earth! And who, I wonder, will be the second?

It took two days for us to travel by dispatch-boat from New Orleans to the bay of Espiritu Santo, close to Tampa Town.

Ardan had the good sense to avoid my company during this brief, uncomfortable trip. My humor was not good. Since leaving England I had steadily cursed myself, and Ardan, for my foolishness in agreeing to this jaunt to Florida.

We could not ignore each other at dinner and breakfast, however. And at those occasions, we argued.

"But," I insisted, "a human occupant would be reduced to a thin film of smashed bone and flesh, crushed by recoil against the base of any such cannon-fired shell. No amount of water cushions and collapsing balsa partitions would be sufficient to avert such a fate."

"Of course that is true," Ardan said, unperturbed. "But then M. Verne did not depict the detail of the arrangement."

"Which was?"

"That Barbicane and his companions in the Gun Club anticipated precisely this problem. The Columbiad, that mighty cannon, was dug still deeper than Verne described. And it did *not* contain one single vast charge of gun-cotton, but many, positioned along its heroic length. Thus a *distributed* impulse was applied to the projectile. It is an elementary matter of algebra—for those with the right disposition, which I have not!—to compute that the forces suffered by travelers within the projectile, while punishing, were less than lethal."

"Bah! What, then, of Verne's description of conditions within the projectile, during its Lunar journey? He claims that the inhabitants suffered a sensation of levitation—but only at that point at which the gravitational pulls of Earth and Moon are balanced. Now, this is nonsense. When you create a vacuum in a tube, the objects you send through it—whether grains of dust or grains of lead—fall with the same rapidity. So with the contents of your projectile. You, sir, should have floated like a pea inside a tin can throughout your voyage!"

He shrugged. "And so I did. It was an amusing piece of natural philosophy, but not always a comfortable sensation. For the second journey we anticipated by installing a couch equipped with straps, and hooks and eyes on the tools and implements, and additional crampirons fixed to the walls. As to M. Verne's inaccurate depiction of this sensation—I refer you to the author! Perhaps he did not understand. Or perhaps he chose to dramatize our condition in a way that suited the purposes of his narrative . . ."

"Oh!" I said. "This debating is all by the by. M. Ardan, it is simply impossible to launch a shell to another world from a cannon!"

"It is perfectly possible." He eyed me. "As you know!—for have you not published your own account of how such shells might be fired, if not from Earth to Mars, then in the opposite direction?"

"But it was fiction!" I cried. "As were Verne's books!"

"No." He shook his large, grizzled head. "M. Verne's account was fact. It is only a skeptical world that insists it must be fiction. And that, sir, is my tragedy."

One hundred and thirty-fourth day. Seven million, four hundred and seventy-seven thousand leagues.

The air will be thin and bracing; it will be like a mountaintop on Earth. I must trust that the vegetable and animal life—whose treks and seasonal cycles have been observed, as color washes, from Earth—provide me with provision compatible with my digestion.

I have brought thermometers, barometers, aneroids, and hypsometers with which to study the characteristics of the Martian landscape and atmosphere.

I have also carried several compasses, in case of any magnetic influence there. I have brought canvas, pickaxes and shovels, and nails, sacks of grain and shrubs and other seed stock: provisions with which to construct my miniature colony on the surface of Mars. For it is there that I must, of course, spend the rest of my life.

I dream that I may even encounter intelligence!—human, or some analogous form. The inhabitants of Mars will be tall, delicate, spidery creatures, their growth drawn upward by the lightness of their gravity. And their buildings likewise will be slender, beautiful structures . . .

With such speculation I console myself.

I will confess to a sense of isolation. With Earth invisible, and with Mars still no more than a brightening red star, I am suspended in a starry firmament—for my speed is not discernible—and I have only the dazzling globe of the Sun himself to interrupt the curve of Heaven above and below me. Has any man been so alone?

At times I close the covers of the scuttles, and strap myself to my couch, and expend a little of my precious gas; I seek to forget my situation by immersing myself in my books, those faithful companions I have carried with me.

But I find it impossible to forget my remoteness from all of humanity that ever lived, and that my projectile, a fragile aluminum tent, is my sole protection.

We stayed a night in the Franklin Hotel in Tampa Town. It was a dingy, uncomfortable place, its facilities exceedingly primitive.

At five A.M. Ardan roused me.

We traveled by phaeton. We worked along the coast for some distance—it was dry and parched—and then turned inland, where the soil became much richer, abounding with northern and tropical flora, including pineapples, cotton plants, rice, and yams. The road was well built, I thought, considering the crude and underpopulated nature of the countryside thereabouts.

I am not the physical type; I felt hot and uncomfortable, my suit of English wool restrictive and heavy, and my lungs seemed to labor at the humidity-laden air. By contrast Ardan was vibrant, evidently animated by our journey.

"When we returned to Earth—we fell back into the Pacific Ocean—our exuberance was unbounded. We imagined new and greater Columbiads. We imagined fleets of projectiles, threading between Earth, Moon, and planets. We expected adulation!"

"As depicted by M. Verne."

"But Verne lied!—in that as in other matters. Oh, there was some celebrity—some little notoriety. But we had returned with nothing: not so much as a bag of Lunar soil; nothing save our descriptions of a dead and airless Moon.

"The building of the Columbiad was financed by public subscription. Not long after our return, the pressure from those investors began to be felt: *Where is our profit?*—that was the question."

"It is not unreasonable."

"Some influential leader-writers argued that perhaps we had not traveled to the Moon at all. Perhaps it was all a deception, devised by Barbicane and his companions."

"It might be the truth," I said severely. "After all, the Gun Club were weapons manufacturers who, after the conclusion of the War between the States, sought by devising this new project only to maintain investment and employment . . ."

"It was not the truth! We had circled the Moon! But we were baffled by such reactions. Oh, Barbicane refused to concede defeat. He tried to raise subscriptions for a new company that would build on his achievements. But the company soon floundered, and the commissioner and magistrate pursued him on behalf of enraged debtors.

"If only the Moon had not turned out to be dead! If only we could succeed in finding a world that might draw up the dreams of man once more!

"And so Barbicane determined to commit all to one throw of the die. He took the last of his money, and used it to bore out the Columbiad, and to repair his projectile . . ."

My temper deteriorated; I had little interest in Ardan's rambling reminiscences.

But then Ardan digressed, and he began to describe how it was—or so he claimed—to fall toward the Moon. His voice became remote, his eyes oddly vacant.

Two hundred and forty-fifth day. Twelve million, one hundred and twenty-five leagues.

The projectile approaches the planet at an angle to the sunlight, so Mars is gibbous, with a slice of the night hemisphere turned toward me. The ochre shading seems to deepen at the planet's limb, giving the globe a marked roundness: Mars is a little orange, the only object apart from the Sun visible as other than a point of light in all my 360-degree sky.

To one side, at a distance a little greater than the diameter of the Martian disk, is a softly glowing starlet. If I trouble to observe for a few minutes, its relation to Mars changes visibly. Thus I have discerned that Mars has a companion: a moon, smaller than our own. And I suspect that a little farther from that central globe there may be a second satellite, but my observations are not unambiguous.

I can as yet discern few details on the disk itself, save what is known from observation through the larger telescopes on Earth. I can easily distinguish the white spot of the southern polar cap, however, which is melting in the frugal warmth of a Martian summer, following the pattern of seasons identified by William Herschel.

The air appears clear, and I can but trust that its thickness will prove sufficient to cushion my fall from space!

"I imagined I saw streams of oil descending across the glass of the scuttle.

"I thought perhaps the projectile had developed some fault, and I made to alert Barbicane. But then my eyes found their depth, and I realized I was looking at *mountains*. They slid slowly past the glass, trailing long, black shadows. They were the mountains of the Moon.

"Our approach was very rapid. The Moon was growing visibly larger by the minute.

"The satellite was no longer the flat, yellow disk I had known from Earth: Now, tinged pale white, its center seemed to loom out at us, given three-dimensional substance by Earthlight. The landscape was fractured and complex, and utterly still and silent. The Moon is a small world, my friend. Its curve is so tight my eye could encompass its spherical shape, even so close; I could see that I was flying around a ball of rock, suspended in space, with emptiness stretching to infinity in all directions.

"We passed around the limb of the Moon, and entered total darkness: No sunlight, no earthlight touched the hidden landscape rushing below."

I asked, "And of the Lunar egg shape which Hansen hypothesizes, the layer of atmosphere drawn to the far side by its greater mass . . ."

"We saw none of it! But . . ."

"Yes?"

"But . . . When the Sun was hidden behind the Lunar orb, there was light all around the Moon, as if the rim were on fire." Ardan turned to me, and his rheumy eyes were shining. "It was wonderful! Oh, it was wonderful!"

We crossed extensive plains, broken only by isolated thickets of pine trees. At last we came upon a rocky plateau, baked hard by the Sun, and considerably elevated.

Two hundred and fifty-seventh day. One million, three hundred and thirty-five thousand leagues.

The nature of Mars has become clear to me. All too clear!

There is a sharp visible difference between northern and southern hemispheres. The darker lands to the south of an equatorial line of dichotomy are punctuated by craters as densely clustered as those of the Moon; while the northern plains—which perhaps are analogous to the dusty maria of the Moon—are generally smoother and, perhaps, younger.

A huge canyon system lies along the equator, a planetary wound visible even from a hundred thousand leagues. To the west of this gouge are clustered four immense volcanoes: Great black calderas, as dead as any on the Moon. And in the southern hemisphere I have espied a mighty crater, deep and choked with frost. Mars is clearly a small world: Some of these features sprawl around the globe, outsized, overwhelming the curvature.

I have seen no evidence of the channels, or canals, observed by Cardinal Secchi, nor of the other mighty works of Mind which many claim to have observed. Nor, indeed, have I espied evidence of life: No herds move across these rusty plains, and not even the presence of vegetation is evident to me. Such colorings as I have discerned appear to owe more to geologic features than to the processes of life. Even Syrtis Major—Huygens' 'Hourglass Sea'— is revealed as a cratered upland, no more moist than the bleakest desert of Earth.

Thus I have been forced to confront the truth:
Mars is a dead world. As dead as the Moon!

We got out of our phaeton and embarked by foot across that high plain that Ardan called Stones Hill. I saw how several well-made roads converged on this desolate spot, free of traffic, enigmatic. There was even a rail track, rusting and long disused, snaking off in the direction of Tampa Town.

All over the plain I found the ruins of magazines, workshops, furnaces, and workmen's huts. Whether or not Ardan spoke the truth, it was evident that some great enterprise had taken place here.

At the heart of the plain was a low mound. This little hill was surrounded by a ring of low constructions of stone, regularly built, and set at a radius of perhaps six hundred yards from the summit itself. Each construction was topped by an elliptical arch, some of which remained intact.

I walked into this ring, two-thirds of a mile across, and looked around. "My word, Ardan!" I cried, impressed despite my skepticism. "This has the feel of some immense prehistoric site—a Stonehenge, perhaps, transported to the Americas. Why, there must be several hundred of these squat monoliths."

"More than a thousand," he said. "They are reverberating ovens, to fuse the many millions of tons of cast iron that plated the mighty Columbiad. See here." He traced out a shallow trench in the soil. "Here are the channels by which the iron was directed into the central mold—from all twelve hundred ovens, simultaneously!"

At the summit of the hill—the convergence of the thousand trenches—there was a circular pit, perhaps sixty feet in diameter. Ardan and I approached this cavity cautiously. I found that it opened into a cylindrical shaft, dug vertically into that rocky landscape.

Ardan took a coin from his pocket and flicked it into the mouth of the great well. I heard it clatter several times against metal walls, but I could not hear it fall to rest.

Taking my courage in my hands—all my life I have suffered a certain dread of subterranean places—I stepped toward the lip of the well. I saw that its sides were sheer, evidently finely manufactured, and constructed of what appeared to be cast iron. But the iron was extensively flaked and rusted.

Looking around from this summit, I saw now a pattern to the damaged landscape: the ovens, the flimsier huts, were smashed and scattered outward from this central spot, as if some great explosion had once occurred. And I saw how disturbed soil streaked across the land, radially away from the hill; from a balloon, I speculated, these stripes of discoloration might have resembled the rays around the great craters of the moon.

This Ozymandian scene was terrifically poignant: great things had been wrought here, and yet now these immense devices lay ruined, broken—forgotten.

Ardan paced about by the lip of the abandoned cannon; he exuded an extraordinary restlessness, as if the whole of the Earth had become a cage insufficient for him. "It was magnificent!" he cried. "When the electrical spark ignited the gun-cotton, and the ground shook, and the pillar of flame hurled aside the air, throwing over the spectators and their horses like matchstalks! . . . And there was the barest glimpse of the projectile itself, ascending like a soul in that fiery light . . ."

I gazed up at the hot, blank sky, and imagined this Barbicane climbing into his cannon-shell, to the applause of his aging friends. He would have called it bravery, I suppose. But how easy it must have been, to sail away into the infinite aether—forever!—and to leave behind the Earthbound complexities of debtors and broken promises. Was Barbicane exploring, I wondered—or escaping?

As I plunge toward the glowing pool of Martian air—as that russet, cratered barrenness opens out beneath me—I descend into despair. Is all of the Solar System to prove as bleak as the worlds I have visited?

This must be my last transmission. I wish my final words to be an utter-

ance of deepest gratitude to my loyal friends, notably Colonel J.T. Maston and my partners in the National Company of Interstellar Communication, who have followed my fruitless journey across space for so many months.

I am sure this new defeat will be trumpeted by those jackals who hounded my National Company into bankruptcy; with nothing but dead landscapes as his destination, it may be many decades before man leaves the air of Earth again!

"Sir, it seems I must credit your veracity. But what is it you want of me? Why have you brought me here?"

After his Gallic fashion, he grabbed at my arm. "I have read your books. I know you are a man of imagination. You must publish Maston's account—tell the story of this place . . ."

"But why? What would be the purpose? If Common Man is unimpressed by such exploits—if he regards these feats as a hoax, or a cynical exploitation by gun manufacturers—who am I to argue against him? We have entered a new century, M. Ardan: the century of Socialism. We must concentrate on the needs of Earth—on poverty, injustice, disease— and turn our faces to new worlds only when we have reached our manhood on this one . . ."

But Ardan heard none of this. He still gripped my arm, and again I saw that wildness in his old eyes—eyes that had, perhaps, seen too much. "I would go back! That is all. I am embedded in gravity. It clings, it clings! Oh, Mr. Wells, let me go back!"

Story Copyrights

David G. Hartwell is a Ph.D. in Comparative Medieval Literature who has been nominated for the Hugo Award fifteen times. He has won the World Fantasy Award in the special professional achievements category, and also for best anthology (*The Dark Descent*). He has taught at Harvard University and New York University, and has edited a dozen anthologies or more, the newest of which is *The Science Fiction Century*. He is the author of *Age of Wonders*, and is presently a senior editor at Tor Books.